Sand and the River

A novel of Oklahoma

Bob Lambert

Cover photograph, Ponca City's Pioneer Woman, by the author

:

DEDICATION

To my wife, Pat, who, darling that she is,
never stopped believing in me.

I must also thank Andrea Ferguson,
Karen Linn, Debbie Koehn, and Alyson Holman,
the owners and workers of Java John's,
the coffee shop in which I wrote
a good portion of the book. Java John's was
not only a good place to work, but the people
were always supportive in every way.
Thank you!

PREFACE

A Few Dead Indians, the novel that preceded this one, told the story, largely through the eyes of a young agent named Walter Gage, of the investigation by the newly-formed Oklahoma Bureau of Criminal Identification and Investigation into the murders of over twenty members of the Osage tribe of northern Oklahoma in the 1920's.

When the federal government moved the Osage into Oklahoma, it had no intention of making the Osage, as a group, the wealthiest people in the world. But it happened.

The land itself was wonderful for cattle, covered as it was with Big Bluegrass, Little Bluegrass, and Switchgrass, some growing to four or five feet in height and highly nutritious.

But it wasn't what was on top of the land that made the Osage rich; it was what was beneath it: oil.

Oklahoma, not long a state, was booming. Oil wells were popping up in many areas of the state. Towns that had existed only as small farming communities or had not existed at all were suddenly bustling cities.

Many of the large—huge?—oil companies that were familiar names in America for most of the twentieth century got their starts in the Oklahoma oil fields. Lots of people got rich.

The Osage tribe was in a rather special position. Their treaties with the United States government meant that royalties from oil taken from Osage land went, not to the landholder, but to the tribe as a whole. That royalty money was then distributed to all tribal members equally.

That meant, in a way, that although a few landholders might have actually received less royalty money than they would have under the usual circumstances, it also meant that every adult member of the Osage tribe rather quickly became wealthy.

Wealthy? Millionaires, each and every one.

What did this mean to people who were, by American standards, scarcely "civilized"?

In simple terms, it meant that they were prey.

And they were preyed upon. Government-appointed guardians stole from them. Merchants took advantage of them. Almost certainly the worst, though, was the plot to sell them life insurance and then murder them for the benefits.

In *A Few Dead Indians*, most of the perpetrators of those crimes were brought to justice. However, evidence to convict the real leader of the group was insufficient to even bring him to trial, and one of the men who had taken part in the actual killings avoided capture.

The novel ended—quite abruptly—with the death of the lead investigator in the case. *Sand and the River* continues Walter's story, but with somewhat greater emphasis on his family—and life in the Oklahoma oil fields of the 1920's and 30's.

The oil boom—and the money that oil meant—brought lots of different kinds of people to the state. There were the workers, of course, and legitimate companies. But there also came gamblers, prostitutes, con men, and violent criminals.

The River

Most, if not all of us, have seen—either in person or in photographs—snow-topped peaks of the American Rocky Mountains. When spring comes in the Rockies of Colorado, that snow begins to melt. If enough snow melts, it becomes a stream and heads down the mountainside.

Sometimes, the stream became a river. In Colorado, it became the Arkansas. At first, the baby river tried to go first one way, then another, seeking always to go down. Along the way it was joined by other streams, at last becoming powerful, ripping southeast through Royal Gorge, then heading east for Kansas, Oklahoma, and, eventually, the Mississippi.

That was then. Today, Colorado dams hold back the river, saving its water for irrigation and for a thirsty Colorado Springs. As a result, the river bed from Lamar, Colorado, to Dodge City, Kansas, and even farther east, is often dry.

But before the dams, before the reservoirs, the light, sandy soil of eastern Colorado and western Kansas meant that the river found it easier, in that flat land, to spread itself into a broad, shallow stream. Flooding in those flat lands covered a lot of ground, but was almost never deep and almost always gradual.

But then, south of Wichita as the river flowed into Oklahoma, floods were often more sudden, and more devastating.

Now, of course, the once wild Arkansas in Oklahoma has been, for the most part, tamed, by Keystone Lake, where the Arkansas meets the Cimarron west of Tulsa, and, to the north, the great Kaw Lake.

PART ONE

THE OLD DRILLER

CHAPTER 1

THE OLD DRILLER
LAKIN, KANSAS 1972

Frank Gage had his last fist fight in Hays, Kansas, in January of 1972, shortly after eleven o'clock.

He was coming out of Jack's Wahoo Tavern into a crisp, icy wind skittering down Fourth Avenue when, in the process of searching for his 1970 almond-beige Coupe deVille, he discovered, just a few feet from his car, two young men carrying out—apparently with some ardor—an assault on a person, invisible to Frank for the moment, but presumably male; for he heard strong thumping sounds and observed both piston-like and hammer-like movements of arms and fists, and it was not in his experience that this was the way men hit women.

He realized at once that the sides were uneven, called out a warning, and, despite his sixty-eight years, joined in with an enthusiasm untempered by either judgment or prescience.

Unfortunately, his addition to the brawl, although contributing somewhat, perhaps, to the leveling of the circumstances of combat, was insufficient to establish either stability or advantage.

His first blow drove one of the assailants back in astonishment and pain; the second boy—for they were indeed boys—had chosen to arm himself with a whiskey bottle. Although he had always been something of a connoisseur of whiskey bottles and their contents, Frank did not have sufficient time to observe the label.

This particular bottle, brought about in a straight overhand delivery Frank later likened to a pitch delivered up by Bob Feller (or maybe this Jewish boy—what's his name—Koufax), just slow enough to see and too fast to duck, smashed through his white LBJ Stetson and brought him to the sidewalk

The rangy old driller who had defeated—always in fair fight—the toughest, meanest, dirtiest roughnecks in boom towns and oil fields from Libya to Wyoming, lay unconscious on the sidewalk of Hays, Kansas, like a downed cowpoke out of his century, with blood seeping from his ear like a scarlet worm.

Lakin, Kansas, was not Frank's notion of the perfect place to live, but it was quiet (and quiet, for the first time in his life, at least for the first time in his memory, seemed somehow desirable) and it was—and this was an important, even vital, consideration—free.

The only cost was one he disliked paying, nevertheless: living here unfortunately required returning to his present wife, to whom he had been married for twenty years, but with whom he had lived perhaps seven, two consecutive years followed by maybe five or so more accumulated in nibbles of time ranging from a weekend to two or three months.

The house was handy, he had to admit. It was right on Main Street, and all he had to do for his meals was walk a block down the street to the north, cross the railroad tracks, cross the street to the west, and there was Margie's restaurant, the City Café, which she owned and operated with her sister Eloise. Margie was either his third or fifth wife, the number depending upon the manner of counting and the social discretion of the counter.

The pool hall was just a half-block farther north. Frank didn't much care for pool, but he listened to the farmers talking about wheat and irrigation and herds, and there was an occasional retired oil field worker. He sat in the pool hall for a couple of hours on most days—when his head wasn't aching—smoking and listening, mostly. Once in a while he'd nurse a beer along, but he really didn't have the taste for anything alcoholic anymore, even beer.

The Caddy was gone, of course; it hadn't even been paid for.

From the front porch there wasn't much to see except the back end of an old maple in the front yard and some kind of overgrown evergreen monstrosity that seemed to own the yard to the north. Nevertheless, Frank spent considerable time on the porch, leaning back in the red, rusty old lawn chair, alone, smoking.

Sometimes, like today, he had company.

"I didn't die," he said to the person in the green lawn chair, rubbing errant pipe tobacco, some still smoldering, off the knees of his gray work pants. "Too mean a son-bitch to die, but it sure the hell cured me a' fightin'."

The young woman sitting beside him on the porch, the daughter of his baby sister Callie, extended her feet and looked at her yellow tennies. "Uncle Frank," she said, "I want to ask you something, okay?"

"Anything you want, Honey." He looked at his niece and waited. Linda—that was her name—looked a little like her mama, only a lot skinnier, he thought. Hair was a lot alike, but Linda's was really long and parted in the middle, kind of hippyish, but nice. He watched Linda pull her long legs up and pull the yellow shoes under her. The chair wiggled, but didn't tip.

"I heard a story," she said. "I wonder if it's true?"

"Depends. Who'd you hear it from?"

"Grandpa. I was real little, and we went—Aunt Mattie and Uncle Nathan—we went down to Okemah for Christmas. There was a lot of company, and the men stayed in the living room and the women all went into the kitchen. You know how it was—the little shotgun house with the big gas stove sort of half separating the living room from the dining room?"

Linda slid her feet out, brought her knees up, and embraced them. Frank half-expected the chair to tip over, and he prepared to grab the back of the chair to hold it in place.

"Anyway, I sat kinda hunkered down by the stove and listened. Grandpa told the men a story about you."

"Don't know," said Frank, wishing he could pull his legs up like she had, "depends on the story. A man don't like to say bad things about his daddy, but the truth is that that man was the very worst liar in Oklahoma. Even Mama said he was a windy old bastard."

Frank gave up fussing with the pipe, which he couldn't keep lit worth a damn, and took out a cigarette. *Tareytons*. He hated the things, but Margie smoked them, and she was buying. He looked at Linda. "What'd he say? What'm I supposed to've done?"

"Well," said Linda. "It was about fighting." Her smile was impish and challenging. "Did you fight a lot when you were younger?"

Frank lit his cigarette and looked at the end of it. "Fightin'?" He leaned forward and reached up with both hands to pull his greasy old hat down over his eyes. "I don't think I fought over-much. Some. I never hit a man that didn't need hittin'." He pushed the brim of the hat back with a thumb. "Of course there were a considerable number of fellas in the oil patch that needed hittin'."

He looked at her and grinned. "I guess I did do a little bit of fightin'. Wasn't half bad, neither. Just didn't know when to quit."

He took off his hat and showed her the flat place above his right temple. "That's where those boys up in Hays tried to do me in. Anyway, they kind of taught me I wasn't near as good as I used to be."

Linda watched as he rubbed the place for a moment, examining by feel, she supposed, the strange new configuration on the skull that had remained the same, familiar in shape, for many years.

Uncle Frank was an old man, she decided. Her mother had always talked about how handsome he was, the dashing older brother who came home bearing gifts of wonderful cast-iron toy ovens and shiny, thin books with pictures of pretty women or pretty little girls to punch out and lots of pretty dresses for her to cut out and for them to wear.

Looking at him even now, Linda could see, if she squinted and threw her eyes out of focus a little, the man she had seen in an old snapshot: a towering man in greasy, rumpled clothes and a shiny metal hat, standing on a rig floor. She couldn't remember what he had been doing in the picture, whether he had been holding something—maybe a big wrench; but she could remember how, even when she was very small, something about the tall man in the photograph had excited her in a way she hadn't understood.

"Grandpa told about one time you had a fight over Aunt Bobbie."

"Don't remember. Had lots of fights *with* her."

"Well, let me tell you what Grandpa said, and you can tell me if it was right. Okay?"

Frank nodded, then replaced his hat and leaned back.

"Like I said, we were down at Grandpa's for Christmas," she said, "and I listened to the men. I think the women kinda forgot me, and maybe the men didn't see me behind the stove—or they didn't care; but I got to stay. And Grandpa told this story. Aunt Bobbie had this friend, and you thought she was, oh, not good enough for Aunt Bobbie, and you didn't want her—it seems funny calling her *Aunt Bobbie*. I don't think I ever saw her, did I?"

"Nah," said Frank. "She was long gone by the time you was born."

"I vaguely remember Aunt Vivian, though—she was tall and she wore her hair—kinda *up-swept* —like this." She cupped her hands behind her head and brought them up over the crown and pivoted her wrists.

"Uh-huh. Vivian's folks had a pot of money. Her daddy had a big old farm down by Ulysses—got rich during the depression. Shoulda stayed married to old Vivian."

"But Bobbie was first, right?"

Frank nodded.

CHAPTER 2

The Flow
Longwood, Oklahoma, 1899

Henry Gage came across from West Plains, Missouri, with a stop-over in Joplin—and another for a little lead mining in Weir, Kansas, until he found that he had to fight an insistent little Italian. Then he discovered that the Italians stuck together, and he'd had to run for it, winding up—on foot, broke, and almost empty-handed on the bank of the Arkansas River, just across the line into what would become Oklahoma. He wasn't really sure where he was. Well, he knew he was someplace he'd heard called "Indian Country"; that was something.

What he did know was that he was tired, that he was hungry, and that he didn't know what the hell he was going to do. He sat down on a little patch of grass and weeds on the riverbank and took off his boots. He rubbed one of his feet, noticing that his sock was almost non-existent. The rubbing felt good, though.

There was shade here, so Henry pushed his hat back on his head and lay back with his head on his old canvas bag, drawing a knee up so he could keep rubbing his foot. "Maybe I can sleep here," he thought. But then he'd thought that before, in a couple of places outside. Usually it had rained and he'd just got soaked for his trouble. Gosh, a real bed would be nice. It'd been a while.

Food would be good, too. Bacon. Ham. Fried eggs. Not beans. He'd eaten enough cans of cold beans lately that he hoped he'd never see another bean as long as he lived.

Slowly, though, hunger or not, his knee settled back to the ground. As his foot lowered, it came in contact with one of his boots and tipped it over the bank into the shallow water. Henry didn't notice that, though, because he was asleep.

When he awakened, sometime later, he at first thought that he was in Weir in the musty old miners' barracks. He sat up abruptly, then looked around him, gradually remembering where he was—if he really knew where he was. He struggled a little to stand up, felt the rough weediness of the ground on the bare sole of one foot, and looked for his boots. One he found easily, of course, so he sat to pull it on. The other one? He stood and looked around for the missing boot.

He didn't see the boot, though the top of it showed above the slowly moving stream. What he did see, though, on the bank about a hundred yards below him, walking on a little beach of river-rolled rocks and clam shells, with her skirts held high and her stockings rolled, was the most beautiful girl he had ever seen.

For a moment, then, he forgot about the boot and being hungry and being lost.

The girl saw him, then, and stopped.

Henry watched her, then mentally shook himself as he realized that this girl, alone on the river bank, would probably be afraid of him, a stranger—and, he thought ruefully—a stranger with dirty, wrinkled clothes and only one boot. He thought that he should say something, something to show that he was harmless, that he wouldn't hurt her. But nothing came; he just watched, his mouth slightly open.

The girl scrambled up onto the weedy bank, off the stones. She looked as if she might run.

Henry didn't want her to run, so he called to her with the first thing that came to his mind. "It's all right! I won't hurt you. I'm just lost. Kinda."

She stopped and looked over her shoulder at him.

"Can you tell me where I am?" he asked, wanting to step toward her but afraid to. "I know I'm in Oklahoma, but beyond that...."

The girl turned toward him, about halfway. She wrapped bits of skirt around her hands. "You're close to Kaw City," she shouted back at him.

Henry was glad that she wasn't running, but he just stood there until she turned away again. When she did, mostly just to hold her there a little longer, he called back to her, "Thank you. Now, if I knew where Kaw City was, I'd know more."

She was moving away now, but she turned back for a second.

Henry bit his lip a little. "What town's near here?" he asked. "Hey, I'm really lost. If you can just point me a direction, I'll get out of here and leave you alone." He wasn't really sure he would do that, but—oh, hell yes, he would. He didn't want to scare such a pretty girl.

She pointed to the west. "Kaw City's over there, just a couple of miles. Or you could just follow the river and you'll come to it."

"Thanks," said Henry, and started to step toward her. Then he felt the ground on his nearly bare foot and remembered that he was missing a boot. He straightened his leg and looked at his foot. When he looked up again, the girl was laughing.

"I seem to be missing something," Henry said.

The girl, apparently not so cautious now, took a couple of steps toward him. Henry put his foot down and looked around him. No boot.

"You're not going to walk to Kaw that way," said the girl. "What did you do with your other boot?"

Henry shrugged. "Lost it, I guess." He heard her laughter over the distance between them, much less now, as she was approaching.

Martha Cantrell had to laugh at the man—boy, almost, standing there looking foolish, body all a-tilt, bootless. He didn't look in the least frightening. He was even good-looking, in a way, tall, like her father, but bigger, broader, strong-looking. But he also looked really helpless, standing there.

"Maybe I can help you find your boot," she said.

"That would be nice," said Henry. "That would be good." He stopped looking at the girl and started looking around him for the boot, standing as he was, but turning his head and shoulders. He looked funny, and Martha laughed again. He looked embarrassed, not angry, at being laughed at.

Martha looked around the area he was standing in—no boot. But then she glanced at the stream, and there was the boot. "Aha!" she said. "I see a boot!"

"Where?" Henry took a step toward her, but his balance wasn't very good and he stumbled.

She pointed. "I'm afraid it's a little tiny bit wet," she said.

"Oh, my God!" said Henry, and started toward the river and the boot. Then he stopped and looked back at her, a concerned look on his face. "I beg your pardon," he said.

"For what?"

"For taking the Lord's name in vain. I really apologize for that."

He reached into the water and drew the boot out, his face, Martha thought, showing genuine regret. "That's all right," she said. "Don't give it a thought."

She laughed again, and Henry thought that her laugh was just about the prettiest thing he'd ever heard.

"It's going to be pretty wet to put on," she said.

Henry dumped the water out of the boot and sat to put it on. "Yes, Ma'am," he said, "but it'll be better than going barefoot!" He stood, and Martha could hear the squishing sound from where she stood.

"I suppose it will," she said.

"Thank you," said Henry, thinking that now he should be on his way, to find that town she had mentioned. But he didn't want to leave her. He sighed. "Which way did you say town was?"

She pointed. "That way," she said. "But it's a long way to walk in a wet boot." She hesitated while Henry watched her—almost too intently, she thought. She bit her lip, but then she had to grin, despite herself and her caution. She gave a mental shrug. "Look," she said. "Our farm is just up over that hill there." She pointed to the northeast. "You could let your boot dry out. I suspect that Mama could find you something to eat, too."

"You sure?" Henry was so startled that he didn't even have time to be pleased.

"Why not?" she said. "Oh, come along." She turned and headed back the way she had come. After a few steps, she looked back at him, over her shoulder. "You coming?"

Her smile was blinding. Henry could hardly speak, but he managed to croak out an affirmative answer and headed northeast with her, his foot squishing in his wet boot.

As they walked, Henry learned that she was Martha Cantrell, that she was eighteen, just a little over two years younger than Henry, that she had an older sister and a younger sister and brother, that she'd been born in Texas, that her father's name was Walter, and that he'd got his farm in the land rush.

Henry heard all this, but it scarcely registered. He knew he carried a completely silly smile on his face all the way to the farm, but he didn't care. If that one boot wasn't so wet, he thought he'd be jumping up and down clicking his heels. This girl was a talker, he realized, but he was glad of that: her voice was as pretty as her face.

Henry was a bit unsure of how he'd be received at the Cantrell house. He knew that he was dirty and wrinkled and probably smelled bad; but he knew, too, that older women, for some reason, usually took to him. So he was hopeful that he wouldn't be summarily turned away or executed.

And, as a matter of fact, Parthie Cantrell actually seemed glad to see him. "It's a while before supper time," she said, after Martha's long and laughing introduction, "but I suspect we can find you a little something to tide you over."

She did. He ate biscuits with slices of ham that Martha had run out to the smokehouse to get and a couple of fried eggs. And a big mug of hot coffee. Henry was very careful about his manners, but he wanted to just swallow everything whole; he definitely did not want them to think worse of him than they probably already did. But both women smiled at him while he ate.

Martha's little brother and little sister came into the kitchen, looked at him, and immediately scampered out. "They don't see strangers much," she said.

"None of us do," said Mrs. Cantrell. "It gets lonesome out here." She smiled at Henry again, and sat down at the table next to Martha. "And Walter has to work so hard. We get to see him at supper, and that's about all." She laid her arms out on the table and folded her hands together. "What do your folks do?" she asked.

Henry put down his fork. He felt a lot better now, with his stomach full. "My mother and her husband have a little general store," he said. "In Missouri."

"Oh," said Parthie Cantrell, with a sympathetic glance. "Is your father—is your father gone, then?"

"Oh, yes," thought Henry, "he's gone all right." He didn't know what to say to the women, though. It was awkward. He reached out and turned his coffee cup around. "Yes," he told them. "He's been gone quite a while now."

"That's too bad," said Martha's mother.

"Yes. Thank you," said Henry. He didn't like to lie, and it wasn't a lie, exactly. He hadn't actually said that his father was dead. And he *was* gone. Just no one knew where. Henry would have liked to know, but so would a couple of husbands and fathers back in West Plains. Henry, senior, had left town in a hurry.

Henry gratefully accepted a second cup of coffee while Martha gathered up his plate and silverware. He couldn't help himself; he had to watch the girl as she walked across the kitchen to the sink. But he caught himself in time to keep from being too obvious, he thought. But he saw Mrs. Cantrell raise her eyebrows a little, so he couldn't be sure.

"I should be going," he said, pushing back his chair. "I suspect it's a long way into town." He took a final sip of coffee. "If you can just point me in the right direction, I'll get out of your way." He put the cup back onto the table and stood. "I'm very grateful for the meal. It was delicious."

Martha was back at the table very quickly. "You're not going already, are you?"

Henry had a flash of astonishment. The girl didn't want him to leave! For a second, he—but, no, he had to leave. He'd imposed enough and he was just somebody—a stray dog—that had followed a pretty girl home. He had to get out of here.

"There's no hurry," said Parthie Cantrell. "Walter will be home in just a little, and you can meet Martha's father."

Oh. Meet her father, and be ordered off the place rather than leaving of his own accord. Not a good idea.

"Ah, thank you, but I'd really better get going. I really do thank you a lot, both of you. You've been very kind."

The back door slammed and everybody looked back at the door leading to the mudroom.

"Home, home, home at last," came a masculine voice from just outside the kitchen door, and then the man came in. He was taller than Henry, not as broad, but he looked strong and, Henry thought, a bit fierce. It was definitely time to go.

Walter Cantrell stopped in the door. "Who's this?" he asked.

Martha almost ran up to her father and hugged him. "I'm glad you're home, Daddy." She turned halfway and gestured toward Henry. "This is my friend Henry Gage."

Friend?

"Oh," said the father. "Proud to meet you." He came forward to shake Henry's hand, but his face didn't say "proud." It said "who the devil is this man?"

But his handshake was firm, so Henry greeted it with a firm one of his own.

"This young man is on his way to Kaw City," said Parthie. "We asked him in to have something to eat and some coffee. Would you like some coffee, Walter? We made a fresh pot just a bit ago." She stood and Henry noticed, really for the first time, how really small the lady was. As she stood by her husband, she was clearly over a foot shorter than he was.

"That'd be good," said Walter Cantrell. He made a "sit down" motion to Henry. "Join me. Parthie makes good coffee, don't she? You could stand another cup, I'd wager."

Henry really didn't know how to respond. He didn't want more coffee, but he'd been asked by the man of the house and it would be rude to refuse. "Thank you, Sir," he said. "Yes, she does."

"I didn't see a horse or wagon outside," said the father, as he sat. "You on foot?"

"Yes, Sir."

"Long walk to Kaw," he said. "Where'd you come from?"

"Missouri, Sir. West Plains."

"Missouri? And how in blue blazes did you wind up out here, a long way from anywhere, on foot?"

Henry shrugged.

"Well, you're here," said Cantrell. He sipped his coffee and blew out a breath. "Gotta be somewheres, I suppose."

Henry could just nod.

As it turned out, it wasn't so easy to leave the Cantrell house. Walter Cantrell was a talker, and, as he told Henry, he didn't get to talk man-talk very much out here in the country.

So Henry listened as Cantrell told him about staking out the land during the land rush and the work he'd had to do to improve the land so that he could actually get the title—and other things that Henry really didn't remember later. But he did listen, respectfully, and nodded when it seemed to be expected. The women were somewhere—Henry didn't know where—and he heard movement sometimes, and the voices of the children in another room. It was warm in the room, and cozy, and he still hadn't had enough sleep. He felt himself drowsing.

Finally the older man noticed that Henry was drifting off, and he laughed. "Parthie!" he called. "Better fix this young man up with a bed! He's gonna fall out of that chair!"

"No," thought Henry. "I have to go." But he didn't. He couldn't. Walter Cantrell actually helped him get up from the chair and led him down the hall where Mrs. Cantrell was turning back some bed covers on a sofa bed. A bed. A real bed. Henry hadn't slept in a real bed for—he didn't know how long. He sighed and looked at the bed with longing.

Mrs. Cantrell smiled at him. "Walt can help you with your clothes, if you like," she said.

Walter Cantrell laughed. "I imagine the boy can undress himself without help. C'mon, Parthie. Let's let the lad get some sleep."

Henry didn't bother to undress. He started to take off his boots, but he didn't have them on. "Oh," he remembered. They were drying in the kitchen. Hell, he'd been trying to leave without his boots. He shook his head in mild amusement. Then he fell onto the bed.

CHAPTER 3

A New Life
Longwood, Oklahoma, 1899-1917

As it turned out, Henry didn't leave the farm for a long time. Walter Cantrell needed help and, for some reason that Henry couldn't figure out, the old man seemed to trust him, even to like him. Mrs. Cantrell treated him almost like a member of the family. And, of course, there was Martha. But Henry was careful around her; he didn't want to make her father have second thoughts.

The farm work was all right; Henry rather liked to strain his muscles, and he could do some heavy things that Walter Cantrell had trouble with. So he felt useful, too. He had his own bed. Of course it wasn't in the main house—that would have been too much, Henry knew. But it was a nice clean bed in the tack room on one side of the big barn.

He found that he genuinely liked the Cantrells—all of them, including Martha's older sister Claudie and her younger brother and sister. The folks were, he admitted to himself, a little strange—Walter Cantrell's politics, for one thing. Their religion, for another.

Henry didn't think he'd ever met anyone who openly admitted to not being Christian. He supposed that he'd known people who weren't, but they'd kept their mouths shut about it. The Cantrells didn't believe in Jesus, but they did believe in some kind of after-life. It was never clear to Henry exactly what they did believe, at least in part because he didn't really try to understand; but he did understand that they believed you could talk to dead people.

Once, when Mattie's sister Claudie had come to visit, some other people that Henry didn't know came to the farm and they all gathered around a table and they held hands and bowed their heads like they were praying while Claudie did some kind of strange talking that didn't make a lot of sense.

Henry went out to the barn, not because he was offended or afraid or anything; he was just confused. He realized that he wasn't all that much of a Christian himself. His father had been a deacon in their church back home, but that hadn't kept him from going off with other women and finally just taking off for parts unknown. If that was Christianity, well....

And, as things turned out, Henry's being careful around Martha didn't make any difference. She simply wasn't all that careful around him, smiling at him, bringing his lunch to him when he was out in the field, even dropping into the tack room when he was alone, asking him if he needed anything.

What he needed, of course, was her. She was still the most beautiful thing he'd ever seen.

Then one day, when he and Walter Cantrell were harnessing the horses to cut some hay, the old man turned to him, one hand on a harness strap, and asked him straight out: "Are you planning on marrying my daughter?"

Henry was almost struck speechless, but he managed to nod. Then—"Yes, Sir. If you'll have me."

Walter Cantrell smiled and slapped Henry lightly on the shoulder. "If I wouldn't have you," he laughed, "my womenfolk would have my hide!"

So, after a short while, Henry Gage and Martha Cantrell were married in the little Baptist Church in the small community of Longwood, Oklahoma, and Henry became, now, for a short time, a real farmer.

For some years. Long enough to father six children: Walter, named after Martha's father, of course, in 1900; Frank in 1904; Tom in 1906, Claude in 1911, Mathilda in 1914, and Caledonia in 1917. But finally there were too many mouths to feed on what they brought from the earth and Henry sought and found work in the oil fields.

CHAPTER 4

Temperature Transients
Okemah and Shidler, Oklahoma, 1945 and 1932

"You all remember Frank—my second oldest boy? Old Slim? He's up in Canada now," said Henry Gage. "Now, Old Slim kinda liked to fight. I mean, hell, he wouldn't go out and push for a fight, but if one started somewhere 'round him—say within fifteen miles in any direction—why, he was right there in the middle of it before you could say, 'bob my tail.' Now I remember one time—he was married to this little bit of a dark-headed girl named Bobbie—that was his first wife—from over at Paul's Valley, I think it was—pretty little thing—and he was drilling for Otis Holtsclaw up north in Osage County. Anyway, he had to leave this here Bobbie alone pret' near all of the time, and this Bobbie wasn't the kind of girl that took kindly to stayin' home." The old man paused, letting the expectancy grow.

Eight year old Linda, small for her age and heavily be-spectacled, wiggled closer to the old brown stove with the flaky isinglass windows and watched the men in the smoky, gas-lit room; she could see them prepare themselves for the story. She knew she liked for Grandpa to hold her on his lap in his rocker and sing to her or tell her stories, but she didn't know that men would like to hear his stories, too.

Grandpa filled his pipe as the men settled in. The room was almost dark, somehow, even though the flimsy little gas mantle on the ceiling seemed to glow as brightly as ever. The smoke was like a warm fog and the men, who were actually moving very little—just shifting, really—seemed to move as if against running water. The heat from the stove was soothing and pleasant, and Linda felt safe—and hidden. The words washed over her like warmth and sleep.

One day in late March of 1932, Frank Gage pulled up in front of Osage County Hauling and Trucking, on the main street of Shidler, Oklahoma, intending to go in and roust out his brother-in-law Nathan, who owed him twelve dollars. However, just as he pulled his Pontiac automobile up next to the sidewalk, he saw his wife Bobbie come out of a honky-tonk with Mildred Perkins.

The two women immediately started to dart back inside, but it was too late, of course. Frank used the old hitching post to boost himself onto the three-foot high sidewalk and came right after them.

He caught them just outside the door. Bobbie's little cloche-hatted head stuck out from behind the Perkins woman, who was at least eight inches taller. He reached around the woman for her and caught her arm.

"Just what the hell do you think you're doin'?" he said, and he jerked her to him, lifting her onto her toes. "How many times do I have to tell you I don't want you drinkin', and I don't want you runnin' around with this whore!"

"Let me go, Frank. You're hurting me. Please, Sweetheart, let me go."

"Frank Gage," said the Perkins woman, "you let her go." When he didn't release Bobbie, the woman pulled at his arm with one hand and punched him a couple of times with the other. "God damn you," she said, "who you callin' a whore? Let her go, you son-of-a-bitch!"

Frank did let her go, then, pushing Bobbie away and shaking off the Perkins woman's grip. He stopped and looked at her. "What did you say?"

"I said for you to let go of her, you son-of-a-bitch."

So Frank hit her.

Actually, it was more a *push*, but it still knocked her back against the screen door of the honky-tonk, maybe breaking the screen a little. She bounced off the door and settled down onto the sidewalk. Frank took Bobbie's arm and started her down the block to the four inset steps that descended to the road. She was crying a little and hollering a little.

"Hold it right there!"

Frank turned to see who was talking, not very happy to be interrupted. The man, standing not ten feet away, was wearing a big old badge and he was pointing a gun straight at Frank's chest.

"Let go of her, fella," he said, coming closer. "I don't know where you're from, and I don't much care, but we don't treat women that way in Shidler."

"Listen," said Frank, stepping toward the policeman. "This is my wife, and I—"

"Shut up," said the policeman. "Just shut your mouth. Let go of that woman and raise your hands. You're goin' to jail."

Frank hit him.

This time he didn't pull the punch. The lawman's shoulder bounced off a Coca-Cola sign; then he made a half-turn, staggered a step, and crashed onto the sidewalk on his head. There was a squelchy, bursting sound. Bobbie screamed. The Perkins woman screamed.

If the policeman had fallen ten feet either north or south, he would have landed on a sidewalk made of rough, unplaned two-by-twelve pine boards. Unfortunately, Ace Holman, the owner of the honky-tonk, fearing that a heavy beer delivery might crash through the wood, had poured, directly in front of his place, a slab of inferior—but nevertheless relatively solid—concrete.

An old man in overalls was suddenly there, standing over the lawman. "He's dead," he said. "You killed 'im!" Bobbie screamed louder, tried to burrow inside Frank's chest, and dug her fingernails into his arm. Other people were coming now.

The gun was almost by his foot, so he pushed Bobbie away and picked it up. "I've done it now," he thought. "I've gone and killed me a man." He waved the gun at them. "Now, you just stay back," he said. "Come on, Bobbie. We're gettin' out of here." He reached for her, but now she squealed and went to the Perkins woman, who grinned at him.

"He killed a law," he heard the old man say. "They'll shoot him down sure."

"Not me," thought Frank, and he jumped down from the sidewalk. The Pontiac was still running, but it didn't really matter. No one tried to stop him.

He started south for Fairfax, where he and Bobbie had a room in a little hotel for a couple of days, but thought better of it and turned back to the plank bridge over Salt Creek and headed for Kaw City. Going back to Ponca wouldn't do any good; Bobbie'd just tell them where they lived. So that left Kaw. They'd figure that out, too, so he had to make it quick. But he had to tell his Dad and Lizzie where he was going and what he had done.

There were ruts in some places in the dirt road and there were a couple of sandy turns, so he had to concentrate some on driving; but he was a good driver. He didn't want to imagine what the folks would say. Dad would probably stand around looking disappointed and angry. Lizzie, though—Lizzie might be able to tell him what to do. Frank nodded

Lizzie Nash had come from a hard family. She'd been an old river-bank whore Dad had taken up with a couple of years after Mama died, and he knew she'd had some experiences with the law herself. Her old man had been in jail somewhere the last Frank had heard. But, hell, she'd been a good wife to Dad, as clear as Frank could tell. And calling her a whore was a little unfair. She'd been a waitress when Dad had met her in Braman. Tough old gal, though. Yeah, she'd have an idea what he could do.

He remembered that there had been a couple of old-time outlaws in his mother's family, way back. Now he was an outlaw. Damn. He slammed the steering wheel with the heels of both hands.

"Jesus," he thought. "I killed a man." He made a right turn into Whizbang, heading north. He slowed down briefly for some old dog to get out of the road. The town itself looked deserted, but he figured someone owned the dog, so he looked around. His Grandma and Grandpa had lived in Whizbang for a while, and he'd worked there himself.

It had been busy then, full of traffic, drunken oil field workers, cheap boarding houses, cheaper whorehouses, with throbbing pump jacks all along the road. He'd been in a few of those whorehouses. Now the town was almost nothing. He saw no one, so he pumped the foot feed and brought the Pontiac back up to speed. There were only a few wells pumping on the edge of town.

"They'll come lookin' for me for sure," he thought. He looked back over his shoulder, but the only dust he could see was his own. "They'll come lookin' for me with guns!"

He remembered the policeman's gun, lying on the passenger seat. He grabbed it and flung it out the window. It landed in some tall weeds at the side of the road. For a frantic second he fought the urge to stop the car and go back for the gun.

When Frank pulled up in front of the little shotgun house between Kaw City and Beal, he just sat in the car for a minute or two. He'd been in trouble before—well, lots of times, he supposed—but he'd never killed anybody. Accused once, yeah. He clenched his teeth. "Gotta do it," he sighed.

His father just stood there, staring at Frank, expressionless. But Lizzie shook her head, bit her lip, took a gunny sack from a nail on the back porch, and started filling it with food.

"Henry," she said, "Get Frank your mackinaw. It'll be a little short in the sleeves, boy, but you have to have a coat; it still gets chilly, especially along towards morning."

Frank sat on a kitchen chair. He felt like crying, and there may have been a tear or two. "What should I do? Turn myself in? Hide out? They ain't dumb; they'd have to know I'd come here."

"Yep," said his father, handing him the red plaid coat. "You got to hurry. Elizabeth, can you get a couple of blankets and fix him a bedroll? Frank, grab some matches off the oven." Frank got up and took a handful of kitchen matches from the holder and stuffed them in a pocket of his father's coat. His father opened the door and looked out.

"Come here, son," he said. "It might look to you like the safe thing would be to just follow the Arkansas River up to Kansas, but if that policeman's really dead, Kansas'll just turn you over. Look, between here and Ponca, you can't go fifteen feet without stepping on some outfit's drilling rig or some pumper out checking wells. You remember old John Blaine?"

Frank nodded. He knew the name, at least.

"The Indian guy, the one your Aunt Claudie worked with, supervised, whatever you call it."

"Oh, yeah," said Frank. "I remember." He did. He didn't really remember the man—at least all that much—but he did remember where the house was. Aunt Claudie had showed it to him, years ago.

"Now, you can't trust him to help you, I don't mean that. But there's a lot of blackjack thicket west of his house, between it and the river. You can hide out there. Won't be very comfortable, but you can stand it."

"More comfortable than that electric chair."

"Right. They may watch me; I don't hardly reckon they will, but they might. Even if they do, I'll find a reason to get up to Newkirk by Thursday and sorta drop in on old John. Meantime, I'll find out what's what and bring you some food. You got a gun?"

"No. Had one. Had the law's gun, but I th'owed it away."

"Well," said his father after a moment, "that's probably all for the best." He looked back toward the bedroom at his wife, just emerging with the bedroll. "Hey, old woman!" he called. "My kid here took a gun off a lawman and then th'owed it away!"

"Good," said Lizzie, the firmness of her words matching the firmness of the set of her mouth and jaw. "Shoulda kept it, though. Now you take this," she said, putting the blankets into Frank's arms.

"Only got two hands," said Frank. He gave her back the bedroll, and, even though it was a fairly warm day, shoved his long arms into the sleeves of the mackinaw. He looked at his father, then at his stepmother. "Better go," he said, "before I bawl like a baby."

He took the roll of blankets, squashed it under one arm, and hoisted the gunny sack of food to his shoulder with the other. "Could you maybe get ahold of Mr. Holtsclaw? I'm supposed to go on evening tour startin' Tuesday, and it don't look like I'm gonna be there."

"I'll do it," said Henry Gage.

Frank just stood there for a moment, wondering how to tell them goodbye and whether this was the last time he'd get to do that. Lizzie came up to him and gave him a little hug. She moved her face close to his ear and whispered, "Do like your dad says. Hide out. It'll be okay." Frank hugged her back, looking over his shoulder at Dad. Then he felt himself tear up. He turned his head, sniffled, and almost ran for the door.

"Drive easy, Frank," his father shouted from the door. "Don't draw no attention to yourself. And get that car back in the woods as far as you can. I'll see you Thursday at the latest."

"Jesus," thought Frank, as he headed for his car, "I wonder who goes after cop killers?" Sheriff? Well, he was out of Osage County. "Oh, sweet Lord!" He stopped and looked back at Henry in the door. The O.B.I! Could this get Walter involved—his own brother? Naw, couldn't be. Might

25

be better, though, really. Walter had pulled him out of messes before. But Jesus! He hadn't killed nobody then!

Frank dumped the stuff beside him in the seat of the Pontiac, started the motor, and looked back at his folks there on the little front porch. He thought, for a moment, that this might be the last time he would see them, and they blurred over. He pulled away fast.

CHAPTER 5

The Damn' Rabbit
Kay County, Oklahoma, 1932

John Blaine's house, located fourteen miles west and a little south of Newkirk, Oklahoma, just across the Arkansas River, was easily the showplace of Kay County—or would have been if there had been anything like a real road to it. As it was, it sat half-hidden in a grove of trees about half a mile off the little farm road that ran north from Uncas.

Old John, who was an oil-rich Osage Indian, would have built the house clear out on the bank of the Arkansas River if only the agent the Bureau of Indian Affairs had appointed to oversee his concerns had agreed. However, the agent, who had happened to be Frank's Aunt Claudie, Mama's sister, had pointed out to Old John—several times—that, since the Arkansas could be counted on to flood with considerable regularity, his house would certainly wind up downstream, smashed up all along the river clear to the hairpin north of Kaw City—which was perfectly all right with her, she'd said, because her folks lived close by, and they could use the solid gold faucets, and the big old yellow catfish would enjoy taking their Saturday night baths in his big old marble bathtub from Italy.

Old John had always wound up doing what Frank's Aunt Claudie said, partially because she was persuasive, but mostly because John couldn't spend any considerable sum of money without Claudie's permission. John liked whiskey and drank it as often as he could, which was every day. That truth, taken with the fact that he was, after all, in the attitudes of the day, an Indian, was clear evidence of need for a guardian. The house was built, in fact, a good three-quarters of a mile from the river.

Frank had driven about halfway up the long, rutted driveway and pulled the Pontiac into a little stand of trees. He wasn't sure yet where he would leave the car, but he didn't think anybody would spot it where it was, almost certainly not from the road. He opened the car door and looked across at Old John's.

Frank had seen the house before, long ago, with his aunt, who had now been long married to Lowell McCracken and moved to Modesto, California. The house was as large as he remembered; it looked like a fancy little hotel, maybe in Tulsa. It was surrounded by a short wall of natural stone. The long, rutted drive turned into a short arc of pavement in front of the house, ending in a slab of concrete in front of the large garage. Parked in front of the garage was a shiny black Packard limousine.

A little road on the south, really just tracks through the grass, snaked west and north, eventually to the river. Hoping that he wouldn't be seen, Frank drove through maybe a half-mile or so of rough pasture before reaching the first stand of trees, where the road looped north again. At a second little grove, Frank pulled the Pontiac off the road and parked it close to an old cottonwood.

He walked out to the little road, looked to see how well the Pontiac was hidden from view, and took some long, deep breaths. He sat on an outcropping of sandstone, lit a cigarette, and looked east to the heavy woods. Off in the distance he could hear the Arkansas River as it rushed southward.

"Just like a huntin' trip," he said aloud, with some disgust. He took a last puff of the cigarette, flipped it away, and stood. "Only I'm the damn' rabbit." He had to dig around in the prairie grass to find the cigarette to make sure that it was out; for a second he'd had the awful presentiment of drawing people from all over the county to put out a prairie fire.

After he'd found the cigarette, extinguished it, and stripped it, he noticed that he'd made a clear trail through some of the long grass. There were tire tracks on the road. He thought of getting a tree limb and brushing out the tracks. Then he shook his head and laughed at himself: he could picture himself flailing a cottonwood branch clear back to Shidler.

He tried to avoid leaving tracks into the woods. There were a few stretches of knee-high grasses that he couldn't avoid, but there were also huge flat rocks, some as large as ten feet by eight feet, that allowed him to avoid even the smallest brushing of vegetation.

In the woods there was a strange kind of silence. Frank had noticed the silence in other woods, but then there had been the scamper and snuffle of a dog, the weight of a rifle on the crook of his arm, and usually the voice of a fellow hunter. Now, alone, he was very much aware of his own noise: the clatter of last year's leaves, even though they were now sodden and blackened; the ripping sound of blackjack and persimmon branches against his sleeves or his pack; the thumping of his boots; the rattle of disturbed stones.

When he stopped, stopped completely, he could hear both the throaty mumbling of the Arkansas and the susurration of, somewhere nearby, a spring.

He found the spring by stepping in it: it was, where he stepped, only a few inches deep, flowing apathetically through an intermingling of broken twigs, blackjack leaves two seasons dead, and some sort of vine with large, heart-shaped leaves, almost the only green in the sun-abandoned spot. He touched the water with long fingers; it was cool, almost cold. He brought the fingers to his mouth. The water bore only the slightest taste of decaying vegetation.

Tracing the spring back to its source was neither difficult nor prolonged: his journey of less than thirty feet ended in a shaded pool, no more than six feet across from Frank's vantage, maybe eight feet long. Water seemed to be seeping from a large slab of gray stone that overhung the little basin.

Frank knelt by the spring, smoked a cigarette, and watched the water. Here in the shadows one couldn't really say the water was clear, exactly, though Frank could see clearly enough that the bottom was nothing more than leaf-strewn mud. Perhaps it was the reflection of the heavy, deep-colored vines climbing the side of the rock that made the water appear green. A single leaf, ancient and soft with mold, floated in the pool. He lifted it out with a finger.

Over his left shoulder, up a small inclination, was another of the large, flat rocks. That, he decided, would be his bed; it might be hard, but he really didn't want to lie down on the softer, moist earth. He put the cigarette out against the sole of his boot and realized that his supply would be gone by morning. He swore a little while he spread his blankets on the rock.

The sack contained an enameled coffee pot and some coffee, as well as food. He was tempted to build a fire, and even gathered some sticks; but it didn't really seem worth the effort. He rummaged through the items in the bag and found an apple. He ate the apple, tossed the core into the brush, and lay down on his hard bed. He could see, he discovered, only various-sized wedges of sky, all small enough to be blotted out by his extended hand.

After a long time, he slept. He awoke to thunder, and, sliding from leaves and pouring down trunks, a hard, cold rain.

Henry Gage, at six feet, was five inches shorter than his second son, and fifty pounds heavier. He had always been an excellent athlete, winning footraces and broad-jumps at county fairs all of his life; his body, at the age of fifty-four, was still robust.

He'd always worked hard, knew what it was to work hard and knew that it was his lot to work hard. He'd gone into debt—actually, to his father-in-law in part—for a good team of horses to haul oil field equipment. The horses could go places trucks couldn't, so there had been plenty of work, but he somehow hadn't gotten along well. He wasn't very good, he knew, about pressing people for payment, and some were slow about paying. And then, for the most part, the drilling slowed down; the outfits that were still drilling hauled their own pipe. Besides, he'd discovered that he really didn't like horses very much.

29

Then he'd spent time on the drilling rigs, first as a roustabout, then a roughneck, and even a chain hand. Hard work. He'd even gone back to Missouri where he'd come from and tried farming, but he'd lost what money he had and quite a bit of his pride. He was working now, as a pumper, for Helmerich and Payne. He'd been with them for quite a while now, through good times and not-so-good.

Almost as soon as Frank left, Henry cranked the old Ford into wakefulness.

"I'll stay in Shidler tonight," he told his wife, "at Mattie's. I can't stomach that no-account Nathan, but I oughta be able to stand him for one night. They'll know *something*, and I'll spy around tomorrow and find out the rest." Lizzie kissed him on the mouth and squeezed both of his shoulders with strong fingers.

It started to rain before he had crossed Salt Creek.

Frank sat huddled in his father's mackinaw. The rain dripped off his hat brim, and unless he sat just so, ran down the back of his neck. The mackinaw was sodden and his cotton trousers were saturated. He couldn't find his blankets in the dark. He had dropped his last cigarette into the spring. He had slept under a tin roof in his day, and he wasn't sure that the sound of the rain on the overhead leaves wasn't almost as loud and maybe more annoying. He could hardly hear himself cuss over the noise.

The spot he was in was actually comparatively dry. He was so completely soaked largely because he had decided, already damp and uncomfortable, to sprint for the car.

He'd felt his way to the edge of the woods in the darkness, pulled his hat down hard on his forehead, then stepped out into rain driven before a strong wind from the west; he had been soaked immediately. Then, as he was turning in indecision, he had tripped against the edge of one of the slabs of rock, stood for a moment with arms flailing, then pitched forward down a short incline. The little draw was already full of fast-moving runoff water. Frank had sworn and splashed and struggled, finally running back into the woods, moving awkwardly because his boots were now full of water. He had leaned against a pin oak to pour the water out.

In his fairly dry place underneath a tree near the Arkansas River in Osage County, Oklahoma, Frank waited for the morning, contemplating, somewhat randomly, misery, death, and the penitentiary.

It didn't take long for Henry to find out that the policeman Frank had hit wasn't dead. Almost as soon as he'd got parked, two people had hollered at him, eager to tell him all about it. By the time he got to Mattie's and Nathan's front door, right there on the main street, he'd been told twice more.

"It was right out funny," said Nathan, clutching his cards so hard they were bending, "Ol' Frank jus' standin' there lookin' like a skunk in the cabbage patch, waggin' that pistol around, and the two women screechin' and hollerin'. I thought I was goin' to fall over laughin'!"

"I'm right glad you find it so funny," said Henry, wanting, as he usually did, to throttle his son-in-law. He'd never understand how Mattie could stand the man, even for a few days. The girl had always *seemed* bright enough. But, hell, she was still just a baby, really. He did some calculations in his head. "God," he thought. "She's nineteen!" He shook his head, sadly. He should have found a way to let her go on to school. Instead, she'd wound up with Nathan.

Nathan pushed a couple of cards together on the table and slapped another on top of them. "Eight and two makes ten," he said, "and, bang, that's Big Casino!"

Henry threw his cards on the table. "I guess I ain't in much of a mood for cards," he said.

"Okay," said Nathan. "I see that."

"Did you see it, Nathan, or did you just hear about it?"

Nathan gathered up the cards and tapped the edge of the deck on the table. "Just heard about it. Hell, everybody's heard about it. And they're laughing about it, too."

"Shut up, Nathan." Henry looked around; Mattie was in the back, probably making up a bed for him. He considered hitting Nathan—just once—before she came back.

"They'll probably shoot Old Slim for sure," Nathan said with a smile. "Hell, you know the law's out runnin' around all over this part of the state lookin' for that guy who killed a bunch of people down by Bixby. Day before yesterday, I think it was. They had this trap set up for 'im and he blasted his way out with a machine gun. Six counties in all directions just rightly swimmin' with law and they ain't goin' to be all-fired careful about who they shoot." He pulled one suspender aside and scratched his belly through his long john top. "I wouldn't want to be in his shoes, I can tell you that!"

Henry arose from his chair and stared hard at his son-in-law. He had learned a few things over the years, and he wouldn't hit Nathan, despite the temptation. He sat on the edge of the table and took both of Nathan's suspenders in one hand and pulled just a little.

"Mattie," he called. "You 'bout got that bed ready?"

Her voice came from the back. "Almost, Daddy. You can come on back any time."

"Good," Henry called back to her. He pulled harder on the galluses and a button came loose. Nathan squirmed, but didn't say anything. "I'm pretty tuckered out, and that bed'll feel good." Henry bent his arm and pulled the suspenders—and Nathan—toward him.

"And I want to thank you, too, Nathan," he said, "for all your hospitality. And I want you to know that I'll make sure Frank knows all about your concern. I reckon he'll want to thank you himself. Good night now."

Mattie met her father in the hall outside the little room just big enough to hold a single bed. Her eyes were wet. He squeezed her hand and kissed her on the forehead.

"I love you, Daddy," she said. "And I'm scared for Frank."

"I know, Sis," he said. "It'll be all right. It will."

Henry lay in the little bed, awake, for a long time, listening to the rain.

Just after dawn, when just a little light began sneaking into the woods, Frank arose, not without pain, from where he had been huddling in the narrow space between the trunk of a chinquapin oak and a great rock. Almost the first thing he saw, just ten feet southwest of the spring, was an old red cedar. He crawled under its branches to its open heart; sure enough, the ground there was dry. If he just had some dry clothes, he thought, he might make himself a *little* comfortable. The thought just caused him to start swearing again.

He broke off some of the dead branches from the underside of the tree, found a suitable spot, built and started a fire, using up almost all of his matches in the process.

As he waited for the coffee to boil, he listened. At first he thought the rumbling was more rain, but it was evident that not much additional moisture was finding its way into the woods. Finally he decided that the sound must come from the river.

The water wouldn't boil. The coffee was terrible-tasting, and he had to spit out grounds after each sip; but he drank it all, then thought of making more. There was some salt pork in the bag, along with a little skillet. He removed the coffee pot from the circle of stones and replaced it with the skillet. Then he cut off a hunk of the salt pork with his pocket knife, dropped the hunk into the skillet, cut another piece, contemplated the skillet, and put the last-cut piece into his mouth.

He was surprised how good raw salt pork tasted, so he ate another piece. Then he fished the warm but still uncooked piece out of the skillet and ate it, too.

As he warmed himself a little over his tiny fire, he examined some choices. The car would be dry inside, but he felt afraid at the called-up image of men with rifles stalking through the tall grass waiting for the eruption of the rabbit called Frank Gage. If they hadn't discovered the Pontiac yet, he imagined that they soon would.

On the other hand, he didn't really want to stay where he was, although he would certainly want to return to the red cedar at night. Again, he listened. After a moment, he knelt over the spring pool to drink, brushed his teeth with a forefinger, then, feeling somewhat better, headed west toward the roar of the river.

The rain was still falling, but not heavily.

CHAPTER 6

D'a-Fon-Tschka
Kay County, Oklahoma, 1932

In south-central Kansas, the Arkansas is fed by Grouse Creek, Slate Creek, and Spring Creek, by the Walnut and the Ninnescah. Though the area's rainfall is not particularly high—about thirty inches per year—heavy spring storms sometimes stall, spilling enough rain to saturate the earth. In days past, these storms replenished rain barrels, cisterns, and farm ponds. Creeks overflowed; tributary rivers quickly filled their narrow channels.

Several miles south of Arkansas City, the banks of the Arkansas begin to rise and the channel begins to narrow and to deepen. The current is faster here, but sometimes there is enough water so that the skilled canoeist can travel the river as far as Salt Creek in Oklahoma. The banks here begin to steepen; even before flood control projects, the river here did not often overflow. Instead, it pushed and shuddered and roiled its way through the narrow channel until it exploded into southern Kay County and west-central Osage County, Oklahoma.

Frank looked down at the river from the bluff. Half the river was still in deep shadow, but he could see that the river was high. Dead trees, or the large limbs of dead trees, having lain long beside the river, had been swept up and were now, depending upon their individual configurations, flailing down the river like drowning men or racing the river, nose down like sleek muskrats.

To the north the woods came to the edge of the bluff, and tentacled knots of root emerged from the sundered rock and dangled over the river. The very edges of the bluff, Frank could see, were crumbly and fragile; the trees there seemed to hover above the rumble and hiss of the river. One spiky sapling canted backward, as if locked in a ruinous tug-of-war, most of its root cluster visible; others seemed to hang precipitously above the river, as if about to dive.

Immediately beyond the clump of roots, however, stood an ancient cottonwood that looked to have sunk roots so deep into the stone that its falling into the river might have caused the whole cliff to disintegrate. Frank stepped behind the aquatic squirm of roots, touched the tree, and slipped by it.

There, just to the north, the earth turned to stone: a foot beyond the cottonwood a huge shaft of red sandstone swept away from the river in a shallow crescent, arcing north and east until it disappeared under a covering of earth. Somehow, the portion of the stone away from the cottonwood had been harder, stronger; the heavily eroded surface upon which Frank now stepped was four feet lower than that to the north, and almost flat.

The shallow bowl, shielded from the north by the less eroded stone and sheltered from above by the cottonwood, was, despite its shape, almost completely dry. There was a slight breeze from the north, still slightly chilling despite the season. Frank hunkered down beside the rock out of the breeze and felt, for the first time in a long while, a little bit of warmth. Then, as he squatted in the little dish of stone, absorbing its heat, he could tell by the changing light on the opposite bank that the sun was coming out.

Frank tugged off his boots and leaned them against the old tree, then removed all his clothing, spreading it high on the rock to the north. The sun would not shine on this spot until late in the afternoon; but the rocks on the opposite bank were changing to the color of straw, and he was made warmer by the color.

The sound of the river seemed directly beneath him here; he was half afraid to crawl to the edge. Careful not to scrape his body on the stone, he moved forward and looked down. Just to the north, some sort of snag in the river was catching debris and breaking the river, temporarily, into two separate streams. A dead tree had lodged against the snag, and bits of brush had quickly filled the space behind it. Patches of foam slid toward the center of the river along the edges of the brush, caught the current, and sped away.

The inner stream, slowed somewhat by a concavity in the cliff, had produced a small whirlpool. While Frank watched, a single branch rotated in the whirlpool for a moment, then was sucked down. He looked for it downstream, waiting for it to bob up again; but, if it surfaced, he didn't see it.

He moved back from the edge; he had, he realized, left himself with few options. If the law found him here, there was no escape route. The river was swimmable, perhaps, by someone, but not by him. He lay there awhile, thinking, his ears full of the sound of the river. He regretted, for a moment, hitting the policeman; but he quickly exchanged that emotion for anger.

He thought of the Perkins woman again, with her cheap orange makeup and her peroxided hair and her snotty expression, and he wished she were here so he could shove her around again. He could almost feel his fist against her soft abdomen, pushing deep into her, pushing her back against the wall.

Then he saw Bobbie's face, tiny and round, white and afraid.

He hit the rock with his fist, then he swore until he was tired of it.

After a while, he noticed carvings in the sheltering rock. Initials, he thought, maybe even a heart. He traced one of the carvings with a finger, but he couldn't make it out. He looked along the stone, over his right shoulder. The little carvings continued along the curve of the stone. He scraped at the edge of one of the inscriptions with a fingernail. He found a circle and a little double zigzag line, but the rest within reach looked like nothing but scratches.

He considered walking back a few steps to examine the other carvings, but he didn't. His body was drying now. Sheltered from the wind, drawing warmth from the rock, tired in body, tired in mind, he retrieved his hat, rested it over his eyes, forgot the carved symbols, and slept.

When he awoke, he was no longer alone. A few yards back from the river, seated on the sandstone ridge, wearing new-looking overalls, a bright green shirt with mother-of-pearl buttons, and a tall black hat with a feather, was an old man. His black hair, loose around his face and hanging long down his back, was uncorrupted with white; but his face, more burnt-orange than red, was heavily lined. He was smoking a cigarette and watching Frank.

Frank scrambled for his trousers, scratching a knee on the rough rock in the process. As he bounced on one leg, trying to maintain his balance and put the other leg into his pants at the same time, he realized that his visitor had to be Old John Blaine.

"Unh," grunted Old John. "White man dance dance of many auto. Indian tourist come powwow, give much money."

Frank looked at the old Indian with dismay. He thought of running, but realized that the old man almost certainly would have a telephone in his big house, and he could call somebody to put on Frank's trail. There was a moment during which Frank considered grabbing the old man by the straps on his overalls and pitching him over the edge of the bluff into the river; the alternative seemed to be to go over that edge himself.

The moment faded: he knew he could not hurt an old man; he knew he was too afraid to try the leap into the river. He stood for a moment, silently, mouth agape, his body, tensed for flight, a long, lean, sinewy skeleton of a white man.

"Sorry I scared you," said the old man, flipping the cigarette in a high arc out over the edge of the bluff. "Name's John. I live over there on the other side of the woods." He straightened his right leg and reached into a pocket. "Since you're my guest in a kind of a way, I suppose I should offer you a drink," he said. The pocket yielded a brown pint bottle. John opened it, sniffed the contents, and took a long drink. "Bourbon whiskey," he said. "Damned good." He offered the bottle.

Frank finished buttoning his pants. "I can use a drink," he said. "You scared the livin' hell out of me." He took the bottle, wiped the mouth with his wrist, and drank. He could sense the old man's eyes on him as he drank, so he drank less than he wanted.

"Mighty grateful," he said, as he returned the bottle.

"Well, now," said Old John. "I come here a lot. I like to hear the river. I like to be where I can have a drink without being told that I shouldn't have a drink. In a way, I own this place." He swept the whiskey bottle in a wide arc, covering the bluff and even the river. He looked at Frank again, tipped the bottle to drink, then held the bottle up to the light. "Seems like I've told you why I'm here. Maybe you could tell me why you're here." He held out the bottle.

Frank's name almost popped out of his mouth, but he clamped down on it. He took the bottle with some caution. "Name's Groves," he said, naming a distant and obscure cousin. "George." He shifted the bottle to his left hand and stuck out his right. The Indian took his hand and shook it gently, as if testing to see how nearly ripe it was, how close to falling.

"Hello, George Groves," he said. "And what are you doing on my bluff?"

"Just watching the river," Frank said.

"And sleeping?"

"Yeah. And sleeping."

"You find this a comfortable place to sleep? You came here from where? Ponca City? If you were from around here, I'd know you. Huh. Just to sleep on Old John's bluff."

"Not exactly," said Frank. "Had a little squabble with my wife." That was true enough, he thought. "Kinda took off mad and just drove around till I wound up here." He made a little twitching, dismissing gesture with his left hand, as if he did this sort of thing with some regularity.

"Go on," said Old John with a wave of the hand. "Drink." He slid forward off the rock and stepped to the edge of the bluff as Frank drank. He glanced at the bottle Frank held out to him and pushed it away. "Finish it," he said. "I have more." He pulled a pint bottle from his right pocket and placed it on the ledge; then he pulled two more from his left pocket. "What do you do, George Groves?"

Frank stood beside him, looking out over the river. "Oil," he said. "I work in the oil field."

"Ah, yes," said the old man. "Oil. Oil is very good." He opened a bottle. "There is much oil on my land. I'm very rich." He took a drink and looked at Frank. His voice changed, got deeper, more guttural. "Much money. Many rooms. Whiskey. Ugh!" He held up his arm, palm toward Frank, and Frank recognized the movie Indian. He almost grinned, despite himself.

Frank finished the bourbon and tossed the bottle out over the river. At the top of its arc it caught a bright ray of sun and returned a bronze flash. "The river's a mean old son-bitch today," he said. It had risen while he slept and was louder and fuller. The tree trunk that had tried to create a dam was gone and the current whipped down the middle of the bed like a giant snake.

Old John sat down on the edge of the bluff, dangling his black-booted feet over the rushing water. He took a package of cigarettes from the bib of his overalls, took one, and offered one to Frank.

"No," he said, after they had lit up. "River ain't angry. It's lookin' to get laid."

Frank looked at him.

"True. It's a little early, that's all." Then John told him, while they drank, about D'a-Fon-Tschka, in the moon of Buffalo-Pawing-Earth, when the river gods rise in great passion to mate with Mo'n-Sho'n, the Mother Earth. He talked for what seemed to be hours, in a strong, quiet voice, about dancing, about giving of gifts, about the gathering of Osage, Kaw, Ponca, Sac and Fox, and Dakota Sioux, about the red dyes, about the hawkbells.

Frank sometimes listened intently to his words; sometimes the words blended with the sound of the river. He may even have slept some, but he knew, at one point, that he heard drums in the river. At the end, there were words that Frank couldn't understand.

"What was that?" Frank asked. "Indian?"

"No," said Old John. "That was Osage." His look, it seemed to Frank, was the kind of look you gave an ignorant kid. "We are not all the same, you know, George Groves. That land over there"—his gesture swept south and east—"is Osage land. But you know that, probably. But every—Indian—is not Osage. There are many tribes." His eyes narrowed. "It's not the same thing, George Groves."

Frank looked at the river. "Yeah," he said. "I've met some Poncas, I know, probably some others. Yeah." He pointed at the carvings in the red sandstone. "These here marks. They signs of some kind? Something from your people a long time back?"

"Who knows?" said John, scratching. "Do you care? I don't. Just a bunch of scratches."

"Your people?" asked Frank. "They make these marks?"

"Before my time," said Old John. "Besides, this right here isn't really Osage land. Well, except that it's mine. Scratches might be Ponca, but I doubt that. Prob'ly even before them. Who knows?" The old man shrugged.

"Okay," thought Frank, but he ran his fingers over them again.

CHAPTER 7

Drill Log
Okemah and Kay County, Oklahoma, 1945 and 1932

Linda looked through the little isinglass panes into the fire. It was blue at the bottom where the gas came out in little streams, but it turned yellow and red at the tops, where it flickered and danced. She was very warm, very comfortable. Grandpa's voice seemed to rock her, cushion her.

"Next morning," said Henry, "I marched myself up to the police station, just to ask around, you know. Walked up to this little fella sittin' behind this railing and said, 'I hear the man that that got hit didn't die. He gonna be all right?'

"Little fella looks up at me and says, 'I know you. You're Henry Gage!' and he got up and come around that rail and shook my hand. 'You're Frank Gage's pa. We been hopin' you'd come in.' He took me around the corner to this little office-kinda thing where I met the chief.

"Chief shook my hand, too. 'Where's Old Slim?' he said, and he was grinnin' big. 'Listen here, Henry, you tell that sorry ol' drink of water to get hisself back into town. There ain't gonna be no charges. Damned old Jim Harris ever' oncet in a while gets to thinkin' he's J. Edgar Fucking Hoover or somebody and goes around pullin' guns on people. Ol' Frank just done what any of us woulda done. Fact is, we had complaints before. This time, we run 'im off. You tell ol' Slim he don't have nothin' to worry about.'

"I have to admit that for a minute I just kinda stood there, with my mouth open." He laughed. "Imagine Henry Gage with nothin' to say!

"Anyway, after that we laughed pretty good, and these old boys wanted to set around and swap stories, but naturally I wanted to get up there and tell Frank he was safe and he could come back in. While I was leavin', this chief hollered out at me, 'Hey, you tell Ol' Slim if he ever wants it, he can have Harris's job. Hell, he can have Harris's badge. Got it right here in the drawer. But, hey, if he don't want the job, tell him to drop off the gun sometime anyway, okay?'"

It hadn't happened exactly as Henry told it. Chief Rowan had indeed told him there wouldn't be any charges, but....

"Henry," he'd said. "You know that we can't just overlook this." He paused a bit, fingering some papers on his desk. "We have a small force here—just three men besides me. Harris was never no shakes as a lawman, but he's better than nothing."

"What do we do?" asked Henry.

"Not much we *can* do," said Rowan. "Harris is going to be all right. He'll get a couple of weeks off—with pay. And he'll have doctor bills—the city ain't going to pay them."

"And?"

Rowan leaned back in his chair. "Frank's going to have to pay those doctor's bills—*and* pick up Harris's pay for the time he's off. Or you can."

"Chief, you know I can't do that. I don't make that much money. And I don't think Frank can do it, either."

"Well, somebody's goin' to have to." Rowan leaned forward again. "Henry, if this was almost anybody else, ol' Frank would find hisself in jail, sooner or later. And we *would* find him." The chief stood up and took a couple of steps to the window and looked out, his back to Henry, then he turned. "What would his brother think of this?"

That brought Henry's thoughts to a full stop. "Walter?"

"Yep. Walter. Oklahoma Bureau of Investigation or whatever that outfit's called. Law enforcement on the state level. That Walter. What's he going to tell the fellows he works with? What's he gonna tell the governor?"

"Don't rightly know."

"We don't intend to embarrass your son—we don't intend to embarrass your family. But Frank's gotta come in. And somebody's going to have to pick up the city's expenses here. And Harris's."

"I see that," said Henry, sliding his hands into his pockets and slouching in his seat. "I'll see what I can do. About getting Frank to come in. And about the money."

"And the gun."

Henry remembered: Frank had thrown the gun away. How much did a police revolver cost? "Yeah," he said. Then he stood. "I'll be in touch."

"You do that, Henry. Soon."

Frank felt something nudging at his ribs and began to wake up. The old Indian was standing over him, kicking at him idly.

"Wake up, George Groves. Wake up."

"What? Hey, quit kickin' me, okay? Damn." Frank struggled a little to sit up on the bare rock.

"I know who you are, George Groves," said Old John, staring down into the neck of the near-empty pint bottle. "I know who you are."

Frank felt a moment of panic, but he managed to keep his composure and look back into the old man's face. "Oh, yeah? Who am I supposed to be, then?" For an instant, the image of the old man going over the edge of the bluff into the river came back to him.

The old man laughed and offered the bottle. Frank waved it away.

"You're the one that killed those fellows east of here. Bixby, I think it was. You're runnin' from the law."

"What?" Frank finished waking and stood up quickly.

Old John smiled at him and offered a whiskey bottle. "No? You're not running from the law?"

Frank couldn't think of anything to say, so he just stood there.

"So," said the Indian. "You're supposed to have some kind of machine gun. Where is it? Here, have a drink."

Frank's hand shook a little as he reached for the bottle.

"So," said Old John, "Where's that gun of yours? I'd like to see it. Don't think I've ever seen a—what you call 'em—tommy gun, except in the newsreels. Let me see it."

Frank took a quick swig; he definitely felt that he needed it. He looked up. "I don't have one." He spread his arms, shocked. Machine gun? Him? "No! Never had one! Wouldn't know how to use it if I did!"

"Then what'd you use to kill those fellers?"

"Hey, I didn't kill nobody!" Jesus! But maybe he had. Probably he had. God damn it!

"Okay," said John. "I ain't callin' nobody a liar. If you say your name's George Groves and that you never killed nobody, I'll believe you." He took the whiskey bottle back. His grin was less than convincing, but it was a grin.

"So," said the old Indian, lowering himself and sitting on the ledge overlooking the river, his legs dangling over the side. "So, set yourself down, George Groves, and tell me what the real truth is. I'm not going anywhere but right here and back to my place over there, so I'm not going to be able to tell anybody else."

Then he nodded toward the river. "Besides, if I was going to do that, would I sit here where you could just push me over? I don't swim all that good anymore." He grinned at Frank, then turned his face back to the river.

Frank watched the old man sigh, then he, too, turned to the river.

So they sat there on the cliff overlooking the Arkansas, each with his own thoughts—one afraid of the future, perhaps; one, mourning the past.

"Wake up, Honey," said Elizabeth Gage, gently shaking her granddaughter. "You have to get up, Sugar. You'll catch your death of cold sleepin' here on this cold floor."

Linda was warm and sweaty and sleepy, and she snuggled in her grandmother's arms as she was carried to the little cot that had been made up for her in the kitchen.

"I want to hear Grandpa's stories."

"I know, Sugar, but you need to go to bed now."

"Okay, Grandma," Linda said, snuggling. "I love you, Grandma."

"And we love you," her grandmother said.

CHAPTER 8

Family Matters
Lakin, Kansas, 1972

Linda sat up and pulled her yellow-shoed feet from beneath her. She looked south at her Uncle Frank and she looked north at the monster of an evergreen spreading hungrily over the lawn.

"Well," she thought, "how about that!" She had forgotten the slipping away into sleep. Had she even heard the end of Grandpa's story? She wasn't sure. The story had always been so clear in her head, one of those family stories, she had thought, that gets passed on through generations. She'd told the story before, in dormitory rooms and in taverns. Now she was no longer sure what was truth—what was remembered from Grandpa, what she had heard from others, and what she herself had unconsciously added over the years.

She grinned at Frank. "How about it, Uncle Wild Man?" She reached out and crushed the crown of his old hat. "Did you knock the policeman out? Did they offer you a job? Tell the truth now."

He shrugged away from her fingers. "Now, damn it, Linda, you leave that hat alone," he said.

"Come on, Uncle Frank. Tell me."

Frank leaned forward, plumping out the old hat. "Naw," he said. "That didn't happen." He looked at her. "I'm sorry, little sweetheart, but I told you my daddy was windy."

Linda grinned at him and pushed his shoulder. "And you're not windy?" She laughed. "Okay, I believe you."

Frank looked at her from beneath his hat brim.

"I do!" said Linda. "My Uncle Frank would never be less than honest with me!"

Frank shrugged, but there was a grin on his face.

Linda sat back in her chair and looked at her feet. "Well, then," she said, "tell me about Uncle Walter."

"Walter?"

"Yeah. I barely remember him, Uncle Frank. Was he like you? More like Uncle Tom? Uncle Claude?"

"Well, now, Baby Girl, that's a good question! So I'll give you a good answer. Hell if I know."

Linda was tempted to pull his hat down over his eyes again, but restrained herself. "When I had my tonsils out," she said, "Uncle Walter came to visit me in the hospital. It was the next day, I think. Anyway, I could eat regular food and they brought me breakfast. Eggs. Runny eggs. I didn't want 'em, and Uncle Walter sat there and ate them!"

"Made you want 'em yourself, didn't it?"

Linda had to smile at herself. "Yeah, it did, kinda. But that's just about all I remember about him."

Frank chuckled, so Linda had to slap at his hat. "What's so funny, wild man?"

"You," said Frank.

"Huh? And just how am I so amusing to my uncle?"

Frank adjusted his hat and then reached down and untied one of Linda's shoes. "I hate to disillusion you, Honey, but that was me. I was the one who ate your eggs. Real good, too, as I remember."

Linda started to re-tie her shoe, but stopped. "Really? That was you?"

"Honey, Walter was gone before you were born."

Linda sat up straight. "Well," she said. "You caught me. I'm stupid, okay?"

"Nah, you're not stupid. You're a bright young woman!" He reached down to try to tie her shoe for her, but her feet were back down on the porch again and he almost lost his balance. Linda reached out a hand to steady him.

"Never mind the shoe, Uncle Frank."

Frank straightened and looked at her. "Natural enough mistake," he said. "You were little and you were probably barely awake."

"I suppose so," said Linda, "but I don't know how I could have thought that I'd met Uncle Walter!"

Frank stretched, throwing his shoulders back and bringing his elbows forward. "Aw, hell, Linda. Maybe you did see him somehow."

"I don't understand. What do you mean?"

"Your mama," said Frank. "She kinda *sees* things. Maybe you do, too."

"See things? What does that mean?"

"Prob'ly nonsense," said Frank. "You remember Aunt Claudie?"

Frank could see the puzzlement on Linda's face. "Sure," she said. "but it was a long time ago. She lived out in California, but I know I've met her. I just don't remember when."

"Well," said Frank. "My Aunt Claudie and your mama and your Aunt Mattie have some things in common. Hell, it may all be bullshit—oh, hell! Pardon the language."

Linda smiled. "I've heard the word, Uncle Frank. May even have used it myself once or twice."

Frank fidgeted for a minute, then laughed. "I'm a crude son-of-a-bitch, Honey. I s'pect you already knew that, didn't you?"

"Yeah," said Linda, "but you're a nice son-of-a-bitch!" She fussed with his hat again. "Now go on. Tell me about this mysterious connection between Aunt Claudie and my mother."

"I will," said Frank. "Provided you leave my damn' hat alone!"

"Done," said Linda.

"How is your mama, anyway?"

Linda shrugged. "Don't know, Uncle Frank. I haven't seen her for—well, at least a year."

"Huh?"

Frank thought that Linda slumped a little. "Yeah," she said. "You know Mama. She does what she wants to do, goes where she wants to go."

She reached for his hat again, but Frank blocked her hand with his. She laughed.

"Now, old man," she said, "you can quit stalling now! What's this stuff about Aunt Claudie and Aunt Mattie and Mama?"

"Okay! Okay! Quit naggin'. Durned women! Thought you was different!"

"No woman ever got away with nagging at you, Frank Gage. Now cut it out and tell me the story, or that ugly old hat of yours is goin' into that bush over there!"

Frank sighed. "I know when I'm beat," he said.

"When I was a kid," he said, "Grandma and Grandpa used to be what they called spiritualists. I never really paid much attention to that stuff, but they held séances or some such thing, and my aunt Claudie was really into that stuff."

"Ah," said Linda. "I think I know what you mean now, by *seeing*."

"You do?"

"I think maybe so. When I was growing up—well, when I was a teenager, living with Aunt Mattie and Uncle Nathan—whenever the telephone rang, Aunt Mattie always seemed to know who it was for." She grinned and reached down to tie her shoe. "I wasn't the most popular girl in school, but I did get a lot of calls. I always sort of figured that she just expected the calls to be for me. You suppose she really knew, somehow?"

"Could be," said Frank. "She seemed to know when Walter died."

"Really?"

"Uh-huh. I wasn't there, of course, but I heard that she woke up screaming and told your Uncle Nathan that something was happening to him."

Linda had finished with her shoe and sat up. "And was it?"

"Yep. He was gettin' shot."

Linda bit her lip. "I'd heard that—that he'd been killed. I don't think I ever knew how it happened, though."

Frank turned just a little to look at his niece. He could almost see her mother in her as she sat there. He'd never really talked to Callie about Walter; it hadn't been easy to talk about for him, and he'd been afraid that it'd be a lot harder on her. He wasn't sure that he wanted to bring the whole thing up now.

"Walt was a good man, Honey. A hell of a lot better man than I ever was."

Linda doubted that. "I have a little time yet," she said. "So tell me about Uncle Walter. Oh! Unless you have to do something, be somewhere!"

"All I have to do," said Frank, "is set here." Frank sighed, deeply. Maybe it was time. He clenched and unclenched his fists. "Okay," he said. "What do you want to know?"

Linda folded her hands in her lap. "Everything. Oh, whatever you want to tell me."

"Huh," said Frank. "Everything'd take a long time."

"As much as you can, then."

Frank let out a long sigh that made Linda think that he didn't want to talk anymore, that he was tired of answering her questions. So she patted his knee. "It's all right, Uncle Frank. We can do this some other time."

"No, Honey. It's all right." Frank straightened his hat again, although Linda thought that it wound up exactly where it had been before.

"If you're sure."

"Sure as rain," said Frank. "Well, first of all, Walter was the oldest."

PART TWO

GROWING UP

CHAPTER 9

Permanent Damage
Mervine, Oklahoma, 1919

Mattie had liked the farm. It had been warm and comfortable, and it felt like home. The house had been big, she realized now. Grandpa lived there. Grandma. Daddy and Mama and Walter and Frank and Tom and Claude and the baby. And there was lots of room. People didn't bump into other people all the time, and you could go someplace to be alone and play without having to listen to the boys running around and yelling. She missed the farm.

But she had to go where Daddy went, and he said he had to move to Mervine where there was work in the oil fields.

There were almost as many people in this house, and it was a lot smaller. Walter had stayed on the farm with Grandpa and Grandma so he could finish school, but Uncle Mac and Aunt Claudie and their son Christopher lived here with them now. Mattie had to share a bed with Claude, and Frank and Tom and Christopher slept in another bed in the same room. Uncle Mac and Aunt Claudie got the bedroom, while Mama and Daddy slept in the kitchen. She didn't think that was fair, especially since Uncle Mac worked for Daddy. But she didn't run the house; she thought, though, that it would be better if she did.

Mama was busy with the baby, of course, besides cooking and washing and cleaning. Aunt Claudie had a job way off in Ponca City—something to do with the Indians, Mattie had heard, but she didn't know what. Anyway, she was gone a lot.

Mattie helped as much as she could. She liked for things to be nice. But she could tell Mama was tired. The baby, Callie, was crawling now, and getting into things and putting things in her mouth. She had to be watched all the time.

Mattie would have liked to help more, but she had to go to school. She liked to go to school, though. She had learned to read right away, and her teacher had told Mama that she was a good student. Mattie wanted to be good, so that made her happy. Tom and Claude were in school, too, but there wasn't a high school here, so Frank didn't have to go. He didn't seem to care. He liked to go to work with Daddy and Uncle Mac.

But today was Saturday. Mama had to go to the grocery store, and Mattie was going along. She liked that. The grocery store was fun to visit. Besides the groceries on the shelves, there were big barrels of pickles and big jars of candy, and, clear in the back, were shelves with bolts of material and ribbons and thread and buttons and even some dress patterns. Mattie liked to embroider when she had time and she liked to look at the material on the shelves and imagine pretty dresses she could make. Then she would help Mama carry things home.

"Are you ready, Matilda?" asked Mama. She was adjusting her hat in front of the mirror that hung by the door. "Your father and the boys will be back before you know it, and I have to get dinner. So come on."

"I'm coming!" Mattie wished she had a hat like Mama's, but Mama said that she'd have plenty of hats—and nice dresses, too, someday. But Mama didn't really have nice dresses.

"Claude!" hollered Mama. "Get in here and watch the baby, *now!*" She patted her tummy as she turned back to watch Claude come in from the bedroom. Mama was getting fat, Mattie thought.

"Can't Christopher watch her?" Claude's voice was whiny.

"No!" Her mama's voice was firm. "She's your baby sister, not Christopher's. So you watch her!"

The grocery store was just two doors down and there was a nice wooden walk, so they didn't have to walk in the mud when it rained. That was good, because Mattie absolutely did not like to get her shoes all nasty and muddy. There were posts all along the street side, with a rail nailed across the top. You could use that to keep your balance, Mattie thought, even though she'd never had to use it. It was a little high for her, anyway. She glanced down at the ground. The walk was a couple of feet high, so the rail could keep people from falling off. Maybe falling off into the mud!

Just before they got to the store, they stepped around the old collie dog that always seemed to be sleeping there. The dog never seemed to bother anybody, but Mattie and the boys had all been told to leave it alone. So they did.

Mr. Carter met them right inside the door with a big smile, and Mattie looked around while Mama told Mr. Carter what she needed and he gathered it up. It didn't take long, but Mattie had time to look at some pink calico that would make a nice dress before Mama called her that it was time to go.

They stepped outside just in time to see the dog leap up and grab baby Callie by the face. He lifted her completely off the walk and shook her. She screamed.

Then Mama screamed and ran toward the dog and her baby.

And the dog turned and ran, still carrying the screaming baby.

Mr. Carter burst out of the store and ran after the dog. Mama and Mattie stood where they were, unable to move. Mama was still screaming. Claude came running out of the house then. He looked at his mother, looked on both sides of the door to the house, looked over the side of the walk. For a moment, Mattie wanted to hit him.

Mr. Carter caught the dog and brought the baby back to her mother. Callie was bleeding—a lot—from several places. There was a big gash on one cheek, all the way to her chin and another, smaller one, just below her chin.

Mama was crying and holding Callie against her cheek. The blood was running down her face, too, and down onto her dress.

"A doctor!" she said. "We've got to get her to a doctor!"

"Yes," said Mr. Carter, "but you need to get the bleeding stopped."

Back in the house, Mama washed Callie's wounds, even though she fought and screamed, and held a towel over them. "Get my purse, Matilda," she said. "It's either on the table by the door or I dropped it at the store. Get it, and hurry!"

Martha Gage wrapped her baby in a blanket, took her purse from Mattie, and headed to the door. "You stay here with Claude and tell your father that I've taken the baby to Ponca City to the doctor."

"Can I go?" asked Mattie.

"No. Stay here." And she was gone.

Mattie followed her out the door and down the block. "Mama," she called, "how're you going to get to Ponca City?"

"I'll have to take the train!" she called back. "Now you get in the house. I mean it! And tell your father where I am!"

Mattie stood and watched her go. She felt bad that the baby was hurt and that Mama was scared, but she really, really, really wanted to go, to ride the train, to go to Ponca City.

The doctor in Ponca City stitched up the torn places and told Martha that the baby would be all right. She'd be scarred, of course, but it could have been worse. He'd given Callie some medicine to help the pain, and she slept most of the way home. Once in a while she'd whimper, but not often. Martha cuddled her and cried a little.

Henry and Mac and the boys were waiting at the depot when she got back to Mervine. She told them what the doctor had said—that Callie'd be all right, that they had to watch for infection, and that she'd be scarred. Henry just looked at the baby with sad eyes. Martha's own eyes were drawn to Henry's face, a face that had its own scars. But he was a man, she thought. Scars didn't matter so much on a man.

Tom just stood there, his face full of pity—for the baby, of course, but mostly for his mother. Frank, on the other hand, was pacing and flailing his arms.

"I'm goin' to kill that son-of-a-bitch dog!" he said. "No god damned dog is going to bite my baby sister!" He turned to face his father. "Does Uncle Mac have a gun? You have a gun, Uncle Mac? You know where I can get a gun?"

Henry just looked at him. Mac backed away a step.

"I mean it! I am going to kill that god-damned dog!"

"No, you're not," said Henry, putting a hand on his son's shoulder. "For one thing, I don't own a gun. Mac doesn't own a gun. We're not goin' to have any guns in our house." Then his voice grew stronger, more harsh. "And we're not killing any dogs!"

Frank lowered his arms, met his father's gaze, then let his head drop. He sighed. "Yes, Sir." Then he looked back up. "But somebody ought to."

"We have to go home!" said Martha. "Can we just go home, please?" There was enough shrillness in her voice that everybody turned to her. Henry nodded, put his arm around her shoulder, and led her around to the front of the depot where the wagon sat.

And they went home. And Callie healed. And the dog, caged up, didn't have rabies. And Callie carried a jagged scar all of her life.

Then Mattie's school year was over, and it was summer. Summer meant that Walter was home, and he had a big leather folder that he called his diploma. He showed it to Mattie, and his big grin told her that it was important.

She asked him if she could hold it, and he nodded and held it out to her. The leather felt good. It was smooth and nice, and the paper inside had Walter's name on it and the year and the name of his school. She liked it.

"You'll have your own someday," said Walter, and he stroked her cheek.

Daddy and the boys were gone even more now. Walter was home, so he could help, too. They were hauling drill pipe, Walter told her.

Mattie was glad she wasn't a boy, because her brothers were always dirty when they came home. And they were tired, too. She was happy to stay home, help Mama when she could, play with her paper dolls, and pretend that this was *her* house—with pretty curtains in the windows and big rugs on the floor and pictures on the walls. She sometimes had to watch Callie, too. Mama was very careful with Callie now, after the dog bite.

Callie's face was healing, but the place on her face was all red and nasty-looking. Poor Callie wasn't going to be pretty, Mattie thought. "But

I'm pretty. Everybody says so." The thought made her smile, until she thought about Callie's scar and how she was going to be ugly, and that made her feel bad.

So summer went. It was quiet for Mattie, for the most part. Uncle Mac and Aunt Claudie and Christopher moved away in July. Aunt Claudie wasn't home much anyway, because her job kept her in Ponca City a lot. So now Walter slept in the kitchen and Mama and Daddy got to sleep in the bedroom. That was good.

But Daddy was sometimes cranky, and Mama looked tired a lot and sometimes sad. Mattie hugged her Mama when she could and helped all she could, but she could tell something was wrong. She didn't want anything to be wrong. She wanted things to be nice.

Then things got worse.

Walter turned the team onto the mud road leading to the Simmons location. The wagon wheels slid sideways in the deep muck for a moment, but straightened out as the horses plowed ahead. Walter flicked the reins lightly, but the team knew what they were doing; they'd plodded through worse mud than this. Walter clicked his tongue at them anyway.

The right front wheels of the wagon hit a deep puddle and muddy water splashed up, spattering Frank, who sat beside him, and almost soaking poor Tom, sprawled behind Frank.

"Ah, God!" squealed Tom and brought his feet back inside.

Frank laughed. So did Walter, a little, though he tried not to. Tom scowled at them, but, as older brothers often do, they ignored him. After all, Tom was twelve, just a boy. Walter and Frank were *men*, seventeen and fifteen.

"How much farther?" Tom asked. "You sure these horses can even get through all this? Gee."

"It'll be even worse when we pull into the location," said Walter. He glanced behind him at the load of drill pipe. Farther back, he could see their father turning onto the road with a second load.

Frank turned around in his seat and swatted Tom's leg, sending up a spray of muddy water. "About a quarter mile, I think," Frank said with a grin. "Boy, will you ever get heck from Mama when we get home! You're gonna spend about an hour under the pump before she'll let you in the house!"

"We'll get there okay," said Walter. "But they've had the rig builders in here—and the drilling equipment. If you think this is a mud pit, wait until you see what it's gonna be like when we hit the location."

Henry's teams and wagons had been expensive, but Martha's father had helped him, partially by lending him some money himself and by cosigning a note for the rest. There was plenty of work right now, hauling pipe and equipment to the drill sites, and he expected to have everything paid off by the end of the summer. And teamstering, though it wasn't exactly fun, was better than some of the things he'd had to work at before. And he had the boys to help him. They were good boys, good hard workers. He watched the team ahead and smiled. They were good boys. And it was nice having Walter home.

Ahead of him, Walter turned the team off the road onto the Simmons farm, where the Marland company was sinking a well. "Well," he said. "Here we are."

"There's the derrick!" shouted Tom, right in Frank's ear. Frank pushed him away. Walter halted the team in front of the barbed wire gate and took a deep breath. He hadn't been all that certain, despite the horses' strength, that they wouldn't bog down.

"Tom, you're already dirty," he said. "Hop down and get the gate for us."

"Huh!" said Tom.

"Go on, do it."

"Not me!" said Tom, peering over at the mud that came halfway up the wheel. "I'm not getting down there in that stuff! You do it!"

Walter laughed. "I'm the driver! I sit up here on the seat and drive the team. You do the other stuff!"

"Says you."

"Jesus," said Frank. "I'll drive the team through and you get the damned gate."

Walter had to laugh. Frank and Tom were already muddy and he was clean, but he was supposed to slosh around in mud up to his knees. What the hell. Okay.

So he dropped into the mud—halfway up to his knees, almost, and slogged through it to the gate. He lifted the baling wire loop off the top post and bent to lift the post out of the bottom loop. As he bent, he looked ruefully at the mud coming over the top of his boot and seeping down over his foot. Wonderful. He should have tossed Tom out of the wagon! Then, with effort, because the bottom of the damned gate was below the surface of the mud, he began to tug it open.

"Okay, Frank," he hollered. "Here she comes."

Frank wasn't paying attention. Usually he would have enjoyed watching Walter flail around in the mud, but right now he was busy rubbing Tom's head with some mud he'd scraped off the top of a wheel. But when he heard Walter's "Okay," he snapped the reins and the team, impatient from standing, moved forward.

With considerable effort, Walter dragged the wire gate aside and let it drop—after all, Dad's team would be coming through, too—and headed for the wagon, intending to climb on before it got through the gate. Frank was sitting in his seat, of course, now, and going around the wagon would take too long and be too muddy, so he'd have to climb in back with Tom. The mud dragged at his boots. He reached up to grab the sideboard and haul himself up, but then his feet slipped in the mud and he fell.

For a second he scrambled to get his feet under him, but then the wheel, carrying its share of a load of drill pipe, smashed his arm and hand. He wanted to scream, but he couldn't because his mouth was full of Oklahoma red mud.

Mattie cried when Walter didn't come home. Daddy was quiet, almost too quiet, she thought. It was a little scary. And Frank, always loud, just sat in a chair next to the stove, with his head down and his hands down between his knees. Every once in a while, Daddy would look over at Frank and shake his head.

Something bad had happened, Mattie could tell, and her big brother hadn't come home. Big Walter, who had carried her around, laughing, when she was littler, and still sometimes picked her up and held her high in the air, even though she was getting big. If Walter was dead, her life was ruined forever.

Walter's arm was broken, and his left hand had been crushed. Healing was slow, and Henry had to do without one of his helpers for a while. Walter, to be honest with himself, despite feeling some guilt, didn't mind that, really. He used the time to do what he really wanted to do: read and study. He hadn't told his folks—he couldn't imagine what they'd think—but he really wanted to go to college. He'd done pretty well in high school. He thought so, and his teachers had told him so.

The farm was quite a ways from the high school in Kaw City, but Grandpa Cantrell had bought an old Model-T Ford, and he'd let Walter drive it to school. Grandpa had been a little afraid of it, Walter thought, and he laughed at remembering seeing Grandpa drive it smack-dab into a haystack, hollering, "Whoa!" all the time. He wondered if Grandpa was driving it now. He supposed that he was, finally. If not—maybe he could use it to take him to Stillwater!

Stillwater. Oklahoma Agricultural and Mechanical College. Mr. Scott, his science teacher, had gone there, and he'd told Walter that he should, too. He might even get a scholarship, Mr. Scott had said. "If you want to go," he'd said. "Let me know. I'll see what I can do. I still know a lot of people down there."

Yeah, it was a dream, and probably a foolish one. But he wasn't any use to anyone here, with his stupid arm and his damned-near useless hand.

As it turned out, it didn't really matter that he couldn't help with the teams. Drilling had slowed in the Mervine field, and Henry wasn't making enough money to feed the family and pay the rent, much less pay off his debt. He sold the wagons and teams for what he could get out of them, and, with considerable regret, took his family to Ponca City, where he took a job working for Lew Winch at the refinery.

Walter's arm healed, in time, but the hand was permanently damaged. He could use it for most things, but there was no real strength in it. He couldn't grip a wrench. He couldn't even hold a hammer with it. His oilfield days were over, he knew. His life would have to be different. He'd have to find another life, another way. That other life might mean a college education and another leather-covered document with his name on it. And some other kind of work—he didn't know what. It embarrassed him a little, but it was exciting.

CHAPTER 10

Something Bad
Ponca City, Oklahoma, 1919-1920

The refinery work wasn't really all that hard, Henry found, but it was dangerous. He didn't have to run the big boilers, but he didn't really trust the men who did. One boiler going off could set off the whole place. With the gas fumes and all that oil, the burning would be fast, devastating, and deadly. Sometimes when Henry thought about that possibility, he'd rub his face, the old burn scars.

But he was feeding his family, and that was the main thing. Mattie and Claude were in school, and he'd been able, this time, to buy their books. Henry knew that there were people agitating to have the state buy schoolbooks, and he hoped that would happen. But it hadn't happened yet.

Frank and Tom had both decided not to go on with their schooling. Henry had gone just through the eighth grade, so he thought that the boys' decision made some sense. At any rate, that meant that he didn't have to buy books for them, too. And they were both working now, bringing home some money themselves. Tom was working at the flour mill, hauling sacks around. Frank had managed to get a job as a roustabout for a drilling company.

Things were going pretty well, Henry thought. The kids were all well, and Martha, bless her heart, was expecting another baby. Henry had to shake his head at that. He could hardly ever have imagined that he'd be the father of six children, let alone seven. A lot of responsibility, but the thought still made him smile. Hell, just thinking of Martha made him smile. He couldn't imagine that anyone could have a better, sweeter, kinder, more loving wife. No, that was impossible. She was his. Life was good, really.

But then came the 'flu epidemic. People were dying all over the country, Henry had heard. And the boys overseas in the war were dying, too. And people in Ponca City were getting sick. Nobody had died in Ponca City, at least none that Henry'd heard of. Thank God.

But men in the refinery started coming down with it. And then Mattie and Claude were sick. And Tom. And Frank. Martha was working herself hard, doing all the work she'd always done and taking care of the sick children besides. Henry caught it himself.

He thought he should go to work; he wanted to go to work. But even when he just tried to stand up, he was weak and he staggered. And threw up. Claude tried to be a big boy, but Henry knew that he cried sometime. Mattie was a brave little girl, her Mama's daughter, for sure; but she was sick, too, and, for the most part, helpless.

With Henry unable to work and with no money coming in, he knew they were in trouble. There weren't any doctor bills, really, because there weren't enough doctors in Ponca City to treat everyone. But interns and medical students from the university in Norman had come to town to help. Henry wasn't sure how much they really knew; the young man who had come out to the house was really only a boy. But he didn't cost anything. That was good, because Henry didn't have anything to pay him with.

Walter Cantrell, Martha's daddy, God bless him, brought them eggs and flour when he came to town to grind his wheat. That was a help. "We'll make it," thought Henry. "We will."

Mattie was glad to be going to school again. Her school here in Ponca City was bigger and nicer. And there were only second-graders like her in the classroom. In her other school, all the kids, big and littler, had been in the same classroom. She thought that she'd do better here because the teacher could concentrate on them instead of having to wander around the room all the time. Her schoolbooks were pretty and clean and she liked to read them and to look at the pictures.

The only bad thing was that they didn't have a sidewalk to the front door, and when it rained the front yard got all muddy. She wasn't about to walk through that old mud and get her shoes all dirty. So either Frank or Tom carried her to the wooden sidewalk that ran along the street.

Then everybody got sick. Mattie hated being sick. She hated vomiting in the slop jar beside her bed. It smelled bad. And sometimes some of the vomit splashed on her and then she smelled bad.

And she got sicker. Grandma and Grandpa had to come in from the farm to help Mama. Mattie wanted to help, but she couldn't. Daddy tried to help, she knew, but he was sick, too. But Grandma was kind to her, washing her face with a cool cloth and patting her shoulder gently and sometimes even singing to her. But Grandma looked tired, too.

Everybody got better, though. Except Mama. Mama was awful sick.

"Get up, Honey," said Grandma. "You have to get up now."

"Why?" asked Mattie. "I'm sleepy."

"I know, Sweetheart. But you have to get up. You and Claude and Callie are going next door to stay with the Allens awhile."

Mattie wanted to know more, but Grandma wouldn't say any more; she just helped Mattie get out of bed and get dressed. Then she and Claude and Grandma, with Grandma carrying baby Callie, walked out in the cold and went to their neighbors. Something was wrong. Something bad.

Henry paced outside the bedroom door. The young doctor from Norman was inside with Martha and he'd told Henry to stay out. The baby was coming, and Martha was very sick. Too sick. A lot sicker than he'd been or than any of the kids had been. "God damn it! God damn it!" Henry thought as he paced, his fists clenched.

Walter Cantrell watched him with pity in his eyes. He knew what Henry was going through, but he knew more. The chances that his daughter was going to survive this were not good. Childbirth itself was a huge risk for any woman, but for a tired, sick woman, the risks were much greater. And Martha was so tired, so sick, that even just looking at her was hard. Walter wanted Parthie to be here, but he knew she had to stay with the children. No, she didn't. She should be here. That was her daughter in there.

The Gage boys, Frank and Tom, were sitting in the kitchen, quiet for a change. They could tell, thought their grandfather, that things were bad.

From across the lawn, at the Allens' house, Mattie and Claude watched their house through a window. They watched Grandma cross the yard. They could see Mama's bedroom window. A shade was down, but they could see some sort of shadow there, moving.

Mrs. Allen was nice. She was rocking Callie in her lap, and she'd asked Claude and Mattie if they'd wanted a cookie. But they hadn't. They wanted to go home. They wanted to see Mama.

At about eight o'clock that evening, the young doctor—if he *was* a doctor—called Henry and the Cantrells into Martha's room. "I'm sorry," he said.

They knew what he meant.

CHAPTER 11

Separation
Longwood Community, Oklahoma 1920

The funeral was hard, of course. Martha was buried, along with the baby girl who hadn't survived, in the church cemetery at Longwood. The Cantrells weren't members of the church, but they were members of the community, so there had been no problem at putting Martha to rest there. The church even allowed them to hold the services in their building, even though there was no minister in attendance.

"We'll see her spirit again," her mother told Henry, and then sought out the children to tell them the same thing.

"Your mother will always be with you in spirit," she told them. "There is no real death." They didn't understand, of course.

Mattie couldn't imagine life without Mama. Grandma said that their mother would always be with them, watching over them, but Mattie couldn't feel her there. She was gone. No matter what Grandma said, Mama was gone. Mattie cried a lot, but she saw her brothers crying, too. Even Walter, home for the funeral, cried. Mattie had seen tears in her father's eyes and that was the most terrible of all. She had never imagined that he could cry, not that big, strong man, the man who protected them all.

Henry, though, wouldn't have thought of himself as a protector. He found it difficult to think at all. He found his thoughts going back and forth from "She's gone. My Martha is gone" to "What do I do now? How do I do right by her children, my children?"

After the funeral, they all went to Walter Cantrell's farm, largely because it was closer, but also because Parthie Cantrell insisted. She would put a dinner on the table. Folks needed to eat, especially in times like these.

By the time they'd reached the farm, Henry had reached a partial, painful conclusion. It was impossible to maintain their home. Henry had to go to work. Mattie and Claude and baby Callie couldn't stay by themselves. The three younger children simply had to stay there on the farm with their grandparents.

There wasn't any other way, really. And he did know that they would get good care and that they'd be loved. Both Parthie and Walter

Cantrell were kind, loving, gentle people. But it was still a kind of failure. A man should be able to take care of his children. He'd send money, he thought.

He shook Walter Cantrell's hand off his shoulder in front of the farmhouse. "I'm sorry, Walt—Dad," he said. "I've gotta be alone for a minute." He saw understanding in his father-in-law's face and walked off back in the direction of the barn.

About twenty feet this side of the barn was an old rusty planter, just off the path. Henry climbed on and sat, his chin supported on one hand. Sending money, he thought. He'd had a hard-enough time just making enough money to keep them going. Hell, he hadn't made enough. If it hadn't been for the generosity of Martha's folks—ah, hell. He'd try. That was all he could do.

It was cold. He needed to go into the house. He didn't want to see anybody, talk to anybody, even his children. Maybe even especially his children. But he had to. Had to. So he straightened up, got down off the planter, pulled his hat down a little, and turned to the house.

In the end, Mattie and Claude and Callie—and Tom, for a while—came back to the farm. For Mattie and Claude, that meant changing schools, but that wasn't that much of a problem. School was farther away, but Grandpa could take them. They were in a classroom with older kids now, too, but the teacher seemed nice. She let them know, quietly, that she knew their Mama was gone. She had a nice smile, Mattie thought. It wasn't going to be so bad. She loved Grandma and Grandpa and she could tell that they loved her, too. She missed Mama, though, and sometimes she still cried when no one was looking.

Henry Gage gave up the little house in Ponca City. With just him and Frank, they didn't need all that room. Besides that, he could still see Martha bustling around, cleaning, ironing the knitted doilies, fluffing up the pillows. In a way, he was glad to leave it.

He and Frank took a room in a boarding house. It wasn't nice, of course. It was barely comfortable, but Henry didn't care much for comfort now. And Frank didn't seem to mind.

But even the town seemed wrong now. The stores, the houses, the kids' school, the refinery—they all reminded him of what was gone—not just his beautiful Martha, but his whole life, as well.

He managed to last out the year; then he resigned from the refinery, and he and Frank packed up their things and headed east to Webb City and jobs in the oil field, picking up Tom on the way.

CHAPTER 12

Roustabouts
Webb City, Oklahoma, 1921

Henry had no trouble getting a job in the Webb City field. Some of the people running operations there had known him when he was hauling pipe, and knew that he was both strong and hard-working. So he went to work for the Marland company, helping to prepare the ground for spudding in a new well a couple miles south of the new little town of Webb City.

Frank and Tom quickly got jobs, too. They were both big and strong for their ages and hard workers. Frank, at seventeen, was six feet, four inches tall. Even Henry thought that he looked twenty, at least. Tom, not quite fifteen, was still growing, but he was still almost as tall as Henry. They were good boys, Henry thought; he was proud of them. They knew what it was to work hard and didn't complain.

Actually, between themselves, they complained a lot. It wasn't the work, so much; Henry was right about that: they did know how to work hard. What they didn't like was Webb City—what there was of it.

The town wouldn't even have existed had it not been for oil. Buildings went up quickly—board and batten shacks, for the most part— some with sloppily painted signs saying "Eats" or "Beds." Henry and the boys shared a single room in an old farmhouse that was just a little bit off the dirt road that was becoming the main street.

The room their father had rented—by the week—was completely bare except for three folding cots. They'd have preferred beds, but a person could sleep on the cots if he had to.

But they'd become accustomed to Ponca City. Ponca wasn't really a big place, they knew, but it certainly beat Webb City. The main thing, though, about being here in this place, and the thing they talked about between themselves, was the absence of one of the major necessities of life: girls.

Frank knew that he was attractive to girls; he'd proved that to himself for a long time. Tom wasn't so sure, himself, but he was quite willing to find out.

Unfortunately, there wasn't any opportunity to prove anything. They got up in the morning, ate breakfast, and went to work. Dad drove

61

himself out to the location; the boys were picked up by one of the bosses and taken in the opposite direction to another drill site, where Tom had the extreme pleasure of running errands, hauling lumber and nails for the men building a storage tank and Frank got to help dig a trench for the pipe that would run to the tank—eventually.

Then, after a bread and cheese lunch and a smoke break in mid-afternoon, they finished the workday tired, but not so tired that they weren't ready to have some fun, and rode back into Webb City.

Fun, fun, and fun. Yeah, right.

Then one day, they discovered Carl's.

Carl's was a red-painted shack on a dirt side-road, just what would have been a couple of blocks from the farmhouse they were staying in, but not in a direction they'd had any reason to go. They hadn't had any reason to go in that direction today, either, but despite their hard day, they were restless. And so they stumbled onto the place.

Frank recognized what kind of place it was, immediately. "Open 2 pm to 2 am," the sign said underneath the name. That meant to Frank that this was a place that sold whiskey. He told Tom so.

"Ain't that illegal?"

Frank cuffed his little brother on the shoulder, fairly hard. "Who cares?" he said. "I don't care. Hell, the law don't care! Let's go in."

"Huh?" Tom looked a bit bewildered, Frank thought. Hell, he was still a baby.

"I'm not goin' to tell Dad," he said. "You won't get a whippin'."

"Dad don't whip us," said Tom, "but I don't think he'd like us goin' in there."

"He's not goin' to know," said Frank, and he pulled the pine-plank door open.

Henry had warned the boys about the dangers of whiskey, of the dangers of being around men who might be doing things that would get them in trouble, and of the dangers of a certain kind of women. Frank had seen that "certain kind of woman" in both Mervine and Ponca City. Some of them looked like any danger they might pose would be worth it.

They didn't dress like farm girls, didn't wear their hair like farm girls, and, unlike farm girls, wore red stuff on their lips. Frank liked to look at them. And, he remembered, some of them—back in Ponca—had looked back. Maybe, he thought, as he held open the door for a reluctant Tom, there'll be one of those evil, loose women here in Carl's. He hoped so.

There weren't. The place did sell whiskey, though. Frank could smell it. He could also smell something cooking; it smelled like bacon and it made him hungry. It was still too early to eat; besides, he realized, he didn't have any money, anyway—wouldn't until Friday. He had to laugh at himself; here he'd pulled Tom into a whiskey joint and they didn't have any money to buy any even if they'd sell it to them.

There *was* a girl in Carl's, though. She was bringing two men at the counter some beer in a pitcher. Frank didn't think she was a "painted woman." For one thing, she didn't have any makeup on, at least that he could tell. Her hair was black and her skin was darker than his or Tom's, even though they were both tanned by their outside work. "Indian," thought Frank. "Part, anyway. But she's a kid." Then he glanced at Tom.

Tom was stricken.

Frank had a little trouble dragging him away. "C'mon," he said. "We'll come back when we have some money."

Tom stopped again outside the door and looked back at the building and at the sign, as if he were memorizing them. "Yep," he said. "We sure will!"

The acreage chosen for the new well was relatively flat and free of brush; preparing the site went quickly and crews began bringing in the rig, the boiler, and pipe. Henry, having shown that he knew what he was doing, was sent to supervise a small crew on different acreage, almost directly across the dirt path. Both Frank and Tom stayed on the same site, unloading, moving, basically doing what they were told by the toolpusher, whose name was Johnson.

Johnson had paid little or no attention to them before, when they'd basically just been cleaning brush or digging. Now, though, that they were handling equipment, he was all over them.

"Do you know what the hell you're doing?" he'd shouted at them as they were unloading wood that would be used to build the supports for the drill pole.

The boys stopped what they were doing, of course. Frank put his end of the planks down, forcing Tom to do the same. "Nope," said Frank, looking the boss in the eye. "I suspect you're about to tell us, though. Right?"

Johnson looked at him for a moment, then laughed. "Go on about your business, boys." Then he turned away and walked over to where a crew was putting the steam boiler into place.

"Jesus, Frank!" whispered Tom. "He's the boss!"

Frank shrugged.

A little later, the man who seemed to be handling the setup of the pulleys—bull wheel and calf wheel, the parts were called—walked by Frank, clapped him on the shoulder, leaned in to him with a laugh, and whispered, "Give 'im hell, kid!"

There was a lot to do, a lot of it heavy work. Frank and Tom helped carry the big spools of cable from the truck to where men who knew what they were doing were installing the drums. The thing they called a walking beam—that was used to raise and lower the bit—was heavy, and Frank could tell that Tom was struggling.

On the second day, a truck brought in a little tin building on a plank base and set it in place close to the rig.

"That's the doghouse," the man who had clapped Frank on the shoulder told them. Well, Tom was there, but it was pretty clear to Frank that the man was really talking to him. "That's where the boss sleeps when he's on site, and it's where we'll eat and take any breaks we can get. Okay, back to work!"

The woman who lived in the farmhouse where they had their room provided their breakfast and their evening meal—usually boiled potatoes or beans, with some kind of meat, for the most part very salty ham. The food wasn't what Frank would call good, but it was edible, and he realized that he was lucky to get it.

Suddenly there were lines forming at the little place with the "Eats" sign. There were more wells being sunk, and a couple had come in—oil was flowing. That meant that the little would-be town was filling up with workers and some other people that Frank couldn't quite figure out. These men didn't seem to do any work; they just ran around talking to people, it seemed. He asked his father, but Henry didn't seem to know, either.

Then, to Frank's utter pleasure, another kind of visitor came to Webb City: women with short, shiny hair, dresses just as shiny, red lips and cheeks, and bright smiles. Oh, he knew what these women were there for! He also knew, though, that he didn't have any money. But he would have! Oh, yes.

Most of their money went to the farm lady for rent and food, though.

Frank had apparently made a good impression on somebody. At any rate, when the rig was in place and drilling was about to begin, the evening driller offered him a job as a roustabout on the rig. He'd paint what needed to be painted, clean up, and help the roughnecks when needed. It would be more money—not a lot—but still more than he'd expected.

"Besides," the driller told him, "you'll learn the business. I think you'll make a good hand. You're strong and you're willing. You know how this thing works?" He gestured at the rig. "You been around a cable tool rig?"

Frank nodded. "I've seen 'em. Never paid a whole lot of attention to how they work, though." He felt a bit ashamed of his ignorance. "Never needed to."

"Okay," said the driller, "we've got a little time so let's give you a quick walk-through. You game?"

"Sure," said Frank. "I'd like that. Thanks."

"First thing—we've got to have power to run things. Jim over there—"he pointed at a dark-skinned man with coal-black hair leaning against the doghouse—"is our boilerman. Everything runs on steam, so he has to keep that boiler running—and running safely. He lets that thing build up too much pressure, that boiler can blow us all to hell. So he has an important job."

Frank could see that. He wondered about where they got the water for the boiler but didn't ask.

"The rest of us concentrate on drilling the hole. Well, the steam does the work, but we have to direct the steam. This thing here we call the walking beam." It looked a little like the seesaw Frank remembered from one of the schools he'd gone to—he didn't remember which one—and just a little like the horseheads moving up and down on the pumping wells he'd seen in the field. "Now come on up here on the deck."

Frank stepped up on the plank platform and looked where the driller pointed—it was just a square opening.

"This is where the hole'll be," said the driller.

"Hey, Ace!" called one of the roughnecks. "Here comes the truck!"

"Well," said the driller, "looks like we'll have to postpone our little run-through. You watch as we set up—when you get the chance. Right now you need to help unload that truck." He slapped Frank across a shoulder. "We'll have you on the regular crew before long, I s'pect."

That sounded good to Frank. The roughnecks—most of them—seemed to be the kind of men Frank thought himself to be: strong, capable. So he went to work helping to unload the heavy spools of cable.

Tom, on the other hand, went to work with a crew digging slush pits, both on this location and then on others. That meant that he would be working different hours than Frank. Henry was still preparing drilling sites; he'd bought an old plowhorse, a plow, and a harrow to even out the ground. He was being kept busy, and the boys saw less and less of him.

CHAPTER 13

Climbing onto the Monkey Board
Carl's Place, Webb City, Oklahoma, 1921

Since Frank was working the evening tour now (he pronounced it "tower," as everybody else on the rig did), he got off work at midnight, "evening" having started at four o'clock. One of the roughnecks, a man named Hiram Moore, who was forty or so, went right by the place Frank was staying on his own way home, so he dropped Frank off. Frank was usually tired enough to fall right into bed.

That meant, when he woke up at nine or so in the morning, he had most of the day to fill. Because Tom went off to work around seven and their father was gone even earlier, Frank was left alone. He didn't quite know how to cope with that; he'd always had family around—brothers, sisters, grandparents, aunts, uncles. Now—just Frank. Most of the men on the evening tour were older; most of them had families; Moore, the man who gave him a ride home, had told him he had a son almost Frank's age.

On the fourth morning after starting the new job, Frank got up, dressed, and went down to the kitchen for breakfast. The lady who rented them the room and provided meals did her cooking earlier—the rest of the "guests" were up and at work before Frank stirred—and she wasn't about to cook again just for Frank. So he ate whatever was left from the others' breakfast—cold ham, cold eggs, cold bacon, cold toast.

This morning he looked down at the big skillet on the stove and at the cold eggs in it, and his stomach suggested strongly to him that it did not want anything whatsoever to do with cold, runny eggs. So he checked his pockets. Yes, he still had a little money.

Of course he did. He smiled, then, remembering that he'd won a dollar and seventy-five cents playing poker in the doghouse with the roughnecks when they took a break. That extra bit of money meant that he could pay for a good hot breakfast.

He'd started to walk over to the main road and the little storefront café when a thought hit him. That Carl's joint. They sold whiskey, but he'd seen food on a couple of the tables there. If they were open and they served breakfast, it almost had to be an improvement on those terrible eggs.

Maybe he'd have some whiskey, too. Maybe not. He'd see after he had some food in him.

The fellow behind the counter at Carl's looked like he hadn't been up even as long as Frank had. He wasn't shaved and he wasn't wearing a shirt, just a kind of yellowish undershirt with a lot of black hair sticking out at the neck. Nor did he seem particularly happy to see Frank walk in the door. But he greeted him, nonetheless.

"Yeah?" he said. "You want somethin'?"

Frank straddled a stool at the bar. "How 'bout breakfast? You serve breakfast here?"

The man picked up a newspaper and spread it over the counter, then he looked up at Frank. "You read, son?"

For a moment, Frank wondered whether the man was asking him if he'd read something from the paper to him, but before he could work up an answer, the man had pointed at the door.

"Well, boy," the man said, "If you can read, you might just have accidentally seen the sign on that door over there." Frank looked. There was no sign on the door. "The outside of the door! Outside! Before you come in! Jesus!"

Frank felt his mouth drop open, but he couldn't come up with anything to say. Sign? Outside? Oh. Oh. When he'd been here before with Tom, there had been a sign.

"Oh," he said. "You're not open, right?"

"Smart kid! You guessed it! We open at two and it's—what?—nine-thirty? In the morning?"

The man was laughing at him, but Frank could see how it could be funny, so he laughed, too. Then he put on a hugely exaggerated whiny voice (copied pretty closely from his little brother Claude). "Does that mean I don't get any breakfast?" The man looked at him, less with disgust now and more with wonder. "But I'm hungry, Mister." Frank tried to make his eyes really big.

The man laughed and swatted Frank on the shoulder with the newspaper. He was laughing again. "Get your ass back here behind the counter," he said, with a huge frown that Frank didn't believe for an instant, "and see what you can find. I'll be damned if I'm goin' to start cookin' somethin' for some snot-nosed kids off the street—not at no god-damned nine-thirty in the morning!"

Frank hesitated a bit, but decided "what the hell" and went around the counter. He didn't know what he expected to find, but he was sure it wouldn't be a hot breakfast. The man—owner?—was reading his newspaper again, and didn't seem to be even watching him. He didn't see any food at first; then he saw, on a shelf beneath the counter, a plate with a couple of home-made doughnuts. He lifted the plate out and held it up to the man.

"May I?" He wiggled the plate a little.

"Help yourself. Go on," the man said, and went back to his paper.

The doughnuts were good. Not as good as his Mama had made, but good nevertheless. He ate them both and ran his finger around the plate to get the crumbs. "Good," he said. Then he put the plate back where he'd found it and went back out front. "What do I owe you?"

"Put the plate in the sink," the man said.

Frank went back and picked up the plate, but he didn't see any sink.

The man waggled the paper at him. "In the back! In the back! Do I have to show you?" He pointed to the open door just to Frank's left. "Door!" he said. "Sink! In there!"

Frank got it, and nodded. There was a sink behind the door, and a stove, and a cupboard, and an icebox. He put the plate in the sink. He was about to turn around and go back into the front of the place when he felt a hand on his shoulder.

"Who are you and what are you doing in here?" asked a feminine voice.

Frank jumped a little. "Huh?" He turned, expecting to see an older woman, perhaps the man in front's wife, but it was the little Indian-looking girl he and Tom had seen the time they'd peeked in. Despite the definitely hostile look in her eyes, she didn't seem much of a threat. For one thing, she was at least a foot shorter than Frank; for another, Frank guessed her age at thirteen or fourteen. She'd looked older carrying that pitcher of beer.

"Oh, it's you," he said.

"Answer my questions," she said. Her hands went to her hips.

Frank had to smile at her. "Your boss told me to put that plate in the sink. You're kind of cute, you know that?" He reached out to touch her hair, but she slapped his hand away.

"He's not my boss. He's my dad!" She stepped back and pointed at the door. "You've put the plate away, now get back in there where you belong!"

"Your dad?" Hell, this girl was Indian, wasn't she? The guy out front sure wasn't.

"Yes! He's my father."

"I'm sorry," said Frank with a big grin and a little bow. "Yes, Ma'am. I'll do that! But you're still kinda cute."

The girl clearly showed that she didn't mind being considered cute, but she kept her face hard, and her pointing arm was straight. "Go!"

Frank went.

He was met with an amused tavern owner. The man was still at the bar, still hunched over his newspaper, but he was laughing. "I see you've met my daughter," he said. "You better watch yourself, kid; that girl eats oil men for lunch. She'd take you in two bites!"

"She's your daughter?"

"Yep. Ramona Glick. Daughter of Charlie and Leonie Glick. I'm Charlie," he said, putting out his hand. "And you are?"

"Uhh...how do you do?" Frank took the man's hand and shook it. He wondered for a bit whether he was in some sort of trouble, but the man was grinning at him.

"I asked you who you were...."

Frank caught himself waving his hands in front of him the way Mama had done. Embarrassing. He forced his hands to stop moving.

"I'm—ah—Frank Gage," he said, extending his hand to shake again, then pulling it back when Glick ignored it. "And you're Mr. Glick? You're Carl?" he gestured at the door.

"Charlie. There ain't no Carl." He turned back toward the kitchen. "Ramona! Get your butt in here!"

The girl came, but she clearly wasn't pleased. Frank took the opportunity to take a better look at her now. Her hair was very black, very straight, but it hung straight down her back, no braid. Her eyes were large and very brown underneath black eyebrows. Her cheekbones were high and her skin was dark, all right. She had some Indian blood, for sure. From her mother—no way Glick was Indian. He was pasty white.

"Monie," said her father. "This is Frank Gage. Go pour him a beer."

So Frank became something of a regular at Carl's. His work hours, since he was on the evening tour, meant that he couldn't get there until after midnight, but catching a ride to the place was no trouble at all; a couple of the roughnecks from the rig regularly stopped there for a drink—or ten—after they got off work. They didn't mind taking "the kid" along.

Frank discovered, somewhat to his pleasure, that he had considerable capacity for whiskey. Beer, he thought, tasted better, but the men seemed to prefer whiskey, so that's what he drank when he was around them. If he got a little tipsy around his co-workers, they laughed at him a little; but it was good-natured and Frank didn't mind.

Ramona wasn't there, of course, after midnight. Instead, Charlie Glick had two other helpers. One was a short little fellow with sallow skin and dark eyes and hair; he didn't look Indian, though.

The other—the one Frank found most interesting—was named Belle, and she was tall for a woman and busty. Frank liked busty. He couldn't tell how old she was, but she wasn't a girl. She was a woman.

She had blonde hair rolled up somehow on the back of her head and she did something with her eyes that Frank couldn't quite figure out. Anyway, whatever she did made her eyes more noticeable, more—interesting, somehow. She had a good, loud laugh and she moved quickly behind the bar and between tables. She laughed with the customers—all men—and Frank noticed that she didn't seem to object to the occasional pat on the behind as she passed by a table. Frank always tried to sit at a table, mostly so he could watch her moving around the room.

Belle called him "Kid," just as the roughnecks did. Sometimes she'd playfully tap him on the shoulder when she passed by. He was tempted to pat her on the behind as he'd seen others do, but couldn't quite work up the nerve.

Then one night, not long before closing time, a man at one of the tables—someone Frank hadn't seen there before—apparently did something, or said something, that amounted to more than a pat. Belle turned suddenly and her hand came around in a really hard slap. Her face, usually so calm and amused, was red and her pretty red mouth was drawn back in a kind of snarl. Everybody in the bar looked up, of course. The sound of her palm striking the man's face was loud. Somebody laughed, but it wasn't a laugh that really sounded amused.

Then the man she'd slapped suddenly came out of his chair, grabbing her and shouting. "You bitch!" he yelled, one of his hands in her hair, pulling her head back. "You fucking whore!"

Frank was two tables away, and there were men closer than he, but he got to Belle and the man in seconds. The fellow was still holding Belle, and now he had his face just inches from hers, and he was still shouting. Almost without thinking, Frank grabbed the man by one shoulder, turned him with a hard jerk, and smashed his right fist into the man's face. The man crashed backwards into a table, sending beer and glasses onto the floor.

By the time the man had struggled to his feet, Charlie Glick was there with a shotgun. He held the gun at his side, not aiming it, but his face was hard. "Get the hell out of my place," he said. "Now."

The man stood, rubbing his jaw. He looked at Frank, clearly wanting to hit back. He looked at Glick and the shotgun. "The little fuck hit me!" he shouted. "You gonna let him do that? And you tell me to leave? Well, fuck you!"

Frank's hand was hurting, but he shook it and looked at Belle. She was crying, and somehow her tears were running black down her cheeks. He started for the stranger again, but by this time the rest of the men in the bar were up, too, and one of the roughnecks from the rig got between him and the man, his hands pushing against Frank's chest. "Take it easy, kid," he said.

"It's all right, Frank," said Glick. "I've got this." He turned back to the stranger, who seemed to be shaking with fury, his face twisted and his hands clenched. "I told you to leave, fellow," said Glick, and he calmly cocked the gun.

Frank heard the other men murmuring, and it was clear that the guy wasn't going to get any support from them. One of the other men that Frank hadn't seen before had taken hold of the man's arm and was saying something to him. Then he was leading him toward the door. He left a string of obscenities behind him, but then he was gone. Two other men who had been at his table turned to leave, too. One of them put some money on the table and nodded to Glick. Then they were gone.

Frank sat down, a little bit shocked at what he'd done. He'd never really hit a man hard before. He'd pounded on Tom, of course, but he'd never hit him in the face and never tried to hurt him. Despite the shocked feeling, something in him wanted to follow the man outside. He looked at his fist, which still stung a little, and felt something like—joy.

He let himself enjoy the feeling for a moment, then remembered Belle. He thought that he should say something to her, to tell her he was sorry for what had happened to her.

But Glick was taking her back into the kitchen behind the bar. He put the shotgun on the bar on the way out, and turned his head to the men, all of whom were still standing except Frank. "We're closing now," he said. "If you owe me for your drinks, pay me the next time you come in. Go." He stopped again in the doorway. "Except you, Frank. Stay a minute, okay?"

Frank stayed, of course. He even got out of his chair and closed and locked the door after the rest had left. He partially expected to be told not to come back. That would be too bad. And he wanted to talk to Belle. For one thing, he wanted to know what the man had said that had caused her to slap him. But that was none of his business. He pushed the thought aside. So he sat there, waiting for Glick to come back, and considered what he'd done. Right or wrong, he decided, he'd enjoyed doing it. He rubbed his fist.

Instead of sending him away, Glick patted him on the shoulder and thanked him.

A couple of nights later, Belle thanked him, too—by taking him to her room and to her bed. He never learned what the man had said to Belle. He hadn't really wanted to ask, and she didn't offer to tell him. Instead, she carefully instructed him—that night and on several successive nights—how to please a woman. That's what she called it, and Frank liked the idea. But he was highly pleased, himself. The physical act was rewarding, of course, but the fact that he could please Belle—and she'd made it obvious that she was pleased—was even better.

The men he worked with would continue calling him "kid," but Frank would no longer consider himself in that way. He was a man.

CHAPTER 14

A Fork in the Creek
Webb City, Oklahoma, 1921

Frank was surprised to learn that Tom had been a bit active in his own way. Since their hours were so different—Tom was asleep when Frank got off work and was gone when Frank awoke—they didn't have a lot of time together. So Frank was really astounded that his brother had also found his way to Carl's. He wondered why Charles Glick—or Belle—hadn't mentioned it to him. Tom had been going to Carl's to see Ramona, Glick's daughter.

"She's beautiful, isn't she, Frank?" Tom's eyes were glistening.

"Jesus, Tom! Yeah, she's—attractive—but what are you doing?" A thought hit him: he was sleeping—if you could call it that—with Belle. Could his little brother...? Nah. "My God," he said, taking Tom by a shoulder. "Are you gettin' some of that?"

"What!? No!" Tom actually looked offended. "She ain't that kind of girl, Frank! She's good and sweet—and beautiful! She has the most gorgeous eyes I ever seen in my life!"

"Okay," thought Frank. "Little brother's got it bad." He thought it was cute, actually. He felt like patting Tom on the head. "She's half Indian," he said aloud.

"So?"

Frank shook his head. "So nothing."

"I'm going to marry her," said Tom. His grin was huge.

Frank laughed. "When you both grow up!"

"No. Now. Soon!"

"You're fourteen, Tom. How old is she?"

Tom pushed Frank away. "I'm *fifteen*!"

"You're still a baby!"

"The hell I am! I've been doing a man's work for a long time now!"

Tom had never been a fighter, but it looked to Frank as if he were almost ready to fight now. He took a step backward and looked at his little brother. He had to admit that Tom was right. They really hadn't been boys now for quite some time. They were both working at hard, tiring jobs— jobs that were usually done by men.

"Yeah, you're right about that," Frank said. "Okay. You're really serious about Ramona?" She was pretty, Frank, thought, but compared to Belle—well, there was no comparing her with Belle!

"I'm going to marry her!" said Tom. "There's a dance tonight and I'm going to ask her tonight! Ask her to marry me!"

This was hard to take in. Married? Tom? He hoped Tom wasn't going to get hurt too bad. If he wanted to screw the girl, that was one thing, and Frank wished him well—but getting married?

"If she says yes," he said, "what about her old man? What'll Glick say? He gonna let his daughter marry some roustabout?"

Tom stood. "We'll find out. If he says no—well, maybe we'll run away!"

"Jesus!" Frank thought. This was weird.

It got weirder. Ramona accepted. Charles Glick, no matter what he thought about it, apparently couldn't tell his daughter no.

"Will he treat her good?" Glick asked Frank one night. "He seems like a good enough kid, but...."

Frank didn't have any doubt at all that Tom would "treat her good," and he told her father so. His own reservations about the whole thing were nothing; it wasn't his business. He did wonder, though, about how Tom was going to support a family.

He wondered, too, what Dad would say. Neither one of them saw much of Henry anymore. He'd taken a pumping job now that the lease-clearing work had run out and he'd moved to a little shack way out of town to the east of Webb City. They'd been to the shack—and it was just a shack—with just room for a little stove and a bed.

"There's not room here for you boys," he'd said, and Frank could hear the apology in his voice. "But I had to take this job. There wasn't anything else." But he smiled then. "And you boys are men now, and I'm proud of you!" He reached out with both hands and squeezed their shoulders.

Dad had looked sad when they left, Frank thought, but then he'd looked sad every now and then since Mama died. He'd just nodded. Tom hadn't said anything, either.

"I know you're not boys anymore," Henry said. "You're men. But you're still my sons, and I feel like I'm deserting you."

They'd both assured him that he wasn't deserting them, and, to tell the truth, Frank felt somehow liberated, more like a man. He was on his own and he was making a living and the men on his job liked him and, he thought, respected him. And there was Belle.

Henry had apparently offered no objections to the marriage. Tom had hitched a ride out to Henry's shack to tell him.

It was going to happen, Frank guessed.

He stood up with Tom at the wedding. It was just in front of a justice of the peace and all Frank and Tom had were their work clothes, but at least they were clean.

The justice told Tom and Ramona that they were married and they kissed. Charlie Glick looked both a little proud and a little sad, Frank thought. Ramona's mother—whom Frank had seldom seen at the tavern— wore no expression whatsoever on her dark, Indian face. Tom looked proud. Ramona looked happy.

Her wedding dress was nice, Frank thought. It was some kind of heavy cloth—maybe muslin—and was plain-colored, not quite white and not quite tan—and there were beads sewn around the neck, all down the long sleeves, and along the hem. Her mother had probably made it; it looked like it was Indian, maybe.

Henry wasn't there; he'd had some kind of emergency on one of the wells he was pumping.

Between the hours spent at work and his time with Belle, Frank hadn't really considered how things would change. But he realized, standing around at the little reception back at Carl's, that things were going to be considerably different.

Somehow, he supposed, he'd thought that Tom would go on living in the little room with him, but that clearly wasn't going to happen. He couldn't imagine Ramona's living there, too. Maybe Tom would move in with Ramona's folks. He shook his head. How could he have been so dumb? He hadn't even asked Tom what he was going to do, where they were going to live. Well, he'd have to find out.

After a few minutes of being congratulated and toasted by the bar patrons and a couple of his co-workers, Tom came back to Frank and, with a huge grin, grabbed him by the shoulder. "Come outside with me! I want to show you something!"

Frank followed, wondering when and how he should ask Tom about what he was going to do, where he was going to live—and probably a bunch of other stuff he hadn't thought of. That all went out of his head, though, when he saw what Tom was pointing at.

There on the street just to the north of Carl's was a shiny Model-T Ford.

"That's our wedding present!" said Tom. "Look at it!" His grin was huge, so huge that it made Frank laugh.

"You're kidding!" he said, almost running to the car and running his fingers over the smooth, black front fender and then down over the chrome hood above the headlight. "Wedding present? Who from?"

"Dad."

Frank must have looked confused—hell, he was confused—because Tom went on: "Well, not Dad only—Dad and Carl, really! They bought it together and Dad cleaned it up and made sure everything was good!"

"Jesus, Tom. I mean—that's great and all, but—you even know how to drive?"

Tom grinned at him. "Ah, nothing to it!" He slugged his brother on the arm. "You know that!" And he made engine sounds. Frank had to laugh again.

"It's got an electric starter!" Tom pulled open the driver's side door and pointed to the floor. "Just step on that and off she goes! No more cranking!" He looked up at Frank and his face was pure joy. Frank had to wonder which was making Tom happier, the car or marrying Ramona.

Whatever. He was happy for Tom, no matter which. He reached down and pulled Tom upright from where he was still looking down at the wonderful electric starter button and hugged him. Tom struggled for a minute, but Frank could tell that he didn't mean it.

"It's nice, Tom," he said. "And Ramona is beautiful."

"I know," said Tom. He pulled back and Frank watched his back straighten and his shoulders lift and his face change. "I'm a man now, Frank," he said. "I have a wife! I have responsibilities!"

"Yeah, you do," said Frank, and he gestured toward the Model-T with a grin. "You got a car, too!"

Tom glanced at the automobile, but he quickly turned back to Frank, his face even more serious. "Need to tell you something," he said.

Frank stepped to the car and leaned against the side. "Well, I s'pose I've got some things to ask you, too, Tom!"

"Well, me first, Brother!"

Frank bowed. "After you."

Tom shuffled a little. Frank thought, with some surprise, that he looked embarrassed. "It's like this, Frank," Tom said. "We're moving."

"Moving?"

"Yeah. I got this job—you know that there's a lot of new production down south of here—around Cushing?"

"Yeah, I've heard that." Frank knew that his mouth had dropped open. "You're going to Cushing!?"

"Well, close," Tom said. "Town called Lovell—it's close by." Tom's face looked almost pleading now. "Frank, they like me. They think I do good work, and they've told me so—and they offered me this job. And

I'm *fifteen years old*, Frank! And they offered me a job—a job that'll pay me enough to support a family!"

The "they" was the company Tom worked for, Frank realized. "Wow!" he said. He needed to say more, but he didn't know what. He looked at Tom. "This will take some getting used to," he thought.

Aloud he said, "Hell, Tom, you're a Gage! What else?" And he tapped his brother's shoulder.

Then Ramona appeared at the door, calling Tom. He smiled at Frank, tapped his shoulder in turn, and went to his bride.

A little while later, Mr. and Mrs. Thomas Gage, their wedding present packed full, pulled away from Carl's place, headed for the highway and their new home. Frank had pressed almost all his cash into Tom's hand before they left, but it wasn't enough, he knew. Despite Tom's clear new maturity and complete willingness to take on what seemed to Frank to be a huge responsibility, he still felt some concern—hell, some *worry*.

People were still drinking and making noise inside Carl's, but Frank realized that it was time for him to go to work. And he didn't have a ride—not from here. He'd have to walk, and that meant that he'd be late! Damn. He took off, wishing that he had the car instead of Tom.

In the next few weeks, things fell apart for Frank. For one thing, he missed Tom, even if their work schedules had meant they hadn't really seen each other much. He also found that he needed Tom's money; he could barely afford to pay for the room by himself, and taking some stranger in to help pay for it didn't appeal to Frank.

So he had less money to spend at Carl's. He didn't think that Charlie Glick was going to toss him out if he didn't buy anything, but— everybody else was buying drinks. So he should, too, he thought. But he could limit how much he spent. He could still go to see Belle. That was a good thing.

Then one night, Belle turned to him in bed and kissed him on the ear. "I have something to tell you, Frank," she said. She sat up, then, and picked up her pillow and used it to cover her breasts.

Belle, it turned out, was leaving, too. She'd miss him, she said, but Frank doubted it. She was going home, she said. Sick mother.

Frank offered to go with her, but she smiled and patted his hand.

The next day she was gone. Frank suspected that the sick mother was more likely to be one of the new oil boom towns and the money that flowed there even faster than the oil coming out of the ground.

When Henry took a job around Braman, over in Kay County, Frank had had enough. He quit his job, packed his few things in an old canvas bag, and caught a ride with a teamster carrying a load of drill pipe to the Cushing field.

CHAPTER 15

Ugly Girl
Whizbang, 1921

Callie had missed the farm when Grandpa and Grandma had moved to Whizbang. (Grandma told her that she shouldn't call the town "Whizbang," even though everybody else did. Its real name was Denoya, she'd said, and that's what Callie should call it. But Callie thought "Whizbang" was more fun.) Grandpa still had horses, but they were big old things and she wasn't supposed to get too close to them.

Back on the farm, there'd been two nice cows, and Grandma had some nice speckled chickens. Sometimes she'd let Callie go to the henhouse with her to gather eggs. Callie hadn't liked putting her hand under the old hens. They got all fidgety sometimes and she thought they might peck her; but she liked the feel of the warm eggs and she liked helping Grandma.

But there weren't any chickens or cows at Whizbang—at Denoya. Instead there was a little house—not nearly as big as the house on the farm—with a yard that was all dirt; Grandma had had lots of pretty flowers on the farm. Callie had especially liked the hollyhocks that grew right beside the back door.

The worst thing, probably, though, was the smell. The air was all stinky. Grandma told her that it was the oil that smelled so bad. Oil was good, she was made to understand, even if it was stinky. She'd thought that the henhouse back on the farm had been a little stinky, but it was a nice, warm kind of stinky—not like those old oil wells!

She didn't think Grandma was happy, either. For one thing, she wouldn't go into town to buy groceries any more; she made Grandpa do that. Grandma kept busy, though, maybe just not as busy as she'd been on the farm. She still did all the washing. Here she had two big tubs and her washboard on the porch. There was a water pump on the porch, so nobody had to bring up water from the well. She baked a lot of things and Callie liked to watch her do that. She liked the smell of things baking—a lot— and, unless she'd been naughty, Grandma let her lick the pan after she'd put cookies in the oven.

But she had to share, usually, with Claude and Mattie, unless they were in school. Callie wished she could go to school. With Grandma working around the house and with Claude and Mattie at school, she didn't have enough to do. She had her nice little oven that big brother Frank had bought her for Christmas and a pretty doll that Daddy had given her, so she could make play cookies for the doll. But she couldn't really play in the yard because the yard was all dirty, and Grandma said that she was tired of washing a new dress for Callie every day.

She loved her big brother and big sister. Claude teased her a lot, but he was never mean. The meanest thing he did was sometimes tickle her until she was silly. Mattie was nice to her all the time. Mattie didn't tease her—ever. She told Callie all about school: what they were reading, who sat next to her, what her teacher was like—she was very pretty and very sweet, Mattie said, but she didn't take any backtalk from the big boys.

The bad thing about Mattie was that she was so pretty. Everybody said so, and Callie could tell that she was. Nobody ever said that Callie was pretty. She knew why. Grandma had a looking glass on the wall over the table in her bedroom, and Callie sometimes climbed up on the little stool and got up on her knees so she could look at herself.

What she saw was an ugly little girl with a big scar running from her cheek to her chin. It made her ashamed, and sometimes it made her cry.

Grandma told her she was being silly, so she didn't cry around people any more. But she still knew she was ugly.

CHAPTER 16

Throwing the Chain
The Oil Patch, 1922

Frank didn't last long in the Cushing field. Getting work hadn't been hard, and he'd watched and learned back on the rigs at Webb City. He was a good hand, and he knew it. So the work itself went well enough.

Tom was pumping now for Shell and the wells in production weren't all that close to where the new drilling was going on, so Frank didn't see him much. Besides, Tom had fast become an old married man and wasn't all that much fun anymore.

The problem was, first of all, with some fellow in a bar in Drumright. Well, to be honest, Frank knew that the problem was a girl.

Her name had been Sarah Jane Prescott, better known as Sally. She'd had curly blonde hair, a nice plump figure, and a good laugh. And she could hold her liquor. She'd been a little older than Frank, maybe just a year or so—or four, but he was tall and, he thought, looked older than he was. Anyway, he'd liked her.

Trouble was, so did a guy who worked the same tour on the rig with Frank. The guy, whose name was Jasper something—Frank had never cared enough for the fellow to bother remembering his last name—thought he owned Sally. Frank disputed that, and one night they came to blows in the bar. Jasper Somebody was shorter than Frank, but probably forty pounds heavier—and maybe fifteen years older.

Yeah, he'd hit Frank a couple of times, but Frank's longer arms and considerable punching power meant that the fellow had wound up knocking one table aside and crashing into another, tipping it over, then lying there.

Frank waited for Sally to run into his arms—hell, he'd been fighting for her, after all—but she ran to old Jasper, instead, kneeling over him and making stupid noises.

Frank just stood watching for a minute, but then the bar owner and a couple of men Frank didn't know were grabbing at him and pushing him toward the door. He might well have fought them, too, if he hadn't looked back at Sally. She was staring at him now, and she looked like she hated him. So he allowed himself to be pushed outside.

Outside, he wanted—really wanted—to hit somebody. He didn't know who—just somebody. So he hit a tree. Fortunately, his anger wrecked his aim and he wound up with skinned knuckles rather than a broken hand.

As he walked back to the room he shared with three other roughnecks, he thought about Belle and wondered what she was doing and where she was.

Of course, the fight with Jasper carried over to the job. The men on the rig had known the man longer than they'd known Frank, and he could tell by how they looked at him whose side they were on. He ignored their looks and concentrated on the job. Jasper himself was easy enough to ignore, because he didn't look at Frank at all, even when they were side by side hooking up a bailer or cleaning gunk off the bit. It was uncomfortable, to say the least, and Frank suspected that something more was to come.

He'd had to stay away from the bar he'd had the fight in. The owner had met him right inside the door and—very politely—told him he wasn't welcome and suggesting that he should pay for the broken table. Frank had tossed a dollar into the room and left. There were other places to drink.

There were other places to work, too. There was a lot of tension on the rig. A couple of the hands didn't talk to him at all, unless they absolutely had to. One of the roustabouts—a guy not much older than Frank—openly sneered at him, so, one night as the tours changed, Frank took him behind the doghouse and taught him a lesson.

Unfortunately, the midnight tour driller, a man Frank really didn't even know, tried to intervene, and Frank had to hit him, too. That, of course, meant that he was out of a job.

There were other drilling companies in the area, of course, and Frank considered asking around for work. He even considered asking Tom if there was a chance he could get on at Shell, but he'd seen what pumpers did and it seemed pretty damned boring. And Tom was busy. So he lay around the room for a couple of days, thinking.

One thing he had to do, he knew, was watch his money. He had a little saved—the pay had been good, and he'd cut back on the drinking. If he was going to move on, he thought, he really needed an automobile. His own. The thought made him smile, and he re-counted his money. Probably not enough. No, definitely not enough.

Even if he had transportation, he had to have somewhere to go. There was drilling going on all around him. Ardmore. Oklahoma City. Sapulpa. Back north in Kay County. Yep, that sounded best. Kay County, where he had people. Grandpa and Grandma Cantrell, after a short time running a team in the Whizbang field, were back on the farm, with Mattie and Claude and Callie. Dad was working in Braman. Somewhere around those places he knew he could find work. He just had to get there.

He got a couple days' work unloading drill pipe, filling in for a fellow who'd smashed his fingers. One of the men he worked with on that job had an automobile he wanted to sell. He'd admitted, ruefully, that he'd lost a lot of money playing poker and was getting a hard time at home. He'd sell cheap, he said. Not cheap enough, though. Frank counted his money again. He tried to get the fellow to lower his price, but that didn't work.

He did get to look at the car, though. It was a rag-top Ford, not new and a little beat up; but it was racy, Frank thought, and he had no trouble at all imagining himself behind the wheel, nor imagining a pretty girl beside him. If the top came down, and it looked like it would, the wind would blow through her hair.

So, although he grimaced inside, he borrowed money from his little brother Tom, a married man with responsibilities. A man who probably couldn't afford to lend him the money.

"I'll send you the money as quick as I can," he'd promised.

Tom had only grinned and said, "Yeah, I know you will, Brother!" And he'd clapped Frank on the shoulder.

"I will," Frank thought. "As soon as I get a job, my first paycheck goes to Tom." And he bought the car—and headed north.

He hadn't really decided where he was heading as he left the Cushing field. He thought that it would be nice to see his little sisters and his little brother again, so he considered heading for Grandpa Cantrell's farm. Dad was in Braman, though, and that was closer. Well, he had time to make up his mind while he was heading north.

He put some gasoline in the tank at Perry and bought a hamburger. That left him almost broke. He considered looking for work there, but decided to head on north. He hoped the gasoline would last long enough for him to get to Tonkawa; he'd heard that there was a lot of drilling going on there. So he crossed his fingers and kept going north.

It soon became apparent, though, that he wasn't going to make it. He needed gasoline. He considered pulling off the road into one of the operating leases and draining some of the stuff that condensed in the pump. He'd seen that done and he knew that the engine would run on the stuff. But he didn't know if he could find a well that produced the stuff—and it was stealing. Frank wasn't worried about the stealing part, but the getting caught part was a different story.

The old car sputtered and died somewhere south of Kay County. Frank got out, stretched, and wondered how far he'd have to walk. He felt like kicking the damned old car, but he knew that, if anything deserved to be kicked, it was him. He shrugged. He didn't have a choice, now; he'd have to find work.

He could see oil derricks up ahead, so maybe there was drilling going on. If there wasn't, well, the oil patch always needed strong hands. He could get something. Earn some money, put gas in the car, and keep going north. He grabbed his duffel bag out of the car and started walking. He wondered whether the car'd still be there when he came back for it.

Several cars went by him as he walked, and one truck hauling a boiler. Nobody offered him a ride, but the swamper in the truck waved at him. Frank didn't consider it a friendly wave. One of the cars had a back seat full of kids, and the driver of the other car looked like he might be an Indian.

But Frank didn't expect anybody to give him a ride. Anyway, he could see a derrick just over the next rise. If the location hadn't been abandoned and the derrick wasn't just sitting there waiting to get torn down, he could probably get some kind of ride, maybe into Tonkawa. He'd probably have to wait until the tour was over, though.

It was a working rig, maybe fifty yards off to the west of the road. There were several cars around the site, and Frank could see men at work on the drilling platform. So he went through the fence and walked to the drill site.

The tin doghouse had a sign on it: Marland Oil Company. Frank felt better. He knew that, once the men on the rig knew that he was an oilfield hand himself, somebody'd give him a ride. Maybe they could even tell him where he could find work.

He was luckier than he believed he deserved.

One of the men on the site was wearing a white shirt and suspenders over a pair of gray slacks—hardly work clothes. Maybe he was the drilling superintendent; a company man, anyway. That probably meant that he wouldn't be staying around here long and Frank could get a ride quicker than he'd thought.

The man was coming down the steps from the platform as Frank approached. He had taken off his metal helmet and was wiping his forehead with a handkerchief. He looked up at Frank. "Hello," he said. "What'd you need?"

Frank thought he should skirt that question for a bit, so he asked the question that he'd heard visitors to a rig ask about a thousand times. "How deep are you?"

"About eight hundred feet. Who are you, anyway? If you don't mind my askin'?"

"My name's Gage," said Frank. "And I've got a little bit of a problem."

"Gage? Huh. Any relation to Henry Gage?"

Frank looked back at that short time with a kind of amazement. Not only did the man know his father; he liked and respected him. Dad had hauled pipe for the man way back at Mervine. So Frank wound up not with just a ride, but with a job as well. Blumenthal—that was the fellow's name—not only gave him a job and a ride, but also took him to an operating well on the same lease and drew out some drip gas that had condensed in the pump, drove him back to his car, put the gas in the tank, waited to see whether the car would start, and told him where to see him in the next town up the road.

"Well," the man said, "It's sort of a town. Anyway, it's just up the road."

The Marland Company's J. H. Smith School Land No. 1 had been brought in and was producing a thousand barrels a day. Marland was beginning to drill offsets, and other drilling and production companies were moving in. There were quite a few men coming into the area looking for work, but the flood hadn't reached full momentum yet; Frank was in the right place at the right time and, through good luck, knew the right people. He got put to work on a Marland rig south of Tonkawa, in Noble County, just on the edge of Kay County.

Blumenthal had had him leave his car in what was going to be a town—they were calling it Three Sands—and drove him out to the rig, introduced him to the driller, told him where to get his pay, got his tour assignment from the driller, who seemed pleased to get a new hand, and took him back to his car.

Frank didn't have enough money to eat, find a place to sleep, and buy gasoline, too. But he had a job. He still had to choose between eating or getting gasoline for his Ford, though. Paying for a bed was out of the question. The car ran on the drip gas, but it sputtered and smoked and he really couldn't trust it. So he chose gasoline—enough to get him to the drill site the next day.

He figured that he could probably sleep in the doghouse after he'd started work. One night sleeping in the car wouldn't hurt him. Food was another matter, but he'd worry about that when he had to.

It was a different world. Frank had seen boom towns before, but this was different; he was here while the town was going up—where no town had been before.

There was a hotel already, a board-and-batten unpainted building, two stories high, with a tar-paper roof. Next door was a hastily constructed place with a sign hanging over the door—"Tyson's," it said—and another, saying "Meals," nailed to the wall. On a pole in front of the restaurant was a sign for a lumber company, offering building materials. Frank looked a bit longingly at both places. A meal would be good. A bed would be good. But he could sleep in his car for a while—or even outdoors; the weather was mild.

His first day on the rig showed him how very much different this new world was. The earth here, at drilling depths, tended to crumble into the hole, hampering the cable tool bit. That meant that drilling had to stop frequently so that debris could be bailed out of the hole—a slow and ultimately costly operation. So the cable tool rig had given way to the rotary rig.

So Frank learned rotary drilling and a set of skills that would serve him for the rest of his working life.

The cable tool bit did its work by simply pounding into the ground. The rotary rig used a turning bit attached to a strong pipe. As the hole went deeper, more pipe was added. Frank's first job on the rotary rig was threading pipe and then helping to move it into place when it was needed.

Everything had been in place when Frank arrived at the rig: the wooden derrick, almost a hundred feet tall, had been built; pipe had been strung; the heavy rotary table that actually turned the pipe and bit was in place. A sheet-metal doghouse had been built next to and attached to the drilling platform.

The doghouse was really supposed to be the toolpusher's bailiwick, but he was handling several rigs at once, so he seldom slept there. That meant that, if he could avoid the times that the crew on duty were taking a meal break, Frank could sleep there—and he did, for the first few days. Days, because he was on the midnight to eight tour. Electricity wasn't yet available at the site, so the men on the evening and midnight tours worked under large kerosene lamps hung from the derrick. The rotary table required steam.

Frank's driller, a man about forty, recognized—as most oil men had—something potential in him and gave him new tasks when he could, handing him off with careful instructions. So Frank learned his trade.

He learned to "trip" pipe, the process of connecting a new piece of drill pipe to the string already in the hole as the bit dug deeper. First, of course, he had to be the "worm," working on the opposite side of the hole from the floorhand, the man who actually did the tripping. Frank's job was to hold the lower pipe in place with a pair of heavy tongs while the new pipe was being put into place. It had to be steady, because an uneven connection could be very dangerous indeed, both to the "worm" and to the floorhand. The tongs were heavy, but Frank was strong.

Soon he found himself on the other side of the hole, tripping the chain himself. This was a trickier job and a bit more dangerous if he did it wrong, but he caught on fast.

Tripping was done by wrapping a special chain around the bottom pipe, then, at the appropriate moment—when the pipe ends were together and aligned—throwing the chain, sliding it rapidly up onto the new pipe. The chain then was tightened and used to draw the two pieces of pipe together.

The job took some genuine skill, and Frank found that, despite some very real danger, that he liked doing it. There was a genuine sense of accomplishment in seeing the drill pipe lengthened, ready to dig deeper into the earth, down where the oil was.

The driller was pleased with his work, he knew. The man told him so, and clapped him on the back at least once during each tour. The other hands treated Frank with respect, as well. Frank puffed himself up a little.

On the next well, he worked for a while as the derrick man. Part of his duties were to climb up the eighty to a hundred feet to the top of the derrick to control the top of new pipe being added to the string or to make sure things were aligned and operating smoothly when pipe was pulled out of the hole. It was a long way down to the rig floor, but he didn't have time to worry about that.

He did get some criticism here, though. Hanging on with one hand was definitely *not* a good idea, he was told. He got chewed out pretty thoroughly when he'd bumped his head against the derrick and knocked his hard hat off his head. The metal hat had bounced off one of the derrick struts and missed the rig floor, or it might have hit one of the hands. Frank kept the hat's strap tightly under his chin after that.

The derrick man's job—when he wasn't either climbing or at the top of the derrick—also included handling the "mud." One of the things Frank had come to dislike about drilling with cable tools was the near-constant mess of pulling the bit out of the hole and using a bailer to haul out the bits of rock, gravel, and just plain dirt out of the hole so that the bit could dig in again. The rotary system worked a lot better. A pump pushed "mud" down the hollow drill pipe and out around the bit; then, when more mud was pumped in, the fluid at the bottom rose, carrying with it the stuff that had to be bailed out by hand on a cable tool rig.

It took almost a year and several different drill sites—every one of which had struck oil—but Frank knew that he was becoming a genuine expert at the job. He could handle some of the tasks better than men who had been working in the oil patch for years. And he knew what he wanted now. He wanted to be the driller—the man in charge. Well, after the toolpusher, of course; but that job didn't interest Frank in the least.

So Frank learned his trade. The respect he got for his skills meant that now, despite his youth, men listened to him.

Life on the rig was one thing, but living in a room he had to share with five other men and actually sharing a bed with two of them wasn't his idea of what life should be like. He'd done that sort of thing for a while back in Webb City after Tom had left, then again for a while in the Cushing field, but he didn't have to like it.

He had to admit to himself that he was homesick.

CHAPTER 17

Worse than Spiders
The farm at Longwood, 1922

The cat went sailing up the tree as if she were being chased. Callie followed her, not quite as fast, because she didn't have claws like Baby did. But she did have a kind of ladder—boards that Grandpa had nailed to the tree so that she could climb it. She was always very careful when she was climbing into her tree, because Grandma had told her to be—and because Grandpa had said that he'd take down the boards if she wasn't.

Callie was very careful today, because she had a new book, and she didn't want to drop it and make it all dirty. So she held the book tightly between her arm and her body and went up the ladder very slowly.

At the top of the ladder, where the trunk met a big limb going almost straight out from it, was a nice hollow little place that was just the right size and shape for a girl to sit and read. Callie had found it a long time ago, when her big brother Frank had just lifted her up—*swoosh*—and set her down on the limb. Now it was *her* place.

Well, hers and Baby's. Because as soon as Callie had got seated and wiggled around just enough to start to get comfortable, Baby came down from the limb above and practically jumped into her lap, purring. Callie might have dropped her book if she hadn't been expecting Baby to do that. But she always did!

Her tree. Her book. Her kitty. Callie looked around her, at the old house, at the barn off to her right. She was home. Grandma was happy to be home, too, she could tell. That old Whizbang was ugly and stinky. But Grandma smiled a lot now, and hugged her a lot, too. Oh, Callie'd got lots of hugs from Grandma wherever they lived, but somehow the hugs were nicer here.

Grandma said they didn't have much money, but they didn't need much. She had a big garden, with lots of vegetables, and Callie sometimes helped her, pulling weeds, mostly. It was good to be home.

So, with Baby purring in her lap, Callie opened her book. It was called *The Adventures of Bobby Coon* and there were pictures in the middle of the book of a fat little raccoon and some of his friends. Callie couldn't read all the words—yet—but she could read enough to make out the story, and the pictures helped. And the book smelled good, too. She felt so good, so happy, there in her spot in the tree with Baby on her lap and a book with pictures of a cute raccoon that she just had to close the book and give it a great big hug.

She could hear cars pulling into the gravel driveway in front of the house. Aunt Claudie had come to visit Grandma and Grandpa and they were going to have company. She'd had her supper early—so she wouldn't be in the way, she supposed. That was all right, though; she'd rather be here with Baby, in her tree.

Claude and Mattie had gone down the road to the Nordstroms' house for the evening. Grandma had wanted to send Callie, too, but she'd whined a little—she remembered that with a little grin—and Grandma had let her go to her tree, instead. But when it started getting dark, she was supposed to come in the house and finish reading in the kitchen. Grandma would light a coal oil lamp for her, she'd said. But she was to stay out of the parlor. Aunt Claudie had hugged her, but it didn't feel like a real hug. But that was all right.

So Callie read. And she scratched Baby behind the ears. The book was nice. Bobby Coon got into all kinds of trouble, but it was teeny, little trouble. No one was hunting him with a gun, for example. Or trying to cut off his tail. That was good, she thought; people shouldn't be mean to animals. She scratched Baby's nose. "Nobody's going to cut off *your* tail," she told the little brownish-yellow cat. Baby looked up at her as if she understood. "Prob'ly she does," thought Callie. "She just can't talk."

But Bobby Coon and his friends could talk. Callie wondered, though, if she could understand them. Maybe they talked in an animal language that people couldn't understand.

Baby could understand her, though, at least some things. She knew that "Kitty, kitty, kitty" meant that she was supposed to come and that she was probably going to get some oatmeal or some milk. Grandpa's horses seemed to understand Grandpa, too. She wondered about that for a while, but then she looked at some of the pictures again and forgot about it.

By the time it was beginning to get dark, she'd finished her book. It wasn't really a big, thick book like Grandpa read, and the print in her book was big, so she'd read through it pretty fast. Next year she'd go to school, Grandma had said. Then she'd be able to read Grandpa's big books. They didn't seem to have any pictures in them, though.

Baby had climbed down some time ago, probably to go make potty, and she hadn't come back. Callie thought that she should probably go potty, too, before it got dark.

She didn't like the old stinky wooden toilet even in the daytime, but she hated it at night. When she had to go after dark she always made Mattie—or Grandma, if Mattie wouldn't—go with her and take a lantern. At least when it was day, you could see things.

Callie had seen big spider webs on the ceiling during the daytime, so she knew there were spiders in there. Spiders weren't cute *at all*! And they were probably down in the hole, too, just waiting for her to put her bottom where they could reach it and bite her.

So, before it got completely dark, Callie climbed down the ladder Grandpa had fixed for her. She was very careful with her book. She'd read it, but she knew she'd read it again, probably lots of times. She remembered what Bobby Coon looked like in the pictures and she thought she'd try to draw him some time. But now she had to go to the toilet before it got dark and she couldn't see the spiders.

As she walked down the path that led from the back of the house and along the front of the old barn toward the outhouse, she had a scary thought: could the spiders talk? To each other? She could imagine the ugly old black things, with their legs all quivery, telling each other that there was a little human girl coming and that pretty soon she'd be putting her bottom right down where they could all bite it at once!

When she was inside, then, she was very careful indeed not to let anything but her hands touch the seat. That was hard, because her legs were too short to reach the floor when she sat on the wooden seat, but she managed by putting her weight on her elbows and pushing her thighs hard against the edge of the seat.

Well, she almost managed. She squealed a little bit when she felt the wood touch her and when she felt the openness beneath her. But the spiders either weren't there or they were sleeping.

She got out of the toilet as soon as she could. Now, she thought, I have to wash my hands! There was an old red pump behind the house, and she could wash there. But sometimes she couldn't make the pump work. If whoever'd used it last had left the handle up, sometimes she couldn't reach high enough to grab the end of it. And you had to hold it clear out at the end. It was kind of a lever—anyway that's what Claude had called it. Sometimes he had put a box by the pump for her to stand on, and she could pump some water that way.

But there wasn't any box there now, and the pump handle was clear up at the top. So she would have to go into the kitchen and wash her hands in the little white basin on the wash stand. That was all right. She was supposed to go into the kitchen anyway, and she'd be very, very quiet! Besides, there were some of Grandma's sugar cookies in the big old cookie jar on the cabinet. She looked around for Baby but didn't see her anywhere.

True to Grandma's word, there was a lit coal oil lamp sitting on the kitchen table. It wasn't really dark yet, so Callie didn't really need the lamp, but she thought it was nice that Grandma had remembered. Of course she always did. And, yes, the cookies were in the cookie jar. She didn't think Grandma would mind if she took two.

She sat at the table and ate her cookies and looked once more at the pictures of Bobby Coon and Jimmy Skunk and Uncle Billy Possum. She remembered—too late, as far as the cookies were concerned—that she hadn't washed her hands. She didn't think she would die, though, but she wouldn't tell Grandma. It was a good thing that Mattie wasn't here, because she would have told.

Callie closed her book. For now, she'd had enough of the cute little animals. Her other books—she had just two others—were upstairs, though, and she'd have to go through the parlor to get them. Grandma had been very firm about her not going into the parlor. So she wouldn't. What she wanted, then, was for Baby to come in, but she knew that Baby would stay outside—chasing things, maybe—until it was bedtime. She always knew when it was bed time and she'd jump on Callie's bed to get petted for a while; then she'd cuddle up next to Callie's back and go to sleep.

"I'm bored," she thought. She looked around the room, thinking—without really thinking—that she might see something interesting, something to do.

There wasn't much, though. There was just an old metal sink, the wash stand, some cabinets that Grandma had told her that Grandpa had built a long, long time ago, and the old wood stove, with a box of cut up tree limbs behind it. And the table she was sitting at, with its six chairs and the coal oil lamp. Sometimes she'd left her doll down here, or her little cast-iron stove, but Grandma always told her to put them away if she saw them. Anyway, they weren't here now.

So she wondered what was going on in the parlor. She knew, of course, that children were supposed to stay out of the way when there was company, but being told to stay out of the parlor completely was different. If she was very, very quiet, she thought, and walked like Baby, she might be able to go stand by the door and listen. Grown people usually were boring to listen to when they were talking to each other. Unless somebody was telling a story!

Maybe someone was telling a story.

The door between the kitchen and the parlor was closed, but the door didn't really fit well in its frame and if Callie put her ear right to the gap, she thought that she could hear what they were saying—unless they were all talking at once, as grown-ups sometimes did.

The voice she heard was clearly Aunt Claudie's. And Callie could hear every word that she said.

"I feel a presence," said Aunt Claudie. It was Aunt Claudie's voice, all right, but it sounded funny to Callie. She couldn't really tell how—just different.

"Yes," said Claudie, "you are here and we await you. You needn't fear us, as we are not strangers to you. Your son is here. Your wife is here.

They seek to know of you, of your path, of your happiness, of your destination."

There was a quiet chorus of "yes" from others in the room.

Callie was very quiet—and maybe just a little bit afraid. Who was Aunt Claudie talking to, and why would whoever it was be afraid, and why didn't he just answer her?

"I sense your presence," said Claudie. "I feel your need to communicate with the loved ones you left behind. I am here to help you do that. You can talk to them through me and they can talk to you through me. All you have to do, Martin Gruver, husband of Molly and father of James, is to give us a sign to acknowledge your presence among us."

There was a pause, then, and Callie wanted to tip-toe away from the door. But she couldn't. She wanted to hear. She wanted to run away. She might have turned from the door and walked away, but being heard by the people inside—no, she had to stay there.

Claudie's voice became louder and now it was almost as if she were giving an order. "Now is the time, Martin Gruver! Speak to us! Give us a sign! If you cannot speak—or are afraid to speak—knock on the table. We will hear it and take it as a sign of your love."

And then there was a rapping on the table and Callie could hear breaths being drawn.

Callie must have squealed a little, because in just a second or two, Grandma had opened the door between the parlor and kitchen, scooped her up in her arms, and carried her through the parlor to the stairs.

Callie knew she had been bad, but Grandma was always kind to her, and she just had to look back at the big table and the people around it. They were all holding hands and staring at the table, except for Aunt Claudie. She had her arms raised to shoulder height; her eyes were closed, and her mouth was open. There was a sound coming out of her mouth, but it wasn't words.

It was worse than spiders.

PART THREE

THE OIL PATCH

CHAPTER 18

Boom Town Woman
Whizbang, Oklahoma, 1924

The Tonkawa field was booming, and there was plenty of work. Frank put aside enough money to replace his car. It wasn't a new one, and it wasn't nearly fancy enough or fast enough to suit him, but it was a Buick at least. Buying it meant that he had to cut back on some other things, like drinking. He could live with that.

Then one day he heard the Marland drilling superintendent talking to the driller on Frank's tour about a new drill site up near Braman. Braman. That's where Dad lived. It'd be nice, Frank thought, to live close to the old man. He'd spent most of his life with lots of people around him—Dad, brothers and sisters, Grandma and Grandpa Cantrell. It'd be nice to be close to family again. So he asked the superintendent about working at the Braman site.

And so he went to work around Braman. It hadn't worked out, though. He loved and respected his dad, but he knew quite well that Henry Gage wouldn't approve of some—hell, a *lot*—of the things Frank did. It wasn't so much the drinking; Frank had cut back on that—not because he had anything against it, but because he had better use for his money. Braman had its usual collection of boomtown whores, and they wound up with a lot of Frank's money.

Hell, he'd rather have a nice girl—as long as she'd fuck him—but there didn't seem to be any nice girls where he hung out. And the whores were fine; some of them were even nice. A couple he'd enjoyed being with, even when they weren't fucking.

But he could imagine the old man's lectures if he found out—as he damned well would—so Frank took off. There were plenty of jobs for a good hand and he'd turned out to be a damned good one, he knew. No more of that climbing around on derricks and threading pipe.

He didn't have any trouble getting good recommendations from the drilling superintendent he'd worked for in both the Braman field and the Tonkawa field, and he didn't have any trouble getting on with another drilling outfit—Helmerich and Payne—at Whizbang. This time, though, with the recommendations and a little story-telling, he'd got hired on to do the job he thought he'd been born to: he was going to be a driller.

The job went well enough. Frank found that most of his crew were older than he was, but they all seemed to accept him. Knowing what he was doing made that difference, Frank thought.

But Whizbang was, even though a lot of wells were already pumping, still a boomtown—and that meant that it had drawn—was still drawing—the usual elements. Grandpa Cantrell had lived here for a while, Frank remembered, hauling oil field equipment. It wasn't hard for Frank to see why he'd taken everybody back to the farm. It wasn't a place that Frank would like to have his little sisters growing up in.

Some of the usual elements Frank approved of: the women. Some of the whores were pretty young things and they were quite happy to take his money; some of them seemed to really like him instead of just pretending to. But some of the other elements Frank didn't care for at all.

There were too many god-damned guns, for one thing. In the first month Frank had been on the job, there were two hold-ups. Nobody had got killed, but somebody sure the hell would if things kept up like that.

What made it worse was that one of the hold-ups took place at a rig. Four men had pulled up to the rig during the midnight tour and robbed the crew at gunpoint. Why they'd done something stupid like that Frank didn't know; they certainly couldn't have taken much off a drilling crew, compared with what they might have got from a bank. But they'd done it, and that might mean they'd do it again.

Frank wasn't scared, exactly, but he really didn't want to face some jackass with a gun. He knew what he'd do if that happened: he'd try to take the jackass's head off, and that'd mean he'd probably get himself shot. He'd rather not.

Nobody tried to rob Frank's rig, but guns still wound up being a problem.

Frank met Connie in one of the speakeasies that lined up on the main drag. She was a little bit of a thing, with big blue eyes and her light brown hair cut in a cute little bob. She'd smiled at him and he'd sat down. He'd figured she was a whore, probably new in town.

She turned out to be a lot of fun. She laughed at his jokes and told some of her own. Some of her jokes would have caused a preacher to have a stroke, Frank thought, but he liked a woman who could cuss.

She threw her drink in his face when he offered her money.

That had made Frank laugh. He reached across the table and grabbed her hand, knocking the empty glass loose. "Little lady," he said with a grin, "for that I am just going to have to pull that little skirt of yours up and spank your ass!"

"You wouldn't dare!" she said. She leaned all the way back in her chair, but she was grinning.

Frank kept her hand. "Look," he said. "I'm sorry. I didn't mean to insult you or anything."

She laughed. "Oh, no," she said. "Calling me a whore isn't an insult!"

"I didn't actually call you a whore."

"Might as well have!"

"Nope," he said. "You ain't no whore. That doesn't mean that I don't want to spank your ass, though."

Her eyes danced. "You think you can?"

"Yup."

The girl—woman--got up and grabbed her little jacket. "Okay, big man," she said. "Let's see you try!"

Frank just looked at her.

"Come on," she said. "You have a room—a place to stay—or not? You have ten seconds, and then I'm leaving!"

Frank grinned as he got out of his chair. "One ass-whipping coming up," he said. "By the way, Sweet Thing, what's the rest of your name? I oughta know that if I'm going to lift that cute little skirt of yours."

"Crocker," she said. "Constance Marie Crocker. But you call me Connie."

Connie Crocker was a terrific lay. She wore Frank out that first night. He couldn't even have told anyone the next morning how many times they'd done it. He remembered doing some things that he'd just heard about but had never done—and a couple of things he'd never heard about. She was some woman—woman enough to make Frank consider forgetting about the whores and even those sweet young things he hadn't met yet.

She couldn't get away the next night, she said. She had something else she needed to take care of. But the night after that he met her at the speakeasy again and took her home again. And the next night. And the next.

Then one day, while his crew was hauling the bit out of the hole, two men pulled onto the site in a new Buick roadster. Folks from the company, Frank thought, and looked around to see whether everything was in place, in good condition, and operating as it should.

They weren't from either the drilling contractor or from the production company, though. Both of the men got out. The driver was dressed in a suit that looked like it was just a little too small for him. He had dark sideburns and he looked too young to be a big shot in either company. The other fellow—the one who'd been in the passenger's seat—a fairly tall man with scruffy hair and dirty khakis—called out. "We're looking for Frank Gage!"

"I'm Gage. What d'you need?"

The man who'd called out started up onto the rig platform, but the other man held him back.

"Come down here," said Suit. "We got some business with you."

"I'm kinda busy here," said Frank.

"I'm not interested in carrying on a conversation with us down here and you up there. Just get down here!"

Frank shrugged. "Cleve," he said to his chainhand. "Watch things for a minute, okay?"

The chainhand nodded, but Frank thought he'd caught a sly little smile.

"Okay," said Frank as he took the four steps down from the drilling platform, "what can I do for you fellas?"

"My brother has something to say to you," said Suit.

Frank turned to the brother. "Talk," he said. Now he noticed that the man's face was very red. Something was wrong. But the man didn't speak; instead he started toward Frank again. Again, the man in the suit stopped him.

"My brother's a little upset," Suit said.

"Yeah, I can see that. What's up?"

"You know a woman named Connie Crocker?"

"Yep. Sure do. Why?"

"This man's her husband," said Suit.

Oh, Christ! Frank backed up and sat on the second step. Then he looked up at the red-faced, furious husband. "Well, God damn it!" he said. "You're not shittin' me?"

"You're god-damned right I ain't shittin' you," said the man who was either really Connie's husband or was pretending to be. "Connie's my wife and I'm not going to have some fucking oil field trash like you puttin' his filthy hands on her!"

"Wait just a minute there, friend," said Frank, getting up from the step. "First of all, I ain't trash—oil field or any other kind. Second, I don't believe you, and third,"—he gestured back at the rig—"I've got work to do. So why don't you two fellers just head back into town where you belong?"

It was like he was seeing two moving pictures at one time. One of them had this red-faced blustering guy, practically slobbering and damned near out of control. The other—the one Frank would have rather lingered on—even though it was really the only one that was painful—was of Connie, rolling over in bed, holding her cigarette in one hand and tickling his chest with the other, then blowing smoke, first in his face, then in his mouth. Connie was married? Bullshit.

Then the man was on him. The man in the suit—the man who'd said he was the brother—made a grab at him, but it was too late.

His first punch was wild, but it grazed Frank's forehead and sent his metal safety cap flying. The second one—quite a bit weaker—cracked Frank on the jaw. That was the last punch the man could throw. Frank hit him in the chest first, just to push him back. Then, with his open left hand, he slapped the man's face—hard, and followed that with a right-handed punch to the exposed right jaw. Crocker—if that really was his name—staggered back a step, then fell.

Then the brother was coming. Despite the suit, he looked to Frank as if he might be a bit tougher to handle, but Frank just wheeled aside and gave the man a little shove as the man slid by him, sending him face down onto the steps to the platform.

Frank waited to see if the fellow was going to get up and charge him again, but he glanced over at the other brother, now trying to get up. His attention was distracted for a second or two when he heard applause coming from the rig platform. But the distraction didn't matter.

The brother who'd hit the steps got up and dusted off his knees. Frank was surprised to see that the fellow actually had a little smile on his face; at least Frank thought it was a smile.

"I see your point," the man said. "Look, I'll apologize for my brother. He shouldn't oughta have called you that." He leaned over and picked up Frank's hard hat and held it out. "Here's your tin hat," he said. "You might need this."

Frank reached out and took the hat, but cautiously. This didn't make a whole lot of sense, he thought, unless this guy was more scared than he looked. "Thanks," he said.

The man in the suit glanced up at the rig. "How deep are you?" he asked.

Huh? What the hell?

"Ah, never mind," the man said. "Doesn't matter. I'll just get my brother and we'll let you get back to work. Okay?"

"Yeah," said Frank. "Okay. No, wait!" He glanced back at the first man, who was struggling to get off the ground. "Is what he said true? Is Connie—is he Connie's old man?"

"Yep. Sure is."

"Jesus!"

"You said it, Buster. Jesus!" The man was still grinning—sort of—but Frank couldn't say that it was a friendly grin—not close.

The husband was on his feet now, and his brother was putting his arm around his shoulder, getting ready to lead him back to the car. Frank watched. His forehead hurt a little, but what really hurt was thinking about Connie.

Yeah, he was a little pissed that she hadn't told him she was married—but, hell, maybe they were separated—but what hurt was the thought that maybe this was it: no more Connie. No more hungry kisses, no more of her slapping his face with her breasts, no more *fun*. He knew that he didn't want to lose her.

So, like a damned fool—he thought later—he stood up straight and told them so. "I ain't a-gonna give her up!" he said.

And that brought both of them back. This time the one in the suit had reached into the car and brought out some kind of a stick that looked something like a little baseball bat—and they came at Frank. They were yelling something, but Frank couldn't make it out.

It didn't matter. Frank took the bat-thing away and threw it into the brush. He had to take a few more punches this time, but the two weren't any match for him. The husband—if that's what he was—wound up on the ground again and Frank had the other brother by the back of the suit between the shoulders and threw him at the car. Then Frank picked up the hard hat where he'd dropped it when they came after him, and went up the steps to the rig.

"Thanks, Cleve," he said to the chainhand, who was waiting with a grin, "Sorry it took so long."

When he glanced out toward the road a minute or so later, the Buick was gone.

CHAPTER 19

Lookin' for Trouble
Whizbang, Oklahoma 1924

As he was driving back to town after his tour, Frank spent most of his time wondering. Connie hadn't *acted* married. Didn't married women go home at night? Hell, didn't they *stay* home? And where the hell was her home, anyway? He tightened his grip on the steering wheel; he was going to have to find out. Damned right.

They hadn't made any specific plans the night before, but usually they just both came to the place they'd first met. He'd try that first. He stopped off at his place to clean up a little, then he started for the speakeasy.

She wasn't there, and the guy behind the bar told Frank that she hadn't been in. Frank took out his watch and checked the time. Well, it was still early; he'd get something to eat and wait. He didn't have anything else to do, after all.

Connie didn't show up that night. Or the next. Frank waited. It was beginning to look like the men who had come out to the rig were right: she probably *was* married.

On the third night, Frank finally decided that he'd better ask around; if she was married, somebody would know. The fellow behind the bar didn't know. Frank thought that a couple of men sitting a table in the corner looked familiar, so he asked them, too. They just shook their heads.

With a sigh, he headed back to his table. But a thought hit him, and he turned back to the men. "Say, fellers," he said. "I'm sorry to bother you again, but I've got another question. You mind?"

They looked up at him.

"The name Crocker mean anything to you? I mean, besides the lady? Anybody else?"

The younger man, about Frank's age he would have guessed, started to say something, but the older man shushed him. He reached across the table and put a big hand on the younger man's wrist.

"No," he said. "We don't know no Crockers. Sorry." The he turned back to the other man and started telling him about some problem or other he'd had with a well.

Frank just stood there for a moment. It was clear to him that the older guy did know something—or somebody—but he didn't want to talk. Damn, but he wanted to let the fellow know that he wasn't stupid and that he'd god-damned better...but he cut the thought off. The man didn't want to tell him, so that was that. Hell with it.

Two nights later, Connie showed up. She sat at a table on the opposite side of the room from where Frank was sitting. He'd seen her come through the door, and he knew that she'd seen him, too. And there was something different about her.

"Don't exist, do I?" thought Frank. "Like hell I don't." And he pushed his chair back, picked up his half-drunk beer, walked over to her table, pulled out the chair opposite to her and sat down.

He saw immediately what was different about Connie. Her makeup was a lot heavier than she usually wore, but it didn't cover up the bruises. There was a big bandage of some kind—it looked hard—covering up most of her nose. "Jesus," he thought.

"Connie," he began, and reached for her hand. She pulled it back, and then looked him in the eyes.

"Go away, Frank," she said.

"What happened to you?"

Connie looked away, first to her right, then to her left. She was shifting in her seat, too. But she didn't answer.

"Connie," Frank said, forcing his voice to be gentle, "what happened? Tell me." He watched her face to see if she was going to reply, but she clearly wasn't.

Frank leaned back in his chair then and folded his hands in his lap.

"I'm not goin' nowhere until you tell me, Connie," he said. "Hell, I'll set here all night if I have to."

She glanced back at him for a second, then lowered her eyes. "Please, Frank," she said. "Just go away. Please. Please!"

He reached across and took one of her hands in his. This time she didn't pull away.

It was true, he thought. She *is* married. But he needed her to tell him. Or he'd just tell *her*. He wrapped his hand around hers and leaned toward her as far as he could, trying to hold her eyes with his. But she turned away.

"Look at me, Connie," he said, and tightened his grip on her hand just a little. "Come on. Look at me." She didn't. "All right, don't, then. But I have to know a couple of things."

She turned back to him, then, sitting straight and pulling her hand away. "I asked you to leave, Frank. Won't you please just go away?"

"Are you married, Connie?" There it was; he'd come out and asked her.

She lowered her head. "Yes," she said, so softly that he could barely hear her.

Frank reached for her hand again. She tried to pull it away, but she was too late. "I think your husband came out to visit me at the rig."

She kept her head down, her eyes on the table between them. "I know," she said. Then she looked up at him quickly. "I'm sorry."

"Okay," he said. "Now you tell me, Connie, what happened? Where'd you get those bruises? What happened to your nose?"

Her face was turned away again; she said nothing.

"Tell me," he said. "Tell me, God damn it! Tell me and I'll go away. Now tell me!" He had to restrain himself from reaching across the table and shaking her. He forced himself to sit back in his chair. "He did this to you, didn't he? Didn't he, Connie?"

She said nothing, but, after a long pause, gave a little nod.

"That son-of-a-bitch!" said Frank. He stood, grabbed his hat, and put his hand on her shoulder. "You stay here!" he ordered.

Frank turned to head to the bar to ask again about Crocker, but then he saw, sitting at a table across the room, the same two men he'd asked a couple of nights before—and had got the run-around. It took him just three long steps to get to the table where they sitting. He grabbed the older of the two—the one he'd suspected of knowing more than he'd been willing to say—by his shoulder and wheeled him around, the chair leg making a loud squealing noise.

"Who's Crocker?" Frank demanded.

"Get your hands off me!" said the man, trying to rise. Frank held him in place.

"I know you know," said Frank. "Now tell me!"

The younger man started out of his chair, but Frank cooled him with a look.

"I don't know who you are, Fella," the older man said, "but I'll thank you to get your god-damned hands off me!"

"Just tell me!" said Frank, and he squeezed the man's shoulders— hard.

"Wait!" said the younger man. "I'll tell you! Leave him alone!"

Frank looked at him and waited.

"What do you want to know?" asked the younger man. His face was pale; his hands were clenched, but not into fists.

"You see that little lady over there?" Frank gestured at Connie, who now had her head lying on her folded arms.

The man nodded.

"If you can't tell from here," Frank said, "you could sure as shit tell if you looked her in the face! Some bastard named Crocker beat the hell out of her, and I want to know where I can find the son-of-a-bitch!"

"He works at the supply store a couple of blocks down," said the man—well, the boy, really.

"Okay," thought Frank. "I know the place." He let go of the older man's shoulder and started back toward Connie.

"Wait!" said the young man.

Frank turned to him. He clenched his own hands into fists; he wasn't going to god-damned *wait* any more. "What?"

The young man looked down. "Mister," he said, "I don't know you, but I know Crocker. He's a bad one, Mister. I don't think you want to go lookin' for trouble."

"That's just it," said Frank. "I *do*." He turned away, walked back to the table where Connie was sitting, lifted her chin, and kissed her forehead.

"You rest," he said. "I have something to take care of."

"Don't, Frank." Her voice was pleading and there were tears running down her cheeks. "Don't. It won't do any good! It won't!"

"I guess we'll have to see about that, won't we?" he said, and walked quickly out the door.

It took Frank, striding rapidly on his long legs, just a few minutes to reach the supply store.

"Where's Crocker?" he demanded of the clerk behind the counter.

"Out in back," said the clerk. If he was disturbed in any way by Frank's tone, he didn't show it. He just gestured toward the rear of the store.

The door at the rear of the store led to a large storeroom full of boxes. At the back of the storeroom was an open sliding door, and Frank headed through that. Crocker was there, helping a couple of roustabouts—Frank thought that he recognized one of them—loading a big spool of cable onto a truck.

"Crocker," he said.

Crocker glanced behind him and almost lost his grip on the spool. The two roustabouts had to struggle for a moment to keep from dropping it. "Damn it, Crocker," said one of them. "Hold on to the damn thing!" But Crocker just let it go. The heavy spool slipped completely out of their control and hit the edge of the truck bed. One of the roustabouts had to jump aside to avoid getting hit.

But Frank wasn't watching the spool or the roustabouts. He was taking Crocker by the front of the shirt and lifting him so that his toes were barely touching the ground.

"You worthless son-of-a-bitch," he said. "What kind of no-account shit beats up a woman?" Then he lowered Crocker, pushed him back a little with his left hand, and slammed his right hand as hard as he could into Crocker's stomach. When he bent over, Frank lifted his right fist into the man's chin. He dropped.

But Frank wasn't through. He leaned over the man, turned him onto his back, lifted his head, and slapped his face twice, hard.

Crocker's voice was weak, but he managed to get something out. It sounded something like "please." So he kicked Crocker in the side. When Crocker's body turned from the power of the kick, Frank kicked him in the back.

When he grabbed Crocker under the arms to pick him up so that he could hit him again, he felt a hand on his arm. It was one of the roustabouts—the one he'd thought he'd recognized.

"Gage," the man said. "That's enough." Frank shook him off, but the man grabbed his arm again. "Come on," the man said. "You're gonna kill him." Frank looked at him. "You don't want that, do you?"

Frank let go of Crocker and pushed him away. "Yeah, I do," he said.

"We're not going to let you do that, Frank. It is Frank, isn't it?"

"He god-damn well deserves to be dead," said Frank, looking the roustabout in the eye. "And if you think you can stop me, feel free to try!"

The man took a step back. He clearly didn't want to fight, and Frank realized that he didn't want to fight the man. Maybe he'd done enough—no, not nearly what the bastard deserved—but maybe all he could do.

"The law here," said the roustabout—Frank still couldn't place him, although he knew he should, "doesn't exactly observe the niceties. You kill this man and you'll probably wind up dead yourself."

He was right, Frank knew. Whizbang didn't have any town law enforcement; they relied on somebody paid by the oil companies. Frank had heard stories about the man, something about gunfights right out in the street, and not necessarily with bad guys. From what he'd heard, Frank figured that the man would be quite willing to shoot him down.

He told himself to relax.

"Okay," said the roustabout, lightly hitting Frank on the shoulder. "Now you get out of here."

Frank looked at him, wondering that they were just going to let him walk off.

"We'll say the cable fell on him," the man said. He looked at the other man who'd been helping load. "Right, Sam?"

Sam nodded.

Crocker was still on the ground, writhing and whining. Frank wanted to kick him again. But he knew that this was over, at least for now. He let his shoulders sag. "All right," he said.

"Okay." Another tap on the shoulder. "Now, go!"

Frank looked from one man to the other. Both of their faces showed concern, but no anger. He knew he should say something—that maybe he should thank them—but nothing came.

"We know why you did what you did," said the man Frank thought he knew. "Or at least we think we do."

Frank just looked at him.

"The son-of-a-bitch was bragging about it," said the man. He aimed a kick at Crocker, but it wasn't hard. "He got what he deserved. You did what you did. Now get the hell out of here!"

Frank nodded. He looked once more at the pathetic devil on the ground, then nodded to the two men. He hoped his nod conveyed his thanks.

Then he left.

He went about his business, trying not to think of Connie or her worthless jackass of a husband. Even so, he wanted to find Connie, maybe even to tell her what he'd done. But he supposed that she'd surely find out. It occurred to him—a bit late, he thought—that Crocker might take his beating out on her. If he did that, Frank realized, he would have to kill the man, no matter what the consequences might be.

CHAPTER 20

God-damned Guns
Whizbang, Oklahoma, 1924

Three days after Frank's little tussle with Connie's so-called husband, all hell broke loose in the little Oklahoma boomtown known as Whizbang.

Frank had been on the job when the whole thing started. The well had hit pay at a couple of levels, but the company man wanted more. So he'd called in somebody to "shoot" the well—to drop a shell containing nitroglycerin into the hole. The drilling was probably over, but they had to wait to see the result of shooting the well.

Apparently the nitro "torpedo" had done its work, because the flow increased. Frank's job here was almost over; all they had to do was gather up their stuff and move to their new location. The production people would take it from here.

When he got back to Whizbang, he found one side of the main street ablaze. The post office, he saw, was almost gone. The buildings beside it were burning. The fire was spreading beyond those, too.

Frank stood on the opposite side of the street and watched. He'd actually been headed for the post office—not that he really expected anything—but sometimes Grandma Cantrell or Mattie sent him a letter. Well, if they had, it was sure the hell burned to shit.

The most surprising thing was that nobody seemed to be trying to put out the fire. The oil company's fire trucks were down at the end of the street, but they were just sitting there. Some of the company firemen were standing around; a couple were sitting up on the trucks. What the hell?

There were lots of people on the street. The girls from Ma Smith's—ostensibly a hotel but really a whorehouse—were all huddled together on the corner across the street from their blazing home—or place of business—or whatever. Most of them look scared. One or two looked excited. Frank knew a couple of them, and he felt that somehow he should do something, something to, well, comfort them. But he couldn't think of anything.

He watched with them while the roof of Ma Smith's collapsed into the fire and broken glass exploded onto the street. The little hardware store next door had flames shooting from the roof and Frank could see through the front of the store that the whole inside was afire. The whole damn town was going up.

The bar where he'd met Connie—and where he'd spent a lot of his time—was down at the end of the block. The fire hadn't reached it yet, but it probably would, unless somebody damned well did something. The damned oil companies paid those men at the end of the street to put out fires. What the hell were they doing?

Frank began to feel as if he himself should be doing something, but—put out that kind of fire? One man couldn't do a thing to stop it, even if he had the right equipment. Hell, it was too late for the firemen to really do anything now. Whizbang—at least one side of the street—was a goner.

Frank looked around at the people, thinking he should ask someone what had happened, why the guys with the fire trucks were sitting on their asses. He saw a couple of people he knew, but they were either yakking away with other people or had looks on their faces like they'd just come back from the war. He thought about asking some of Ma Smith's girls, but he figured that they wouldn't know. They'd have been busy at work or lounging around in the parlor until either the noise or the smoke rousted them out.

There was a crash and a huge billow of smoke as the front wall of the whorehouse fell in. The roof of the hardware store was totally in flames now, and the little eating joint beside it was burning. No more bacon and eggs from that joint, Frank thought. Then he felt a little ashamed. That was somebody's business. Old man Heffner was a grouch and not much of a cook, really, but, damn it, a man had to make a living.

Where the hell was the law? That sumbitch should have been making those firemen do their jobs, even if he had to do it at gunpoint. Then Frank saw him. The sheriff or marshal or whatever they called him—the oil people paid his salary, so they could call him any damn thing they wanted to—was standing in the street, just off the sidewalk, watching the town burn.

Raul Dominguez was his name, but he didn't look a damned bit Mexican, Frank thought. Anyway, the bastard was just standing there with his damned boots and his two guns and his bandolier of bullets across his chest, watching. He did not look displeased, Frank thought. He might even be enjoying himself.

The fire hadn't reached the bar yet, and there were men still standing in front of it. They wouldn't have long to wait, though, for the fire to reach the place; it was probably already hot as hell over there.

Frank started across the street. He certainly didn't think they were doing any business—although a cold beer would taste damned good. But— he admitted to himself—he wanted to see if Connie was there, if she was all right. He hadn't heard anything at all about his little visit to Crocker; it was as if it had never happened. But he was sure Connie would know; what she thought about it was a different story. And, whatever was going to happen between them in the future—if anything—he still wanted her to be safe.

There were cars stopped all along the street, some of them empty, others with people in them—all watching Whizbang burn. He walked around them and went up onto the wooden sidewalk. That was probably burning, too, he thought, and looked back up the street toward the fire. Yep, the sidewalk was on fire, too.

"Somebody'll have to build a new sidewalk," Frank thought, then caught himself. "Crazy bastard, there ain't gonna be nobody building any sidewalks around here for a long time!"

The men standing around the door of the tavern were sweating, but they didn't seem to want to leave. It was hot. Frank reached into his back pocket for his blue bandanna and wiped some of the sweat from his face.

"What the hell happened?" he asked. A couple of the men looked at him, but then turned their eyes back to the fire. Their faces were slack. Some of them looked either dead drunk or out of their fucking heads with that Mexican dope—Mary something. One fellow, though, a roughneck Frank recognized, told him.

If what Frank learned from the roughneck, and, later, from others, was the truth, the post office had caught fire—nobody seemed to know how. The oil company fire department had shown up fairly quickly, but they'd been stopped by Dominguez, the man the company themselves hired to do their law enforcement, and three of his deputies. Guns were holstered, but very obvious. The firefighters backed off.

Why Dominguez and his men kept the firefighters from saving the post office wasn't known—if there was a good reason; nobody seemed to have any ideas. Some of the oilfield bosses had shown up, ready to order Dominguez and his men to step aside. But it was too late. The post office was essentially gone.

The fire had spread to the adjacent buildings, and Dominguez and his men had stepped aside finally and told the bosses that they could have their people put out the fires now.

But the bosses had apparently had enough. They told their fire crews to stay put, so the men on the trucks had sat and watched the street burn for a while before finally turning their trucks around and leaving.

It was getting too hot there in front of the speakeasy, and Frank could see the flames on the wooden sidewalk moving toward them. Time to go. The roughneck he'd been talking to stepped off the walk and headed down the street. A couple of the other men followed.

"Think it's time to skedaddle," said Frank. "You boys gonna stay here and roast wieners?" One of the men looked at him; the others didn't even seem to have heard him.

Frank stepped off the sidewalk, but before he'd taken more than two steps, a man came bursting around the corner, almost colliding with him. Frank recognized him immediately; it was the other Crocker—the brother with the sideburns. "Oh, Jesus," he thought, "not this guy again!"

The Crocker brother stepped back when he saw Frank and his hand went inside his coat.

Frank stopped. "I don't have no quarrel with you," he said.

"Yes, you do," said Crocker, and his hand came out of his coat with a revolver. But before he could lift it to aim, Frank had his hand on Crocker's wrist, twisting it down and to the side. The gun bounced off the wooden railing lining the sidewalk and fell onto the street.

"No," said Frank, twisting the arm up and behind the man's back. "You don't have any quarrel with me. This's been between me and your shit of a brother."

"Let me go, you fucker!" said Crocker, trying to twist free.

Frank kicked the gun back toward the building and sent it skidding underneath the sidewalk. Good. Let the bastard crawl in the dirt to get his god-damned gun and burn his ass while he was getting it. He used the man's arm to turn him around and pushed him away.

As he walked away—rather pleased with himself, actually—he heard the man shouting behind him.

"You're dead!" the man shouted. "You wait! You don't have any idea who you're fucking with! You are one dead son-of-a-bitch!"

Frank turned for just a moment. He grinned at the fellow. "Yeah," he said. "I think I do have an idea." He walked away. Only later did he think about Connie.

Five days later, at the new location, just across the road from the old one, a car carrying four men pulled up next to the pipe rack. Frank glanced at the car, but he was busy; they were adding a joint of pipe to the drill string—an operation that could be dangerous. Then he was aware of a sharp *ping* as something struck the rotary table. Then he heard the shots. He ducked behind the rotary table and heard the chainhand grunt.

Bullets clanged off the drill pipe, off the rotary table, off the derrick. Then they stopped. Frank looked over at Cleve, his chainhand; he was holding his shoulder and blood was pouring from beneath his hand. Frank reached for him, but Cleve flinched away.

Frank took a chance, then, to look over the rotary table. The car was still sitting where it had been, but only one man was outside it, standing beside it, holding the driver's side door open: the damn brother again!

"I told you," the man yelled. "This was just a tiny little warning, Gage! Next time, you're dead!" He got into the car and backed it away from the pipe rack. Then it was gone.

Frank's car had four flat tires. The windshield and the headlights had all been shot out. The rest of the hands, who'd scattered quickly, were unhurt, thank God. Frank had some of them load Cleve into one of the hands' car and take him to town. Then he and the others shut down the rig. It'd have to be checked for damage. Frank needed to get to a telephone to call his toolpusher. And, he supposed, he'd have to talk to the law in Whizbang. But, from what he'd heard and seen at the fire—that probably wouldn't mean shit.

He looked over the damned car. It'd been a good old car, but he really wasn't in the mood to buy four new tires and get the windshield and headlights fixed. He kicked one of the flat tires. "Well, old girl," he told the car, "I guess this is goodbye."

He got a ride into town with the derrickhand. They didn't talk much on the way; there was plenty to think about. For one thing, Frank wondered, why hadn't the men with the guns come right up on the rig? Everybody up there would have been a sitting duck. Well, he couldn't worry about that now. There was plenty of other stuff to worry about.

Cleve was going to be all right. The bullet had gone through the upper arm. It might have nicked a bone the doctor thought, but he hadn't had to dig out a bullet, thank God. Frank did his own thanking, but not for quite the same reasons.

The toolpusher had to drive down from Ponca City, so Frank had to get hold of the drillers from the other two tours and tell them what had happened, and that all the pipe and the rig itself had to be inspected for damage. He checked with his own crew; they all seemed okay. Not particularly happy with him, Frank thought. He damned well didn't blame them; he'd got them shot at.

He got a ride out to the rig with the evening tour driller and helped look over the rig. Several joints of pipe had bullet holes in them, so they had to be moved out of the rack. The rotary table had a couple of nicks in it, but nothing that would prevent its working all right. Myers, the evening driller, thought they could get the bit back into the hole and start drilling again.

"Up to you," said Frank. He thought they ought to wait for the toolpusher, but it wasn't for him to say. He stayed during the evening tour—helping out when he could. This crew wasn't nearly as good as his own, he saw. They'd barely got the new joint tripped onto the chain by quitting time, much less getting the bit back into the hole. He would miss his crew.

He got a ride back into town with Myers. He just left his car there. Somebody might salvage it, he thought, or it might just sit there. Too bad.

At his rooming house he settled up with his landlady, checked the cash in his billfold, realized that it wasn't enough. A replacement for the old car would have to wait. He packed what he could of his belongings into the one beat-up suitcase he owned.

Outside the rooming house, he looked back at it and up and down the street. He didn't see anything threatening, but he knew that he had to be careful.

Damned guns. God-damned guns!

He'd have to hitchhike, he guessed. Where? The only choices were back to Dad's at Braman or back to the Tonkawa field. Well, they were in the same direction.

He went by to see Cleve—to apologize for getting him shot and to tell him that he was leaving. He made sure that Cleve would tell the rest of the crew and, more importantly, the toolpusher. Frank wasn't worried about his reputation—as far as dependability and competence were involved; he suspected, though, that, given the circumstances, everybody would be glad to be rid of him. Cleve told him that he'd be missed, but his tone of voice and facial expression told Frank otherwise.

In Whizbang, the block that had burned was completely gone. The little joint on the corner was rubble. Even after five days, the smell of burned wood was still strong. He wondered what had happened to all Ma Smith's whores. Well, they'd probably just find another place to conduct their business. You had to be tough to be a whore in the first place. They'd probably all be okay.

He wanted a beer. And he needed a ride. The beer was easier. There was a little place on the side of the street that hadn't burned. Frank had gone there a couple of times when he first came to town, but he hadn't been back since. It was open.

He had his beer. It was cold and good. Connie wasn't there, of course. He had thought, somehow, that she might be, but he hadn't expected it. He'd probably never see her again.

But there was a piece of luck. A Marland landman headed for Ponca City was there, and he agreed to let Frank ride.

As it turned out, the landman had had a little too much to drink, and he was happy to let Frank drive. The man slept, leaning against the passenger door. Frank was a bit concerned that the fellow might fall out, but didn't worry about it much.

At first he tried to concentrate on his driving, but his thoughts kept going back to Connie. Was she all right? Had Crocker beat her up again?

Was Frank deserting her? Would she miss him? Was she all right? Was he a bastard for just taking off and leaving her there? Damn, damn, damn.

Should he go back? He gripped the wheel and shrugged his shoulders. He wouldn't do her any good if he was dead. One Crocker he could handle. Even two Crockers. But not four men with guns.

God damned guns.

They wouldn't find him where he was going—if he knew where he was going.

CHAPTER 21

A New Site
Kay County, Oklahoma, 1924

The landman Frank had caught a ride with was awake enough by the time they got to Ponca City to tell Frank how to get to the Marland office, so Frank drove him there, thanked him for the ride, got his old suitcase out of the back seat, and watched the man—staggering a little, still—go into the building.

Frank stood outside and checked his wallet. They'd stopped to eat once along the way and Frank had felt obligated to pay for the man's food. There wasn't much in the billfold. He could eat for a while. Depending on what was available, he might be able to pay for a room for a week or so. He needed to get some work fast. But he had no transportation.

He looked back at the Marland office. Maybe the job hunt could be taken care of right now. Old Blumenthal worked out of here, didn't he?

As soon as he entered the building, though, Frank could tell that this wasn't the place to find a job on a rig. The only person in the large room inside the door was a receptionist behind a big desk. She was talking on the telephone.

While he waited, Frank looked around. The room had a row of fancy-looking chairs lining one wall. There were large photographs of oil wells and derricks on the walls. There were several glass-fronted offices to the right and another behind the receptionist. "Business office," Frank thought. But maybe somebody could tell him where he should go to apply for a job.

He could tell from the look the receptionist gave him that she wasn't used to seeing men in work clothes at her desk. She was polite, though, and gave Frank the address of the drilling office. He thanked her and left.

Outside, he realized that the address he'd been given was clear across town. He could walk it, sure; but when he looked at his watch, he realized that he wouldn't make it before closing time. He looked up and down the block. He wasn't even sure where to go to get a place for the night. He shrugged his shoulders; he didn't really have a choice. He'd have to call his dad.

He went back into the office. The receptionist was kind enough to let him make a collect call to Braman. There was one good thing about

Dad's job, he thought while he was waiting for the operator to get done ringing: the company had put a telephone in Dad's house so if there was trouble on a well people could get hold of him quickly. He realized then that he didn't know Dad's hours. He might not even be at home. He was surprised to hear a woman's voice answering.

Henry was surprised to hear from Frank, and even more surprised that he needed a ride, but got ready to leave for Ponca as soon as he could.

"My boy Frank needs a ride," he told Lizzie. "I s'pect he'll be stayin' with us for a while."

Lizzie grinned at him. "I figured," she said. "It'll be nice to see ol' Frank again."

"Huh? You know Frank?" Henry was surprised. "How'd you know Frank?"

"C'mon, Henry," she said. "He came into Barney's all the time."

"Oh," he said. "Sure." That was interesting. If Lizzie knew Frank, that meant that Frank knew Lizzie. He wondered what Frank would think. Well, it didn't matter what his son thought.

He kissed Lizzie goodbye and started for his Ford. Before he got there, though, he heard the telephone ring again—a long and two shorts. He recognized his ring and turned back toward the house. Lizzie met him at the door.

"Telephone, Henry," she said, holding up the receiver. The telephone was on the wall right next to the door, so all Henry had to do was step inside the door and lean forward to speak into the mouthpiece.

All Lizzie heard were a couple of "uh-huh's," one "yes," and an "I'll tell him. Yes. Right away. I'm leaving to pick him up right now."

"Who was that?" she asked as Henry was putting the receiver back on the hook.

"You don't know him," he said. "Fellow name of Billy Payne. Frank works for him—or I guess he used to work for him. Apparently there was some trouble on the rig." He leaned to kiss her goodbye again. "I need to get on the road, Lizzie," he said. "I'll be back as soon as I can."

"Be careful, Henry," she said, and pulled him to her again. She kissed him hard, then pushed him away with a grin. "Now, go!"

Frank was happy to see his Dad's Ford coming down the street. For one thing, he was getting damned cold standing out here. For another, he was tired. He'd tried sitting on the curb for a while, but that had put his long legs up around his chin and wasn't restful at all.

He'd been a little bit ashamed to have to call his dad for help, but all that went away with the pleasure of knowing he'd soon be seated in the warm car. At least he hoped it would be warm.

Their greetings were perfunctory. Neither man really showed it, but they were both glad to see each other and each knew it. Henry got out and tried to take Frank's suitcase, but Frank pulled it away from him, opened the rumble seat and tossed the bag in. Henry gave him a look and closed the hatch.

"Well, then," said Henry. "Get in and tell me where you want to go."

Frank seated himself—there really wasn't room for him in the passenger seat, but then there usually wasn't. He just spread his knees to keep them from bumping the dashboard.

"I need a job," he said, after Henry started the car.

"So I hear," said Henry.

Frank turned to him, startled. "You heard? What did you hear?"

"Billy Payne called," said Henry, backing into the parking lot to turn around.

This was bad, thought Frank. Billy Payne was one of the two owners of the drilling company he'd worked for back at Whizbang. Hell, he'd never even met the man. Well, this *could* be bad. Probably was. "What did he say?"

Henry pulled out onto the street. "He didn't say nothin'," said Henry. "He *asked*."

Frank just looked forward.

"What happened, Frank? It must have been something bad for the head man to call me like that." He looked over at his son, who seemed to be just staring out the window. "Are you in trouble, son?"

"I guess so, Dad," said Frank, and he felt and heard the whole story began to burst out of him—well, almost the whole story; he left out Connie.

"They *shot* at you?"

"Yep."

"Then you did the right thing, gettin' out of there." Henry reached over to pat his son's leg. "I'm glad you're home. Well, I'm glad you'll be home in a little bit."

"Me, too, Dad," said Frank, and he began to relax.

"You'll have to call Billy Payne when we get back to the house."

"Yeah. All right. I'll do that." He squirmed in his seat. This car wasn't as comfortable as his old car. Damn, he'd liked that car and now it was gone for good. Well, he'd just have to get a new one when he had the money. Maybe a Buick like the one the men with the guns had had. Then he thought of something else.

"Dad," he asked, "who was that woman who answered the phone?"

"That was Lizzie—Elizabeth."

Frank chuckled. "Okay," he said. "She's Lizzie or Elizabeth! Now who the hell is she?" His dad didn't make enough to hire someone to come in and clean for him, that was for sure—and Frank couldn't imagine why any other kind of woman would be in his dad's house.

Henry didn't look at him; he just looked on down the road. "She's your new mother, Frank. Well, she's my wife anyhow." Then he looked over at Frank, clearly wondering how his son would take that particular bit of news.

Frank laughed and slapped his knees. "Bullshit!" he managed to get out. Then he reached over and tipped his father's hat, almost over his eyes. "You always were a windy sumbitch!" He pushed his father's hat back—no sense in causing a wreck—leaned back, spread his legs wider, and gave himself a good laugh.

"It's not bullwhatever," said Henry. "She's my wife." She wasn't, actually; she'd just moved in with him. But Henry didn't see any reason to tell Frank that.

Frank stared at him for a minute. Henry just drove.

Finally, Frank got some words out. "You're kidding me, right? Jesus!"

"Nope. God's truth." (Well, almost.)

Again, Frank had to be silent. Dad married? Again? No. Couldn't be. He looked over at Henry, but there wasn't anything to tell from his facial expression. His eyes were on the road. There wasn't a trace of smile, but his mouth wasn't set like it became sometimes when he was angry. Okay, he thought; I'll play along. "All right," he said. "If you say so. God!"

"I do say so, Son."

"Who is she, Dad?" Frank took off his hat and tossed it on the floor between his feet. "Tell me about her. Where'd you meet her? How long has this been goin' on?"

Henry turned his head to look at Frank, then turned back to watching the road. "She's a good woman, Frank. She's not your Mama. No one could ever take Martha's place, but Lizzie's not trying to do that, Son. She couldn't if she wanted to, but she doesn't want to. She just wants to be with me."

"Brother! I am going to need some time to get used to this!" said Frank, and he reached over and tipped Henry's hat again.

"Lay off the hat," said Henry, and he reached over and pinched Frank's thigh, hard enough to make Frank flinch.

"Ow! Quit that!"

Then both men laughed. Frank had felt that pinch many times when he was growing up. It had usually come at a time most of the fathers that Frank had known would have gotten a board. The only time Frank remembered getting a whipping from his father was for talking back to his mother. He'd tried not to do *that* again. But the pinch had been there quite often. Sometimes it had been playful; sometimes it had been serious. Frank had always been able to tell the difference, even when one stung about as much as the other. This one was playful.

"You'll meet her soon enough," said Henry. "I suspect you're tired now, considerin' all that you've been goin' through, so why don't you just lean your head back and take a little nap?" He reached over and patted Frank, just about where he'd pinched him. "It's only about another twenty miles or so, but you could sleep a little bit."

"Yeah, I'll do that," said Frank. He was tired, he realized, plum' wore out, as Brother Tom would say. He leaned his head back and closed his eyes. But a grin spread across his face. "Lizzie, huh?" This was a definite new look at the quiet, serious man that he'd known all his life. "What the hell," he thought, as he began to drift off, "the old man deserves to get a little, too." That made him think of Connie, of course, but he was too close to being asleep to deal with that. So he let it go.

CHAPTER 22

The Pumper's Wife
Kay County, Oklahoma, 1924-1925

Frank woke up as they were pulling out of Braman. It took a minute or so for him to figure out where they were; by the time he had, they were out of town.

"Where we goin', Dad?"

"Home."

Out here?" Frank looked back up the road to town. "Out in the country?"

"Yep. And here she is." Henry was turning into what looked a little bit like some of the oil camps Frank had seen. He lifted his right hand and pointed.

"Here?" The house looked like one of those row houses that some of the oil companies had built for their crews back at Whizbang. It was a board-and-batten affair, with what looked like a tin roof. One big difference here that there wasn't any row. The house sat, instead, by a pipe rack on one side and a pumping well on the other. A drive went right beside the house, between it and the pipe rack. Frank could see some kind of metal building at the rear of the drive—some kind of warehouse, he thought—and the usual outdoor toilet back there. Behind the pipe rack was a windmill, turning slowly.

Henry pulled through the drive and then turned the Ford into a parking space behind the house.

"Here we are, Son," he said. "Home. Let's get you unloaded."

"This is where you live? Huh!"

"Oh, no," said Henry, with a straight face, "This is where Harry Sinclair lives. We're just going to drop in on him for a chat."

Frank knew that he didn't know much, but he was damned sure that Henry Sinclair—who had to be worth a million at least—didn't live in any little shotgun house in the country. His leg was being pulled. The thought made him grin—having his Dad pull his leg was like being a boy at home again. He popped open the door of the Ford and swung his legs out.

"Good enough," he said. "Let's go see how ol' Harry is doin'!"

He had forgotten—for the moment—that he was indeed going to meet someone: not Harry Sinclair, but Dad's new wife. Right now, though, he was curious.

"How come you're living out here?" he asked.

Henry was out of the car and walking around it toward Frank. "I'm pumping, Frank. Have to live close to the wells."

"Pumping? Oh, yeah. Right." He shook his head. "God, I couldn't do that," he said. "How the hell you stand it?"

"Gettin' old, Son. That crawlin' around on a rig floor was gettin' to be too much."

Frank looked at his father. Getting old? Hell, how old was he? Forty-something? And he was still one of the strongest men he'd known.

"Yeah," said Henry. "Time to settle down." He gestured at the house, then at the pipe rack, then at the warehouse behind them. "This is a job that'll last. No more hauling my rear end all over the country from drill site to drill site."

Frank thought that his father looked somehow satisfied—calmer. Huh. Well, okay. It made sense—some, anyway. Frank couldn't imagine himself being a pumper: making sure engines were working, gauging tanks, goosing grass from around tank batteries. The work had to be done, but— well, not by him, for damned sure. "Huh," was all he could think of to say.

"It's not as much money," Henry said, "but the house there is part of the deal. No rent." He gestured then at the windmill. "And that old windmill there gives us electricity. Now, come on in the house and meet Lizzie."

Lizzie. Oh, yeah.

She met them at the back door, holding the screen door open and standing at the top of the two-by-six board steps.

"Oh, my God!" thought Frank. "It's *that* Lizzie!" His heart sank.

"Hello, Frank," she said. "Come in."

Frank looked back at his father, just a step or two behind him. Was this some kind of joke? No. It was real. Jesus.

"Go on in," said Henry. "I'll get your bag." He made a shooing motion with one hand and turned back to the car.

Frank just stood there, first watching his father opening the rumble seat, then watching Lizzie waiting there at the door. Her greeting had been friendly, but Frank thought he could see some uneasiness there, too. Well, there damned well oughta be.

Lizzie sort of waggled the screen door. "Come on in, Frank," she said. "We're lettin' the flies out!" She stepped back then, and waved him in. "It's good to see you again, Frank."

Frank didn't know what to say to her, so he just grunted.

119

Lizzie looked out into the yard where Henry was boosting Frank's suitcase out of the rumble seat, then turned to Frank. "I know you're surprised, Frank."

"You got that right!" Frank tried to keep the hostility out of his voice, but he could tell that he hadn't. Lizzie seemed to flinch back a little.

"Give me a chance, Frank," she said. Then she held her finger to her lips. "Shh. We'll talk later."

Frank walked through what would have been called the mudroom back on the farm—he supposed it was called a porch or something here—and into the kitchen. There was something cooking on the stove. Beans, it smelled like. Ahead he could see, down the hall, a living room. There was a door along the hall that he supposed led to their bedroom. Their bedroom!

"Go on to the front," Lizzie said, "and set down. I'm fixin' supper."

The living room was pretty bare. There were two old chairs, a gas heater, and, on the wall just to the left of the front door, a wooden telephone box. Seeing the telephone reminded him that he had to call Billy Payne. He hoped Dad had the number written down someplace.

The ham hock and beans were good, and Frank was too hungry to talk. He just listened, spooning food into his mouth while Henry did the talking. Lizzie sat quietly at the end of the table. She wasn't eating much, Frank noticed. Frank's father was making up for all of them, though, between bites.

"You saw the well beside the house," Henry said, gesturing over his shoulder with his fork. "That's one of mine." He returned the fork to his plate, then back to his mouth. "There's eight more. They're all back there." He gestured back in the direction of the warehouse—if that's what it was. "And I have to take care of the pumphouse."

Frank looked up at him then. He hadn't seen any pumphouse.

"It's back at the rear of the tin building," said Henry.

"Sounds like a lot," said Frank, reaching for another piece of cornbread. Whatever Lizzie was, she was a pretty good cook.

"I suppose so," said Henry. "Keeps me busy." He reached over and patted Lizzie's hand. "Don't it, Honey?"

Again, Frank felt himself cringe. His daddy was really married to the old whore. Damn.

Henry *had* written down the number; so, after they'd finished supper, they made the call to Billy Payne while Lizzie gathered up the dishes.

"I understand there was some trouble at the rig down at Whizbang," said Payne. "You wanta tell me what went on?"

Frank told him about the men with the guns—and about his car—but he didn't mention Connie. Wasn't none of the man's business.

"That's pretty much what I got from the hands," said Payne. Then there was a pause. Frank waited; he expected that he was going to get a good bawling-out. Hell, he probably deserved it.

But he didn't get what he expected.

"Look, Gage," said Payne. "We're sorry about what happened out there. You're a good hand and we don't really want to lose you."

Frank didn't know what to say to that, but he managed a choked "Thank you."

"You still want to work for us?" Payne's voice over the telephone sounded muffled, and Frank wasn't sure he'd heard right.

"What was that?"

Payne's voice grew louder. He was probably shouting into the phone, Frank thought. "I said: Do you still want to work for us?"

"Yes, Sir!" Damned right he did.

"Good," said Payne. "We got a location starting up down at Three Sands and we can use us a midnight tour driller. You interested?"

Frank held the receiver out and put his hand over the mouthpiece. "He's offering me work." Henry nodded and smiled. Frank uncovered the mouthpiece. "Damn' right!" he said.

"Okay," said Payne. "Here's who you see. You got a pencil?"

"Just a minute," said Frank. He got a pencil and pad from Henry. "Ready." He carefully copied down what Payne gave him: the name of the toolpusher at Three Sands and some directions on how to find him. "Got it," he said.

"Good. He'll be expecting to hear from you," said Payne. "Oh, one more thing: I understand you left your car at the rig."

"Yeah," said Frank. "It's pretty shot up."

"What you want we should do with it?"

Frank grimaced. He'd loved that damned car, but he sure the hell didn't want to see it again—not with the bullet holes. "Junk it," he said. "Fix it up. I don't want it."

"All right," said Payne. "They'll be expecting you at Three Sands. Get there tomorrow, okay? Or the next day at the latest?"

"I will," said Frank, realizing that he'd have to ask Dad to take him. He didn't have any doubt that his father would do it, though. "And thank you. I really appreciate it, Mr. Payne."

Laughter came over the phone. "Call me Billy," said Payne. "Everybody does. I imagine that we'll be meeting soon, Gage." And he hung up.

"I have a job," said Frank, putting the receiver back on the hook. He was surprised; no, he was amazed. And Payne had said that they didn't want to lose him, that he was a good hand. Frank had to grin.

That night Frank slept on a pallet that Lizzie made for him on the living room floor. He slept well, although it took him a little time to drop off. His negative thoughts about his father's new wife were completely overwhelmed by the fact that he had a job—that he was *wanted*. Things were looking up. He'd go to work on that rig down at Three Sands and put some money aside for a new car—maybe a Buick this time. He had a smile on his face when he slipped away.

He went around the lease with Henry the next morning. Everything was running like it was supposed to, so it didn't take all that long. Henry showed him every well and Frank could tell that his father was genuinely happy and almost proud of those wells—as if they were his own. Life was good, he thought. Damn!

It wasn't all that far to Three Sands, on the border of Kay County and Noble County, but the roads from Ponca on weren't all that good, so Henry was a little tired when he got back to the Braman field. He had to replace a belt in the pumphouse, and he thought he'd better check all the wells again before he actually went back to the house. It had been a long day, but a good one. And Lizzie would have supper ready for him when he got home. She might have to heat it up; he hoped that wouldn't make her mad at him. No, she wouldn't be. That made him smile.

"Frank's not happy that I'm here," said Lizzie that night in bed.

"What?" said Henry, turning to her and sitting up. "What makes you think that?"

"He knew me, Honey—from before. From Barney's."

"Huh? So? I don't understand."

Lizzie slid over to him and put her head on his chest. "He don't think I'm good enough for you, Henry."

"What?" Henry laughed. "That's plum' foolish, Lizzie!" He bent a little and kissed the top of her head. "And it don't make any difference what Frank thinks, nohow."

Then a thought hit him and he put his hands on her shoulders and turned her around to face him. "Did he say something to you? He better not have!"

"No, he didn't," she said, "but I can tell."

She had tears in her eyes, and Henry pulled her to him. "It don't matter what Frank thinks—or what anybody thinks, Lizzie. It don't matter at all."

"It matters, Henry," she said. "It matters."

"Naw," he said. "The only thing that matters is right here beside me in this old bed." He bent to kiss the top of her head again, then lifted her chin to kiss her forehead. She was warm in his arms.

"Thank you, Henry," she said, her voice soft. "I love you, you know."

"I know," said Henry. And he sat up suddenly, throwing Lizzie off balance. She kept her head from hitting the headboard, but just barely. The he turned to her, apparently unaware that he'd thrown her. "We're not married," he said. "But we could be!"

Lizzie didn't speak.

Henry took her hands in his and looked her in the eyes. "Shall we?" he asked. "Shall we get married?"

Lizzie moved into his arms and put her mouth to his ear. She kissed the ear, then whispered, "We are married, Henry. Maybe not in the eyes of the law, but in our own eyes. It's good enough for me." Then she kissed his mouth.

Henry and Lizzie were married, at last, although thirty-five years passed before their little ceremony before a justice of the peace. Their only witness was his daughter Callie, who was herself thrice married and thrice divorced.

PART FOUR

YOUNGER BROTHER

CHAPTER 23

Brothers
Three Sands, Oklahoma, 1925

Frank was having breakfast—such as it was—at a dump called Sal's Eats in Three Sands, when his brother tapped him on the shoulder.

He hadn't seen Walter for a while, and it was a surprise. A pleasant one. The funny older brother—well, maybe not so funny now that he was some kind of law enforcement type. Anyway, Frank was glad to see him, so he scooped him off his feet and gave him a bear hug.

"God damn it! Walter!" He shook his brother a little.

"You might consider putting me down," Walter said. Then he said something about what he'd do if Frank kissed him. So Frank kissed him. On the mouth. Loudly. The he put him down, pulled his hat off, and messed up his hair.

"Jesus, Walter," he said. "You're gettin' kinda thin up on top!"

"You know," said Walter, "a minute ago I was darned glad to see you. Right now, though—well, not so much!" But then he returned the hug.

"Now," said Walter, "eat your breakfast and we'll talk."

"Jesus, I don't know if I can, after seeing that shine off your head!"

Frank sat, though, and scooped a big forkful of pancake into his mouth. But some of the damned syrup ran down from one side of his mouth onto his chin. Walter grabbed a napkin and wiped it off.

"There. That's better."

"Thank you, Daddy," said Frank. He grabbed a menu from between the sugar jar and the triangular glass pie rack, now holding cinnamon rolls. "Order something. I hate eatin' alone."

"Sure you do," said Walter, taking the menu. "Just absolutely hate it."

Frank called the waiter over and Walter ordered some coffee and some whole wheat toast.

"Sal might have some lettuce or somethin' in the back," Frank said. "Let me holler and find out."

"Ah, Frank, the toast'll be enough."

"No trouble," said Frank. And he shouted. "Hey, Sal, you fat bastard! You got any rabbit food back there in that filthy kitchen?"

Walter objected. "Damn, Frank!" he said, leaning as close to his brother as he could without falling off the stool. "That's no way to talk to a woman! What's got into you, anyway?"

"Huh? Sal ain't no woman. He's some kinda Eye-talian fella."

Sal didn't come out of the kitchen. Instead he just yelled back.

"I recognize that voice!" he shouted. "That's that skinny half-wit Gage! Ever'body out there just kinda pretend he ain't there! That's what I do!"

Frank grinned at Walter. "We're buddies. Kinda."

"Yeah, I see you are," said Walter.

Frank ate more pancake and then took a mouthful of sausage. "What are you doin' here, anyway, Brother?" he asked. "How'd you even find me, anyhow?"

"The lady at your rooming house told me you'd probably be here."

"I'll be damned," said Frank, and took another mouthful of pancake. Damn syrup dribbled down his arm. "How'd you find out where I live?"

"I'm a detective, Frank."

"Huh?"

"Okay. Dad told me."

Frank stuffed the pancake into his mouth, chewed and swallowed. "You ain't goin' to arrest me, are you, Mr. B.I. man?"

"O.B.I." said Walter. "Oklahoma Bureau of Criminal Identification and Investigation."

"Yeah, whatever," said Frank. "So, you gonna arrest me or not?"

"Dunno. Should I?"

"Prob'ly." Frank speared another chunk of pancake. "Rather you didn't, though."

"Okay," said Walter. "I won't."

Frank turned to him then, putting the laden fork back on his plate. The grin was gone. "Dad's proud of you, Walter. Damned proud. And, you know, so am I." He reached back for the fork. "Truth is, though, I'm a little scared of you, too!"

Walter laughed. "Sure you are!"

"So, you come for a visit, or passing through, or what?"

"Actually, Frank, I'd like to ask you a favor."

"Speak, Little Brother."

"Little brother? I'm a year older than you are, Frank!"

"Yeah, but you're five inches shorter, too." Frank waved a hand as if he were wiping the remark away. "Go on," he said. "Tell me what you need."

"Okay," said Walter. "You go ahead and finish eating, and I'll babble. Okay?"

Frank had already turned back to the pancakes and sausage, but he nodded.

Walter blew out a mouthful of air. "I own this farm, see? Wait. This is—what d'you call it—*hypothetical.*"

Frank looked at him over a forkful of sausage.

"I mean—I don't really own a farm," said Walter. "Oh, hell. I'll start over!"

Frank chewed and swallowed.

Walter blew out more air. "This is a pretend farm, all right? And I own it. I lease the mineral rights to somebody, and a company comes in and drills a well."

"Okay," said Frank through a mouthful of pancake. "You struck oil."

"Yeah," said Walter. "And now I get a royalty check. Now, here's my question."

Frank paused in his eating and turned to Walter. "Where is this farm?" he asked.

"Huh? It doesn't matter where the farm is!"

"Sure it does! If your farm's down around Seminole, you're getting about a dollar or so less a barrel for your oil."

Walter sighed. "It's a pretend well, Frank."

Frank shrugged. "It's your well. Put it wherever you want to. I don't care."

"Okay," said Walter. "As I was saying, I get a royalty check. Now here's my question. Suppose someone is stealing oil from my land—how would they do it?"

"How much oil?"

"Does that make a difference?"

"Yep. If they're just stealing a couple of barrels at a time, they might just tap the Christmas tree."

"The Christmas tree?"

Frank shook his head. "Never mind that," he said. "Right from the well—you know, where the oil comes out of the ground and before it goes into the pipeline?"

"No, not a couple of barrels. Lots of oil. Thousands of barrels, say."

"Well," said Frank, "they could haul it off in a tank truck, I guess. Used to have to do that in some places, anyway."

"Then what would you do with it?"

Frank shrugged again. "Haul it to a refinery, I guess."

Walter leaned back on his stool and slapped his hands together. Frank watched him and wondered what the heck was going on. His brother didn't come around asking questions as a rule—hell, never, as far as he could remember. So this must matter somehow. Stolen oil? Was this police thing Walter was a part of looking for oil thieves? Seemed unlikely given all the killings and robberies going on. "Oh, well," he thought. "I'll play along."

So he put down his fork and wiped his mouth with the napkin. "This is a pretend well, right? Right. So we have a pretend refinery."

"What do you mean?"

"Well, if we take our pretend oil to a real refinery, they're just going to look at us like we're out of our heads—and not because our oil is pretend oil!"

"Why's that?"

"Because, Little Brother—oh, excuse me! I mean 'Shorter Brother'—nobody, at least in this part of the country, hauls oil to the refinery in trucks anymore. It gets to the refinery through pipelines."

"Oh, yeah."

"And the refinery people would wonder just what you had in that truck. Might be oil. Might be the run-off from a pig farm."

"So the refinery wouldn't buy the oil?"

Frank rubbed his fork in the remaining syrup on his plate and licked it off.

"'Tain't likely, 'less of course they knew you and'd done business with you like that before. And they'd damned sure want to know where the oil come from!"

"Yeah," said Walter. "I think I see that. Now—could they haul the oil from my well to—say, a tank battery on a different lease and empty the truck into their own tanks?"

"Could, I guess," said Frank. "Hard to do, though. They'd have to run a hose clear to the top of the tank and pump the oil up through the hose—and not many tank trucks'd have pumps that can do that. Try to pump it into the tank from the bottom and all you'll get is a tankful of oil in your lap."

Walter took a long, deep breath.

"Thanks, Frank. You don't know how helpful that is."

Frank raised one eyebrow.

"Now," said Walter. "That was the question. Here's the favor. I need you to walk through—or ride through, if we can—some farmland to see if you can see where somebody's taking oil that doesn't belong to them."

Frank turned on his stool; this had his attention. "You're saying this is *official*, then? O.B.I. business?"

"Yep."

"God! I'm flattered and all, but if you really need somebody who knows the production end, Dad's the one in the family to do that. Hey, I'm a driller. I run a bit into a hole. Dad knows about the kind of shit you're talking about."

"I know," said Walter. "I asked him. He can't get away."

"Huh! And you think I can?"

Walter rested his elbows on the counter and folded his hands beneath his chin.

"Yeah," he said, with a little grin. "I checked at the office in Ponca to see where you were—and right now your site is taken up with the rigbuilders. That'll take another day, at least. So you *can* get away!"

"Shit!" said Frank. "Okay. Where we goin', Little Brother?"

Walter punched Frank lightly on the shoulder. "Frank, you can call me 'little brother' all you want to if you'll help me out on this!"

Frank shrugged. "You got a deal."

He turned back to the counter, reached into his billfold for a dollar bill, tossed it on the table, and called out. "Hey, Sal! I'm goin' to use your phone!"

Sal shouted back from somewhere in back, "Yeah, go ahead! Put your nickel in the jar!"

Frank stood and crossed behind the counter to the phone on the wall behind the cash register.

"Doin' it, Sal," hollered Frank. "Just so you know, I'm calling Switzerland! That okay?"

"Sure," came the voice from the back. "Just don't forget the nickel!"

Frank made his call.

"Guess you're right," he said after he hung up the receiver. "I don't have to be on the location until day after tomorrow." He looked at Walter, sitting there at the counter, looking innocent. "You know," he said, gripping Walter's shoulder enough to hurt a little, "it looks to me like somebody did some *official* persuading! Know anything about that, Little Brother?"

"Not a thing, Frank," said Walter.

"Okey-dokey," said Frank. "Lead on, Mr. O.B.I. Where you lead me, I shall follow."

CHAPTER 24

Drilling Operations
Northern Oklahoma, 1925

Later, back in Three Sands, back on the rig, Frank found himself thinking—over and over again—about his trip into Osage country with Walter.

Drilling was going well, and Frank's crew were, for the most part, old-timers who knew their jobs and did them without any prompting from Frank. Everything was working. Adding additional drill pipe went smoothly. The sands at the level the bit was cutting through weren't likely to clog the bit, but they flushed the hole with drilling mud periodically, anyway. At times there simply wasn't much—much to do with drilling, anyway—to do. The crew spent the downtime cleaning the doghouse, drinking coffee, threading drill pipe, whatever. Of course somebody had to keep watch over the steam boiler, but the man whose job that was was careful and dependable.

Frank had to watch the hole, the drilling procedure, of course. If the bit hung up down there, the turning pipe could tear itself away from the bit, resulting in a bit of fairly expensive "fishing" and a considerable loss of time. So Frank stayed near the rotary table, just in case.

But his mind wandered.

Mainly about that damned Crocker again. The pumper fella back on that lease up in Osage County, where Walter had taken him—Frank couldn't remember the fellow's name—had said something about four men in a car coming out to visit the lease. The sons-of-bitches were probably the same ones who'd shot up the rig and ruined his automobile. He wondered whether Connie's husband had been one of them. And guns. Frank hated those damned guns, too. Something needed to be done about those bastards.

And it looked like that maybe ol' brother Walt and those O.B.I. guys had their eyes on 'em, too. Something about killing a bunch of Osages for their oil money. Frank grinned. Ol' Walt'd catch the bastards and put 'em away.

And Walter—Frank had to smile. Sure, Walter had been the oldest; but even when they were kids, he'd been quiet—shy, even. He'd allowed Frank to take the lead on anything they'd done together; and quite often when he thought whatever Frank was intending to do was likely to get them in trouble, he'd quietly backed away and gone off somewhere to read a book.

But now Walter was investigating murders, wearing a suit, driving a state car, dealing with dangerous people like the ones Frank had run away from at Whizbang. Damn.

And ol' Walt had apparently figured out something on that lease. It was odd, Frank had seen. Pipelines running from one lease to another would've been strange in any case, but when the leases were being operated by two different production companies—now that was really strange. And probably illegal as hell.

He scraped the toe of one of his boots with the heel of the other one. Hell, he hoped he'd been a little help.

"Hey, Gage! You awake?" The voice interrupting Frank's reverie was that of Don Jameson, the toolpusher and Frank's immediate boss.

"Huh? Oh, yeah." Frank took a quick look at the rotary table, even though he'd been staring at it, anyway. Everything seemed normal. "Just thinkin'."

"Yeah, about what? About some old gal or what?"

"Nah," said Frank. "There a problem?"

"No," said Jameson. "I just came out to check around. Looks like everything's going smooth enough here. How deep are we now—close as you can tell?"

"About two thousand feet," said Frank. "Close to that, anyway."

"About what I figured," said Jameson. "Good enough. There'll be a geologist fella out tomorrow to look at whatever you bring up. You ain't had any flow of any kind, have you?"

"Nope."

"Didn't think so. We got a little show in the Hoover, but most of the locations around're going clear to the Wilcox. We got to check the Endicott, though, and you should be at that depth for the geologist fella, unless you have a hangup."

"We'll try to keep that from happenin'," said Frank, resolving to keep his mind on his job.

"Okay," said Jameson. "Carry on." He started off the drilling platform, but looked back at Frank. "I'm headed over to the Chaney lease," he said. "Let me know if you get a flow and tell the hands on the next tour that I'll be in to check on things later. Okay?"

"Got it," said Frank.

Jameson hadn't been gone five minutes before Frank felt his mind wandering again—the men with guns, his shot-to-shit car, the dead Osage Indians, Walter. And Connie. Was she all right? That bastard husband of hers had beat her up at least once; there was no telling what he might have done to her since.

"And, damn me to hell," thought Frank. "I run off like a damned yellow-bellied coward and just left her there!"

The well came in from the Endicott sands. It wasn't anything like a gusher, but the flow was constant even without "shooting" the well. But the bigwigs decided to shoot it, anyway; so, because it happened on Frank's tour, he watched the shooting crew lower the nitroglycerin "shell" into the hole. The nitro would blow the hell out of the rock formation down at the bottom of the hole, and that would let the oil flow more freely. Frank thought that in this case it was a waste of time and money. But it wasn't his money, so what the hell?

Cleaning up the site and moving the rig were, for the most part, somebody else's responsibility. So the next thing was—another location, more drilling, more of the same.

Ordinarily, Frank really liked his work; there was real satisfaction in watching the drill pipe and the bit going deeper and deeper into the earth— and a genuine feeling of accomplishment.

Right now, though, Frank wasn't really eager to start drilling in a new spot. What he wanted to do, he realized—with a little shiver at his idiocy—was to go back to Whizbang. Not to work there. That was over. But he wanted to check on Connie—hell, she'd probably turn him away, but that was all right. Even if her husband was a shithead, she was still married. But he'd run out on her, in a way. And maybe, just maybe, she needed help.

And even if she wasn't there anymore, he'd like to look around— maybe find the husband. Maybe even his brother—the man Walter thought was in on the Osage killings. He'd need a car. Yeah. He didn't have enough money to buy anything like what he'd like to have, but he could scrounge up enough to buy some old piece of junk that could get him to Whizbang.

And a gun? He shrugged. Maybe even that.

They could move to the new location without him, he decided. And if they wanted to find somebody to take his place and fire his ass, well, that was their right. He was going to Whizbang.

Frank found a car he could afford. It was a piece of junk, but it ran—at least enough to get him to Whizbang. After that, who knew? He left a message for the toolpusher, gathered a change of clothes and his razor and headed out.

He had a lot to think about during the drive. Connie. Would she be there? He realized that he didn't know if he even really wanted her to be there. Even if she was—and if she was glad to see him—he wasn't sure he wanted to get involved with her again. Not that he was afraid of her husband; he knew he could take care of that asshole if he needed to. He actually looked forward to that: any man who'd hit a woman like he'd hit Connie deserved to get his ass kicked.

The men with guns were a different story. The husband's brother was somehow involved in this thing that Walter was working on. Hell, Frank knew the man was dangerous; he'd seen that for himself. But it looked like he might be even worse than Frank had thought. Shooting at somebody who'd screwed your brother's wife was one thing; killing for money was something else.

Frank shrugged. They could only kill him once.

Maybe he should have bought a gun. He shrugged that off, too. He'd never really had anything to do with guns. Dad had never had guns around the house, not even to hunt with. Grandpa Cantrell hadn't ever had guns, either, at least to his knowledge.

The only gun he'd ever seen around home was one belonging to Uncle Mac—and he didn't even know what kind that was. He remembered—with a little bit of amusement at himself—trying to get Dad to let him get Mac's gun to shoot that damned dog that had bitten Callie. The memory of his baby sister's screaming and the ugly scar came back to him; he pushed it away.

He'd check the bar first—if it was still there. Who the hell knew whether it was still standing; it may have burned to the ground. The supply store where her husband worked might still be there; he'd look in there for Crocker. And he'd ask around. He damned well didn't have much faith in the law in Whizbang after watching that son-of-a-bitch with a badge stand around watching the fucking town burn, but he supposed he could be nice and polite and ask some questions.

Well, he'd just have to see what happened. Who the fuck knew?

CHAPTER 25

Unfinished Business
Whizbang, Oklahoma, 1925

Whizbang had changed even more than Frank had expected. He'd known there would be changes, of course: after all, at least a block of the town had burned. There would have been some re-building and probably some of the businesses would have moved. But he came into the town quicker than he'd thought, because the business section had been extended about half a mile.

The new buildings were still board-and-batten shacks, really, but they were all painted up and shiny new. There were new wells, too. Derricks all over the place. He hadn't been away from Whizbang all that long, so all this had had to have happened damned fast. Well, money to be made, he supposed.

He recognized a business name or two. The outfit that sold lumber and hardware had a much bigger place now, out on the north of town. There was what looked like a dance hall next to it, the parking lot almost empty at this time of day. A little beer joint on the opposite side of the road was doing quite a bit of business, though. Not surprising; the oil field hands worked three tours—twenty-four hours a day—so the evening tour folks had to do their drinking during the day. He was tempted—just for a minute or two—to stop. He could use a drink. But he had things to do.

Most of the burnt-out section had been re-built, too. The whorehouse was gone, but he suspected it had just been set up somewhere else. Probably, though, some of the girls had moved on.

The little bar he'd met Connie in was gone, too. In its place was some kind of general store. There were women's clothes showing through a big glass window in the front of the store. Frank wondered how long that window would last, considering all the fights that probably still broke out.

The supply store hadn't changed much. It had been most of a block away from the main fire, so it might have got singed a little.

Frank angled into a parking spot in front of the building. It still had an old hitching post in front of it. Frank tapped it with one hand as he walked by it. Wonder it was still standing, what with all the drunks. He'd have probably knocked it down himself at one time or another, if he'd had a reason to park in front of the store.

A man Frank didn't recognize was on a ladder behind the wooden counter. It looked like he was stacking work gloves on a shelf. He turned to look at Frank when the little bell hung from the door lintel tinkled.

"Yeah?" he said. "You need somethin'?"

Frank looked around the store, but nobody else was there, at least in the front part of the store. Maybe in the back where the heavier stuff was stored. "I'm looking for a fella named Crocker. He around?"

The man placed the rest of the gloves he was holding on the shelf. "Crocker?"

"Yeah. Crocker."

The man gestured to some boxes on the counter. "You mind handing me some of those gloves? I'm gettin' tired of runnin' up and down this ladder!"

Frank shrugged, reached into the box of gloves, took a handful, walked around the counter and handed them up.

"Crocker? He around?"

The fellow irritated Frank by just turning around and putting the gloves in place. Then he turned again and put his hand out for more gloves. Frank stepped back. "Never mind," he said. "I'll just look in the back."

He headed toward the door that led to the warehouse section, but the man stopped him before he reached it. "He don't work here no more," he said. "And you need to stay out of the back. Nobody there, anyhow. All out on a job."

Was the sucker lying? Frank turned to watch the man, who kept his eyes on Frank's for a minute then started down the ladder.

"I'll just have a look-see," said Frank and pushed the door open. As far as he could tell, the fellow was right. There wasn't much room for men, anyway. The room was full of equipment—squirrel-cage motors, bits, bailers, plug valves, packing heads, reels of cable. This outfit was obviously doing some good business.

The little man came right up to Frank. "I told you you needed to stay out of there! Who you think you are?" But when Frank turned around, his eyes got big and he backed away. "I told you Crocker don't work here anymore. Far as I know, he ain't even in town no more!"

"Know where he went? How 'bout his brother? He around?"

The man went back to the counter, picked up another handful of gloves, and started up the ladder.

"Don't know no brother. Bosses fired Crocker. Don't know why. But he's gone. Now s'pose you leave."

Frank was tempted to go shake the ladder a little, just for fun. But he just closed the door to the back and headed out of the store. He stopped at the entrance, though, and turned again. "Thanks for your help," he said, though he knew that the tone of his voice was absolutely empty of gratitude.

"Glad to be of service," said the man, without turning.

Outside, Frank looked up and down the road. He didn't really know who Crocker hung out with, but somebody would've known him. He shrugged. He'd try the bars; that was the best bet.

Turnover on the rigs was high. The work was just flat-out too hard, even too dangerous, for some of the young men who tried it. Some of the crews moved to new locations, new fields. The Whizbang field was still booming, but there were new outfits, new rigs, new crews. Frank had to hit three bars before he found anyone he even recognized.

In a little bar called Shorty's, the new-looking place that Frank had passed coming in to town, he found a couple of hands that he'd known—more or less. They didn't seem to recognize him, but both of them stood and shook his hand when he stuck it out.

"Hi," he said. "I'm lookin' for some folks and you fellas might be able to help me out."

"Well, we'll sure enough try," said the older of the two men, a stocky fellow with brown hair that needed cutting. "Have a sit-down and we'll see what all we can do."

"Thanks," said Frank, and pulled out one of the rickety wooden chairs.

"Want a beer?" asked the younger hand. "Somethin' stronger?"

Frank was tempted, but he knew what one drink often led to, and he had things to do. "I'll pass," he said.

"Suit yourself," said the young man. Frank thought of him as a kid; he looked about twenty or so, tops. Well, he'd gone to work a hell of a lot younger than that.

"I'm tryin' to find a couple of people," he said. "Main one is a fella named Crocker—used to work in the supply store downtown. But I hear he's gone. You men know anything diff'rent?"

"Ain't even heard of 'im," said the younger one, and his companion just shook his head.

"Figured as much," said Frank. Dead end. Crocker was gone, and that meant that Connie was gone, too—probably. But asking wasn't going to cost him anything.

"How 'bout his old lady? Connie Crocker? She still around? No? Pretty little thing, dark hair, dark eyes?"

They just shook their heads.

Frank leaned back and took a deep breath. This was just not working out. "Okay," he said. "One last question and I'll get out of your hair. You know a fella named Cleve Marshall? He's a derrickman, or was, anyway. Worked for Helmerich and Payne. Got shot up a while back. Know him?"

"Hey," said the older man. "Sure, I know ol' Cleve. He's drillin' now. Don't rightly know where, though. I ain't seen him for some days now. I s'pect he spends most of his time out at his rig since he ain't much of a drinker."

Frank perked up. Maybe this wasn't going to be a complete waste of time after all. He wasn't going to find Connie, it looked like, but it'd be good to see old Cleve at least. "Still with Helmerich and Payne, I imagine?"

The older man shrugged.

"How about a driller name of Moore?"

The two men looked at each other, then back at Frank.

"Guess not," said the older man.

"Any idea where Cleve's rig is right now?"

"Jesus," said the younger one. "There's fifty or sixty of 'em goin' all the time. It could be any of 'em."

"More like twenty, twenty-five," said his companion. "But the boy's right. It could be any of 'em. I 'magine you could find out where any of their rigs are operatin',' though, if he works for 'em."

"Yeah," said Frank, pushing his chair away from the table. "I'll keep lookin'. Thanks for your time."

Back outside, before he started his car, he got a thought. Hell, he hadn't talked to the guy behind the bar—probably the guy who owned the place! The fellow probably didn't know the names of too many of the hands that came in and went out, but he'd damned sure know Connie if she'd been there more than a couple of times.

This time he figured that he should buy something from the guy, so he ordered a glass of whiskey. When the man running the bar—he looked to be thirtyish, dark skin, bushy eyebrows, a little gut—brought him his drink, he asked the question. "You know a woman—might have come in here—named Connie Crocker?"

"Yep," said the man. "Shore do. She ain't around anymore, though. She and that worthless old man of hers took out of here right after the fire. Heard they went to Ponca, but I don't know for sure."

"No shit?"

The bartender laughed. "No shit."

"Huh," said Frank. "Say, you don't know where—no, I s'pose you couldn't...hell, if I wanted to find her in Ponca, you have any idea how? Where'd she be?"

"Nope." The man shrugged.

Frank looked around the room, looked at the glass of whiskey, looked back at the bartender—or owner, whoever he was. Connie'd bound to have some girl friends here—well, probably, anyway—but she'd never mentioned anybody, or at least Frank didn't remember if she had. So—there didn't seem to be anybody he could ask.

Well, okay, he thought, Ponca City was a lot bigger place than Whizbang, but it was on his way back to Three Sands, anyway. He stood and tossed a dollar onto the bar. "Thanks," he said, and headed for the door.

"Don't you want your drink?"

"You drink it," said Frank.

In the car, Frank considered asking around for Cleve. It'd be nice to talk with some of the old crew, if he could find them, but if Connie was in Ponca City and that no-account husband of hers was there—well, he supposed he'd just head down the road to Ponca.

"While I'm this close, though," he thought, "I'd better stop by Grandpa's in Shidler." After all, he hadn't seen his grandparents for a while now, and he had a little brother and two little sisters staying with them.

"Hell's bells," he said aloud as he drove, "I ain't seen Claude or Mattie or Callie for a long time." The thought made him smile. Heck, ol' Callie might not even remember him.

CHAPTER 26

The Stream is Quiet, but it Still Moves
Shidler and Kay County, Oklahoma, 1925

Frank was a little surprised to see how Shidler had grown. He should have expected it, of course. Find oil and new towns spring up and old ones grow. Hell, look at Whizbang. Not many years ago, it'd been a road going through pasture land. He suspected that Webb City had grown a lot, too, since he'd lived there with Dad.

The streets were how he remembered them, at least, so he expected that he could find Grandpa's house easy enough. "Need to watch my language," he thought. He knew that nobody would say anything to him if he cussed, but he knew, too, that they wouldn't like it. He'd never heard a single cuss word out of Grandpa Cantrell. "Dad blast and Tom Walker" was his idea of rough language.

They were good people, he thought, his grandparents. Even if they do go in for that spiritualism shit. Oh, well, that didn't hurt nobody. He tapped the steering wheel as he looked for his turn. He remembered Grandpa's coming into town, bringing them groceries in his old wagon when they'd been living in Ponca and things weren't going so good. He'd brought his wheat into town, too, to be milled; then he came bringing Mama a couple of big sacks of flour.

And Grandma had to be the gentlest soul he'd ever come across. Well, unless it was Mama.

The house was where he'd remembered it. That surprised him a little; he couldn't remember when he'd been here last. When he'd seen it last, though, it had been one of only three houses along the road. Now the houses were all jammed up against each other—mostly just shacks, but pretty new-looking. "Better than a lot of places I've lived in," he thought as he pulled up in front of the little house.

He didn't even have a chance to knock. He'd barely got both feet on the porch when Mattie pushed open the screen door and ran shrieking into his arms.

Frank picked her up and hugged her, then put her down and pushed her away. "Who're you?" he asked.

Her face clouded for a second, but then she caught on. She played the game. "I'm your sister," she said. "I'm sorry you don't remember me." Then she laughed and came into his arms again. This time Frank twirled her around and they laughed together.

Then Grandma was in the door, smiling. Frank put Mattie down and hugged his grandmother. The top of Grandma's head didn't even come up as high as his breastbone. He could remember seeing Grandpa standing with his arms held straight out to the sides with Grandma standing under an outreached arm as if she were standing under a tree limb. But she fit nicely into his hug.

"Oh, Frank," she said against his chest. "It's so good to see you!"

"You, too, Grandma. Grandpa here?"

Grandma Cantrell opened the screen door and motioned Frank to go into the house. "You come in the house right now, Frank Gage. Mattie, you run to the kitchen and see if there's some coffee left—or I could make you some tea, Frank!"

"I don't need nothin'," said Frank, "but thanks."

Mattie had already darted between them and was headed toward the back of the house. Well, if she came back with something, he'd drink it.

"After you," he said to Grandma.

"She's sure grown," he said as he came into what he knew Grandma called "the parlor." It might be a parlor, but it was pretty clear that it was also a bedroom. It'd have to be, with three kids living with them in the little house. The small bed, though, was covered with a pretty quilt— he suspected from Grandma's own hand—and some nice pillows. There were crocheted doilies on table tops and antimacassars on the backs of the three chairs. Frank suspected that Grandma could make a cave comfortable and attractive if she had to live in one.

Grandma reached up to pat him on the arm and headed for the kitchen. "Sit down, Frank," she said. "I'll just see what's keeping that girl!"

"Hey," said Frank, but she was already going. He looked around and wondered where he should sit, where he'd be least likely to leave some of his dirt behind. Before he could decide, though, a small blonde bundle of energy came swooping out of the back of the house and leaped at him.

His sisters were certainly good jumpers, Frank thought, as he hugged Callie. She was still yelling his name—over and over—while he kissed her cheek. When he bent to put her down, she leaned over to kiss *his* cheek with a very loud smack.

"I'm sorry, Baby," he said to her, kneeling so that his face was level—more or less—with hers. "I don't have a present for you this time. Next time—I promise! Okay?"

"I don't need any presents," said Callie. "You're my present!"

Mattie and Grandma came back from the kitchen with a cup of coffee, a sugar bowl, a cream pitcher, and some kind of sandwich on a plate. Frank wasn't hungry in the least—or thirsty, for that matter—but feeding people was important to Grandma and he knew she'd be hurt if he refused. So he took the coffee and put the plate down carefully on a table beside the biggest chair. He supposed that chair was Grandpa's.

"Thanks," he said. "Room looks beautiful, Grandma, as usual. And, Mattie, you're growin' up to be a beautiful woman!" She really was, Frank thought. Mama had been pretty and Aunt Claudie was, too. Ran in the family, he guessed.

He looked at Callie. No, she wasn't really pretty. The scar dominated her face. But it was a sweet face. She was looking at him expectantly.

"And you, little girl," he said, "are going to be the most gorgeous of all!"

"I'm not pretty," she said.

"You have a pretty soul," said Grandma, "and that's what matters."

Time to change the subject, thought Frank. "Where's Grandpa?" he asked. "He around? Claude?"

"Frank, Frank!" Callie was demanding his attention.

"What, Honey?"

"Can I sit on your lap?"

Frank patted his knee, but Grandma said, "No, Callie! You let your brother eat his sandwich."

"It's okay, Grandma," said Frank, but Grandma shook her head at Callie, who settled for snuggling up to one of Frank's legs.

"Your grandpa's out on a well," said Grandma, "and Claude went with him. Now you eat your sandwich and drink your coffee!"

Frank looked at the sandwich. Ham, it looked like, with a slice of tomato. He suspected that he'd find a bunch of tomato plants outside the back door if he looked. He took a bite. Good.

"How's Grandpa doin'?" he asked.

"Good," said Grandma. "No, I'll tell you the truth. Your grandfather's wanting to go back to the farm. His heart's not in this. The good Lord knows he's tried" She sighed. "His heart is back on that farm."

"I can see that," said Frank. "I'm glad you got out of Whizbang when you did, but Shidler ain't so bad." Grandma was looking around the room, perhaps seeing if a doily was out of place. "What about you? What do you want?"

Grandma smiled. "I want what your grandpa wants," she said, "and he doesn't like being a pumper. So we're goin' back. I s'pect soon as they find somebody to fill his job here." She plucked at the crocheted thing on the arm of her chair. "We keep going back again, Frank. He tried hauling.

That didn't work so good, and we went back to the farm. Now he's pumpin' and he's hatin' it. So here we go again!"

"Farm is good," said Frank. "I always liked it there."

Grandma smiled again. "Yes," she said. "A long way from town, but it's, well, cleaner. This's a dirty old place. Oil's good, I s'pose, but it's dirty!"

"You get used to that," said Frank.

"You, maybe," said Grandma. She fiddled with a doily, then smoothed it down. "There's something else, Frank. Your grandpa's mama and daddy. They're old, and they need somebody to watch over them. So they're comin' to live with us when we get back to Longwood."

Frank looked up at her with a bit of surprise. He'd never even met his great-grandparents; he'd not even heard much about them. Grandpa Cantrell had never said much at all about his family.

Frank had heard little hints from people—back when he was a kid—that there were people in Grandpa's family that were, well, a little questionable. A couple of his cousins had come to the farm years ago, Frank remembered. Big, tough-looking men. They looked like cowboys—hats, boots, even big guns in holsters strapped around their waists.

Grandma looked around the room again. "And the old place isn't hardly big enough for all of us."

"It's nice, though," said Frank. "Your house always looks good."

He thought Grandma was looking a little sad, now. She was fingering the doily again, crumpling it up in her hand.

"I don't want you to think less of your Grandpa and me, Frank," she said. "But we can't keep Claude and Mattie any more. There's not really much of a chance for them to go to a good school out there. And they're smart, Frank!" She smiled at him and lifted a finger to point at him. "All of Martha's babies are!"

Well, all but me, thought Frank.

"So," Grandma went on, "they're goin' to live with their daddy."

Frank felt his jaw drop. He'd seen Dad's house and he'd met Lizzie—his step-mother, he supposed—and he couldn't imagine prissy little Mattie living there. Claude, sure. Claude could make it anywhere. But Mattie? She'd hate it. But Grandma was right, too. They could go to a real school in Braman.

Grandma smoothed the doily then moved it a little. Then she smiled. "Your grandpa and Claude'll be back before too terribly long. You have to stay for supper, Frank! He's proud of you and he'll want to see you!"

Frank doubted that Grandpa would be very proud if he knew everything that Frank had done, but, well, he didn't need to know. He tapped the sandwich plate. "This'll do me for quite a while," he said. Then he took a bite. "I can't stay, Grandma. I have things I have to do. Really. I'll come back soon, though. I promise."

They really hadn't wanted to see him go, he thought. They'd all hugged him again and he thought that he'd seen tears in Grandma's eyes. Callie had cried openly. He would definitely have to remember to bring them all presents when he came back. Back to the farm, he supposed.

He tried to shake off the whole family thing. It mattered. It mattered a lot. But now he had to think about what he was going to do in Ponca City. Where was he going to find Connie—if he could find her at all?

The road to Ponca City took him through a lot of familiar territory. Webb City was just about a mile and a half up to the north. Webb City, where Frank and Tom had first gone to work—except for working with Dad—in the oil patch. Where Tom had met Ramona and married her. He hadn't seen ol' Tom for quite a while, either; he'd have to run down to Cushing sometime. Yeah.

The road came pretty close to the farm, but he wasn't tempted to make the necessary turn to get there. And Mervine—that was where he'd run over Walter's hand. Damn!

Then he saw something and had to stop. The Longwood cemetery, where Mama was.

There wasn't any Longwood. Frank supposed there had been once, otherwise there wouldn't be the name. But the graveyard was there, and a little church just across the road from it. He pulled to the side of the road. He hadn't visited her grave, he remembered, since the day they buried her. Time to say hello.

The cemetery had been mowed, but it was mostly weeds. His mother's grave was on the far east side. It was the only grave there. Dad had bought up several lots there, he remembered. Or Grandpa had. Probably Grandpa; he'd have had the money.

The gravestone was reddish-brown. Granite? Marble? Frank didn't know which was which. The only kind of rock he really knew anything about was the kind brought up in little chunks by the drill bit. There was a heart carved on the stone, her name—Martha Elaine Cantrell Gage—and the years that spanned her life. Too damned short. Too damned short. Just thirty-eight god-damned years.

"Well, Mama," he said. "Save me a space, okay?"

He spent most of the time on the rest of the way into Ponca City just remembering.

CHAPTER 27

A Flower in the Stream
Braman, Oklahoma, 1925

Mattie had mixed feelings about going to live with Dad. In one way, it was just a little exciting. She didn't think she'd ever been to Braman, but it had to be better than Shidler, with oil all over everything; and, when it wasn't oil, it was mud.

When it rained—and it rained a lot—the road in front of Grandpa's house was just awful. She didn't know what kind of dirt it was, but it got all slick and sticky when it got wet and water ran over it instead of sinking into it the way water was supposed to. So sometimes, after a rain, the water was a couple of inches deep and she couldn't even cross it without ruining her shoes.

Braman would have to be better. Of course she'd miss Grandma and Grandpa, and she hated to leave Callie behind; but it was still, well, an adventure, kind of. And she'd heard Grandma say that school would be better. And they had a high school in Braman! Claude had had to take eighth grade over because there wasn't any high school in Shidler. She'd heard people talking about how they needed one, but it hadn't happened. So now she and Claude could go to high school together! She was just a little proud that she'd caught up with Claude in school, even if it hadn't been because of anything she'd done.

When she got there, she was a little disappointed with Dad's house. It was nice enough, she supposed, but it didn't have the nice little touches that Grandma's had. The arms on Grandma's chairs might have been worn, but they'd been covered by the nice doilies Grandma had crocheted. The arms of Dad's chairs were just worn, period. She could fix that, though. She had her own crochet hooks and she'd make doilies!

Lizzie seemed nice. She wasn't pretty like Mama and she was, well, kind of fat, really. That was all right, though. Grandma was kind of fat, too. But Mattie wasn't ever going to let herself get fat. Never. Anyway, Lizzie seemed to welcome her and Claude and she had a room ready for them.

She was too old to be sharing a room with Claude, she thought, but it wasn't like he hadn't seen her without any clothes on. After all, they'd taken baths together a lot of times over the years. And she knew she could get Claude to leave the room when she needed to undress or change clothes. She could get Claude to do almost anything.

High school turned out to be fun and exciting. Her classes weren't too hard and the other students seemed to accept her right off. In fact, she was getting lots of attention from the boys. A couple of older boys had even asked her to go out on dates with them, but Dad had said no. That had been all right, because Mattie didn't think she had the kind of clothes that girls wore on dates.

She kept her clothes neat and clean and ironed, but they were mostly things Grandma had made for her and, as much as she loved Grandma, the woman didn't have much sense of style. Mattie did what she could with them—shortened some skirts and sewed on some pretty buttons. Lizzie didn't have a sewing machine. Dad should buy her a sewing machine.

Dad's house was in a kind of camp. The people who worked for the company all lived in houses that looked just alike and there was a big warehouse and a big yard with pipe on racks. The houses were close together and there were quite a few children.

It wasn't long before one of the women who lived close to Dad had asked Mattie to baby-sit with her two little ones while she and her husband went to a dance. Mattie would rather have gone to the dance herself—she and Claude danced together to Lizzie's record machine and she thought they were pretty good—but she was glad to get the money. If she could get more baby-sitting jobs, she could save money until she had enough to buy her a nice dress and some nice beads and maybe some earrings.

Mattie heard bad talk at school, but she didn't listen to it. It wasn't nice. Even some of the girls used bad words when they went to the outhouse behind the school, but Mattie didn't. Oh, she'd heard cussing. Dad didn't cuss, though, at least not often. If he hurt himself somehow he might—just a little.

She'd heard Frank say a lot of bad words, but then he was a boy—a man, now, she guessed—and it was different with boys. They did things like that, and it was okay. She wished they wouldn't, though. Someday she'd meet a boy that she loved and wanted to marry, but he wouldn't cuss. Not even when he hurt himself.

Dancing! Dad was calling square-dances again—and there was a dance at the camp once a week. They didn't always play square-dance music. Usually, now, Mattie had to stay with somebody's children during the dances, but once in a while she got to go.

145

Lizzie liked to dance, too—although Mattie didn't think she was very good—so Dad couldn't say much when Mattie and Claude went out on the floor and did one of the new dances. She could tell by the look on his face, though, that he didn't like it very much.

Sometimes boys asked her to dance, but she always said no. She and Claude danced really good together, she thought, and most of the boys at the dances stomped around like horses.

So life in the Braman oil camp wasn't so bad. Oh, the house wasn't as pretty as Grandma's, but Mattie tried to make sure that the room she shared with Claude was done nicely. She kept it clean and she'd found some nice pictures in some magazines and cut them out and tacked them to the walls. She could tell that Claude didn't like her pictures much, but he didn't say anything—at least not much.

School was good—mostly. The classes were interesting enough and she enjoyed the social life of the school. There was one big problem, though.

For the last couple of years the state had provided some of the school books, but the new governor, who was just plain mean according to Grandpa Cantrell, had been against spending the money and the state had stopped. And Dad hadn't been able to afford to buy all their books.

Since it was more important for boys to get an education than it was for girls, it had been Mattie that didn't get all her books. Some books she could share with Claude, but almost as soon as they'd enrolled, he'd been moved to a couple of more advanced classes and she couldn't use those books.

There were assignments every day in algebra and, since she didn't have a book, she had to borrow one from somebody in her class just so she could copy down the problems. Then she had to give the book back before she caught her ride back to the camp. So sometimes her homework didn't get done. English class was the same way, but without the problems. The English teacher gave them time in class to do their homework, and usually Mattie could look over Sally Bryson's shoulder and see the sentences they were supposed to correct or find the right verb tense for or whatever. Not always, though.

Tests. Usually she did all right—if passing was all right. But it was getting harder and harder and she'd gotten a C on a couple of tests.

She considered telling her teachers what her problem was; but it was embarrassing, so she didn't.

So instead, one day, instead of catching her ride home, she walked uptown to the bookstore. The nice man there let her buy her books on time. She had to go into the store once a week and pay him fifty cents. He'd smiled at her all the time she was there, and she smiled herself as she walked away, carrying the two books that she had to have, even if the trip to the bookstore meant that she'd missed her ride and would have to walk the three or four miles back out to the camp.

Lizzie didn't have a sewing machine, and sewing everything by hand took an awfully long time, and Mattie needed new clothes. It wasn't just that her clothes were old—and old-fashioned looking, too. She was growing, especially around her top, and that made some of her dresses really tight there. Lizzie had a lot of clothes, but they were way too big for Mattie.

She sat at the kitchen table where she was trying to figure out how to do the stupid algebra problems—why did she have to learn algebra, anyway?—and fretted about her clothes. She needed money to buy clothes, and she had to pay for her books, and she had to pay the boy she and Claude rode to school with. None of that amounted to much money, but her baby-sitting money wasn't enough to pay for those things and certainly not enough to buy even a single new dress.

She sighed a long sigh. If she didn't go to school, she knew she could get a lot of baby-sitting jobs—and some house-cleaning jobs. She could return the school books; maybe the nice man would even give her some of her money back. The books had been used, anyway.

Probably he wouldn't, though. But at least she wouldn't owe him anything more. And maybe she could make enough money to buy her some clothes she wasn't embarrassed to wear.

School was important, but maybe not that important. "I'm pretty," thought Mattie, and the thought embarrassed her as soon as she'd thought it. It wasn't nice to think you were prettier than anybody else. But the algebra problems were just meaningless blurs, and the face she looked at in the mirror in the morning was sharp and clean.

She closed the algebra book and sat looking at it for a long time.

CHAPTER 28

Another Flower in the Stream
The farm near Longwood, Oklahoma, 1925

Callie was happy, happy, happy to get back to Grandpa's farm. The big old elm tree to the south of the house was still there and now she didn't have to have Grandpa boost her up into the crotch where she liked to sit. She could climb into it herself. So she'd sit there with one of the nice books from Grandma's collection and read as long as she wanted to.

Baby was gone. Grandma told her that cats ran away all the time. But one of the barn cats had had kittens and Callie had found a little gray-colored cat with white paws and a pink nose. He'd nuzzled her finger when she poked it at him and she fell in love with him right then.

She could have named him Baby, but the real Baby was a girl kitty. So she named him Blue Boy, even if he wasn't really blue. The kitten sat with her in the tree, just like Baby had done, snuggled against her while she read. Sometimes she'd read aloud to him and he seemed to listen to her. Sometimes he just slept and she read silently to herself.

Great-Grandpa Cantrell was blind, so Grandpa had put posts in the ground and fastened rope to them and made a path for Great-Grandpa to follow to the outhouse when he needed to go. Sometimes he had trouble finding the first post, though, and Callie had helped him find it several times. He never said much. He just grunted, mostly. Callie thought that he looked sad. Great-Grandma was very sick and she stayed in her bed almost all the time. Getting old was bad, probably.

But Grandma and Grandpa were old, too, and they didn't seem sad. Grandma always smiled at her and hugged her. Grandpa called her "his little angel" and patted her on the head a lot. Grandpa worked hard every day and Callie could tell that he was tired when he came in for supper, but work was hard. Callie got tired herself sometimes, when she helped Grandma clean the house.

There weren't any of those séance things any more. Callie was grateful for that. They'd been scary. She'd heard Grandma say that Aunt Claudie was in California now, so she suspected that she was holding her spiritualist meetings out there. She didn't know what California was like, but it was a long way away and that was good. All that table-knocking and whispering voices and stuff couldn't be too far away for Callie.

She missed Mattie and Claude some. There wasn't anybody to play with here, but she had Blue Boy and her tree and her books. School was all right. Grandpa usually took her to school in the morning, but if he couldn't for some reason, it wasn't too far to walk. Grandma didn't like for her to walk to school, and she fussed over it. So Grandma had talked to one of the neighbors who had a girl going to the school and they gave her a ride home.

The school was just one big room and all the grades sat in rows in front of the teacher's desk. Miss Harmon, the teacher, gave each grade a little talk and an assignment and then went on to the next grade. She was nice, though, thought Callie. If you had a problem with what you were studying and raised a hand, Miss Harmon would stop what she was doing and come right to you. Callie tried not to bother her, though.

The school work was almost too easy, so Callie made sure she had one of her books to read when she'd finished her arithmetic problems or her reading assignment or whatever else. But she listened, too. The eighth grade sat right in front of her, and sometimes what they were studying was a lot more interesting than what her grade was studying.

The eighth grade boys were studying agriculture and they were going to take some sort of county test. Miss Harmon was trying to get them ready for it, but the boys seemed more interested in hitting each other and making each other laugh than in doing well on the test. But Callie found it all interesting, so she listened.

A week before the test, she managed to stay after school for a little bit and made herself walk up to Miss Harmon's desk. The teacher was looking at school work, but she looked up at Callie and smiled.

"What do you need, Callie?"

Callie shuffled her feet. "Miss Harmon, I...."

Miss Harmon raised her eyebrows. "What is it, Callie? You don't want to miss your ride!"

Callie took a deep breath and forced it out. "Can I take the agriculture test? I know I'm just in the third grade, but I'd like to try."

Miss Harmon chuckled a little, but then her expression turned serious and she seemed to be studying Callie. Then she smiled, tapped the edge of her desk with her wrists, and leaned back. "I don't see why not," she said.

A week later, when Miss Harmon passed out the county agriculture test, some of the boys looked puzzled when they saw the teacher walk around where they were sitting and put some papers on Callie's desk. But they had the test in front of them and went to work. So did Callie.

Callie finished her test, handed it in, and forgot about it. She had a lot to read when she finished her own school work, so that old agriculture test wasn't important, really.

On the Monday of the week after the test, Miss Harmon distributed the test scores to the eighth graders, told them that they had done well, and then went on with the lesson. Callie was reading about George Washington, so she didn't really pay attention.

At the end of the day, Miss Harmon asked her to stay after school for just a minute. Callie went up and stood by her desk, but Miss Harmon didn't say anything. She just walked to the door and stood there while the rest of the boys and girls left the classroom. Then she closed the door and came back to her desk, wearing a big smile.

"Sit down for a minute, Callie," she said. She saw Callie hesitate and she gestured to a front row desk. "You can sit in an eighth grade desk. It may be a little large, but you're a big girl for your age. I think it'll fit."

Callie sat, wondering, first of all, if she was going to miss her ride, and then what Miss Harmon was keeping her for. Sometimes the teacher made pupils who had been naughty stay after school, but she hadn't done anything wrong. At least she didn't think she had. And Miss Harmon was smiling.

Miss Harmon had some papers in her hands and she was looking down at them. Then she looked up at Callie, then back down at the papers. She sort of laughed, then, real lightly, as she put the papers aside.

"Young Miss Caledonia Gage," she said, "I think that you would like to know how you did on the county agriculture test. Am I right?"

Callie nodded. Sure, she'd like to know. She didn't want to miss her ride, though.

"Well," said Miss Harmon, "you did well." She took the top paper off the stack and held it up. "No," she said. "You didn't do just well. Callie, you had the highest score—not just in the school—but in the *whole county*."

"Really?"

"Really."

Missing her ride wasn't important any more. Callie beamed. She had beaten all those boys! She felt herself wriggling in her seat.

"Just one thing," said Miss Harmon. "This is going to have to be just between you and me."

Callie's head came up. What? What did that mean?

"You should be very proud of what you've done," said Miss Harmon, "but you have to remember—we have to remember—that this test was for eighth grade boys."

Callie nodded.

"And, Honey, their scores are really the only ones that count." Miss Harmon took her pencil from behind her ear and tapped the eraser on the desk. "The boys did their best—well, some of them did—and the scores go on their records. We don't want to embarrass them by telling them that they were beaten by a third grade girl."

Yes. Yes, we do, thought Callie.

She could tell that Miss Harmon read her expression accurately. The teacher's grin just got wider.

"They may even deserve to be embarrassed," she said. "But the fact is that some of them wouldn't like being beaten by a girl, especially one so much younger. And, Honey, they might take it out on you."

Miss Harmon looked serious and Callie realized that she was right. If she did what she really felt like doing—shouting "I beat you! I beat you!"—especially at old Arthur Jergens, some of the boys would really be mad. They might even hurt her and they'd certainly make up lies about her! She had to nod.

"So this'll have to be our little secret," said Miss Harmon. "But I want you to know that I'm very proud of you."

Callie looked down and bit her lip. Proud? Nobody could really be proud of her. She had known for a long time that she was ugly and that no one was ever going to marry a girl with an ugly old scar all over her face. But it was nice that Miss Harmon liked her. So she smiled up at her teacher.

"I have written a little note," Miss Harmon said, "to take home to your parents."

"Grandparents," said Callie.

"Yes," said Miss Harmon, and she sort of waved her hands in a dismissive way. "So they'll know, too, just how smart their daughter—their granddaughter—is, and they'll be proud, too!"

They would, thought Callie, especially Grandma. She could see how big Grandma's smile would be.

"Now," said Miss Harmon, "you'd better hurry and catch your ride. They're waiting for you. I told Sarah to ask them to wait."

Callie nodded and got up from the desk. "Could I," she started. "Could I have my test? I mean, if it doesn't count or anything, could I just have it to keep?"

"Of course," said Miss Harmon, picking the test paper up and holding it out. "To tell you the truth, I rather wanted to keep it myself, to remind myself of the very, very smart girl I had in my third grade class. But you deserve it, so here. Take it."

"Thank you," said Callie. At the door, she turned. What she really wanted to do was run back and hug Miss Harmon, but she didn't think that would be, somehow, *right*. "I mean," she said, "thank you for everything. Thank you so much!" Then, of all the stupid, stupid things, she was crying.

And then Miss Harmon was by her, pulling her into her arms, and stroking her hair while Callie wept.

CHAPTER 29

Female Connections
Ponca City, Oklahoma, 1925

Frank considered, as he came into Ponca City, that he really had no idea where to look for Connie. Bars, he supposed. But there had to be a lot of bars in Ponca.

Like all of the oil towns, the place had grown. Maybe even more than most of them. After all, this was the base for old Marland with all his money. Dad had worked at his refinery for a while; Frank couldn't imagine what working in a refinery would be like—nothing like the feeling of seeing that oil coming up out of the ground; he was certain of that much.

The building they'd lived in, back while Mama was still alive, was still there, but he'd have never recognized it if he hadn't remembered where it was. It was some kind of clothing store now, with glass windows in the front. The old wooden sidewalk was gone, too. Concrete. All that had been—what? Five years? Six? By the look of the street it might as well have been fifty. Hell, there'd even been some hitching posts for horses back then.

He decided that he'd just start looking for bars. He chuckled to himself at the sheer number of places selling liquor, right in the next block. Selling liquor was illegal all over the United States and Okla-by God-homa had prohibition written right in its fuckin' constitution. All these places selling just plain ol' beer? Yeah, right!

But he wasn't after hard liquor—not right now—so that didn't matter. He'd just drop into a couple places, have a look around, maybe ask some questions. Hell, he was probably wasting his time, but he wanted to find her. He laughed at himself; he wasn't even sure why he wanted to find her. He was sure that, whatever the reason, it was complicated. That damned husband of hers. Not only beating her up but probably involved in a bunch of killings, too.

He laughed out loud at himself as he pulled into a parking spot. "Here I am," he said, "a grown man just out lookin' for trouble!" Hell, he realized, he was at least as interested in finding her husband and maybe even the men who'd shot up his car as he was in finding Connie—not that he'd mind a little roll in the hay with her for old times' sake.

He began his little journey through the bars. Part of him expected to see Connie at a table, a glass in front of her, her purse on a chair beside her, and a welcoming smile on her face. He was pretty sure that wouldn't happen, though; for one thing, she damned well wouldn't be waiting for Frank Gage.

None of the places on the street were helpful. A couple of them were far too dirty and rough for Connie to hang out in. One of them looked like its customers were farmers, mostly, and old men. There were a couple of fellows in overalls at the bar—too clean to be oilfield workers, he thought, and not all fancied up like land men or company men.

He asked about Connie in a couple of places, but nobody seemed to know her or to have heard of her. The name Crocker got a response from one barkeep, but he claimed not to know any Connie Crocker. Frank didn't have any reason not to believe him.

It had gotten dark while he was going in and out of the places. The last place, just like all the others, had been a bust. He looked down the street toward the next block. If there was a bar down that way, it didn't have any kind of electric sign, at least that he could see—looked like all stores. He'd have to start looking on side streets or at the edge of town. Probably the places oil folks would hang out in would be out there, anyway. But now, he thought, he probably needed to start thinking about finding a place to spend the night.

Frank found a place—a row of dirty, run-down cabins on the southern edge of town, with a little beanery right next door. He ate, wanted a drink, decided that he didn't need one, and went to bed. He lay there for a while, wondering whether he should even bother looking for Connie any more and just what the hell he thought he was doing, anyway. But he shrugged it off. He'd started, so he'd finish. Old Walter'd told him he was working out of Ponca right now, so tomorrow he'd look him up. Shoulda done that in the first place, he thought.

In the morning, while he was eating some bacon and eggs with a couple of big pancakes, it struck him that he didn't have the slightest idea where Walter lived. He thought that he had Walter's Oklahoma City address somewhere, but that wouldn't do him much good here in Ponca.

The gal who'd waited on him was a cute little thing and she seemed to like him. At least she'd grinned a lot when he joked with her, and he'd caught her glancing over at him while she was waiting for some guy to make up his mind about what he was going to order. Have to come back by here later, he thought. But first things first.

The outfit Walter worked for—Oklahoma Bureau of something or other—had to have some kind of office here. They wouldn't have some kind of big electric sign up, though, so he wouldn't find them by driving up and down the street.

Aha, he thought. The cops would probably know!

He finished up his last pancake and held up his coffee cup and shook it a little. The cute little waitress came bouncing right over.

"More coffee?" she asked.

"Uh-huh," said Frank. "Couple of other things, too."

"Oh? Like what?" The grin was back. Really a pretty grin, thought Frank.

"First, the coffee," he said.

"Coming right up, Sir!" she said, taking the cup and bouncing off to the other end of the counter where the coffee machine was. Frank watched with considerable pleasure. Pretty grin. Pretty face. Nice, tight, twitchy little bottom! He would definitely have to come back by here.

When she came back with the coffee, she pushed the cup toward him and stood back, her hands on her hips, waiting. The grin was still there, but it was different now somehow.

She thinks I'm going to ask her out, thought Frank. Yeah, she probably gets that all the time, good-looking gal like that. Oh, well. He put his hands around the cup and took a breath. He was going to have to change the order of the things he was going to ask her. Okay.

"I was wonderin'," he said, "if you could tell me where I'd find the police station."

The girl dropped her hands and took a step back. "Why? There some kind of trouble?"

"Naw," he said. "Just lookin' for somebody. My brother, actually."

"And you think the police have him?"

Frank laughed and moved the cup in a little half-circle. "Nah. He's some kind of police himself. Just think they might know where I can find him."

The girl seemed relieved a little, Frank thought. At least the smile came back.

"Yes, I guess I could tell you," she said, and did.

Frank thanked her and took a sip of the coffee. Then, as she turned away, he asked the other thing. "Hey, could you tell me your name?"

She turned and smiled. "It's Roberta," she said, "but everybody calls me Bobbie."

The police station turned out to be easy to find. Bobbie's directions had been clear, and it took Frank only a few minutes to find the place.

The police station was a little more impressive than he'd expected. It looked pretty new, for one thing, and it was bigger, too. Well, he supposed, Ponca'd need a pretty good-sized jail with all the oil stuff going on. Frank had been in a couple of jails himself—just to sleep it off after he'd had a couple too many—but this place didn't look too bad. At any rate, it had to be a lot nicer than that rat hole in Shidler. He'd spent one night there a long time ago. Most of the time he'd spent brushing off spiders and sweating like a pig.

He chuckled at his thought. The Ponca City jail might be nice enough, but he damned well didn't plan on spending any time there. First time I ever went into a police station when I wasn't under escort, he thought, as he opened the door.

There was a young fellow behind a desk. He looked like he might be seventeen or eighteen, thought Frank. But he was wearing a uniform, so he was probably older.

"Wonder if you could help me with somethin'," he said.

"I'll try," said the young officer. "What you need?"

"I'm lookin' for Walter Gage. You know where I might find him? Hey, he's with the whatyoucall it? State police, kinda."

"O.B.I.?"

"Yeah, that's it. You know where I could find him?"

The young man's expression was decidedly neutral. "Why do you want to know?"

Frank thought about giving a smart-alecky answer, but thought better of it. "He's my brother," he said instead.

"Ah, okay. I don't know where he lives or anything," the young officer said, "but I can tell you how to get to the O.B.I.'s office. That do?"

Frank nodded. "That'll be good. Thank you much."

"It's not hard to find," said the man, "but there won't be a sign on the door or anything." Then he told Frank the street address. "It'll be on the second floor, the last door in the back. Want me to write this down?"

"I think I can remember it," said Frank. "Thanks again."

On the way out, he had a sudden thought and turned. "Say," he asked the helpful young man, "you know a gal named Connie Crocker?"

The officer's jaw dropped. "Yeah," he said. "Sure do. She's here."

"Here? You mean right now?"

"Yep. Women's cell in the far back."

"Jesus Christ!"

"You a friend or somethin'?"

"Somethin'," said Frank. "Look, can I see her?"

"Sorry," said the officer. "No one can see her. Fact is, ain't nobody allowed back in the jail section at all, 'cept for us and maybe a lawyer or two."

Frank could see that there was no use arguing, so he thanked the man again and left.

He sat in his car for a little while, just thinking. Connie in jail? Her old man, certainly. Bastard belonged in jail. But what the hell had Connie done to get herself pinched? He dropped his hands between his legs and leaned back in the seat, knocking his hat off in the process.

"Fuckin' wasted trip," he muttered while he was fishing in the back for his hat. He finally dug it up and adjusted it—more or less—on his head.

"Well, shit," he said. "Might as well go see old Walter, anyway, long as I'm here."

It took him quite a while to get any information from the guys in the place where Walter was supposed to work. For one thing, it was clear that they thought he was some kind of intruder. He'd had to knock at the door a couple of times, and then the guy who answered it—a burly sort of fellow—put his arm out to keep Frank from going in.

"We're kinda busy here," said the man. "You probably got the wrong place. Okay?" And he started to close the door.

"Hey, wait up!" said Frank and pushed against the door. "This's the state police place, right?"

The man scowled at him. "What if it is? I told you: we're busy here."

A voice came from somewhere in the back. "What is it, Gravel?"

"Just some guy."

"Find out what he wants," said the voice. "Maybe he's got something for us."

The burly guy let go of the door, but he didn't step aside. "Okay, fella," he said. "What'd you want?"

"Hey," said Frank. "I'm just lookin' for my brother."

"Brother? And just who might that be?"

"Walter Gage."

The man's eyes grew even more suspicious. "You're shittin' me," he said.

Ridiculous, thought Frank. "No, I ain't shittin' you! I'm lookin' for my god-damned brother and I was told he'd be here!" He pushed on the door and shouted into the room. "Hey, Walter! You in there?"

The man pulled the door all the way open and took a step forward. He put a hand on his belt, pushing his jacket aside just enough that Frank could see a gun. His first reaction—one he was extremely glad later that he hadn't acted on—was to grab the fellow's arm and yank him out of the room.

"Look," he said. "I'm gonna ask you real polite again. My brother here or not?"

Then another man came up behind the first one and the whole thing started over. It took quite a while for Frank to convince them that Walter really was his brother. They'd asked for identification, but Frank really didn't have anything with his name on it. Then they asked him a bunch of questions—who he was, what he wanted with Walter, stuff he couldn't even remember later.

Finally the second man shrugged. "We've got things to do, Jim," he said, patting the other fellow's shoulder. "Let's go back to work."

"Fine with me."

But they did finally give Frank an address, a place on South Fourth Street, and the information that Walter wasn't in the office. They didn't tell him why, though.

The place turned out to be just another set of cabins, a little nicer than where Frank had spent the night, but certainly not very damned fancy. Damned state ought to provide their people decent places to stay!

Then he got met by another hostile face when he knocked on the door.

This time, though, it was a nice-looking, dark-haired woman—a little on the hefty side, maybe, but still okay. The look on her face wasn't okay, though. Maybe he'd knocked on the wrong door. The gal was dressed, though, so it didn't look like he'd interrupted somebody's sneaky fun.

"What do you want?"

"Look," said Frank. "I'm sorry. I might've knocked on the wrong door. I'm looking for my brother."

The woman came damned near sneering. "And what's your brother's name?"

"Walter Gage, Ma'am," said Frank, wondering which door he'd need to knock on next.

But there came from inside the room a very familiar voice. "Frank! Is that you?"

CHAPTER 30

Moving On
Ponca City, Oklahoma, 1925

The Crystal woman wasn't exactly what Frank would have chosen for himself—a bit on the wide side, but she seemed to care for Walter; she damned near hovered over him, asking if he needed anything, if his hand hurt, stuff like that. And Walter seemed to like her, too. So it looked like old Walt had finally got himself a gal.

"What the hell happened, Walter? You look like you been drug through a cow pasture!"

"Not exactly," said Walter. "Just doing my job."

"Yeah, right."

"O.B.I. business."

Walter was cradling his left hand and it was clearly hurting. Frank remembered running over that hand, years ago, with Dad's wagon, and here it looked like it'd got hurt again.

Walter seemed to want to talk, and he seemed happy to see Frank. His words were a little slurred, Frank thought, but he was making sense; and, even though he gritted his teeth from time to time, he seemed pleased to be telling Frank about what had happened: the arrests of a bunch of people who'd been killing Osage Indians for their money.

It might have been Walter's slurring of the words, but Frank had a bit of a hard time following it. But he got most of it.

His brother, the damned O.B.I. agent, had gone out and arrested a bunch of Indian murderers! Damn! Frank wanted to grab Walter's hand and shake it, but he held back.

He could see why Walter'd be damned pleased. He knew from his own experience that these were really bad people, and from what his brother had told him, even worse than just bad. Bunch of Osage Indians killed for their money. Bastards deserved anything they got, including that old electrical chair they had down at McAlester.

That the Crocker brothers were a part of it was a little surprising, but it really wasn't at all hard for Frank to see that Simon Crocker bastard as a killer. Jail was a good place for him and Frank hoped he'd die there. Well, what he really would have liked was to remind the rat what he'd done to Frank's car back at Whizbang while the jail cell was clanging shut.

The whole thing was spoiled just a little bit by the news that the other Crocker brother—Connie's old man—hadn't been found. Shit, he might have to look for the bastard himself.

The news about Connie herself—that she'd had some kind of fake marriage to an Osage man so she could get hold of his allotment money—was a little disappointing to Frank, but even while he was shaking his head he didn't have any trouble believing it.

Even if her husband—her real husband—had forced her to do it, he knew she wouldn't really care—if there was enough money involved. Maybe she'd thought if she had some money she could get away from the bastard. Now, though, she was sitting on her ass in the jail. Nothing he could do about that, though. At least she was safe there.

Walter's woman had just sat and listened, but now she rose from her chair and sat down on the bed beside Walter. She put a protective arm over his shoulder and leaned in to kiss him on the cheek. "He needs to rest," she told Frank. She smiled. "You can see that, can't you?"

Frank could, and said so. He stood, walked over to the bed, and stuck out his hand. "I'll take off," he said, "but before I go, I just have to say somethin'."

Walter took his hand and looked up at him.

"Yeah," said Frank, shaking his hand—gently. "Little brother, I am damn proud of you!"

Walter pulled his hand free and feinted a punch at Frank's chest. "I'm not your little brother!"

"Oh, yeah," said Frank. "I meant my shorter brother."

"Get out of here," ordered Walter with a grin.

Frank headed back to Three Sands. He needed to work, after all. But the trip into Ponca wasn't a long one, so he could drive in every day if he had to, to check on Walter. And maybe to drop in on the place that little Bobbie girl worked.

Frank was back at work on a new drill site. Three Sands wasn't all that far from Ponca City, though, so Frank managed to get back there quite often—almost every day, in fact. The little waitress—Roberta-you-can-call-me-Bobbie—was the attraction, of course.

Frank had been a little bit surprised that Bobbie wasn't willing to just crawl into bed with him, but he decided, after some initial disappointment, that he liked her better for it. He'd even taken her with him to old Walter's wedding in Oklahoma City, and it felt good to have her on his arm. Walter'd probably worried that he was going to bring some old whore. Those days were over, Frank thought. They weren't, of course.

CHAPTER 31

Light, Sweet Crude
Ponca City, Oklahoma, 1927

It hadn't been just that he wanted to get her into bed. Yeah, he wanted to do that, Frank knew. But it was more. It was that perky little smile, that bounce in her step, the way that her hair kept slipping down over her eyes, the cute little knees showing beneath her short little skirts. His mind had run back through the women he'd known, the women he'd been with. Belle, back in Webb City, Sally Whatever-her-name-was, even Connie. Not the whores. He shrugged them off. Bobbie was different.

He'd spent a lot of time driving back and forth from the Three Sands pool where his work was and Ponca City, where her work was. Not once had she ever suggested that he spend the night. He'd hinted some, but there was something—he didn't really know what to call it—that kept him from pushing too hard.

Then one day, after putting in a hard and fairly frustrating day on the rig—a bit had hung up in the hole and then they'd lost a damned fishing tool down there, too, a real mess—as he was driving in to Ponca, he began to wonder just what in the bloody hell he was doing.

He was dog-tired. He was driving to Ponca City to see Bobbie, when what he really needed to do was to have a couple of drinks and hit the sack. He thought for a second or two about turning back and doing just that.

Ah, but he wanted to see her, to see that big welcoming smile, and feel her arms around his neck. Despite how tired he was. Then a thought hit him. If they just—lived together. Lived together. He could come home from the rig, and no matter how hard the day had been, she'd be there. No driving clear across hell and gone. Go home and Bobbie would be there. Bobbie and home together, all wrapped up in one package.

It sounded good.

He didn't mention it that night. He even forgot about it for a while. They went to a moving picture show and he slept through part of it. She teased him about that and told him when they were saying goodbye at her door that she was worried about him, that she was afraid he'd go to sleep on the way home and wreck his car and hurt himself.

Frank managed to grin and suggest—as he often had before—that maybe he should just stay there with her. As usual, she seemed to take that as a joke at first, but after she'd kissed him goodnight, he could tell from the look on her face that she was really concerned for him. As he turned to leave, she put out a hand to touch him.

"Please be safe, Frank," she said. "I don't want anything to happen to you. Please?"

Frank's drive back to Three Sands and his little rented room might not have been all that safe, but it wasn't because he was sleepy. There were a lot of things to think about, and he thought about them.

He didn't go back into Ponca for a couple of days. He went back to his room. He slept. He thought. One evening he tried to call Dad, but there wasn't any answer. He thought about calling Walter and decided that he couldn't do that; he wasn't certain at all what Walter would think. He went into his usual drinking spot one night, but stopped before he even sat at the bar. He just turned around and went back out.

He had a day off then; on the drive to Ponca he used the time alternating between what he was planning to say and talking himself out of saying it.

But he did say it, and Bobbie threw herself into his arms. She was crying, of all things, but she was also saying, "Yes! Yes! Yes!"

Being married turned out not to mean any less driving. There were places to live in Three Sands, rows of board-and-batten shacks; but the town, such as it was, was noisy and vulgar and over-run with drunks and whores.

Bobbie would have been willing to go—she'd made it clear that wherever Frank wanted to live, that was where they'd live. But he didn't want to put Bobbie there. So they found a little apartment in Ponca City, and he drove back and forth to the rig.

To Frank's utter surprise, he found himself the happiest he could remember being.

PART FIVE

SHORTER BROTHER

CHAPTER 32

Sudden Rapids
Oklahoma City, Oklahoma, 1926

Walter had slept late the morning Taylor's body was discovered. The lateness hadn't been intentional; Crystal had just let him sleep. He'd probably needed the extra thirty minutes or so, he thought. He'd still be able to get to the office in time, and he had to admit that he'd come home tired.

"You're going to take me dancing!" Crystal had told him the night before, right after dinner. She had a suit laid out on the bed, all brushed and ready to go, and he could see a shiny black dress draped over the chair at her dressing table. Dancing?

He'd laughed at first. It wasn't like Crystal to play jokes on him, but this certainly had to be a joke! Dancing? Him? Hardly!

But she wasn't joking. Even when he protested that he'd heard some of the music people were dancing to now and that he knew damned well that he'd just embarrass the pants off her if he tried doing—whatever it was called—in public.

"It's the Charleston," she said, with a smile, "and you've never had any trouble with getting my pants off in the past, in any way you could!"

He'd gone dancing, naturally. Crystal had tried to get him onto a dance floor before, but he'd always managed to resist. This time, though, he found that he couldn't get away with it.

The only real dancing he'd ever done was square-dancing, and that had been a long time ago. Sometimes Dad had called the dances and he'd danced then, of course. But just with his brothers and sisters. And nobody laughed at kids dancing, at least not in a mean way. But maybe he could maneuver his way through a slow song or two. Maybe.

The evening had gone better than he'd thought. Yes, Crystal had dragged him onto the floor when the little band played something called "The Collegiate." He'd mostly just stood there, lifting one foot then another, more or less to the beat of the music, and watching Crystal.

The black dress was almost tiny—so tiny, in fact, that he might have been embarrassed if she hadn't looked so damned pretty. And she could definitely dance! He'd have to learn, he thought; he owed that to her.

So he tried. Fortunately, there were some slow things; the slow dances were the rest period. Then back on the floor to "Yes, Sir! That's My Baby!" or something else he'd never heard—or heard of—before.

It was worth the effort, definitely; the grin on Crystal's face was worth all the embarrassment and all the breathlessness. She'd leaned into him a couple of times—during fast dances rather than the waltzes—to kiss him on the mouth with a loud smack.

He hadn't been too tired when they got home sometime after midnight to take off the little black dress and toss it on the floor. Crystal had poked him in the stomach and got away from him long enough to hang the dress in the closet. Then she made him undress and put his suit away. But then she came into his arms.

"I love you, Walter," she'd said. "And thank you for a wonderful evening!"

So the dancing wasn't the only reason the extra thirty minutes of sleep had been welcome.

Crystal had given him a quick kiss and was out the door before Walter had finished tying his tie.

"I'm going to be late to work, Walter Gage! And it's your fault!" Then she patted him on the behind and left. Walter just stood for a moment, grinning at himself in the mirror.

He managed to get in to the office on time—or almost on time. As he'd climbed the stairs to the fourth floor, he reflected on his job. What was there to look forward to? Not much.

Since the Osage murders, things were getting a bit routine. Sure, one of the Crocker brothers—Jack—was still on the loose somewhere, but the chances of his even being in Oklahoma were slim. The sleazy Ponca City lawyer, Joshua Lennon was still out there, too, but he'd slipped through the investigation and the trial without getting a scratch on him. He had to feel relieved enough about that to be laying low.

Crime went on, of course. But getting his hand re-injured during the arrests out at that banker's ranch had caused Duncan, the agency's head, to keep him in the office. He was getting a bit bored. Oh, yes, he knew the work was important. Categorizing evidence, checking reports from the field for accuracy and clarity, even doing some investigating via telephone. But he wanted to get back to doing what he thought he should be doing: enforcing the law—in person.

His hand was better. The pain was mostly gone, but he had to admit that it was still weak—probably always would be.

He sighed as he opened the door with the gold lettering: Oklahoma Bureau of Criminal Identification and Investigation.

The office was quiet. Walter looked around. Taylor, the chief agent, wasn't around. Nor was Duncan. Jim Gravel was at his desk, on the telephone with someone. The new girl—not so new, now really—was typing away. The clicking of the typewriter keys was just about the only sound in the place.

Walter found his desk and looked at the folders on it with some distaste. But he took off his coat and hung it on the rack next to his desk, rolled up his sleeves, and settled in to do some work.

In a few minutes he heard Gravel hang up the telephone. "That's enough for a bit," thought Walter and pushed the paper he was looking at aside. It was nothing, really, just a report from one of the new agents on duty down south in Ardmore, reporting on an attempted bank robbery. The gist of the report was that he hadn't really learned any more than he'd started with. File and forget.

So he stood, stretched, and took the few steps it took to leave his desk and cross to Gravel's.

"Hey, Jim," he said. "Where is everybody?"

Gravel looked up with a grin. "We're it, looks like," he said. "You and me and Nancy and her typewriter."

"Huh," said Walter. "Where's Taylor? You know?" He didn't ask about Duncan for the reason that Duncan was often out of the office—at the governor's, possibly, but nobody ever asked.

Gravel shrugged. "No idea."

"You have anything new?" asked Walter.

"Nope," said Gravel. "Quiet day. Maybe all the bad guys are taking a vacation. Say, you look like shit, you know that?"

At that moment, the door to the front office swung open and Director Duncan burst into the office.

Agent Lucas Taylor was dead. Murdered.

Even though Lucas Taylor was an O.B.I. agent, the investigation into his murder was conducted by the Oklahoma City police. Duncan had tried to get the police department to share, but he had to settle for insisting that the agency be kept informed. Walter managed, after several tries, to contact Charles Clinton, his old partner when he'd been on the force; but Clinton didn't know anything or was under orders not to give out information.

So they had no choice but to wait.

There were, of course, other things to deal with.

The Ardmore bank attempt, although unsuccessful, led to a couple of suspects who, if they were indeed the same men, had had better luck with a bank in Maud. Agents had been dispatched to Maud and a second group to the little oil town of St. Louis, just a few miles away, where one of the men was supposed to be living.

A third group, led by Agent Dark, now apparently back in good graces after a questionable performance at the apprehension of the Osage killers, was in Cromwell, investigating the death of a U.S. marshal.

The office, then, was nearly empty. Duncan had kept Jim Gravel in the office, although some of the agents out in the field were relatively inexperienced. He'd wanted both Jim and Walter on hand, he said, in case anything broke on Taylor. There was enough for them to do, but Walter could tell that Gravel's attention—like his own—wasn't really on the paperwork. They were waiting.

It took only three days. Walter's telephone rang. As he picked it up, he could hear another ringing, probably in Duncan's office.

"Walter Gage," he said into the receiver.

The caller was Charles Clinton. "Thought I'd let you know," he said. "We've made an arrest in the Taylor case."

The Oklahoma City police had arrested Marilyn Taylor for the murder of her husband.

Before Walter could even thank Clinton for calling him, he heard a shout from Duncan's office.

"I have to go," he told Clinton. "But I really appreciate your letting me know."

Duncan had received a similar call. He stepped out of his office, yelled that Taylor's wife had been arrested, and burst out into the reception area, and, presumably, out of the office altogether.

Work stopped. Both Walter and Gravel got some coffee from the front office and took it back into the workroom.

"Think Miss Nancy's cryin' out there," said Gravel.

"Yeah."

"Well, she's got a right."

Walter drained his cup. "We all do," he said.

Gravel put his elbows on the table and rested his chin on his interlaced hands. "Hard to believe, ain't it?"

Walter toyed with his empty cup. He sighed. "Damn near impossible," he said. "Man's spent most of his whole damned life risking his neck—dealing with cold-blooded killers—then this!"

Gravel looked up. There was a grin on his face, but it was obviously forced. "Apparently married life ain't as safe as it's suppose' to be. You better watch out for that Crystal gal."

"I will," said Walter. "Damn. You know—as much time as I've spent with Taylor over the last couple of years—I didn't even know he was married!" The thought made Walter feel a bit ashamed. He should have known that.

"Met her once," said Gravel. "Didn't like her. Don't really know why. Just somethin' about her." He tipped up his coffee cup and drained it. "But kill him? Wow!"

"I owe him my life," said Walter. "And, hell, I owe you, too."

Gravel drew back in false terror. "Don't say that, Gage! That could mean that I'll be next!"

Walter had nothing to say to that.

Gravel leaned forward, lifting his shoulders and sighing. "Nah," he said. "I always do what ol' Bessie tells me to do. Obey, obey, obey, that's me! First time in my life I felt that was a good thing!"

CHAPTER 33

Toolpusher
Oklahoma City, Oklahoma, 1926

Lucas Taylor's death had an enormous impact, of course, on the agency itself and on all the members.

Walter hadn't even been aware that Taylor had had a *title*. He'd just been "in charge." It turned out that he was "Chief Inspector Taylor."

Other things—the routine work—went on, pretty much as usual, except that there was a certain quietness in the offices that hadn't been there before and the fact that Director Duncan busied himself on things that he hadn't before. People kept breaking the law, sometimes in reckless, dangerous, and even deadly ways. So the work went on.

Then, about a month after Taylor's death, Duncan called Walter into his office.

"Sit down," he said. "We need to talk." He gestured to the chair in front of his desk. His expression was serious. Walter's first thought was that he had done something wrong or that there was some sort of serious problem, but Duncan lounged back in his chair, picked up a pencil and twirled it between his fingers. It might be something else, then.

It was.

"Lucas—Inspector Taylor—ah, damn!" Duncan let out a big sigh. "Shit!" he said. "I didn't think this would be all that hard."

Walter just watched.

"Here it is," said Duncan. "Taylor's job—his *position*, if you will—has been open since he died." He put the pencil down and leaned forward, both elbows on his desk. "As you could probably tell, I've been sorta handling things that he would have ordinarily handled." He sighed again. He looked at Walter, then away, then back to his desk top.

Walter nodded. "I know," he said.

Duncan straightened in his chair and his face became his business face. "I have other duties, Gage. I have to meet with the governor. I get called to talk to legislators and their damned committees. I just can't do both things, so we need to fill Taylor's spot."

Of course, thought Walter. That just made sense.

"So," said Duncan, "the job's yours—if you'll take it."

"*What?*"

He had to be joking, Walter thought. Really bad joke, in really bad taste. Part of him wanted to get out of his chair and just walk out of the room.

"I'm serious," said Duncan. "I'm offering you the title, the raise in pay, but mostly a huge increase in headaches."

Walter felt his mouth fall open. It had to be a joke. It didn't sound like a joke.

"Wait a minute," he managed to say. "Why me? Look, I know I'm—well, probably just too damned young, too inexperienced! There have to be better people, more qualified people!"

Something occurred to him, and he sat up straight. "What about Jim? What about Gravel? He's experienced. He's good at this stuff. I won't know the things he knows when I've been at this for ten years!"

Duncan leaned forward and smiled. "You've got me there," he said. "I'll tell you the truth. I offered him the job and he turned it down."

"Jesus! Why?"

Duncan sat up and picked up the pencil again. "You'd have to ask him," he said. "But right now, we're talking about you. Yes, you're young. Yes, you're inexperienced in some ways. But I've watched you, both here and during the Osage investigation. I wouldn't offer you the job if I didn't think you could do it."

Walter wiped his sweaty hands on the knees of his trousers. This was darned near as scary as facing Simon Crocker's gun had been.

"A lot of what you'll be doing," Duncan continued, "is pretty much what you've done here for a while—evidence, reports, that kind of thing—but with some more responsibility. You'd make assignments—oh, you'll check with me, I suppose, but I think I'm showing you that I trust your judgment. And you'd handle all the field reports, examine them for clarity, that kind of thing. Mostly office stuff, but important office stuff."

"You really think I can handle this?"

"Damn it, Gage! Don't insult my intelligence! You think I'd offer you the damned job if I didn't think you could do it? Now tell me yes or no. If it's no, then get the hell out of my office and let me think!"

Walter bit his lip. Part of him wanted to get up and run. Part of him wanted to stand, straighten his shoulders, and reach out across the desk to shake the director's hand. Instead, he found himself nodding, once, twice, three times. Then he looked up.

"I'll try, Sir," he said.

Walter tried to concentrate during the next twenty minutes while Duncan elaborated on what his new duties would be, his compensation. Some of it registered; some of it didn't. His mind kept going to other things: what Crystal's reaction would be; how the men would take it;

whether he was up to the job. He sweated and tried to listen, to keep calm. But, he had to admit to himself, he was just a bit scared.

When he came out of Duncan's office, Gravel was waiting, a big grin on his face.

"Took it, huh?"

Walter had to force himself to look Gravel in the eye. "Yeah," he finally said, the words forced. "I had to, I guess. Some ugly son-of-a-bitch who should have taken the job turned it down."

Gravel laughed and whopped him on the shoulder. "Yep," he said. "that ugly son-of-a-bitch was too fuckin' smart to saddle himself with all that shit you're going to have to deal with!"

He stepped back and let his face return to something like neutral; then he smiled again. "So," he said, "how about we go down the street a bit and I'll buy you a drink. What say, *Boss?*"

Walter had to chuckle himself. "Uh," he said, "what about that little thing called prohibition?"

"Fuck it," said Gravel. "Let's go."

Walter went along, but he ordered a soft drink.

CHAPTER 34

Two Boats in the Water
Oklahoma City, 1926

Crystal was pleased, even excited. She jumped at him and threw her arms around him, almost causing him to lose his balance. If it hadn't been for the door frame, they'd probably have gone right through the door and down the three steps to the front lawn.

"This calls for something special for dinner," she said, after she'd let him go and he'd managed to take off his hat and jacket. She stood watching him. He just watched back, thinking how lucky he was to have her. Then she folded her arms.

"Any ideas, Mr. Chief Inspector? Want to take a lady out to dinner? Celebrate a little?"

They had dinner at one of the nicer restaurants, but Walter could scarcely remember what he'd ordered. He knew that he'd mostly just picked at his food while Crystal told him how proud she was of him and how she knew he'd do just an absolutely brilliant job. He told her something about his worries, his concerns, but he wasn't able to really tell her how genuinely frightened he was. He suspected that she sensed that, though. Several times during the dinner, during one of those moments when she wasn't talking, she'd reached across the table to squeeze his hand.

When they got home, Crystal started removing her clothes almost as soon as they were through the door. "I have never had sex with a chief inspector before," she said, "and I am looking forward to the experience. Now get those clothes off and get your rear end into our bed before I jump on you right here in the living room, with the blinds open!"

So, for a while, Walter forgot about responsibilities and worries and plans. When they'd finished—to both of their satisfaction—Crystal snuggled against him. "I love you," she said, "and I am so proud of you!"

Walter lay there, his arm around her shoulders, and smiled up at the ceiling and at the world.

Crystal had her own concerns, it turned out; and over the next few days, she shared them with Walter.

"My job," she said one morning. "I don't think I'll have it much longer."

Walter looked up from his scrambled eggs. "Oh?"

"Well, you know that Governor Trapp isn't eligible for re-election and whoever takes his place will probably want his own person."

Walter hadn't considered that, but he knew that it was true. "It doesn't matter," he told her. "I'm making more money now. We'll get by."

Crystal put her coffee cup down on the saucer with a clank. "That isn't it, Honey. It isn't the money. I like to work. I want to work. I need to work."

Walter took another bite of his eggs and pondered. He knew from working with her in the bureau office just how damned competent she was. The new governor—whoever he turned out to be—would be a damned fool not to keep her on.

"Well," she said, picking up her cup again. "It's too early to worry about that now. But I thought you ought to know. You're not the only Gage family member who's going to be making some changes."

Walter watched Crystal as she lifted her cup, stared into it, and then put it down with a smile. "All gone," she said.

Walter wanted to go around the table and take her in his arms. He'd had a thought. "Maybe it's time we started thinking about starting a family," he said.

To his enormous surprise, Crystal pushed the saucer away, tipping the empty cup onto the tablecloth. She rose abruptly from her chair and walked away. Walter heard the bathroom door slam.

Walter sat for a moment—just sat. Did the job in the governor's office mean that much to her, or was it something else? He tried to remember if he'd said anything—done anything—to upset her. He couldn't think of anything. But something was wrong.

He tapped on the bathroom door, very lightly, and called her name. There was no response, but he could hear her crying.

"Crystal? What is it, Sweetheart? What's the matter?"

The door between them muffled her words, already distorted by her sobs, but he made them out. "Go away, Walter," she said. "Just go away."

He tried again, and this time her response was strong and clear.

"God damn it! Just get the hell away from me!" Then her tone softened. "Please, Walter. I'm all right. Just go on to work. Please. Please."

Walter hesitated at the door for a long time. Twice he raised his hand to knock, then pulled it back. The sobs had ended, but he suspected that she was still crying. He walked around the living room, then the kitchen. He looked at his unfinished breakfast, but the thought of sitting down and eating it was repugnant. He dumped the eggs into the trashcan and rinsed his plate in the sink. He started to pick up Crystal's saucer and tipped-over cup and began to feel angry. He thought, for just a moment, about going back to the bathroom door, banging on it, and demanding that she come out.

But instead he put on his suit jacket and his hat, looked around for his gun, and then realized that it was at the office. At the front door he looked back down the hall, half expecting Crystal to come out to kiss him goodbye. He stood there, waiting, for a minute or so, then stepped out of the house and went to work.

When he got home—the day had been routine—Crystal met him at the door, put her arms around him and nestled her head against his chest.

"I'm so sorry, Honey," she said. Then she stepped away and gestured toward the little dining room. "Dinner's ready," she said. "It's a little early, I know, but I'm hungry and you're always hungry, you!" She poked him lightly in the stomach and walked away.

Walter just watched her for a moment, caught somewhere between wondering and admiring.

"Well, are you coming or not?" she asked.

"Yeah, yeah," said Walter, hanging his hat on the rack by the door.

Dinner was some kind of steak—well, beef of some kind, anyway. There were mushrooms over it, and some kind of sauce—maybe it was gravy; he didn't always know the difference. There were fresh-baked rolls and some kind of spinach casserole. Walter looked at the food and then at Crystal.

"This all looks really good," he said, "but how'd you find time to do all of this? I mean, this must have taken a couple of hours at least!"

"Sit down," said Crystal. "I didn't go in to work today. So I had lots of time to cook for the man I love."

"Uh, you—well, it looks delicious."

"I hope so. Now sit down, Dummy Dear, and eat Mama's cooking, or Mama will be very, very angry!"

Walter had to grin. It looked as if whatever had been so wrong this morning had somehow been straightened out. He wondered about her not going in to work, but he managed to put that aside and split his concentration between the food—which really was delicious—and the somehow glowing but also hesitant face of his wife.

Finally, after he'd mopped up the last of the gravy or sauce or whatever it was with a piece of bread, he sat back and patted his belly. "Jesus," he said. "I should be damned glad you have a job, woman! If you stayed at home and cooked like this all the time, I'd get to be too damned big to fit in one of these chairs!"

Crystal smiled. "I'm glad you liked it, Walter. I just think that you ought to know that there's dessert."

"Ye Gods!" exclaimed Walter. "You are kidding, woman! I couldn't eat another bite of anything if I had to!"

"Devil's food cake?"

Walter felt like dropping his head into his plate. Devil's food cake. He hadn't had devil's food cake for years—not since, well, his mother had died. He'd told Crystal how much he'd liked his mama's devil's food cake, and now she'd remembered and baked it for him. He looked up into her face, but there were no words.

Crystal moved her plate a little and stacked her silverware on top of it. She hadn't eaten much herself, Walter saw. "We'll wait for the dessert, then," she said, "if you want to."

Walter nodded. There was no sense in wasting the pleasure of eating that cake when he was stuffed already.

"But, before that, and before I scramble up from here and do the dishes—unless you plan on helping me, of course—there's something I need to tell you."

Crystal wept again when she told him. They'd left the remaining food and all the dishes on the table and sat together on the little sofa in the living room. Crystal had sat at the far end of the sofa, right up against the arm. She'd folded her hands together and rested them on her thighs. And told him that she couldn't have children, that she'd never have children, and if he wanted a family she'd understand if he wanted her to go and—"

He stopped her, astonished. As he moved toward her on the sofa, she moved, too. Then his arms were around her and she wept against his shoulder. Walter patted her shoulder and wondered what to say.

Crystal forced the issue. She sat up, leaned back, and looked Walter in the eye. "Do you want me to go, Walter?"

Of course he didn't. He pulled her to him again and held her. Saying anything seemed impossible. He rocked her a little, listening to her very quiet sobbing. Then he stroked her hair and finally got out the words that he needed to say.

"Please don't," he said. "I need you. I love you."

She looked up at him, her cheeks wet. "Are you sure, Walter? Do you mean it?"

He did, and said so. He wondered a bit about the children he'd never have, but they didn't seem at all important at the moment. He put his fingers under her chin and lifted her face to kiss.

"Ah, sweetheart," he said after a moment. "All I need is you—the way you are. I love you."

The expression on her face was both somehow happy and somehow expectant. So, for no reason that he could understand, Walter put a forefinger on the tip of her nose, pushed just a little, and said, "Besides that, where could I find a woman who could cook a meal like that and bake me a devil's food cake besides?"

The old Crystal—the one he was used to—was suddenly beside him on the sofa. She punched him in the stomach, stood up, put her hands on her hips, and said, "Just for that smart-alecky remark, Walter Gage, you get to do the dishes!"

CHAPTER 35

Re-opening the Hole
Oklahoma City, 1928

It had been a fairly long and decidedly grueling procedure, but at long last—after one hung jury and a second trial—Marilyn Taylor had been found not guilty in the death of her husband.

None of Taylor's co-workers had been called as witnesses in either trial, and the work of the agency—crime certainly hadn't stopped—prevented any of them from anything close to regular attendance at either.

Walter had managed to listen to some of the prosecution's case during the first trial, and the hung jury wasn't much of a surprise. The case was clearly weak—at least far weaker than the *Oklahoman* made it out to be—and a guilty verdict would have been questionable at best. In Walter's opinion.

No one from the Oklahoma City office was in the courtroom when the final verdict in the second trial was announced. Instead they learned the verdict from the governor himself.

Governor Tripp was gone; he hadn't been eligible under Oklahoma law to succeed himself. Walter understood that he was practicing law somewhere, but if he'd known where, he'd forgotten it. Perhaps almost as bad, Samuels was gone from the government as well, cutting the most useful connection to the governor's office.

The new governor was clearly a different animal. There had been some trepidation at election time that Tripp's successor would either try to shut down the agency or to cut some of its funding. Johnston might have had some sort of negative opinions about the need for the agency; but if he had, they hadn't heard of it. The legislature had very quickly provided their funding; there had been a few wildly praising orations, based almost totally on the Osage case.

As for everything else, the state was still in a mess. The legislature had supplied the bureau with money and given it the power to do its job, but sometimes the whole damned legislature seemed to be populated by jackasses.

Governor Tripp had gone into office the first time when his predecessor was impeached and tossed out on his ear. Now the legislature had been after Johnston for months now. Whether the man could stay in office very long was a question.

Walter had found the legislature's first and major complaint a little amusing. He had no idea whether the complaint was justified or not, of course, but he and Crystal had discussed it a number of times.

Crystal had been replaced, of course, as they knew she would be. The new governor would certainly choose his own office staff and anyone who'd worked for the previous tenant of the governor's chair would be out. Apparently, the legislature—at least a number of them—thought that Crystal's replacement was too powerful, that she was making decisions that the governor should be making.

"Oh, I had no idea being the governor's secretary could be so powerful," Crystal had said with a grin. "If I'd known that, I'd have had him get that school book money back into the state's budget!"

The withdrawal of state money to buy schoolbooks had been one of the major criticisms of the Tripp administration. Walter himself doubted the wisdom of that decision, and he'd listened to Grandpa Cantrell ranting about "that pawn of the big companies" a number of times.

On the other hand, Walter knew that his very job existed only because of Tripp. Since he considered the work the agency did and was doing to be important, he felt that he owed Tripp his loyalty.

He wasn't so sure about Johnston. The whole business about the all-powerful secretary had struck him as foolish. He knew that, if he were governor, he'd definitely be looking for advice. If the advice was good, it didn't matter whether it came from the clerk at the grocery store or the President of the United States. But when Johnston had called out the National Guard to prevent the legislature from going into session to impeach him, that struck Walter as a bit much. Quite a bit.

All of that had convinced Walter that he'd be a lot better off if he just didn't get involved. Even voting became questionable.

There had been some concern—unvoiced around Duncan, of course—that the head of the agency might be replaced. The job was a political appointment, after all, and the new governor had been very clear during his campaign and afterward that his opinion of Tripp was not very much short of contempt.

But Duncan was still around, and it was he that took the telephone call from the governor.

He immediately called a meeting of the agents who happened to be in the office at that moment, just Walter and one of the newer agents.

"The case is now in our hands," he told them after giving them the news of the acquittal. "If his old lady really didn't do it, we have to find out who did. Just between us, our new governor sounded fairly thoroughly pissed about the decision, but that's neither here nor there."

"I never thought that she'd done it," said Walter. "Hell, I don't know the lady and I don't have any idea whatsoever about what kind of relationship the Taylors had. I've always thought that this probably had something to do with the Osage murders. Some kind of revenge or just plain fear that Taylor would come up with something new, something we don't know about."

Duncan just nodded. Walter couldn't tell, really, whether he agreed or not.

"Anyhoo," said Duncan. "It's back on the case and it's our top priority at the moment. Has to be."

Walter nodded. "Okay," he said. "Who does what? Gravel's somewhere in Okfuskee County. Dark's still chasing himself down in Seminole. You want me to call either of them back?"

Duncan came as close to glaring as Walter had ever seen.

"You're in charge," he said. "Do what you need to do. Call back anyone you need to call back! Now, I'm going to get the hell out of here. There's some people on Capitol Hill I need to talk with." He pushed his chair back and rose. "You know what needs to be done," he said. "Do it."

Then he was gone.

Walter and the newer agent—Sparks was his name—sat at the table for a while, neither speaking. Finally Sparks asked, "What you want from me, Chief?"

"Nothing right now." Walter felt a little bit like pounding his head on the table. "I need to think," he said. "You go do what you were doing, or whatever you need to do." He didn't look up as Sparks left the room. He heard the man say something as he was leaving, but it didn't really register.

In a way, Walter was glad to have the chance to go after whoever had killed Taylor. The missing Crocker brother? Lennon, even. Someone connected to the whole Osage murder-for-money scheme whose name hadn't turned up the first time?

Oh, he knew that it might not be related to that at all. Taylor had almost certainly made a lot of enemies during his years of arresting people and hauling them in front of a judge. Maybe his wife really *had* killed him. If that was the case, they'd all be wasting their time; but even finding that out for certain would be worthwhile.

He knew that he'd need to go back over every single bit of evidence from the first investigation—re-read all the notes, Taylor's, Gravel's, his own. Duncan's, too, if he'd made any. And he definitely needed to get on the telephone to Jim Gravel and get him in here. Yeah, Gravel would need to go over all that material again, too. And he'd need a couple of other men, too. Maybe some fresh eyes would help.

He pushed back from the table and went out into the front office. There he asked the new girl to see if she could reach Jim Gravel. "I think he'll be in Weleetka," he told her. "If not, Okemah."

The girl looked up at him with a baffled expression.

"Yeah, I know," said Walter. "He could be at either place, but he left you the places he'd be staying, didn't he? Hotels? Cabins? If he didn't, just call around. It's important that we get hold of him." He went into his own office, then, and closed the door, probably leaving the poor girl mumbling under her breath about what an unfeeling bastard he was.

It wasn't at all difficult to come up with the names to start with.

The missing Crocker brother and, of course, Joshua Lennon. That didn't make things easy, though. Crocker had been charged in the original indictment and he was on the federal agency's wanted list as well as the state's. As far as Walter knew, though, nobody was actively searching for him. If the man was smart, he was probably out of the state, as far away as he could get.

Lennon was another story. There hadn't been enough to tie him directly to any of the Osage deaths, and what they had had on him hadn't apparently impressed the federal prosecutors enough to charge him with anything else. Okay. Lennon was the place to start. Walter got up, pulled open the top drawer of his filing cabinet, and began looking for the folder on Lennon.

He stopped for a moment and just rested his hands on the file drawer. He sighed. Lennon, having escaped getting sent to prison once, probably wouldn't risk his neck for revenge. He might be an unscrupulous bastard, but he was a smart unscrupulous bastard. Something else then?

If Taylor knew something that would have been dangerous to Lennon, Walter couldn't imagine what it would be. Taylor didn't usually keep secrets from the men; even if he just had a suspicion, he'd always shared it. At least as far as Walter knew. But they had to look at Lennon very closely indeed.

Walter dug out the files and tossed them on his desk. He'd have to go over everything in them, page by page, line by line. Then, even if that really didn't lead anywhere, somebody—probably Walter himself and Gravel—would have to go to Ponca City and confront the man.

If he was really innocent, he might have some ideas about who might have been angry enough or afraid enough to kill Taylor—or where to find Jack Crocker. If Lennon himself were involved, well, they'd have to talk to him about that possibility, too. From Walter's experience with the man, he couldn't really expect any cooperation. But then Simon Crocker was sitting in a cell down in McAlester, rather than acting like Lennon's gatekeeper. That might make a difference. Walter sat down and began going through the files.

It was almost five o'clock when Gravel called back. Walter had closed the file he was reading and was rubbing the back of his neck, trying to ease what was threatening to become a major headache.

The conversation was brief. Gravel started to report on what he was finding—or not finding, but Walter cut him off.

"Tell me later," he said. "Right now I need you to get back to Oklahoma City. We're going to find out who killed Taylor."

Walter would recall those words with chagrin quite a few times in the following months. The agency has started with the supposition that the death of the man who had been their immediate superior was connected to the case that had made his and the bureau's reputation. Revenge, quite possibly.

True, Marilyn Taylor might still have been the shooter. Even if they could prove that she had been, of course, she was a free woman and would continue to be.

Walter had tried to talk to the woman; perhaps she could shed some light on Taylor's life outside of the bureau—enemies, anything he might have told her, anything she might have witnessed.

She'd simply refused to see him at all. She'd hung up her telephone as soon as he'd identified himself, and she'd simply closed the door in his face when he went to their—her, now—house. Now, she was completely out of reach; she'd moved from the city, apparently back to Indiana where her relatives were.

There was a lot of talk in meetings about the second Crocker brother. Everyone familiar with the Osage investigation thought that Jack Crocker had been a very minor player, just someone who'd done what he was told. There had been no signs that he was a party to any decision-making. But he was still a fugitive. He had to be considered.

If Simon Crocker hadn't been in prison, he would have been the perfect suspect. But he was in McAlester, locked up.

Jim Gravel had gone south to the prison to talk to Simon Crocker and, probably more importantly, to find out who his visitors had been, if any. That had been a bust, too. Crocker wouldn't talk to him; he just sat at the table and stared at the wall until Gravel gave up.

Visitors had been, apparently, practically nonexistent. They'd known from the original investigation that the Crocker brothers' parents were both dead; the two brothers had both come to Oklahoma at least in part because their aunt was married to Willoughby, the banker who'd been involved with the Osage killings. No cousins, no other brothers or sisters, at least none that showed up in the investigation. Mrs. Willoughby herself had visited her husband and her nephew just once. Like Taylor's wife, she too had now moved out of the state.

Willoughby had refused to speak to Gravel at first, but then he'd changed his mind. All that Gravel got from him, though, was a fairly lengthy description of all the wrongs that had been done to him by "the damned socialists" who'd been out to get him just because he had some money and some prestige.

Lennon, of course, had to be considered. He had plenty of money to hire a gunman, quite probably from out-of-state. Some Chicago gangster? But motive? Why would he have Taylor killed? Doing that would just put him back in the attentive eyes of law enforcement. Unlikely, but it had to be looked into.

The man himself had been personally cleared early as far as the Taylor murder was concerned. He and his family were off somewhere in North Carolina at the time of the murder. That had been handy, of course.

Taylor had arrested other men, some of them dangerous, and some of them had been released from prison. Those who could be found didn't seem to have had the opportunity to be in Oklahoma City at the time of Taylor's death. Some were simply gone—out of Oklahoma or simply disappeared somewhere in the oil fields or boom towns or cotton farms. Dead end.

Walter had even made a couple of personal trips up to Pawhuska to talk to the people at the Osage agency and then back through Gray Horse to talk to Sam Persomoie, the young half-Osage whose cooperation had helped break the case. Those trips had stopped abruptly when Director Duncan saw the expense vouchers. Walter had to agree that the trips had been a waste of time and money.

The Indian agent and the Osage leaders Walter had talked to were sympathetic and perhaps even shocked over Taylor's death, but they were of no help, really. There had been no threats, no new tribal deaths, at least any suspicious deaths. Nothing.

He'd really driven down to Gray Horse for the sole purpose of seeing Sam Persomoie and to warn him that he might be in danger. The young Osage had testified at the trial, and he could possibly be a target. That is, if revenge was the motive.

The Crocker woman, the justice of the peace who had made out the fake marriage certificate that had given her access to Persomoie's money, and all of Willoughby's old ranch hands that they could find—the ranch itself was now owned by someone else—were interviewed. Nothing.

There hadn't even been any real rumors. Walter had had some of the newer and therefore supposedly unknown agents hang out in some of the speakeasies, mostly just listening. Nothing.

Nothing.

But there were other cases, and the agency had other work to do. So they did it, and gradually the Taylor case simply faded away—except in the minds of the original agents, of course.

CHAPTER 36

Old Acquaintances
Ponca City, Oklahoma, 1928

By 1928 a lot had changed in Frank's world. Being married to Bobbie had made him happier—or at least more content. He loved her, he knew, and she was a good wife. She was a little antsy, though; she got bored doing housework and cooking and sitting around. She'd talked several times about going back to work.

"I've worked around people since I was fifteen, Honey," she'd said. "I like people and I like keeping busy!"

"You don't need to work," Frank had said, every time.

Bobbie had pouted for a while, but she always came around. But the asking was coming more often now, and it was beginning to get downright aggravating. "No wife of mine is goin' to work outside the house!" he said, and he'd stormed out of the house. Durn woman had probably cried, but he'd made up his mind.

Frank had a lot of time to think on the drives back and forth from Three Sands. The field there was tapering off and some outfits had moved on, mostly farther south. He expected that there would come a time— probably not too far off—when his rig—and his job—would be moving, too. Where? No idea. Not Seminole, he hoped. From what he'd heard Seminole was more of a hell-hole than Whizbang had been. But he'd have to go where the work was.

Moving seemed to be what everybody was doing.

Dad had quit pumping and hauled Claude and Mattie back to somewhere in Missouri. He'd been going to try to farm, like Grandpa Cantrell. Well, that had worked out like a toad playing fiddle, and they were all back in Braman. Except now Callie was with them, too.

Grandpa and Grandma were back on the farm. Tom was still pumping down in the Cushing field, and ol' Walter was still in Oklahoma City, playing cop. Well, he was some kind of big shot now. That was good, Frank supposed, and he was proud of his brother, even if he did think that he was damned dumb to have risked his god-damned neck on that Osage thing. But that'd worked out. Good enough.

He hadn't thought about Connie Crocker—even in passing—for a long time. Then, one afternoon—he was on the evening tour—as he was driving down the street in downtown Ponca City, running out for bread that he'd forgotten to get earlier when Bobbie had sent him to the store, he saw what he thought was a familiar face behind the wheel of the black Packard automobile that had just gone past him, headed the other way.

Could it be?

By the time he'd reached the end of the block, he'd decided that he wanted to make sure. The bread wouldn't be running off anywhere, and it would just take a minute or so to find out. He made a quick—and probably illegal—U-turn and followed the Packard.

It pulled to the curb and a woman got out. Yes, it did look like Connie! Her back was toward him, but the shape was familiar and the hair. Frank hesitated a minute and pulled to the curb behind the Packard.

The woman didn't even glance his way. She closed the car door and went into a clothing store. As she turned halfway in the entrance to the store, for just a second she faced the street.

It was her. It was Connie.

Frank sat in his car and considered. He didn't have any interest in Connie Crocker any more—*that kind* of interest. But he was damned curious. He figured that Bobbie wouldn't understand why he was sitting here, but, hell, she didn't have to know and he damned sure wasn't going to let anything happen.

"I'll just wait here for a minute or two," he thought. "Hell, damned women take forever lookin' at clothes. She'll probably be in there a hour." He drummed on the steering wheel and sat there. Twice he decided to go, and twice he told himself just a couple of minutes more.

And then she came out of the store, carrying a dress of some kind on a hanger. She seemed to be having some trouble juggling the dress and the keys to the car, so Frank got out of his car and opened her door for her.

"Frank!"

Connie Crocker's arms dropped abruptly and the tail of the dress dragged across the dirty sidewalk. Frank reached out and took the hanger from her hand.

"Better let me take care of that," he said.

They stood there on the sidewalk for a while, just looking at each other. Frank was trying to figure out something to say, what to ask. It looked to him as if she was doing the same. There wasn't any of that damned electricity on her face and he was sure there wasn't on his. That was good.

Finally Frank found some words. "How you?" he managed to get out.

Connie just nodded, and reached for the dress. For some reason Frank pulled it away.

Connie's mouth tightened. "Give me the dress," she said.

"Oh," said Frank, looking at the dress as if he didn't remember that he was holding it. He sort of shook it, but didn't hand it to her.

Connie put her hands on her hips and just stared at him.

Frank managed a grin and opened the back door of the Packard and hung the dress inside. "There," he said. "That do you?"

"Yes," she said, her voice cool, even cold. "Thank you."

"Seriously, how you been, Connie? It's been a long time."

"Yes," she said. "It has."

Frank shuffled his feet. "Look," he said, "I'm not after nothin'. I mean, well, that was a long time ago, and, hell, I just want to know that you're okay—that things are all right with you."

For some reason that brought a smile to her face. "Why do you care, Frank Gage?" she said, but the words weren't hostile.

"Maybe we could go somewhere and have a drink—no, coffee'd be better—and you could bring me up to date."

Frank was a little surprised to see her smile. "I suppose coffee would be all right," she said. "There's a little place right down the street. Just let me lock the car."

The little café was nicer than what Frank was used to, and he realized that his clothes weren't really all that clean. Bobbie did a good job with his clothes, washing them out, starching the shirts, and ironing everything, but Frank didn't change clothes every day and you couldn't drill an oil well without getting something on your clothes—grease, if nothing else. The waitress looked at him as if she was having the same thought. He didn't think that Bobbie had ever looked at her customers that way.

They ordered coffee and the waitress seemed to sniff a little bit, so Frank ordered a piece of apple pie.

There didn't seem to be anything to say while they were waiting for the coffee. Frank looked around the place, not really noticing—just looking. Connie played with her napkin.

"You seem to be doing well," Frank finally managed.

Then the waitress was back with the coffee and the pie. "Want cream?" she asked. She gestured toward the sugar jar on the table. "Sugar's there."

Frank looked at Connie. He didn't think they'd ever shared coffee before; it'd always been whiskey. She shook her head, so Frank did, too.

"Enjoy your pie," said the waitress, and she flounced off. Bobbie could show this gal how to do her job right, Frank thought. He sipped the coffee, thinking that he always used cream.

"Like I said, you seem to be doing all right."

Connie had a little smile, but it didn't really look like a happy smile. "The Packard? That what you mean?"

It hadn't been, really, but Frank nodded. He had wondered about that. Packards were expensive automobiles.

There was a long pause while Connie took a drink of coffee, then unfolded her napkin and put in on her lap, then looked up at the ceiling. Frank waited.

Connie took a deep breath and sighed. "I'm living with someone, Frank. He takes good care of me. It's his car."

Living with somebody! That meant somebody other than that son-of-a-bitch she'd been married to. That was good. It might not please the church folk, but, hell's bells, it was one hell of a lot safer.

"I'm glad he takes care of you," Frank said. "Not married to the guy, though? I mean, hell, I don't give a shit if you're married or not. Ah, fuck, forget the question. I'm sorry."

Connie's laugh was the old laugh, the one he remembered.

"Oh, Frank," she said through her laughter. "You haven't changed a bit, have you? Still the same old Frank!"

He didn't correct her. As far as he could tell, he'd changed one hell of a lot. So he just lifted one shoulder and opened his eyes wide.

She grinned at him. "Well, to answer your question, no. For one thing, he hasn't asked. For another, I couldn't even if he did ask; I'm still legally married to Jack."

Frank smiled inside, but made an effort to keep the smile off his face. Being married hadn't ever stopped her before. She'd married that Indian guy—or at least there was some kind of legal document. Maybe she'd never fucked the guy. Who knew?

"Where is old Jack?"

Connie looked at him over her coffee cup. "Are you goin' to eat that pie?"

"Help yourself," said Frank and pushed the pie across the table to her.

She smiled her thanks and said, "Uh, Frank, if I'm going to eat your pie, I'm gonna need your fork!"

"Oh, yeah." He found the fork and handed it to her.

"Thank you," she said. "I don't know where Jack is, and I'll say the same thing to you that you said to me a minute ago: I don't give a shit."

Frank chuckled. "Yeah. Well, between you and me, I think that's a damned good thing. I hope the bastard is down at the bottom of some farmer's well."

Connie put the fork down and looked up. "You know I had to go to jail for a while, don't you, Frank?"

"Yeah. I heard."

"That wouldn't've ever happened if I hadn't been so damned stupid. Over and over stupid. Marrying him in the first place was stupid. Staying was stupid. Doing things—bad things, really—just because he told me to."

"You were scared," said Frank.

"Boy, are you ever right about that!" said Connie. "I spent my whole life being scared." But now her smile was big and clearly genuine. "But I'm not afraid anymore! Jack Crocker be damned! He can't touch me now!"

"You look happy," said Frank. And she did.

"I am, Frank. Probably for the first time in my whole rotten life!"

Frank felt himself wanting to get up from the table and take Connie in his arms and squeeze her hard. He knew that he couldn't do that, though. And he didn't *want* her—not in that way. But it was good, good, good to see her happy.

"Who's the guy?" he asked. "If you want to tell me, that is."

"I don't mind," said Connie. "He's a lawyer. His name is Josh. Joshua. Joshua Lennon."

PART SIX

BABY SISTER

CHAPTER 37

You're Not My Mama!
Braman, Oklahoma, 1928

Callie loved her Daddy, but she hadn't wanted to leave the farm. She loved Grandma and Grandpa, too, and she'd have to leave them behind. And her cat, Blue Boy. He'd have to stay on the farm, too. She wanted him to go with her, but Daddy had a big dog and so she'd been told that Blue Boy couldn't come. She'd miss her tree, too. And her school. Miss Harmon was really nice, and Callie supposed that she loved her teacher, too.

Grandma had packed up all of Callie's clothes, her little stuffed rabbit that she didn't play with any more but that she still loved, her school books, and the framed picture of her mama. Then Daddy came to get her and they went to Braman where Daddy lived.

Callie was happy to see Mattie and Claude and they both gave her big hugs. Daddy's new wife was named Lizzie, and Callie didn't quite know what to think about her. She wasn't pretty like Mama, but she told Callie that she was happy that she'd come to live with them.

The house they lived in was like the house Grandpa had lived in at Shidler, but it didn't have any paint. There wasn't any grass in the yard at all, and there were old pieces of machinery—oil stuff, she supposed, but didn't know what—all over the back yard and all along one side of the house. The inside of the house was clean enough, but keeping the house pretty clearly wasn't something that Lizzie considered important. Callie looked the place over and decided that she didn't like it.

Her bed was a sofa in the living room. She'd thought that she probably would be sleeping with Mattie, but Mattie's bed was a little thing with not enough room for two people, and it was in the same room with Claude's little bed. The sofa wasn't really uncomfortable, but sleeping wasn't always easy; Daddy and Lizzie came in and out of the room early in the morning and it always seemed to wake her up.

School was different, too. For one thing, it was bigger. At the Longwood school, everybody had been in the same big room; this school had several rooms and Callie's classroom had just two grades, the fifth grade and the sixth grade. That meant that the teacher spent more time with each grade. Callie thought that was good sometimes. Some of the people in her class seemed to need a lot of help, and some of them didn't have any of their books. Callie had hers from back at Longwood, so sometimes she let the girl who sat next to her borrow a book—as long as she gave it back before school was over for the day. Books were precious things, even when they were too easy and written for little kids.

School was sometimes kind of boring, so she spent a lot of time drawing pictures.

The school had the high school in it, too, so there were lots of big kids there. Including Claude. Her brother took her to school with him every morning and didn't seem to mind a bit.

Callie wondered why Mattie didn't go to school any more, but Mattie told her not to mind, that she was working, making money, babysitting for the women in the camp and cleaning houses.

Lizzie had made it clear, after a couple of days, that everybody in the house had chores to do and that Callie had to do chores, too. That made Callie a little bit mad, because she'd never had *chores* to do at Grandma's. Daddy worked hard all day, Mattie did the sweeping and dusting, and Claude brought in firewood and burned the trash. Lizzie did the cooking—lots of boiled potatoes and chick peas, which Callie definitely did not like—and did the washing with water from the rain barrel beside the house.

That left washing the dishes, and that was now Callie's job. After supper, the sink was full of dishes from breakfast, dinner, and then supper. Callie had to haul the heavy iron pot to the pump out in the yard— rainwater from the barrel had little mosquito babies in it, so they didn't drink it or wash dishes in it—fill the pot, then put it on the stove to get the water hot. The pot was heavy when it was full, and Callie sometimes spilled some of the water when she was trying to lift it onto the stove. That made Lizzie kind of mad.

Having to do the dishes made Callie a little bit mad, too. She knew that everybody had to do some work and she recognized that that was fair, but it didn't seem like it was fair. And she found out that she did not like for Lizzie to tell her what to do. Over and over.

One day, when Callie had not only spilled some water on the kitchen floor, but had also tripped on the wooden platform the pump sat on, dropped the pot in the dirt, and skinned her knee on the boards, she felt like she'd had enough and was naughty.

Lizzie saw the dirt on the pot and told her that she'd have to wash the pot before she put any dishes in it. That was when Callie was bad.

"You're not my mama!" she yelled, threw the pot down on the floor, and walked out of the kitchen.

Lizzie had followed her out of the kitchen, yelling at her, but Callie just kept going. Out the front door. She didn't know where to go from there, but she was not going to go back into the house. And if Lizzie came out and tried to drag her back or whip her, she was going to fight!

There wasn't really any place to go. Her tree was back on the farm. Grandma's arms were back there, too. And her kitty. She looked around. The front porch sat on concrete blocks, and Callie could see under it for a long way.

Daddy's dog, a Collie named General, slept under there a lot, but he wasn't there now. Probably he was with Daddy, wherever Daddy was. Would Daddy spank her when he got home? She knew that other boys and girls were spanked sometimes. Some of them she'd known had come to school with bruises, even.

But Daddy wouldn't spank her. He never had, and he'd never seen him spank any of her brothers or sisters, either. But he'd be mad.

Callie crawled under the porch and stayed there in the dust and the spiders' webs until her father got home.

"She shouldn't talk that way to me," Lizzie told Henry when he and Claude came home. She'd waited for them to stack the firewood they'd gone after and then for Claude to go into the house, probably to get his school books and put them on the kitchen table to study. Mattie was off somewhere, babysitting or something.

"I know I ain't her mama, but this is my house and I think that girl needs to do what I tell her. Doing the dishes isn't such a terrible thing to have to do, is it?"

No, it wasn't. Henry had to agree. "I'll talk to her," he said. "You know, it's got to be hard for her, being pulled away from Grandpa and Grandma Cantrell like that. I suppose you'd have to say they spoiled her some, but that's Parthie Cantrell for you."

Lizzie sniffed as if she could smell spoilage. Then Henry could see her shoulders slump.

"I know this ain't what she's used to, Henry. I know it's got to be hard for her. But I try to be a good mother to all of 'em, like I try to be a good wife to you."

"You are," he said, putting an arm around her and pulling her to him. "And I'll talk to her. This is your house and she has to learn to do what you tell her. She'll learn."

What Callie learned, though, was that she could get away with it. She did what she was asked to do. She hauled water. She washed dishes. She cleaned the table. But she didn't have to like it, and she didn't have to like Lizzie. Sometimes she really, really didn't want to do what she was being asked to do, but she did it, anyway. That didn't mean that she had to be nice about it, and she wasn't. Telling Lizzie that she wasn't Callie's mother, with the implication that Callie didn't have to obey her, happened more than once.

Lizzie talked to Henry about it, and Henry talked to Callie. But nothing changed. Callie was still surly and she still, once in a while, wheeled around and shouted, "You aren't my mama!"

Lizzie had never liked to have the photograph of Henry's first wife in the house. There hadn't been a picture of the woman until Callie brought it in, and now here one sat in her own parlor right there on the old bookcase Callie'd put it on.

Lizzie'd caught Henry picking it up and looking at it from time to time, and she didn't like the look on his face when he did. And that girl was constantly picking up the picture; she even kissed it good night. She came to hate that damned pretty woman in the photograph.

So one night, after everybody was in bed asleep, Lizzie rose from the bed she shared with her husband and went into the parlor. She looked down at the sleeping girl all curled up on the sofa, holding that ragged old rabbit that she'd outgrown years ago. "You need to be taught a lesson, girl," she thought.

She walked over and picked up Martha's picture. So damned pretty. Lizzie felt a wave of pure hatred. She tossed the picture frame onto a table and went to her sewing kit to get her scissors.

The next morning, when Callie woke up, stretched, and turned over on the sofa where she'd been sleeping, she saw her mother's picture in pieces, scattered across the floor.

CHAPTER 38

Turbulence
Braman, Oklahoma, 1928

The pieces of the photograph were gone when Lizzie came in from the kitchen to make sure that Callie was up and getting ready for school. The pieces were gone, and so was Callie. The girl was probably someplace trying to glue the pieces back together; the frame and the piece of cardboard that had been the backing for the picture were gone, too.

So be it. If the girl was hiding someplace and wasn't getting ready for school, there wasn't anything that Lizzie could do about it. She had biscuits in the oven and pieces of salt pork in the skillet, so she went back into the kitchen. Breakfast had to be on the table for Henry and all the kids.

She checked on the biscuits. About ready. So she needed to hurry. She removed the pieces of salt pork from the skillet and stirred some flour into the fat. She poured some milk from the can she kept it in into the skillet and stirred it. Pork gravy for the biscuits. It smelled good, and so did the biscuits.

Henry's children, she thought, as she pulled the baking sheet with the biscuits from the oven. One of them had an important job with the state, and, with the exception of Callie, they were smart and, well, she couldn't complain about their behavior. They did what they were asked, helped around the house, and helped their dad, too. She scooped the biscuits out onto the big old platter that she'd got as a present from, of all people, Henry's first wife's folks.

Mattie came into the kitchen, then, all ready for the day.

"Set the table, will you, Mattie?" Lizzie asked while she scooped the gravy into a big bowl.

She glanced at the girl while Mattie was getting plates from the old buffet cabinet. Pretty girl. Sweet, too, really, even if she was maybe a little silly. Well, that was Henry's opinion more than hers. So the girl liked to dance and she seemed to like the boys. Lizzie liked to dance herself. Nothing wrong with that.

Callie came to breakfast with the rest of them, and she was dressed for school. Lizzie started to ask her where she'd been, but decided that she'd better not, at least right now. She didn't need another explosion, not at the breakfast table.

While the kids were bustling around getting ready to head off to school, or, in Mattie's case, to do some cleaning in one of the big houses where the company big shots lived, Lizzie put a hand on Henry's arm.

"I know you need to go to work," she said, "but I need to talk to you a minute."

"Good enough," said Henry with a smile. "The old pumping units aren't goin' anywhere, so why don't I just help you clean the table while we talk?" Then he popped the last biscuit into his mouth.

Lizzie started stacking the plates. Callie had taken just one biscuit and what had looked like a single spoonful of gravy; Mattie had taken more, but it looked like most of it was still on her plate. So Lizzie took it to the garbage can and scraped what was left into it.

"Henry," she said. "I think maybe you're going to hate me."

"Huh? Couldn't hardly do that!" He was picking up the next-to-last piece of salt pork.

"I hope not," said Lizzie. Then she told him about the picture.

Callie almost never got in trouble at school. There had been a few times that the teacher had told her to pay attention, but sometimes it was just boring to have to listen to other people being asked over and over stuff that she knew the answers to. She'd learned not to raise her hand to answer any questions, though. She'd done that at first, but she'd found out that if she was going to have any friends, she'd better just shut up in class and be bored.

Today, though, she'd been called down three times. Twice it had been for not paying attention, but once it had happened when Katie Johnson had poked her in the back with a pencil and called her a crybaby. Callie had turned around and thrown a book at her.

She didn't like Katie Johnson, anyway, and she'd been a little disappointed that the book hadn't hit her in the face. And if she had tears in her eyes, it wasn't any of that stupid girl's business.

So she'd had to stay after school for a few minutes and get a lecture. It didn't matter that the teacher—who definitely was not as nice as Miss Harmon—said things about how good a student she was and all that other stuff. It didn't matter, either, that the teacher had asked her what was wrong; it was none of her business.

She didn't go into the house when she got home. She'd considered not going home at all, but she didn't know where she could go. The farm was a long way away and she wasn't even sure how to get there; it was too far to walk, anyway.

So she sneaked around the side of the house and down the little path to the old tool shed next to the pump house. In her pocket she carried the little jar of library paste that she'd taken from Mrs. Nyquist's desk when the teacher looked away for a minute.

She'd got up really early that morning, gathered up all the pieces of Mama's picture and taken them out to the shed. She'd had time to put the pieces together before she'd had to go in to breakfast, and now she could glue the pieces to the cardboard backing. It wouldn't look as good as it had before, but it would still be Mama.

She could hear the swish-swish-swish-chug-chug-chug from the pump house. Dad had shown it to her once, and then told her never to go in there, that it was dangerous.

Callie'd never been tempted to go inside, but she sometimes opened the door and watched the big, wide belt moving. The belt was almost as wide as she was tall and ran in a big loop around some wheels, big ones clear at the back and littler ones right inside the door. Daddy had told her what the building was for and what the belt did—something to do with the oil wells, probably something to do with pumping—Daddy was a pumper—but she didn't remember exactly what it did. It was sometimes interesting to watch for a while, though.

The old tool shed was different, though. Daddy had shown her the inside of the tool shed, but he hadn't told her not to go inside it. She was pretty sure that he thought that she wouldn't, though, because he'd grinned when he showed her the nest of baby mice back in one corner. But Callie wasn't afraid of grown mice, much less babies. Mice were cute, she thought.

But the baby mice were all gone the first time she went into the shed with her book. She thought that was too bad, and wondered if they were all grown up or maybe dead. She hoped they were all grown; she didn't have any idea how long it took for baby mice to grow up.

The shed was dirty and if there were no baby mice—or grown-up mice—there were definitely spiders. She'd brought one of Lizzie's fly swatters from the kitchen to take care of the spiders, but every day or so there was a new web in one of the corners. The shed wasn't her tree, then, by a long way, but it was private and she could read there in peace. All she needed was her book and her fly swatter. Well, and her kitty.

No Blue Boy. Okay. No book today, either. Except for her school books, and she left them outside the shed. Today she was going to fix Mama's picture.

Bob Lambert

PART SEVEN

FAMILY MATTERS

CHAPTER 39

A Damned Fool
Ponca City, Oklahoma, 1929

Over the months, Frank had maintained some contact with Connie Crocker. He hadn't had any particular reason to do it; he didn't really even think she was a good woman. Usually he'd made certain that they wouldn't be alone together; she was still a damned good-looking woman and he didn't want to take any chances that he'd fuck up.

He'd even brought Bobbie along a couple of times, and she and Connie actually seemed to hit it off. At any rate, Bobbie had seemed to accept his explanation that she was just an old friend. The two women had even met on their own a couple of times, shopping, Bobbie had said.

Frank hadn't been sure that he liked that all that much. For one thing, Connie had a lot more money to spend and she might lead Bobbie to spend more than they had. And old Connie could certainly be a bad influence in other ways if she chose not to behave herself.

But he hadn't been able to find a way to stop it. Bobbie clearly liked Connie—they laughed together a lot; and Frank recognized, with something between amusement and frustration, that if it was all right for him to have Connie for a friend, he could hardly object to Bobbie's doing the same thing.

The big thing, though, was the thought that Jack Crocker might catch the two of them together and that Bobbie might get hurt.

He'd finally figured out who Connie's "gentleman friend" was. He hadn't recognized the name right away, but it finally came to him. This Lennon guy had been involved somehow in that Osage thing Walter had worked on. Got off, though, if that meant anything.

The guy was loaded, it looked like. He kept ol' Connie in fancy clothes—even a fur coat that must have cost—well, a lot. Frank had no idea how much fur coats cost, at least when they weren't made out of rabbits. And there was the Packard.

Connie'd said they were living together, but that turned out to be not exactly true. The guy was married, so Connie had to kind of sneak around. But she was pretty good at that, Frank knew. And he didn't care if Lennon was out screwing people while his old lady sat at home and knitted or whatever rich women did. No skin off his nose.

So old Connie was being a kind of whore by sleeping with Lennon for what she could get off him. Frank didn't have anything against whores. He'd known some pretty nice ones in his day. As far as he was concerned, they were just making a living, same as he was doing.

Connie had a nice little five-room apartment over a drug store just off the main drag. She had a parking place back behind the building, just off the alley, so she didn't have to leave the Packard out on the street. And there was room for Lennon to park there, too, when he was of a mind to make a little visit.

Or for Frank to park.

He had to admit to himself that he was being a damned fool even seeing the woman, even they weren't doing anything but talking. Part of the trouble, though, was that he knew damned well that what went through his head sometimes was a long way from being innocent. Sure, he loved Bobbie, and he damned sure wanted to keep her. Connie wasn't nowhere near the woman his Bobbie was, but—he couldn't help remember those nights in bed, a long time ago now.

So he'd finally slipped. He wasn't proud of it, but he still found himself in Connie's bed. Just twice. Maybe twice wasn't so bad.

CHAPTER 40

Blowout
Oklahoma City and Ponca City, 1929

Walter sat at his desk in the Oklahoma City office, relaxing for a bit, and reading the city paper. Oklahoma was, he thought, in its usual state of chaos.

The legislature had finally managed to impeach and convict Governor Johnston. It was just about all they'd managed to do since the poor bastard had been elected. They'd called him "incompetent," but Walter really didn't think he'd had much of a chance to be anything else with the legislature on his behind almost from the day he'd taken office. Well, that was neither here nor there. The bureau was still working and crime was still filling the newspaper and filling his time.

The federal counterpart of the O.B.I. was back in the state, alternately demanding things of Walter and ignoring his requests for information. Some *hoodlums*—the federal agent-in-charge's word—had killed a couple of notorious gangsters in Kansas City, and the gunmen were supposed to be in Oklahoma. The rumor—and it was nothing but a rumor, in Walter's opinion—was that they were hiding out in either Oklahoma City or Guthrie. There'd been lots of looking, but no finding. Naturally, the story in the paper was full of quotations about how arrests were near and that the federal agents were hot on the trail.

That was nonsense, Walter was certain. As far as he could tell, the federal folks were having about as much luck chasing their pet gangsters as his own bureau had had finding Lucas Taylor's killer. Either the thought of that failure or his weakened hand caused the newspaper to shake.

Walter's hand had healed, but *healed* was a word that had a different meaning than what Walter would have considered accurate before.

The hand didn't hurt any longer, but it was twisted, somehow. His fingers curled inward permanently and he could hold something in his left hand—something small and light—only by smashing it against his fingers with his thumb. He could hold the newspaper, but he had to almost put it down just to turn the page.

He couldn't feel sorry for himself, though. He had a job, and he had to recognize that it was a good one. He got paid more than he deserved, he thought, and if he'd been an Oklahoma City cop—well, he probably wouldn't have been one now. The injury would have meant, at best, that he might have been sitting around the jail checking prisoners' property before locking them up. If that.

And, of course, there was Crystal.

He tossed the newspaper aside and considered what he should do next. He glanced at the file containing the federal bureau stuff and dismissed it.

There'd been another bank robbery, this time over in Sallisaw. Nothing from that, so far. The Oklahoma City police were overwhelmed. A huge oil gusher had erupted, sending oil over whole city blocks, and practically the whole force was out trying to keep order. At least they hadn't asked for help, not that Walter could have found enough men to really do much.

There was paperwork to do, but it was routine and utterly boring. He shook his head at himself and said aloud, although he was alone in the office, "Yeah, yeah, yeah. Boring is good!"

He dug out the folder containing the expense records from the past month, sighed, and began looking them over so that he could make out a report to Director Duncan.

Then he heard the telephone ring in the outer office.

"It's for you, Mr. Gage," called the secretary.

"Okay, thanks, Sally," Walter said, and picked up the telephone.

Suddenly things were anything but boring.

"Walter? Walter?" came the voice on the line. The connection wasn't good, and Walter didn't recognize the voice at first.

"Yes," he said, wondering who would be calling for Walter instead of Agent Gage or whatever. Then he thought that he recognized the voice.

"Dad? Is that you?"

"Jesus!" said his father. "Thank God you're there!"

"I'm here," said Walter. What was going on? He couldn't remember his father ever calling. Something had to be wrong.

"What is it, Dad? Are you all right? Grandpa? Grandma? What's wrong?"

"No," said Henry Gage. "They're all right, least as far as I know. Walter, you'd better get up here. No, no, no, not here. Ponca. You need to get up to Ponca. They've got Frank in jail!"

"What?"

"They say he killed some old gal, Walter. You and I know Frank isn't above bustin' a few heads if he has a good reason—or thinks he has a good reason, but you know he'd never kill a woman!"

"I'll get there as soon as I can!" Walter almost shouted into the telephone. "Where are you? Are you in Ponca?"

"Just hurry, Son."

200

"I'm coming, Dad," said Walter. "Tell me: where will you be?"

But Henry had hung up the receiver.

Walter swept all the files into the top drawer of his desk and stood. Yes, he'd have to go. He looked around the office, although he didn't know what he was looking for—or at. At last he grabbed his hat.

He told the office girl—Sally, that was her name—that he would be gone for a while and that he'd give her a contact number as soon as he could. She just looked at him with a mouth-open stare.

"Wait!" he said at the door. "You have my home telephone number. Call my wife for me and tell her that I'm going to be out of town for a while and that I'll call her!" Then he was out the door, hoping that the girl had caught all of that and would follow the instructions. He was halfway down the stairs before he thought that he should have left some kind of message for Duncan.

The trip to Ponca City seemed to take forever. Walter spent the time wondering what Frank had done, or not done. He knew that Frank had a temper and that he often hadn't hesitated to use his fists. Could he have hit some woman? Hit her too hard? He hated to think it, to admit it, but it was possible.

Finally he let out a long sigh and tried very hard to concentrate on his driving.

Henry Gage was waiting for him in front of the Ponca City police station. He'd probably driven like a mad man to get there and had been out here pacing since the call.

"Thank heavens you're here," said Henry. "They say he killed some people, Walter. You're the law. Get this fixed. You can fix it, can't you?"

Walter patted his father on the shoulder. "We'll see," he said. Fix it? No, he couldn't fix anything. He'd find out what was going on and that was probably all he could do. A look at his father's face—tired, enflamed—told him, though, that he'd better just let Dad—for now—think that he *could* fix it.

"Let's go see the chief," he said, and pushed open the glass door. It was good that this happened in Ponca, he thought. Chief Galloway's assistance during the Osage murders arrests had been invaluable, and Walter was thankful that their relationship had been a good one. If that made any difference.

Galloway seemed pleased to see him until he found out why Walter was there. Then that changed.

"Your brother? Damn. I knew the name was the same, but I didn't make the connection. And this is your father?"

Walter nodded. "No reason you should have," he said. The long trip had calmed him down some, so he was able to keep his tone level. "But I need a couple of things. I need to know what he's charged with and I need to see him."

Galloway shrugged. "I can let you see him," he said, "but you have to realize—oh, Jesus, this is harder than I could've imagined—ah, you're a relative here, not an officer of the law. This is our investigation. I'm sorry, but it has to be that way."

"God damn it! I understand that!" Privately, though, Walter was thinking "Like hell it is!" He felt himself straining forward, his good right hand clenched into a fist. "I'm not here to take anything away from you! I want to know what the hell you've got him in here for, and then I by God want to see my brother!"

A glance at Henry showed Walter that his father was on the verge of doing something he'd regret, so he put a hand out, pushed lightly against Henry's chest.

Galloway gestured toward a chair. "Sit down," he said. "I know this is hard, but yelling at each other isn't going to accomplish anything."

He was right about that, Walter knew, but he damned well didn't want to sit down. "Just tell me," he said, "what he's supposed to have done."

Galloway threw up his hands. "Okay," he said. "You asked. I'm tellin'. Your brother's been arrested for two murders."

"Jesus."

"Yeah," said Galloway, "and you'll probably say 'Jesus' again when you hear who they were."

What Walter actually said when he heard—under his breath—was far worse than "Jesus!" Aloud, he managed to get out, "You can't be serious!"

Galloway just nodded. He was serious indeed.

Lennon dead, murdered. The Crocker woman who'd faked the marriage with Sam Persomoie for his allotment money, dead, murdered. Lennon had belonged in prison, damn him, but murdered? By Frank? By his brother? Hell, that made no damned sense at all! Frank had known the Crocker woman, he remembered—something about her husband, but Lennon? Put that aside, he told himself. Later.

CHAPTER 41

A Different Kind of Doghouse
Ponca City, Oklahoma, 1929

"Can we see him?" asked Walter. He'd decided fairly abruptly that Dad didn't need to hear any of the details; they'd deal with that later—after they'd heard what Frank had to say.

"Suppose so," said Galloway. He stood, then. "Come with me."

Frank was alone in the cell, sitting on the bunk, head down, arms crossed over his legs. He looked up only when Galloway put the key into the lock.

His look at first seemed almost like relief, but Walter could tell the exact moment that Frank saw Henry. The relief was gone in an instant.

But it wasn't the look that got Walter's attention; it was Frank's shirt. It was bloody. His first thought, then, was as an officer of the law. "They should have taken that shirt," he thought. "Evidence." No, no, that wasn't his problem.

It was to Henry that Frank spoke first. "I didn't do it, Dad," he said. "I swear!"

"I know, Son. I know." Henry sat next to Frank and put an arm over his shoulder. Frank looked like he wanted to cry, and Walter couldn't ever remember seeing his brother cry, even when they were kids.

Business. "What happened, Frank?"

Walter could see Frank struggling for control. Then, suddenly, he had it. The old Frank was back, if just for a moment. "They think I killed ol' Connie—you remember Connie, don't you—and that Lennon fella. Jesus! I ain't never killed no man and I damned well wouldn't kill no woman." He shuddered then. "Not like that. Jesus! Not like that!"

"We'll get you a lawyer," said Walter. "It'll be all right." And I'm a damned liar, he thought. "Right now, though, why don't you tell us what happened?"

Frank shrugged. "I found 'em. I was goin' to see her, to see Connie, goin' up to her place—hey, it wasn't like that! I wasn't cheatin' on Bobbie or nothin'!"

"It's okay, Frank. Just go on." It didn't really matter to Walter about whether Frank was catting around; he knew his brother and catting around was one of the things he did.

"Anyway, I went in and they was both just layin' there." Frank picked at his shirt and lifted it away from his body. "I didn't pay much attention to the man, but Connie was bleedin' bad and—well, that's how I got her blood all over me. I was tryin' to help her, I swear!"

The tone, the words, the expression on Frank's face: Walter believed him. Whether anyone else would, of course, was the question.

"They was *shot*, Walter! You know what I think about guns! I hate them sons-of-bitches!"

"I know," said Walter. He wanted to pace up and down the little cell, trying to think what to do, but of course there wasn't any room. No, Frank didn't like guns; he was probably even afraid of them. That didn't mean that he couldn't use one, though.

"You need anything, Frank?" he asked. Of course he did, but there was very little that Walter or their father could give him right now. Some tiny degree of peace? Probably not even that.

"Out of here," said Frank.

"First thing we have to do," said Walter, "is get you a lawyer."

Henry looked up from the cot. "You're an O.B.I. agent, Walt! Do something! Get your brother out of here!"

Walter grimaced. He wished he could. "I can't do that, Dad," he said. "This isn't a bureau case, and even if it were—"

Galloway was at the door. "That's probably enough for now," he said.

Walter nodded. There were things he needed to do and he couldn't do them here. Henry, on the other hand, wasn't ready to go. He pulled Frank up from the cot and wrapped his arms around him, patting his back.

"We'll get you out of here, Son. We promise that we will! We promise!"

Walter shook his head. That was something that his father shouldn't promise.

Galloway was waiting patiently, but he *was* waiting. Walter gently separated Henry and Frank. "We need to go, Dad," he said.

Henry nodded, but he was slumped, beaten. Walter didn't think he'd ever seen his father so whipped-looking, even when Mama had died. This was going to be very, very hard.

"Come on, Dad. We'll come back." He turned to Frank. "We'll be back, Frank, and it won't be long. I promise you that."

"Walt! Walt!" Frank called from his cell, just as the door was closing. "It was prob'ly that stinkin' no 'count husband of hers!"

That stopped Walter. He turned back to Frank, ignoring Galloway's hand on his arm. "What? Wait a minute, Chief! Frank? You've seen Crocker around? Where?" Walter jerked his arm loose and took a step to the cell door. God, if Crocker was around here, after all this time!

"Ain't seen him," said Frank, "but that don't mean he ain't around."

Walter slumped. "Yeah," he said. "We'll be back."

"Where'll we get a lawyer?" asked Henry when they were outside the station. "Who'll we get?"

Walter had no idea. He'd have to ask around. Right now, though, he had other things to do; finding an attorney would wait.

"Where's your car?" he asked.

Henry gestured. "Around the corner. Back there."

"Okay," said Walter. "Parked legally?"

Henry nodded. "Think so, anyway."

"It'll be all right, then. Leave it here and come with me, okay? We'll get a place for the night first thing, because we aren't going to get out of Ponca City tonight!"

CHAPTER 42

Permission to Drill
Ponca City, Oklahoma, 1929

Walter found a room for himself and Henry at one of the sets of cabins where he'd stayed before, then practically forced his father to eat something. Henry had picked at his food at first, but his appetite improved as he went. Walter pretended to eat, even taking a mouthful now and then. He couldn't have told anyone later what he'd eaten.

Finally, when he could tell that Henry had eaten all that he was going to, he pushed away from the table. "I'm goin' to take you back to the cabin, Dad. You need to get some rest."

Henry nodded at first; but by the time he was standing, he was shaking his head. "No," he said. His voice was firm, in control. This was Dad, thought Walter. He was back.

"You're here now, Son," he said. "I can leave things in your hands. I know you'll do what you can. I know you won't let your brother down. But I have to get back home. I have a job and I have your brother and your two sisters back there to take care of. I don't know what I'll tell Claude and Mattie, but they've got to be told. I don't know what Callie'll do. She thinks Frank is Jesus or somebody." He let out a long sigh.

Yeah. Walter didn't envy Dad that little chore. Mattie would be hysterical, he thought, and they'd have to watch Claude to make sure he didn't take off hitch-hiking to Ponca City.

"It's awfully late, Dad. We should call, and you should get some rest."

"No, take me back to my car," said Henry. "Then do what you can. And call me. Okay? Call me?"

Walter dropped his father off at his car, watched him crank it into life, and pull out. He hoped the old wreck would last long enough to get him back to Braman. Well, there was enough to worry about without worrying about Dad getting stranded somewhere.

Lawyer. No, that could wait. He walked around the corner and pushed open the door to the police station. He thought about pulling out his watch and checking the time, but didn't bother; if Galloway had gone home, Walter would either just talk to whomever he'd left in charge or go find the police chief.

He expected Galloway to be in his office, though, unless there'd been some other kind of emergency, and he was right. The look on the chief's face said very clearly that he'd known Walter would be back.

"He didn't do it," said Walter.

Galloway looked at Walter and shook his head. "You have any idea, Gage, how many times I've heard that?" He leaned forward, hands on his desk. "How many times have you heard it yourself?"

Walter tossed his hat in the chair. "Ah, hell, Chief. I know it. Everybody says it. But in this case I'm pretty damned sure it's true."

"Couldn't be because he's your brother, could it?"

Walter picked up the hat and sat down, running his finger around the brim. Was it? Was it just because it was Frank? He knew Frank could be violent, that he'd fought men, even hurt men. But, no. It wasn't because it was Frank that was locked up. Not altogether, anyway.

"You know who the woman is, don't you?" he asked.

"Hell, yeah," said Galloway. "In case your memory's been fried or something, you might recall that she sat her shapely little butt in my jail for quite a while!"

Walter nodded. Of course. "Frank says they were shot. That right?"

"He should know."

"Something's not right here," said Walter. He looked at his hat, wondered what he was doing with it, and tossed it on the floor. "We have two dead people. One of 'em was arrested for—hell, you know what she was arrested for. The other one was under a damned lot of suspicion for the Osage killings, and the man who was one of the actual murderers was something like his right-hand man. Lennon was involved, and you know it. I know it. Both of these dead people were part of the whole damned Osage mess, and now they're dead!"

"Yep. They sure are," said Galloway. "Right down dead."

"Why was Lennon there? It was the woman's place, right?"

"Rumor is that he was screwing her."

"So why Frank? Look, we didn't bring in all the people involved. Jack Crocker's still out there somewhere, and the dead woman was his wife! Why not him?"

Walter realized he was sweating and brushed his forehead with his shirtsleeve.

"Look," said Galloway. "What you're saying would make sense, except for two things."

Walter looked up and waited.

"First of all, your brother's been seen around town with the Crocker woman. Maybe he came in, found 'em together and just went off!"

Galloway shook his head in what looked like frustration. "Gage, your brother was found in the room with them, with the gun, and with blood all over his clothes. It was almost like catching him in the act." Galloway shuffled in his seat, then leaned forward. "Look, I know this is hard. It'd be hard for me if it was my brother. And I don't like it. I like you and I respect you for the work you did. I don't want it to be your brother. But proof is proof."

He sat back, then, and rested his elbows on the arms of his chair. "I'm sorry."

Walter felt himself slumping and pulled himself upright. Yes, what the chief said made sense. But.

"I understand," he said. "One thing, though. I know it's asking more than you'd like for me to ask, but I'd like to see the place they were shot. Can you do that for me?"

Galloway clearly wanted to say no, but after a second or two, he nodded. "I can't take you myself, but I'll have an officer take you. You know damned well that you can't touch anything, don't you?"

"I know that."

"Okay, okay, okay. The officer that answered the call and made the arrest is off and I don't want to drag him out for this, but I'll have Sergeant Cook take you out. Thank God it's a slow night."

"Thank you," said Walter.

"Don't thank me," said Galloway. "If I thought your going there would mean a damned thing, then maybe it'd be worth a thank-you. As it is, you'll just be wasting your time and Cookie's time."

CHAPTER 43

Safety Slide
Ponca City, Oklahoma, 1929

The trip—in a patrol car—was made largely in silence. Cook was an older man, probably mid-forties, Walter thought, not all that much younger than Dad. He had a competent air about him, but that might have been nothing more than years of experience. He was polite, almost deferential, to Walter, probably more because of Walter's badge than anything else.

"Guy's your brother, huh?" he asked, and then was silent after Walter had told him that yes, he was.

Connie Crocker's apartment was up a flight of stairs and the second apartment down a narrow hall. It looked to Walter as if there were four apartments over the drug store; at least there were four doors down the hall.

"Here we are," said Sergeant Cook, unlocking the door. "It's a mess, but I s'pect, your bein' a state agent and all, that you've seen as bad or worse. Prob'ly. Thought I'd better tell you, though. Some folks get kinda— well, you know—when there's a lot of blood."

The living room and small dining room seemed undisturbed. The furnishings were nicer than Walter had expected. He didn't know much, really, about furniture, but this all looked expensive.

Cook gestured toward the rear of the apartment. "Bedroom," he said.

Walter had indeed seen worse, but there was a lot of blood. The bodies were gone, of course, but the pools of blood showed clearly where they'd been. The bed itself was soaked with blood, and there was a fairly large pool of dried blood on the floor beside it. Other than the blood—and the fact that the bed was unmade—there wasn't, so far as Walter could tell, anything else amiss.

"Who was where?" Walter asked.

Cook took a couple of steps into the room and pointed. "The woman in the bed; the man, there beside it." He shoved his hands into his trouser pockets and seemed to be jiggling some change. "It looks like, well, that they were either going at it in the bed there, or were gettin' ready to. The woman was naked, and the man was just wearin' his shorts."

Walter stepped very carefully into the room and looked down at the blood on the rug and then at the bed. This didn't look good. If Frank was still thinking of Connie as *his*, somehow, and caught her in bed with somebody, there'd be a definite potential for violence.

"All right if I touch this?" he asked Cook as he reached out for the bloody sheet. Okay, so he'd told Galloway he wouldn't touch anything.

"Don't see why not," said Cook. "It ain't gonna tell you anything, though."

Walter didn't expect it to tell him anything, but he pulled the sheet back anyway. Just more blood, soaked through the top sheet and then through the bottom one. Probably fairly deep into the mattress.

He carefully lowered the top sheet, trying to put it back exactly as it had been.

"You seen enough?" asked Sergeant Cook.

Walter shrugged. He'd seen too much, really. He let out a long sigh, still staring down at the bloody bed.

"How'd you know about this? How'd you know there'd been a crime committed here?"

"Lady down the hall heard shots and called it in."

Oh, yes. Other apartments. Somebody would certainly have heard the shots. Not everybody would have called the police, though. For one thing, not everybody would have a telephone and going out looking for one when somebody had been firing shots either next door or down the hall might not be exactly a wise thing to do.

"Could I talk to her?" Walter couldn't expect anything new, really, but—well, anything to help him understand. He felt a wry smile cross his face; he was investigating even though he'd been told not to. So be it.

"Be my guest," said Cook, "She's right down the hall."

The apartment of the lady in question was the first apartment at the top of the stairs, right next door to the Crocker woman's.

The woman who answered the knock looked to be in her late fifties, early sixties. She held the door open just far enough to show her eyes, but Walter could see that she was wearing a hairnet, probably getting ready for bed, even though it was early for that—by four or five hours.

"Mrs. Larkin," said Cook. "This here gentleman is Agent Gage, with the O.B.I., and we wonder if we could talk to you again about what went on next door?"

"O.B.I.? What's that?"

"Oklahoma Bureau of Identification and Investigation," said Walter, showing his badge. "We're sort of state police."

The woman's eyes got wide. Walter felt a little guilty because he was probably frightening the woman. He was certainly misleading her: he had no standing to be asking her any questions.

The answer was apparently satisfactory, though, because she pulled the door open and stepped back.

"I'm not dressed for company," she said. "Forgive me."

Yes, her hair was up and in a hairnet. She was wearing a blue housecoat, made out of some sort of shiny material. She looked comfortable, but she was clearly embarrassed.

"I was supposed to go to my daughter-in-law's for supper tonight, but after all of what happened, I just didn't want to. So I just got comfortable." Then she blushed. "Oh, forgive me!" she said. "Please sit down. I should have asked you to do that! But, oh, I know you'll forgive an old woman who's been scared out of her wits!"

"You look just fine," said Sergeant Cook, and gestured for her to sit first.

"I know this is difficult," said Walter, after they were all seated, "but would you please tell us again what happened?"

The woman nodded.

"Just a step at a time," said Walter. "And take your time."

Mrs. Larkin nodded again and gnawed a little at her lower lip. Walter happened to glance at her lap. Her hands were writhing.

"I was just cleaning in the kitchen," she said. "Mopping the kitchen floor. I'd made biscuits this morning. I don't do that every morning, but this morning I did, and then I noticed flour I'd spilt and after I swept it up, I decided that the floor could use a good mopping, so—"

"And then?" Cook interrupted her.

"Yes," she said. "I'm sorry. I'm just a babbling old woman."

"No," said Walter, leaning toward her. "You've had a shock and it's natural that you'd be nervous. And, just between the three of us, I hardly think you'd exactly qualify as being an old woman." He sat back then. "You were mopping. What then?"

"I heard two loud bangs. One bang, then a little bit later, another bang. Loud. Awful loud. Bang! Bang!"

Walter nodded. "And then you called the police? Is that right?"

The woman nodded. Then her mouth came open and her eyes widened. "No, wait!" she said. "No, no, I didn't call right away. I don't hear a lot of gun shots. I mean, I grew up on a farm, and my daddy and brothers hunted some, so I've heard shooting, but, well, I wasn't sure."

"Mm-huh," said Cook. "When did you call, then?"

"Well," she said, "I put my mop in the sink and I was getting ready to wring it out, and I got to thinkin'. Maybe it was just somebody slammin' the door. The man lives across the hall does that sometimes."

Walter kept himself from fidgeting.

"I looked out, but his door was closed, and I got to thinkin'. Fellow'd be at work, so he couldn't be slamming his door. Then this man came in the front door and up the stairs he came." She looked up. "Then I thought I'd better call. I did right, didn't I?"

"Yes, you did," said Cook. "Thank you."

"Wait," said Walter. "This man—the man who came up the stairs. What'd he look like?"

"Oh, gosh. I didn't pay a whole lot of attention. Tall fella. Khaki clothes. Big ol' hat. Think he had on work boots. Leastwise sounded like that."

Walter sat up very straight and looked over at Cook. Cook was looking at him, too. The sergeant raised an eyebrow and Walter nodded to him. That description, limited as it was, sounded as if the man who'd come up the stairs might well have been Frank. And if it had been....

Cook let out a long exhalation. "Jesus Christ!" he said. Then he shook his head. "Oh, sorry, Ma'am. I apologize for my language."

The woman looked confused, Walter saw. She just nodded at the officer, then shook her head.

Cook turned to Walter. "We'd better tell the chief about this," he said. "Right away. What do you think?"

Walter agreed and said so. If the man on the stairs had been Frank, then he'd come in *after* the shots. So, maybe—just maybe.

He leaned forward to meet the woman's eyes. "Did you tell the officers who came out about the man on the stairs?"

"No. Didn't seem important. I just told them about the gun shots. That's all they asked about! Did I do somethin' wrong?"

Cook hoisted himself out of his chair. "No, Ma'am," he said, "You didn't. You were a big help. But now I hate to trouble you any more than you've already been troubled, but could you come with us? Tell the chief what you told us? It could be important."

"Well," said the woman, "I s'pose so, but I don't see how anything I said could matter none."

Cook smiled at her. "It might be very important," he said.

"Well, all right. I have to fix up some, though, if I'm gonna go out in public and all."

"That'll be fine," said Cook. "There's no big hurry. We'll just wait for you."

When the woman had gone down the hall and closed a door behind her, Walter saw Cook's hands on his knees, squeezing. The muscles in his arms stood out as if he were holding something heavy. Walter understood the tension, but the tension he was feeling himself was strongly tempered by hope.

"Whoever took this lady's story in the first place didn't do a good job," Cook said. "Looks to me like there's a possibility that we might have the wrong fellow sittin' in jail."

None of this cleared Frank, of course. He'd been found in the room. He'd been bloody. The gun was lying right there and he could easily have dropped it where it lay. If somebody else had been in the apartment when he'd come up the stairs, he should have run into whoever it was. And if he had seen somebody, he damned well would have said so. Even so, things looked better—a little better.

Chief Galloway agreed that Mrs. Larkin's new revelation meant something. "I'm not sure what, though," he said. "Maybe he shot 'em, left, then remembered that he'd left the gun."

"And come back for it," said Cook, nodding.

"If it wasn't your brother, Gage," said Galloway, "then who was it? He says himself he didn't see anybody else—on the stairs, in the hall, in the place. I don't want to dispute what Mrs. Larkin said, but maybe she's not remembering things right. Maybe she saw the man going up the stairs before the shots and just got confused. It's not every day that most of us have someone murdered right next door."

"I know it doesn't prove anything," said Walter, "but it does create some doubt."

"Well," said the chief, pushing himself back from his desk, "that's something you can tell his lawyer, I guess."

"You're definitely going to charge him, then?" asked Walter. "Right now? Before you've checked out all the possibilities?"

"What other possibilities? That's all we've got." Galloway stood. "I'm sorry," he said, "but I think we've cooperated with you, probably more than we should have. I know that you understand our limitations here and that the fact that the prisoner is your brother can't count for anything."

"I do know," said Walter. "But I have one more request."

"Yeah? And what would that be?"

Walter stood, too, so that Galloway wouldn't be standing over him. "I'd like to see the apartment again."

Galloway rested his hands, palms down, on his desk. "And why would that be?"

"Chief," said Sergeant Cook. "I'd like to look at the place again myself. This new stuff might not mean anything when it comes right down to it, but what Mrs. Larkin told us says to me that maybe not enough was looked at the first time around." He glanced at the closed chief's door. "Besides that, Mrs. Whoever is sittin' out there waitin' for a ride home. Somebody's gotta take her, and it might as well be me." He paused then, and looked over at Walter. "And Gage, too."

Galloway looked at each of the men in turn, holding Cook's gaze longer. Then he straightened. "Very well," he said. "We'll *all* go."

It was Walter who found it. The open window in the back wall of the bedroom.

"Look," he told the others. "This window—look what it leads to."

"Shit!" said Cook.

"Yeah," said Walter, pointing through the window to the steel fire escape going down to the alley below. "Exactly."

Galloway nodded to Cook. "Better have a look," he said.

Cook was outside on the landing for just a minute or two. His eyes were cast down, then he bent from the waist to look more closely at something. Then he knelt, and rubbed his hand over the metal.

"Blood," he said, looking up. "And I can see blood on a couple of steps farther down, too. Footprints. Bloody footprints." His eyes met Walter's, and he nodded.

"We'll need to get someone out here to take some pictures," Galloway said. "Sorry, Sergeant, but you'll need to stay here 'til we can get somebody." He gestured back toward the door leading to the hall. "Gage, you come back with me."

Walter followed, but first he put a hand on Cook's shoulder, wordlessly thanking him.

At the door leading into the hall, Galloway stopped. "This isn't conclusive," he told Walter, "but it looks like your brother just got lucky."

"It wasn't luck," said Walter. "Your Sergeant Cook's a good man and a good cop."

"Yeah, well, I hope that means you're not goin' to try to steal him from us!"

"Never know," said Walter with a grin. Yes, he definitely felt like grinning. There was a killer out there, and that the killer was probably connected to the old Osage Indian murders. And that made this his job.

CHAPTER 44

Out the V-Door
Kay County, Oklahoma, and Southern Kansas, 1929

Jack Crocker was seething. The bitch was dead. The bastard that was screwing her was dead. Bastard. Not only was he screwing Crocker's wife, the son-of-a-bitch was responsible for putting his brother—his only brother—behind bars while the son-of-a-bitch walked away free with no telling how much money. Bastard!

He'd driven up to Newkirk, headed for Kansas, but he'd had to stop and pull over for a while. He'd caught himself driving too fast, and the last fucking thing he needed was to get pulled over for speeding.

And he'd left the fucking gun behind. If some god-damned cop stopped him, he couldn't even defend himself! Fuck! He'd liked that gun, too. Ol' Simon'd bought it for him—birthday or something, he couldn't remember exactly what. And it'd done its job just right, too. How many people had he shot with it? He tried to count them off.

Well, hell, start with the big ones. That fuckin' Indian sheriff down at Okmulgee—dumped that fucker down a creek bed. They probably hadn't even found him yet. He found himself grinning.

Then that god-damned state cop that'd been all over their asses, that Taylor. That was a good one. Just walked into the house like he owned the damned place and put one right in the bastard's forehead. Eight or nine injuns. That Korbelik guy in Oklahoma City.

Ah, shit. He could get another gun. At least that bitch Connie was dead, out of his life forever now and good fucking riddance.

As he sat there, pulled off the highway onto some kind of oilfield road, he thought of what he needed to do. Kansas. He'd been holed up in some rat trap up in Caldwell, but there wasn't any reason to go back there. Besides, he'd left without paying what he owed.

Gun. He had plenty of cash left. There'd been a whole box full of the stuff at Simon's place and he'd taken a chance and got there before the fucking cops. So he could buy damned near anything he wanted. Guns were easy enough to come by. He could probably get away with just walking into a general store in one of these little farm towns and buy one. Okay. Get a gun.

He was gripping the steering wheel so hard that his hands were beginning to ache.

Fuckers. Fucking whole god-damned world. The whole god-damned Indian thing. Made his uncle rich, sure, but that did the poor bastard a whole lot of fucking good down in McAlester. Lennon. He could still see that scrawny bastard's hands on Connie, there in the bed. Fucker deserved to die.

Then he remembered that other fucker. That long-limbed bastard that had humiliated him in front of his brother and then again in front of the guys at work. Gage, that was his name. And Connie had screwed him, too! He'd have to take care of that bit of business yet. And while he was at it he'd get rid of that asshole justice of the peace that'd fucked Connie over. Probably ought to kill her so-called injun husband while he was at it. He'd probably screwed her, too!

Crocker had to take his hands away from the steering wheel; they were hurting too bad. He shook his head. He didn't have anything left. His old man and old lady had died a long time ago—not that they'd been any big loss—and his brother was in the pen, his uncle was in the pen, and his wife was dead. For a moment he saw Connie's face, smiling at him, long ago. Then the face changed. There was no smile. There was just a look of terror when she'd seen the gun.

No reason to live, thought Crocker. For some reason, that made him smile. There was no reason at all for him not to do just what he wanted. Yeah, they'd probably kill him for it, but what did that matter? He was dead anyway.

First thing, then. Gun. Then that damned driller that'd caused him so damned much hurt, probably the reason that Connie had snuck off from him in the first place. His hands were caressing the steering wheel now. Yes. One more dead bastard. If the bastard had a wife, well, he'd take care of her, too. Fuck the bitch, kill her. Kill 'em all.

He nodded to himself and started the car. No Kansas. Some little town to find a gun and a place to stay for the night and then, look out!

But then things went to hell. He tried to buy a gun in Kaw City, but the shop owner had looked at him funny and said that he didn't have any revolvers, even though Crocker could see a couple of them in the glass case right in front of him.

He'd pointed down at the guns, but the bastard just shook his head. Crocker had to admit to himself that he'd lost it a little bit, then. He'd grabbed the guy by his shirt and punched him a good one in the mouth. He was tempted to break the glass and just grab one of the guns, and he might have if some old farmer hadn't come in the door. So he'd shoved the old man aside and got the hell out of there.

So now he'd had to high-tail it out of Kaw City. And he figured the law would be after his ass now—again—so he'd have to lay low for a while.

Kansas again.

He'd got as far as Burlington in Kansas, where he stopped and asked around for a bootlegger. Then, like a damned fool, he'd drunk too much and run his fuckin' car into a damned bridge.

No gun. Now no car. He still had plenty of money, though. Well, not plenty. Damn. Enough to buy a car all right, but nothing he'd like to drive, especially if he had to outrun some fuckin' cops.

Well, Burlington was a good enough place to lay low for a while. He'd done hard labor before and it hadn't hurt him, so he supposed he could get some kind of job in Burlington. For a while. Just for a while. Might even make a little visit to some little burg bank—after he had a gun, of course. Shit.

He took the registration from the steering column and pried off the license plate and tossed both of them off the bridge into the Neosho River. Then he hitched a ride back to Burlington, and left the car where it sat, crumpled up against the bridge abutment.

He didn't really listen to the old farmer's babble on the way into town. "Oklahoma," he thought. "I'll be back."

He would. But it would take a while.

Maybe he'd go east for a while. See some of Simon's old buddies. Maybe—just maybe—he could get some help.

CHAPTER 45

Slant Drilling
Kay County, Oklahoma, 1929

"It doesn't look like we have enough to hold your brother on," said Chief Galloway, "so I'm turning him loose." He gave Walter the familiar cop stare. "That doesn't mean that he's off free as a bird. You know that we're going to have to consider everything here, and that includes your brother."

"I know," said Walter. "And I appreciate your consideration here." He paused, then, and considered. Yes, he'd say it.

"I think you know," he told Galloway "that we have the greatest of respect for you and your work, and that we don't want to interfere—well, any more than I have already." Walter felt a rueful smile cross his face.

The look on Galloway's face was expectant. "And?"

Walter lifted both hands and held them toward the chief, palms out. "Yeah, *and.* This is your case, your investigation. I just want you to know that if want the bureau's assistance, all you have to do is ask."

Galloway laughed. "The way you say that sounds like I had some sort of choice!"

Walter shrugged.

"It's fine," said Galloway. "We'll keep looking here, but the main thing—the important thing—is to find out who did this and put 'em away. So anything you come up with—well, I'd like to know."

"Of course," said Walter. "I'll guarantee that."

"Fine," said Chief Galloway. "And we'll do the same. Now let's go let that brother of yours out of his cell."

"What now?" Frank thought when Walter and that head cop showed up at the door of his cell. Maybe Walter had found him a lawyer. Or something.

Then, after Galloway had unlocked the door and swung it open, the man said, "All right, Gage, you're free to go—for now."

"You're letting me out?"

Galloway nodded. "I said you could go, didn't I?"

"It's all right, Frank," said Walter. "Come on. We'll talk in the car. Get up."

God! Whatever he'd done, ol' Walter had done it! Frank's impulse was to jump up and hug his brother, but, well, not in front of the cop. So he shook his head and got up from the cot.

"We'll need to get you a clean shirt, at least," said Walter. Then he turned to Chief Galloway. "You need the shirt? Evidence?"

"What? Oh. Yeah, we should, I suppose. Just in case."

"Take it off, Frank," said Walter, "and then let's get out of here."

"You know you have to stay in town," said Chief Galloway while Frank was undoing the bloody shirt.

"Huh? What? I gotta go to work!"

Galloway nodded. "Yeah, yeah, I get it. So where do you work, then?"

"Down at Three Sands!"

"Okay," said the chief. "Kay County, though, right?"

"Barely," said Frank. "Work's in Kay sometimes and in Noble sometimes. Rig's in Noble County right now."

Galloway shrugged. "No problem, far as I can see. I'm gonna need your address, though."

Frank undid the last button and shrugged out of the shirt. "There ain't any house numbers or nothin'," he said. "It's a camp—just a bunch of houses lined up along the road 'bout a quarter-mile or so just south of town."

"Camp," said Galloway, reaching for the shirt. "Okay. I suppose we can find you if we need you? You're a driller, right? Who you work for, then?" The police chief held the shirt away from himself as if it smelled bad. Maybe it did.

"Helmerich and Payne," said Frank. "Hey, brother. Can I go out of here half nekkid like this?" Frank spread his arms, apparently to show that his chest was bare—as if they couldn't tell.

"It'll be all right," said Walter. "The chief here isn't likely to arrest you for public nudity."

"Better not," said Frank. "I ain't too crazy about the accommodations 'round here."

"Then let's go," said Walter. Come on, Frank, he thought. Enough. You're out of jail, probably out of trouble altogether, so quit acting like a jackass. "We'll talk in the car. Come on."

"Said that already," said Frank.

"So I said it again. Now get your skinny rump out that door before I tell Chief Galloway to close the door to this very cozy little cell and lock it up."

"Okay," said Walter when they'd gotten Frank into the car. "Where's your car?"

"Out front of...her place."

Walter turned to look at his brother. It didn't look like Frank, at least not much. He was pale and his eyes had a dead look. And he hadn't called the woman by name; she was "her." The anger would come later, he thought, and then—well, he hoped he could be around when the anger came out.

"I probably should drive you home," said Walter, "and we could talk on the way—and, Frank, believe me we need to talk."

"I'm goin' to need the car," said Frank. "I still gotta go to work, you know."

"You up to driving?"

"Hell, yes! What you think I am, some kind of baby?"

"Okay, okay! I'll take you to your car!" Walter had to grin a little; this was more like the Frank he'd known most of his life.

Frank's car was where he'd said it would be, next to the curb in front of the Crocker woman's apartment.

"You always park here?" asked Walter. He was thinking about the parking spaces behind the building and the fire escape. That was a more logical entry, especially if you didn't particularly want to be seen.

"Nah," said Frank. "In back, usually. Easier."

"Why'd you park out here this time?"

"Hey, Mr. Officer! This one of those what you call *interrogations*?"

"Necessary, Frank. When we get back to your place, I'm going to have some more questions."

"You think I killed 'em? That what you think?" Frank was pulling on the door handle, ready to get out of the car.

"No, no, no," said Walter. "but I want to know who did, and I'm sure you do, too."

Frank let go of the door handle and slumped in the seat. "Yeah," he said. "I do." He took a breath. "I parked out here because I wasn't plannin' to stay. I was just goin' up to tell her I was goin' to go on the evening tour so I wouldn't be seein' her for a while."

"Uh huh. So you didn't even go through the alley? You didn't see Lennon's car there?"

Frank grimaced. "If I had, I wouldn't'ta gone up." He turned in the seat and looked at Walter. "Should've looked, huh?"

"Drive careful," said Walter. "I'll be right behind you if you start feeling shaky or anything."

"Damn it, I'm all right!"

"I know you are! I know that! But I have to talk to you some more, and I'm gettin' tired of looking at that bare chest of yours! So get yourself home, kiss your wife, and put a shirt on!"

"Jesus! Bobbie! She don't know any of this!"

Walter reached across and patted Frank's bare shoulder. "She'll be glad you're not in jail, Frank."

"Yeah. I suppose so. Not goin' to be easy to tell her all this stuff, though."

"I'll help," said Walter. "If you want me to."

"Up to you," said Frank. He opened the door and wheeled in the seat to put his feet out onto the street.

Walter had a sudden thought. "Frank? Frank, you have a telephone?"

Frank turned to him, a puzzled look on his face. "Hell, no. Why?"

"I need to make a telephone call, one I should have made a long time ago. Look, you tell me how to find your place and I'll be out as soon as I can. Okay?"

CHAPTER 46

Revenge?
Ponca City, Oklahoma, 1929

Bobbie, as it turned out, already knew a lot of what happened—almost everything except the fact that Frank had been released. They might not have had their own telephone, but that didn't mean that there weren't any in the camp. Mrs. Sawyer from just down the road had come pounding on her door with the news. The woman had seemed to enjoy telling Bobbie.

Then she'd had other, more frightening visitors: a couple of Ponca City policemen.

Bobbie met Frank at the door with a little scream and threw herself into his arms. Then she was crying. Frank found himself patting her back while she sobbed against his bare chest.

"Honey! Honey!" he said. "What's goin' on? What's the matter?"

Bobbie pushed herself away. The look on her face turned from joy to something like anger. "What do you mean, what's the matter? Frank, I've been sitting here scared to death, and you ask me what's the matter?"

Frank reached out and took her by the shoulders. "Did something happen?" Good God, had something else gone wrong? This was turning out to be a hell of a day!

"The police were here, Frank! They searched the place, and they wouldn't even tell me what they were looking for! And they told me you'd killed somebody!"

"I didn't, Honey. I swear."

She came back into his arms, then. "Oh, Sweetheart," she sobbed, "and I'm so glad!"

Walter found a telephone in a little grocery store and persuaded the owner to let him use it, promising to reverse the charges. The owner, a short little fellow with yellowish-gray hair and a considerable belly, took some convincing, but the badge helped.

Walter had a moment when he thought that whoever answered the phone back in the city might refuse to accept the charges. If Duncan was there, he might well be pretty upset—even angry—that Walter had just taken off and left him with all that unfinished paperwork.

Duncan wasn't there, though, and the secretary/receptionist told Walter that the director hadn't been in, that she herself was the only person in the office, and that she was about to leave, had her purse in her hand, in fact, and what did he want?

Walter asked her—very careful to sound polite, rather than like a boss—to leave Mr. Duncan a note telling him that he'd been called to Ponca City and that he'd be back in the city tomorrow. She agreed to do that and hung up. Walter hoped that she'd take the time, but he couldn't be certain. Oh, well.

He thought that he should call his father, but one look at the storekeeper told him that the request to use the telephone again would not be met with a happy smile. Very well. He should probably tell Dad in person, anyway. He'd drive up to Braman. He could still get back to the city tomorrow.

And Crystal! Damn! He needed to call her, too. He hoped to hell the girl had remembered to call her. Maybe he could call her from Frank's. No, damn it! Frank had said he didn't have a phone.

At any rate, he still needed to drive out to Frank's. He wasn't at all optimistic that his brother would tell him anything useful, but he'd said that he'd be there. So he'd go. Frank needed his support, probably, though he could easily imagine Frank's just putting on a clean shirt and going to work. Come to think of it, Walter wasn't even sure what time the evening tour started; he might not even be at home when Walter got there. And that was provided he could find the place

Frank seemed to be doing fine. Walter had knocked at only one wrong door before he'd found the right place, and Frank—newly shirted—was sitting at the table eating pork chops and mashed potatoes, with Bobbie hovering over him like a new mother. So far, so good.

"Sit down, Walter," said Bobbie with a big smile. "You want some dinner? We have more!"

The pork chops smelled good, and Walter was tempted. However, a glance at the kitchen stove showed a single pork chop in the skillet and an empty plate where Bobbie would be sitting. He'd be taking her food, he realized.

"No, but thank you," he said, sitting at the end of the table. "I won't stay long. I just wanted to make sure Frank was doing all right."

"I am," said Frank through a mouthful of mashed potatoes.

"Has he told you everything?" Walter asked.

"I think so," said Bobbie. Then she gave Frank a hard look. "Have you, Frank? Told me everything?"

Frank put down his fork and nodded. "I think so," he said. He looked at Walter. "Anything you know that I don't?"

Walter reached over and put a hand on his brother's shoulder. "Looks to me like you're doing fine," he said. Then he turned to his brother's wife. "Your husband just stumbled into a bad situation," he said, although he was pretty sure that wasn't the entire truth. "He's home now and he's safe, and that's what counts."

Walter watched Frank eat for a moment and watched Bobbie's eyes that never moved from her husband's face. The questions he needed to ask could wait, he decided.

"I'm going up to Braman to tell Dad you're all right," he said. "Anything you want me to tell him?"

"Yeah," said Frank. "You tell the old man that if I'd wanted to kill that Lennon bastard I'd've done it with my bare hands, not with no gun!"

Walter felt himself laughing. "Yeah, I'll tell him that. That'll make him feel real good." He pushed himself away from the table. "Bobbie, thank you for the offer of dinner. I hope I can take you up on that sometime; everything looks right down delicious."

"Dessert?" she asked. "We have some peach cobbler."

Ouch. Peach cobbler. Mama used to make peach cobbler and Walter could feel his mouth watering.

"No," he said. "I've gotta go, but I thank you. Frank, I'll see you in a couple of days—and if I were you, I'd keep close to home for a while."

Frank reached over and took his wife by the waist, pulling her closer. "No reason to go to town. I got everything I need right here!"

Walter knew that he needed to be heading back for the city—back to Crystal and back to the damned office—but talking to his father, reassuring him, seemed important right now. He checked his watch. By the time he got to Braman and talked to Dad, it'd be dark. Driving back to Oklahoma City at night wasn't an appealing prospect.

He spent a good part of the trip north thinking about what had happened. And what it meant. He had no pity, he found, for Lennon. The woman, though. That was too bad. She'd apparently been quite willing to break the law; what she'd done with the fake marriage amounted to fraud, of course. But that wasn't enough to die for. And Frank had seen something in the woman. Knowing Frank, though, that something might have meant only that she was good in bed.

And which one had been the target? Both? Lennon was the more likely of the two. And who'd want Lennon dead? Walter didn't doubt that there might be any number of people who wouldn't mind putting a couple of bullets into the man.

One of the Osage? Possible. If someone from the tribe, unhappy because Lennon hadn't gone to prison, had killed the pair, finding out who would be enormously difficult. The tribe certainly didn't sanction murder—

if they ever had—but they'd be unlikely to give up someone who had killed Lennon.

Somebody that Lennon had got the best of—quite possibly unfairly—in some legal matter? If that was the case, there'd be a lot of legal stuff to look into, and it wouldn't be easy to find. Somebody—the Ponca police or his own agency—would have to talk to a lot of people, listen to a lot of rumors, most of which would come to nothing.

Walter took a deep breath and tried to concentrate on the highway.

Then there was the woman's missing husband. Oh, yes. Yes. Walter almost felt as if he needed to pull the car to the side of the road. Jack Crocker. A known killer. Wife in bed with another man. And Crocker was already on just about every "wanted" list in the country. But he hadn't shown up in any of the nets.

If it had been Crocker, Walter thought, forcing his concentration back onto the road for a minute or two—Crocker. Crocker.

And that brought him back to the killing that meant something to him personally as well as professionally. Lucas Taylor.

Mrs. Taylor had been acquitted; that didn't mean that she hadn't killed her husband, though. But the Crocker brother. Revenge. That made a lot of sense. Of course the killer might just be someone else Taylor had arrested. Who among the arrested were out of prison now? Did the ones in prison have angry brothers or fathers?

"I'll have Gravel look into that," he said aloud. But his own hunch was that he needed to keep looking for Jack Crocker and to look harder.

CHAPTER 47

A Drifting Branch
Braman, Oklahoma, 1929

When Walter pulled up in front of Henry's board-and-batten house, his father was standing on the front porch. It was dark, and there were no yard lights, but Walter could tell that it was his father by his silhouette. "He's probably been there for a long time," Walter thought, "just waiting to hear from me."

Walter had barely had time to turn off the engine and shut off the lights before Henry was there, pulling open the car door.

"Walter! God, I'm glad you're here!"

"I should have called, Dad, but—"

"Get out. Come in. How's Frank?"

For a moment Walter felt that his father was going to yank him out of the car. "He's all right, Dad," he said. "He's out of jail. Let me get out of this car so I can get some feeling back in my legs and I'll tell you all about it."

"Yeah, sure." Henry stepped back and put out a hand to Walter. "Grab hold, Son."

Walter let his father halfway lift him out. He'd been serious about his legs and the help was appreciated, although not really needed. "Thanks," he said.

"Come in the house," said Henry. "Lizzie's got some coffee on. You look like you could use some."

"Yeah," said Walter. "Good idea."

Henry took Walter's arm as they started toward the house.

Walter felt himself smiling. "I can walk, Dad. Yeah, I really can."

Henry let go of his arm, with some reluctance, Walter thought. Then he felt his father's hand under his elbow as they started up the two steps to the porch. He was surprised that he felt just the smallest bit of resentment and wanted to pull away. That made him realize just how tired he was.

Walter sat on the old, lumpy couch—he suspected that it was somebody's bed—and Dad sat in his usual rocker. Lizzie came in then with a percolator and two cups. Walter tried to wave the coffee away, but Lizzie poured it, anyway, and pushed the cup at him. So he took it and sipped the coffee. Hot, but good. Lizzie touched Henry gently on the shoulder and went back into the kitchen. Giving them privacy, probably.

"All right," said Henry Gage. "Tell me, Son. Everything. Don't try to protect me now!"

Walter looked at his father over the raised coffee cup. Henry was gripping the curved wooden arms of his chair as if he were going to break them off.

"He's out, Dad. And it doesn't look like he did it." Walter forced himself to speak slowly and carefully. He told Henry the names of the people who were dead, that Frank had been discovered in the woman's apartment with her blood on him, but that the evidence seemed to show that he'd come into the building after the shots had been fired, and that there was evidence that someone had left the apartment by the fire escape. That that had made Frank look like a victim of circumstance.

The look of relief on his father's face, though, prompted him to caution. "It's not over yet, Dad. Frank's still a suspect—just not necessarily a strong one." He sipped his coffee while he searched for words. "Honestly, I think that if Frank hadn't been my brother—even with the evidence that he came in after the shots—well, he'd still be in jail."

"But he didn't kill those people! He didn't. Ain't that right?"

"No, Dad. I don't think he did. I mean—yes, you're right. I think you're right. If they charged him and put him on trial, I'm fairly certain that he'd be acquitted." Walter put the cup down on the worn coffee table; he had to push aside what looked like some school books to find a place for it. "What we need to do is find out who really did kill those people. When we find that out, and have them in jail—well, that'll be the end of it."

Henry sighed, a long, deep sigh.

"I know you'll do your best, Son. You always do. I'm proud of you, you know. And your mama would be proud of you, too."

But Henry's fingers were kneading the chair arms again.

"Well, thanks, Dad," said Walter. "I'll always try; you know that. You do have to understand, though...this is Ponca City's case. We can't come into it unless Chief Galloway asks us to."

Henry looked up with something like a scowl. "Doesn't sound right to me," he said. "These people—the dead ones—were involved in your big old Indian case, right?"

Walter nodded.

"Then it looks to me like it'd still be your case!"

"It doesn't work that way, Dad."

"Well, it oughta!"

Walter really had to agree. There might or might not be a genuine connection between the murders of Lennon and the Crocker woman and those of the Osage, but he knew he could easily make a case that the O.B.I.

should be involved. He did not want to step on Chief Galloway's official toes, though.

"I'll do what I can," he said.

Henry just sighed. "I know, Son. I know you'll do what you can."

Walter watched his father for a bit then—the kneading fingers, the eyes that darted from Walter, then to the front door, and then back to Walter.

"Something else, Dad? Something else is bothering you. What is it?"

Henry rose from his chair, walked to the door, and stood looking out. Then he turned back. "Callie's gone," he said.

"Huh? What d'you mean?"

Henry opened the screen door and leaned out. "Told her about Frank—that he was in jail—and she just took off crying." He stepped back into the house and let the screen door bang. "She loves her brother," he said.

"Of course she does." It was natural that she would be afraid—how old was Callie? Twelve? Eleven? "I'm sure she'll be back soon, Dad. She's probably at a friend's, crying on her shoulder."

"Don't think so," said Henry. "She's been gone a long time now, and I looked everywhere I could think of. Claude and Mattie are out looking now." Henry made a waving motion with his hand, dismissing what must have seemed to him like Walter's lack of concern.

That was fair, Walter considered. He wasn't worried, not really, about what a twelve-year-old girl might do when her big brother was put in jail. She'd hide someplace and cry; that's all. But his father was clearly concerned, so....

"What do you want me to do, Dad? Want me to look for her? Drive you around? Places you think she might go?"

Henry came back and sat back in his chair, so hard that it rocked back strongly enough that Walter thought that it might collapse.

"We've been to all of those places," said Henry. "Friends—she don't have all that many. The school. Her teacher's. Even the company buildings. Nothing."

"I'm sure she'll come back, Dad. When she's ready. Be patient and don't worry. She'll get hungry and come home."

Henry took a long, deep sigh.

"Maybe," he said. "But there's something else, Son."

"What?" Walter leaned forward to hear his father's answer.

"Ah, shit!" said Henry, and he dropped his head.

Walter had seldom heard his father swear at all, and he couldn't remember ever having heard that particular word come out of his mouth. He immediately got up and went to Henry's chair. He put a hand, gently, on

Henry's shoulder. When his father looked up, Walter realized that Henry was close to tears.

"It'll be okay, Dad. Frank's going to be fine, and Callie'll be back soon. You'll see."

"Frank," said his father, "Frank'll be all right. I believe you. But Callie? Walter, I'm really afraid she's took off and she's out there somewhere, hitchin' a ride or...or...."

"Why would she do that?"

"Ah, darn. Darn. Darn." Henry sat up straight again and gripped the chair arms again. "There was some kind of trouble with Lizzie and I think maybe my baby's run off. Maybe tryin' to get back to Grandpa Cantrell's place. I don't know, Son. But I'm scared."

"What happened, Dad?"

"Callie's never really liked Lizzie. She's been a trouble—not doin' what she's told, sassin' back."

Walter nodded. He didn't have any trouble understanding that. The girl had been taken from the Cantrells' and transitions like that were never easy. Walter didn't know Lizzie all that well—she seemed nice enough, but she certainly wasn't anything like Grandma.

"Kids, Dad," Walter said. "Sometimes we don't behave like we should. I can remember a few times...."

Henry waved it off. "None of you were ever out-and-out disrespectful."

Walter wondered about that, but he wasn't about to argue with his father. "It's been hard on her, I know," he said. "Moving and all. She was used to what it was like at Grandpa and Grandma's."

"Mattie didn't act that way," Henry said.

"Mattie's different," said Walter. "People react differently to things. And Callie's the youngest—the baby. Probably Grandma spoiled her some."

"Yeah, yeah, yeah. I know," said Henry. "But, well, there was some trouble. Some trouble with Lizzie."

"Uh-huh. She disobeys. You told me."

Henry grimaced and turned his whole upper torso in the chair, as if he was in pain. Then he turned back. "I love Lizzie," he said. "She's a good woman. But she did something dumb. I understood it, but it was dumb."

Walter raised his eyebrows.

Henry sighed again. There was a lot of sighing going on, Walter thought.

Walter waited. And watched. And waited.

Finally Henry met his gaze. "She cut up your mother's picture. The big one."

"What? Callie cut up Mama's picture?"

"No, no, no. Lizzie did. Lizzie cut it up."

"Why in the world would she do that?" Walter remembered the photograph. He wasn't sure when it had been taken, but it had been around the house when he was a boy. It might've even been older than he was himself. And it was Mama. Walter, for just the moment he allowed himself, wanted to walk into the kitchen where he could hear Lizzie making kitchen noises and...and do *something*.

"Got tired of hearing 'You're not my mother,' I s'pect," said Henry.

"Jesus!"

"Lizzie feels real bad about it."

"I'm sure she does," said Walter. Having Mama's picture cut up would definitely give Callie a reason to run away. Walter felt that, were he younger and still living with Dad, he might do that himself.

Walter sighed. He needed to get back to the city. Paperwork. Crystal. Restart the process of finding Jack Crocker. Talk to the federal people again, even if that wasn't something he looked forward to. He looked up at his father. The man was worried, deeply worried. First Frank, then this. So he stood, reached for his hat.

"All right," he said. "Let's go look for her."

They drove around the camp, going by all the houses, by the office, through the yards where miles of pipe were stacked. They stopped at the warehouse and asked the men working there if they'd seen a twelve year old girl.

Henry said that Callie sometimes went across the road to play with the Nelson girls, so they asked about her there.

They drove by the school. It was closed for the day, and locked up, but they walked around the building and even tried to look through a few darkened windows.

They checked the pump house and sheds behind Henry's house.

Nothing.

"I don't know where else to look," said Henry. "God damn it! Where did that girl go?"

Walter didn't know, of course. What he did know was that it damned well wasn't safe for an almost teen-aged girl to be out on the roads. If Callie were trying to hitchhike back to the farm, she was definitely in some kind of danger. He leaned far back in his seat and looked up at the car's roof lining. He'd have to go to Longwood, looking for Callie all the way. "Any place else you'd like to look, Dad?"

"No," said Henry. "We've looked ever'where I can think of—most of 'em twice. Let's go home. Hell, maybe she's there!" Walter could see hope in his father's eyes. Yes, it was possible.

But she wasn't. She hadn't been there, said Lizzie. No calls. No knocks on the door. She gave Henry a little hug and disappeared into the kitchen again, although Walter suspected that she had nothing, really, to do in there.

"I don't know what else to do," said Walter. "I'll drive over to Grandpa's place, I guess, and look out for her on the road."

"Come sit," said Henry, and headed for the porch.

Walter waited while Henry sat down, filled his pipe, and lit it. "I really should go, Dad."

Henry gestured to the second chair, smoke wreathing about his head. Walter started to sit, then changed his mind. Henry gestured toward the chair again, and took the pipe out of his mouth.

"Sit down, Son. Please."

Walter nodded. Sitting on his father's front porch wasn't going to help find Callie—or do his paper work, or explain to Crystal why he was out so late—but he sat.

"You've done all you could," said Henry.

There was some sort of scratching noise from beneath them, from under the porch.

General, Walter thought, Dad's collie. He hadn't seen the dog since he'd got here.

But then a blonde head appeared. Callie.

"Oh," she said when she noticed the men on the porch. "Daddy! Oh, *Walter*!" Then she was scrambling up over the edge of the porch, lifting herself, ignoring the steps. Walter had barely managed to push himself out of the chair before she had run into his arms.

Henry just looked at her, apparently speechless. So Walter took the girl gently by the shoulders. "We've been looking all over for you, Callie."

His sister gave a little shrug. "I've been sleeping."

"Under the porch?"

"Yeah. Why not?" Then her expression changed from sullen to worried. "Is Frank all right? Is he out of jail? Do you know? Tell me!" Her eyes darted from Walter to her father and back again.

"Frank's all right," said Walter, hoping that it was true. "Dad can tell you about it." Walter looked at his father, whose face now showed, at the same time, both relief and anger. Walter suspected that the anger would soon dominate. He didn't need to stay around to listen to the lecture, he decided.

"Dad, she's home, and she looks like she's all right." He looked at his little sister again. "Well, except for the dirt and the spider webs in her hair. Now I need to get back to Oklahoma City."

Walter watched Callie rather frantically rubbing at her hair. "I'm glad she's home safe, Dad."

The good-byes were quiet. Henry walked him out to his car and held out his hand. "Thank you, Son," he said. "For everything." He was clearly uncomfortable, probably about what looked like some serious upcoming talk with his daughter, but he still looked relieved.

Walter shook the hand and then patted his father's shoulder. "Things'll work out, Dad."

"Yeah. Probably. Drive careful, Son."

Walter nodded and slipped behind the wheel. Henry simply stood watching as Walter pulled out. Callie was on the porch, holding onto one of the columns; she was obviously in tears. Walter almost stopped the car.

No, there was nothing he could do here; this was between father and daughter. Dad had given very few whippings, even when he or Frank—especially Frank—had done something either utterly outrageous or very dangerous. Callie might get one now, but he couldn't really imagine his father taking a belt to the baby of the family, the baby girl of the family. But she would definitely get a good talking-to.

So he didn't stop. Instead he waved at the two as he pulled out of the drive.

He had plenty to think about on the long drive back to the city. He'd have to start looking for Crocker; that was the main thing.

He hoped that Crystal wouldn't be waiting up for him. Or maybe that she would be.

She was up, waiting and worried and loving. And the job went on. And on. And on.

PART EIGHT

CONTINUING OPERATIONS
Three Years Later

CHAPTER 48

Bluestem Rancher
Gray Horse, Oklahoma, 1932

Sam Persomoie sat on top of the short stretch of wood fence at the edge of his pasture and looked out over his land. The rest of the fence was barbed wire, but he'd left this section just so he could sit on it.

There was a little wind from the southwest and the bluestem grass was just tall enough to begin to ripple. Before long it would be tall enough to wave. His Hereford cattle were nose down in the grass, except for one heifer that was drinking from the water tank about twenty feet or so from where he was sitting. He wondered whether he needed to go check the water.

Sam had spent part of his allotment money to drill a water well there by the side of the fence and put up a small windmill to pump water into the tank. Sometimes, though, the water level got low and he had to prime the pump. And the water got dirty, too, so sometimes he had to drain the tank and clean it. That seemed silly to him sometimes—when he was down in the tank; cattle drank out of muddy creeks all the time and it didn't seem to hurt them.

But these were *his* cattle, bought with *his* money, grazing on *his* land. He'd even been tempted to name them all before he realized that he really couldn't tell the difference between all of them.

He was getting his allotment money from the oil now, right on time, every three months. The agency had even gotten back part of the money that his so-called wife had collected. Not all of it, but some. So he had plenty of money. Not rich like some of the older folks, but still....

He looked to the south, where he could see a couple of pumping oil wells. Production was down around here, he'd heard. Oil was giving out. Two of the wells on his own land had stopped producing altogether—or at least not enough to be profitable to the oil company. So they'd been plugged.

Oil prices were down, too, according to the folks at the agency. He'd heard that there was a whole lot of oil being pumped out of the ground down south somewhere—so much oil that it had caused a big price drop. The more oil there was, the cheaper it was. He could kind of see that. He'd got his cattle for less than he'd thought he'd have to pay because the man he'd bought them from had had too many cattle for the grazing land he had. So it all made some sense.

But then prices for everything seemed to be down. He'd heard the people at the agency in Pawhuska talking about financial things off and on for several years now. Other than the fact that his allotment was smaller, it hadn't really meant much to him.

The allotment *was* smaller—quite a bit, actually. But it was enough. Plenty. Less oil combined with cheaper oil meant less money for the Osage. Not that they needed it, he thought. At least most of us. He let his eyes travel over the cattle again and felt himself smiling.

He'd thought about rebuilding the house, but there hadn't been enough money to do that right and still buy the cattle. So he'd cleaned out a part of the old barn—where the old tack room had been—and put in a bed, a chest of drawers, a table and chair, and a gas cook stove. The stove ran on natural gas from his own wells, so that was free.

The cow that had been drinking wandered off and headed back in the general direction of the herd.

The grass was good. Lots of it. He had a good hay crop stored in the barn; there'd be plenty for winter. He hadn't cut as much as he could have; there wasn't any need to fill the barn. Not yet. Maybe when the herd was twice as large or three times as large. It would be, sometime.

Right now, there were other uses for the barn. Most of the equipment his father had kept in the barn hadn't really been used all that much—his dad hadn't been much of a farmer—and a lot of it was all rusted out. So Sam had gotten rid of most of it; he didn't know how to use some of it, anyway. Now he kept his automobile in the barn.

It was just a Ford—not a Cadillac like some of his people bought, just to leave it sitting in the yard—but it was good enough for him. And he needed it to drive up to Pawhuska to get his allotment and, well, just to buy some things he couldn't always get in Gray Horse. Besides, he kind of liked the lady who ran the store there. Her husband, too. And they always seemed glad to see him.

Cadillac? Hell, no. He had better use for his money.

He looked out across the fields again, imagining ranch hands on horseback moving cattle toward a loading pen, getting them ready to ship out to market somewhere.

Horseback. Shokah was getting old, he supposed. Not really all that old, even for a horse, but the old fellow'd had a kind of rough life, out on the prairie like that, being ridden for hours at a time, living on whatever he could find and put his nose to.

Oats now. All he could eat. Sam took him out every day, saddled him up, and rode him out into the pasture. Took it easy, though. He needed to go check to make sure that none of the cows were down and to look out for coyotes—not that the coyotes would take down a full-growed Hereford, but there'd be calves someday. And the exercise was good for Shokah.

Sam smiled and rocked a little bit on the fence. Anyway, the horse always seemed glad to see him and was still eager to go.

Calves. Sam supposed that he'd have to get a better bull sometime. Now, that would require some thinking. He'd seen some mean bulls and he damned well didn't want a mean one. And there was the cost.

The agent fellow up at Pawhuska had told him when he'd talked about buying cattle that he had to be careful about what he bought and who he bought them from. There were still folks out there, the agent had told him, who'd try to cheat him just because he was an Indian. Things had changed, sure, but not that much.

But he'd wound up buying his cows from another Osage man—well, half-Osage, like Sam—from up around Barnsdall. The fellow still called the town Big Heart, but they'd changed the name to Barnsdall a couple of years back. Then he'd had to hire a couple of trucks to haul them all back to his place.

Sam sighed. So he'd probably have to buy a truck, too. Cattle'd have to go to market sometime and the cattle market was clear up at Grainola, where the railroad was.

Sam shook off thoughts of bulls and trucks and money and climbed down from the fence. Time to take old Shokah for a ride. He dusted off his pants and headed for the barn and Shokah's stall.

Shokah was glad to see him and whinnied a greeting.

"Hello, old pal," said Sam, and pulled the bridle off the hook on the wall next to the stall. "Want to go for a ride?"

He led Shokah out of the stall, put the bridle on, and took the old saddle from atop the barrel where he kept it. Shokah puffed and stamped a little while Sam got him ready.

"Good fella," said Sam, patting the horse's flank. "Easy now."

Outside the barn, Sam stroked Shokah's neck. He had just turned to mount when the bullet struck him in the back of the head.

CHAPTER 49

Hydrostatic Pressure
Oklahoma City, Oklahoma, 1932

Walter pulled into the parking lot at 7:45, his usual time to get to work. Work was different, these days. Having a parking lot was itself a difference, actually. He looked up at the building in front of him and the sign. *Oklahoma Bureau of Investigation.* More change. New building. New sign— partly because the agency had a new name.

The lady at the telephone desk smiled at him as he came through the door. He thought her name was Wilson, or maybe it was Williams. He hadn't had much contact with her, really, even though he'd hired her. She was night staff; that was another difference—operating twenty-four hours.

The lettering on the door to his office was different, too: *Director Walter Gage.* His desk was empty, but he knew that would change pretty rapidly. He glanced around. Well, same old furniture, at least.

The damaged hand had almost, in a strange way, turned out to be a blessing. Walter had missed being in the field at first—he still missed it from time to time—but being stuck at a desk had seemed to bring out his real talents. He'd found that not only was he good at organizing and administering but that he found satisfaction in those things, too. The higher-ups had apparently thought that he was, too, because when Duncan retired, he'd been offered Duncan's job.

And there was plenty of organizing to do.

Duncan's retirement and Walter's subsequent appointment to the head of the bureau had fairly closely coincided with the legislature's changing the name of the bureau and passing the bill that provided funds to buy the new building.

The building wasn't really *new*, of course; it had been a small warehouse at one time. It looked good, though, Walter thought; the state had done a nice job of fixing up the place, despite a very tight money situation. Walter's own salary, despite the promotion, was almost the same as it had been; money, though, went farther now than it had in the past. Prices, like everything else, were down.

Walter felt a bit lucky that his salary was as good as it was. He certainly wasn't going to get rich on what he made, but he knew that he was far better off than many, perhaps most, people. Banks had failed, wiping out the savings of thousands of people. Farms had been foreclosed on—or sometimes just deserted.

His own family had been affected, too, just not as much as some others. Oil production was down in a number of places, but there was still drilling going on. Brother Frank still had work. Brother Tom was now in Lovell, still pumping and still raising a family. Walter didn't know how much money they made now, and he wasn't about to ask. But they were surviving—doing a lot better than some.

The bureau had needed the added space. New building. New technology. Increased staff. There were usually more support staff in the building than actual agents. During the day there were three women handling telephone calls.

Besides Walter's office, there were offices for the chief inspector and the man in charge of the firearms division. There were also a fairly large space that held the desks of the agents assigned to the Oklahoma City office, an office-work area for the new fingerprint people, another large room used for meetings, a smaller meeting room adjacent to Walter's office, and a couple of yet smaller rooms that were called "interrogation rooms."

Then, too, there was a locked store-room in the back filled with weapons—a lot of machine guns. Walter had never fired one of them and didn't plan to.

Thinking of the machine guns reminded Walter that he expected to hear from Jim Gravel today. Gravel loved the guns and made sure he always had one in the back seat of his car. He'd gone to Konawa to check on another, all-too-common, bank robbery there and should be reporting in.

The O.B.I.'s function now was mostly support, providing information to the various law enforcement agencies and, when possible, coordinating their efforts. Even though agents spent less time actually investigating crime, there was still a heavy workload for all of them. Crime in the state had always been at a high level, made worse by the oil boom and now, maybe even more so, by the depression.

So Gravel would have been working with the local police around Konawa. No doubt there would be federal marshals involved and quite possibly the F.B.I. Walter had already been in touch with the local federal agent about the Konawa robbery, and he'd need to call him back after he'd talked to Gravel.

The federal agency had changed, too. Expanded. There were local offices all over the country now. And they'd had a name change, too. They were now officially the *Federal* Bureau of Investigation. They had a new chief, too, somebody named Hoover. Walter hadn't had any contact with the man, but the agents he'd met or talked to who worked under the man seemed to respect him.

Walter opened the file drawer in his desk and took out the first folder: the list of his agents, where they were currently located, and what they were working on. The murder of a Tulsa attorney who was reputed to have gangland connections. Bank robberies in McCloud, Anadarko, Inola, oil towns of Fairfax and Earlsboro, more. Walter looked at three robberies on the list and sighed.

Castle, Meeker, Stonewall. All high priority. Walter had four agents assigned, but they were a very small part of the investigation. The bandits in this case were well-known, and not only in the state of Oklahoma. Charles Floyd, George Birdwell. Killers. They'd almost been captured several times, but had always escaped. At times leaving dead officers behind.

Walter put the list down and sighed. Some people, he knew, were protecting Floyd. He'd supposedly torn up mortgages at the banks he'd robbed. Walter had heard stories of his giving food and money to farmers in trouble. Hell, even his sister-in-law Ramona, Tom's wife, liked the man. Her car had stalled out on the road, and he'd given her a ride into town. He was "charming," she said.

Yeah. Charming. And deadly.

The telephone rang. Ah, Gravel.

But the voice didn't belong to Jim Gravel. "Walter Gage?" said the voice.

"Yes."

"You may not remember me," the man on the other end of the line said. "My name is Brown. I'm the chief of the Osage Nation police force. We met some years back."

"Ah, yes," said Walter. "I remember." He'd met the man just once, back when they were investigating the Osage murders, but if he remembered correctly, Brown hadn't really been any help. "What can I do for you?"

"This isn't really official business, but I thought you'd like to know. Sam Persomoie was found murdered yesterday afternoon."

"What?"

"Yes," said Brown. "He was found by the fellow that pumps the wells on his place. Sam'd been shot in the head and his horse was limping around the barnyard."

"Any idea who shot him?"

"Not one. Look," said Brown, "I've gotten to know Sam Persomoie pretty well over the past few years. He was a good guy. All that stuff from the past—that was over. The tribe took him back in, and they don't do that very often."

"I see," said Walter. "Look, I don't know what the bureau can do about it. We can't really even look into it without an official request. Hey! Is this an official request?"

Walter heard the man's sigh over the line. "No, it's in the hands of the sheriff. The only way I can be officially involved myself is if we find out another member of the tribe shot him. And that didn't happen."

Walter was silent for a moment, thinking of what to say.

"Well," said Brown, "I thought you'd want to know. I won't bother you any longer."

"Wait," said Walter. "If there's any chance—any chance at all—that this is involved with the murders of your people, then we *are* involved. I don't know right now, right off the top of my head, what we can do, if anything, but I will get back to you and I'll put in a call to the sheriff's office as soon as we hang up. Where can I reach you?"

"You may not be able to. I'm at the agency office in Gray Horse right now, but I'm not going to be here long and we don't have a phone out at our place."

Well, thought Walter, maybe somebody would have to go to Gray Horse. Then something occurred to him.

"Hold on a second," he said. "Did Persomoie marry? I mean, really marry—not that fake thing. You know who gets his oil allotment now?"

He heard something like a chuckle on the line. "No," said Brown. "He didn't marry anybody and he didn't have any living relatives that we know of, so his allotment just goes away—back to the tribe."

"How about his land, then?"

"Goes back to the tribe, I suspect. I imagine it'll be sold."

"Really?"

"Yep. I'd hope it could stay in the tribe, but I don't make those decisions."

"Umm. All right. I see. Thanks."

"I thought you'd want to know."

"I did. I do. We *are* going to look into this. At least I am."

After Brown had hung up, Walter sat for a moment, just looking at the telephone. It could be just some sort of random killing. Persomoie had lived a kind of rough life and maybe he'd made enemies. But one enemy that Walter knew of was still at large.

Crocker had probably killed Taylor and he'd probably killed Lennon. And Sam Persomoie had testified against his uncle and his brother. Revenge was a motive, even after six years.

Walter thought, just for a second, about calling the Osage County sheriff. He started to reach for the telephone, but a thought stopped him. If the damned fool was looking for revenge there were more people in danger!

He considered for a moment. Gravel, yes. McMurray and the other federal agents weren't around any longer; they were probably out of the man's reach. Darden, definitely. Carstairs, the justice of the peace that had issued the fake marriage certificate. Duncan. They'd all have to be warned. And me.

Oh, God. Frank, too.

The morning girl—her name was Daisy—stuck her head in the door.

"You have another call," she said. "He says that he's agent Donahue of the F.B.I."

Walter nodded his thanks and picked up the receiver. "Hello, Max," he said.

"Hey, Gage! Just thought I'd touch base with you on a couple of things."

"Always good to talk to you, Max. What's up?"

"First thing: our people in Indiana picked up Jake Morrow last night, so you can wipe that Tallequah bank job off your list."

Walter hadn't thought about the Tallequah robbery for some time. Morrow had been identified by people at the bank; after all, he'd been a local boy. But he'd gotten away and nobody had known where up until now.

"That's good," he said.

"He got shot up a little bit," said Donohue, "but we'll be shipping him back to you when he can travel."

"We'll be looking for him," said Walter. "Thanks. You told the folks in Cherokee County?"

"Nope. Thought I'd leave that up to you!"

Walter laughed. "Well, you need to send him there. That's where he'll be tried."

"We'll see about that," said Donohue. "That's not up to me."

"Well, we'll get that worked out," said Walter. "Thanks for letting me know; I appreciate it."

"So, Gage, you have anything for us on that Konawa job yet?"

"No, I'm waiting for a call from Jim Gravel—he's our agent in charge of that."

"Okay, let me know when you hear something. And, oh, yeah, one more thing. Old Pretty Boy and his sidekick pulled a job in Wisconsin a day or two ago, so he's apparently out of your hair."

"Yeah," said Walter. "If they really did it!" Pretty Boy Floyd and George Birdwell had been accused of almost every crime committed in the state of Oklahoma for some time—even for robberies that took place at the same time a hundred miles apart. "And I'm not so sure he's out of our hair. He killed an ex-lawman in McIntosh County about a month ago."

"Yeah, well, there was positive identification this time," said Donohue. "Didn't kill anybody for once, and it looks like they got clean away. But we'll get 'em. Sooner or later."

"Let's go for sooner," said Walter. Floyd might be charming, all right, but he was still a killer. "Anything else, Max?"

"No, that does it, I think. Let me know when you hear from your man."

"Wait a second," said Walter. "I've got a question for you."

"Shoot."

"Max, I know you weren't around for the Osage murders investigation, but we're still missing one of the men involved. I know he's on your wanted list. Fellow named Jack Crocker. You have anything new on him? Could you find out?"

"Nothing comes to mind, but I can check. Why him in particular?"

"Something's come up," said Walter. "A man who testified against those people in court was murdered the other day. It's possible that Crocker's doing some pay-back."

"Yeah. That doesn't sound good. Look, I'll check our records here—not that I think that'll help—and then I'll call Washington. Any idea off the top of your head where he might be, where he might have gone?"

"No," Walter said. "We haven't had a good line on him since the arrests back in '26. There's a good chance, though, that he was responsible for a pair of murders in 1929—so there's a fair possibility that he's still in the midwest, at least."

"Okay," said Donohue. "If you don't hear from me in a couple of days, give me a shout. And, hey, guy, don't be impatient with me. We're just a little busy here. But that kinda fits us all, doesn't it?" A few pleasantries and promises to stay in touch ended the conversation.

Daisy came in with a stack of papers, put them on his desk with a smile, and retreated to the front. Walter could hear movement in the outer office, so he supposed that all the day shift was present. He glanced at the wrist watch that Crystal had given him for Christmas. Meeting in fifteen minutes and he needed to look at the papers he'd been brought. So with effort he pushed Jack Crocker out of his mind as he tried to remember what he needed to tell people at the meeting.

Ah, hell. He'd bluff it. He'd done that before.

He took his notebook out of his top drawer, gathered the papers, and headed for the meeting room.

"If Agent Gravel calls," he told the girl at the desk, "interrupt the meeting. I need to talk to him."

She nodded and smiled and Walter went to his meeting.

CHAPTER 50

Back to the Reservation
Northern Oklahoma, 1932

The meeting was routine, and it came off without any complications or interruptions. Gravel hadn't called. Walter gathered his papers and turned to Dougherty, the new (fairly new) Chief Inspector. The man had been a successful federal marshal and had been, in Walter's estimation, a valuable addition to the staff. He'd pushed to get Jim Gravel, but that hadn't happened. Gravel had turned down the job before, when Walter had been appointed, and he'd turned it down again.

"Anything you need from me, Ralph?"

Dougherty grunted, and Walter took that for a "no."

"I haven't heard anything from Jim. You going to be in the office today or are you headed somewhere?"

"I'll be here this morning, but this afternoon Garner and I are headed down to McAlester. Goin' to talk to old George Bell about some of his buddies still on the outside."

"Yeah. Good luck with that." Bell was serving a life sentence and Walter couldn't imagine that he'd be all that willing to help law enforcement.

"Gotta try," said Dougherty. "Shit, Gage, even if the bastard gives us names, we probably couldn't find 'em." Dougherty shrugged. "Gotta try, right?"

"Yeah," said Walter. "Good luck. Look, I think I may be going out of town myself. I'm going to tell the girl out front to transfer any of my calls to you for the rest of the morning. That be a problem?"

Dougherty grunted again. This time Walter took it for a "yes," but that didn't matter.

"If Jim calls, take some notes for me. Put one of the women on the line if you think that'll help."

Dougherty grunted again. Walter smiled at him and went back to his office.

He tossed his meeting notes on top of the stack of papers Daisy had dropped on his desk earlier. For a moment he considered moving the notes and looking through what she'd brought. It wouldn't do any good, he thought. The Persomoie killing was running through his head, twisting, turning.

"I'm going to have to go to Gray Horse," he said aloud.

It was probably going to be a waste of time. His place was here, in the office. Men in the field would probably be calling, and he wouldn't be here. Dougherty was leaving this afternoon. Well, Morgan could run the office if he had to. "I can call in," Walter thought. "I will."

He told Agent Morgan that, after Dougherty left for McAlester, he'd be in charge of the office for the rest of the day and then all day tomorrow. He stopped at Daisy's desk and told her where he was going and that he'd call in when he knew where he could be reached. He started out, then remembered that he hadn't told Dougherty where he was going.

"No," he decided. "He didn't need to know."

The trip to Gray Horse was going to take a couple of hours at least and he'd almost certainly have to spend the night, either there or, more likely, at Pawhuska. So he'd need his razor and a change of clothes. So he headed home.

Crystal was at home all the time, now. The job shortage had been such that it was simpler for her to be a housewife. He knew that she'd rather be working. She'd hinted that he could, considering the fact that the Bureau was hiring new employees, give her a job himself. He knew that he really couldn't, though. Even if he'd somehow managed to do it, the criticism he'd have gotten for it—and there definitely would have been criticism—would have made both himself and the office less efficient. And they didn't really need the money. She'd understood, as she always seemed to.

He told her where he was going and why, listened to her reasons why he shouldn't go, and packed a change of clothes. Then he took her in his arms, told her that he loved her, that he'd be back as soon as he could, and that he'd call. She hugged him back and kissed his neck. Then he left.

He didn't know what he might be able to accomplish in Gray Horse. But if Persomoie's death had anything to do with the old Osage case, then it was definitely Bureau business. If what Brown had told him was accurate—and he had no reason to think it wasn't—then there probably wouldn't be any useful evidence. But he could ask around town, at least. And at Pawhuska. Maybe somebody would remember seeing Jack Crocker—if he'd been there at all. He had photographs to show, so maybe....

If Crocker was really back... Damn! He'd forgotten to call Duncan. Darden needed to be warned, too. And that justice of the peace. Hell, he didn't have any idea where Darden had gone. Was he still in Ponca City? The j.p.? Ah, Duncan was probably safe, at least for a while. Since his retirement, he'd moved out of the city and pretty much out of public view; Crocker probably couldn't find him, at least not easily.

So Walter would have to go to Ponca City after he'd been to Gray Horse, to see if he could find Darden.

Jesus! He'd need to talk to Frank, too. Frank hadn't been involved in the Osage thing, but he had been involved with Crocker's wife. So he might be a target. The killing of Crocker's wife and of Lennon was still open. Frank had been cleared, but whoever had actually killed them was still out there. And the odds were damned good that it had been Jack Crocker.

Frank was in Ponca, so he'd look him up while he was there. If he could find the place. Hell, he'd been there just once since Frank and Bobbie had moved from the camp into an apartment in town. Well, anyway, he'd find him.

He could imagine how Frank would take to being *warned*. He'd probably tighten his fists and his face and try to go looking for Crocker. Well, he'd have to be warned, anyway.

The road had been improved since the last time he'd driven to Gray Horse, and so had automobiles. He wouldn't have to stop at a creek to get water for the radiator this time. How long ago had that been? Eight years. A lot had happened in eight years.

Depression. Dust bowl. Crime. Oklahoma had gone through governors like water down a drain pipe.

But his own family had done well enough. Luck, maybe, a little. Certainly some of them deserved to do well. Grandpa and Grandma deserved more than they'd ever got, but they were all right. Grandpa was, he knew, looking forward to the Presidential election. Roosevelt was going to be the savior of the country, he'd insisted. He'd hated Hoover. Of course Grandpa had always pretty much hated whoever held power. Walter had the feeling that he was pretty close to right this time, though.

Dad had always worked hard, and he'd raised a family under some trying circumstances. He'd probably not gotten what he deserved, either, really, at least in terms of money. But Dad hadn't ever really seemed to care that much about money, as long as there was a warm place for the family to live and food on the table.

Things hadn't gone so well for his father lately, though. Production in the Braman field had almost stopped, and the wells Henry Gage had been taking care of weren't putting out enough oil, considering the low oil prices, to keep them pumping. So Dad was back in Kaw City, working for an outfit named Big Chief Drilling. Walter thought he remembered that there was some sort of connection between Big Chief and the company Dad had worked for before, but he couldn't remember what it was.

Like almost everyone, his father was probably getting by on quite a bit less money than he was used to making. Walter hadn't wanted to ask. At least Dad was close enough to check in on Grandma and Grandpa Cantrell.

Walter's brothers and sisters were all doing well enough. Walter had felt good about going to college, getting a degree, but he suspected that Claude was going to put him to shame. His youngest brother was at the university at Norman now, majoring in petroleum engineering, and he was a straight A student. He'd probably wind up rich.

Mattie, the beauty of the family, had married. A good man, as far as Walter knew—another oil field hand; so at least he had a job. Tom was still old steady Tom, raising his own family, much like Dad, except without the complications.

Of course there was Callie. Walter had to chuckle, even if doing it made make him feel a little guilty. Callie was quite possibly the brightest of them all, but she'd turned out to be a handful, giving Dad fits.

She'd skipped a couple of grades, so at fifteen she was a senior in high school. So she'd graduate a couple of years early—if she managed not to be expelled first. She'd been in trouble at school a couple of times. She certainly hadn't looked or acted fifteen the last time he'd seen her. Bleached blonde hair, high-heeled shoes, lipstick. Walter could just imagine what his father was going through with the girl.

Walter didn't know the half of it.

CHAPTER 51

Wildcatting
Northern Oklahoma, 1932

At the time Walter was driving toward Gray Horse, Callie Gage was on the back of a motorcycle that was tearing across the country on the way to Ponca City. She wasn't particularly happy about it: the wind was playing hell with her hair, for one thing.

For another, she really didn't trust the guy she was holding onto. She'd liked the idea that he was twenty years old, that he was fairly good-looking, and that he seemed to think she was some kind of catch.

It wasn't so much that he was trying to get her to go to bed with him; she'd been fending guys off for a couple of years. It wasn't the drinking so much, either; Callie didn't mind having a drink or two herself. But there was something about him.

Dad had warned her about him. She admitted to herself that that was probably one of the reasons she was on this damned motorcycle with her carefully permed and molded hair turning to a blur around her head.

The immediate reason, though, was that she'd been suspended from school again. It had been that damned Barney Roland's fault. He'd put his hand on her breast at a dance once and she'd slapped his face; he'd been trying to get her into trouble ever since. Today he'd succeeded.

It hadn't been much. She'd been walking toward the front of the room to turn in her English theme and he'd dropped a handful of beans on the floor in front of her. Naturally she'd stepped on one, right on one of the heels of those high-heeled shoes that her dad hated. Her ankle had turned, the damned heel had snapped off, and the bean went flying. Then she'd said, quite loudly, "Shit!"

That might have gotten her some time after school and a lecture, but unfortunately it hadn't ended there. She'd managed to keep from falling on her butt and she'd wheeled around and was giving the little asshole a piece of her mind, when Mr. Logan interrupted. And he made the mistake of calling her "oil field trash."

When she'd finished telling him what she thought of him, she'd guaranteed herself a two weeks' vacation. Dad would have a fit, of course, so Callie hadn't decided whether or not to tell him. There wasn't a telephone at home anymore, so the school couldn't call him—if they would even bother.

And if Callie was on her way to Ponca City, she wouldn't have to answer any of his questions about why she wasn't in school. Johnny had promised her he'd get her home at the usual time, and he'd better!

Dad was too hard on her, she thought—almost mean. It was that darned Mattie's fault. Mattie had gone to dances and stayed out late. She'd never gotten in any trouble that Callie knew about, but he'd heard Dad tell Lizzie a lot of times that he was afraid that they were giving Mattie too much freedom.

And that meant that Callie didn't get *any* freedom. Damn it. She didn't even get to play basketball on the school team—just because Mattie had played basketball.

Then Mattie had gone and married that Nathan guy and left home. Things immediately got worse.

She knew that she loved her Daddy. It just seemed like he didn't want her to grow up. Yeah, she knew that she tried to look like the women she saw in the picture shows, especially Jean Harlow, and that Dad didn't like it. He'd told her, over and over again, until she was sick of it, that she was pretty without all that makeup and the bleached hair.

But she knew better. Mattie was pretty; Callie was ugly. The old scars had faded a little, but they were still there. If the makeup and the bleach fooled people into thinking she wasn't disgusting to look at, then good.

Johnny swerved to pass an old Chevrolet and Callie jerked. "Hey! Careful! I almost fell off!"

He looked back at her. "Didn't, though, did ya?"

"For God's sake watch the road!"

"Yeah, yeah, yeah," he said, but he did turn around.

Callie didn't like her face, but she was proud, a little, of her mind. She was smart; she knew that, whatever that counted for. Not much, though. Claude could go to college, but he was a boy. She'd never get to go herself. Mattie had had a woman she cleaned house for offer to pay Mattie's way to go to nursing school. She'd wanted to go, but Dad had said no. Apparently the school was run by Catholics and somehow that was bad; Callie didn't know why.

Callie liked her makeup and her hair. Boys seemed to think she looked all right and she wasn't about to disillusion them, at least if she could help it.

But sometimes—just sometimes—she wouldn't mind being a little girl again. Growing up was scary. Hell, being anybody was scary, no matter how old you were. Aunt Claudie's spiritualism stuff was scary. Rattlesnakes were scary. And spiders.

And this damned motorcycle was scary! Johnny was making it go faster and faster!

"Slow down, Johnny! Slow down!" She yelled at him, but he just laughed.

CHAPTER 52

I Did a Bad Thing
Kay County, Oklahoma, 1932

"Don't know 'bout you," said John Blaine, "but I'm gettin' hungry."

Frank Gage turned from the river and looked at the old man. Hungry? He hadn't even thought about food since that salt pork in the morning. What time was it, anyway? He brought up his arm to look at his wrist watch, and almost lost his balance in the process.

"Careful there!" said John Blaine. "You fall in that river, you're a goner!"

"Yeah," said Frank. "I s'pose so."

"Whiskey's gone, too." The old Osage man fidgeted a little and stood up, pulling his legs back from the ledge. "Don't know about you, but when I don't have neither whiskey nor food, I get right antsy. I'm goin' back to the house."

Frank looked back down at the river. It was still roaring away to the south, but the speckles of white had faded. The trees behind them and the bluff itself were cutting off some of the sun's rays now. Sun was going down. How the hell long had he just been sitting here in some kind of fucking trance like his Aunt Claudie?

"You comin'?" asked Blaine.

Frank stretched. "Might's well," he said. What did he have to lose, anyway? They'd find him, sooner or later, and this time there wouldn't be anything old Walter could do to haul his ass out of the fire.

"C'mon, then." Blaine reached out a hand to help Frank up.

Frank was a little surprised that he needed assistance. He was stiff from sitting so long. But the old man was stronger than he looked and Frank had to scissor his feet to keep from being dragged. Between them, though, they finally got Frank to his feet.

"Let's go find us some whiskey," said Blaine, gesturing off toward the house.

"Food?"

"That, too."

Frank followed Blaine up and out of the sandstone hollow and around the old cottonwood. It was quite possible that the old man would use his telephone to call the law when they got to the house, but it didn't seem to really matter.

When they were on level ground, Blaine looked back over his shoulder at Frank. "I know you," he said.

"Yeah, you told me," said Frank. "I'm Dillinger or somebody."

"No. Really." He pushed aside a blackjack limb and stepped onto a path, one that Frank hadn't seen, hadn't known about. "I remember you from when you was a boy. Took me a while to place you, that's all."

Frank ducked under the limb. "Huh?"

"Yeah. Same gawky body, same eyebrows—and somethin' behind the eyes, too. You're Miz McCracken's boy."

"Naw," said Frank. "I'm her nephew. How the hell you remember me? That was years ago!"

"Oh. All right. But you was here once. And I remember."

Back at his house, Blaine called out to someone to get some food on the table and to someone else to get a fire going. Then he led Frank into a large parlor and told him to sit.

"Be right back," he said, and left the room.

Frank leaned back in the leather chair and watched a young white man arranging logs in the fireplace. Servants. Hard to imagine what it'd be like to have people paid to wait on you. Wouldn't be too bad, actually, he thought.

Old John came back with two glasses and a bottle of whiskey. "I think we both could use a little of this," he said, "and food's comin' up. Be a little while, though, so we can just set." He put the glasses on the table by the chair Frank was sitting in and poured the whiskey. "And while we drink, you tell me your story. All of it."

Frank was glad to have the drink. He let the whiskey dance around in his mouth while he wondered how much to tell the old Indian and how much of it should be the truth. Out on the trail he'd just grunted and Old John had, for the moment, let it go. But now he was asking again.

The old man could certainly call the law. Frank didn't see a telephone in the room, but there almost had to be one in the house. He sighed. A jail cell. For how long this time? Maybe forever if the policeman had died. Frank finished the whiskey in the glass and held it out for more.

"I did a bad thing," he said while Old John re-filled the glass. "Something really fuckin' stupid."

CHAPTER 53

Tripping Pipe
Ponca City, Oklahoma, 1932

Walter pretty much drew a blank at Gray Horse. He hadn't expected more, really, but he'd still hoped.

The man at the agency was distressed. He had nothing but good things to say about Sam Persomoie. It seemed that Jack Brown had been right about the man's being re-accepted by the tribe. That was confirmed by a visit to one of the tribal elders. But no one had any idea who might have killed him.

And no one recognized Jack Crocker from the picture he showed them.

He debated with himself about whether to drive out to Persomoie's place to look things over for himself, but finally decided against it. The murder itself wasn't a bureau case—at least not yet. His interest—and the bureau's, really—was in Jack Crocker. So, instead, he drove on to Pawhuska.

Pawhuska didn't prove to be any better. The sheriff's office was "investigating." The Osage County sheriff's department had been notoriously lax in its handling of the Osage tribal killings. Walter wouldn't even have called what they'd done "investigating." "Ignoring" was more like it. At least they'd put on a better front this time. Walter reminded himself to be fair. All they had was a man killed by a single rifle shot. No gun. No witnesses.

No one had seen Jack Crocker—or anybody else suspicious. Some knew Sam Persomoie. A lady in a little general store had tears come into her eyes while Walter was talking to her. "He was a good young man," she'd said.

Walter thanked the woman and started out, but she stopped him.

"Does this have anything to do with the murders in the past? The Osage?"

"I don't know," said Walter. "I'm trying to find out."

Outside the store, he looked at his watch. There was still time to drive to Ponca; he might still be able to find Darden tonight. He'd try.

Johnny didn't get Callie home by the time she usually got home from school. He didn't get her home at all. He'd taken her to a party with some people he knew and everybody was sitting around drinking and smoking something Johnny called "mary jane."

Callie had taken a puff or two, but it didn't taste good. Tobacco was all right; Callie smoked regular cigarettes once in a while, but the mary jane stuff just plain stunk. So she'd tossed it away. That'd made Johnny mad at her for some reason. He'd called her a "fucking bitch" and then got so drunk that he passed out on the floor.

She was tempted to just take his damned old motorcycle and go home. Unfortunately, she didn't have the slightest idea how to make it go. So how the heck was she supposed to get home?

Walter checked his watch again as he neared Ponca City. It was a lot later than he'd hoped. He'd run into a construction mess on the highway, with one-way traffic for several miles, and then he'd been stuck behind an old farm truck that was weaving all over the road.

Not much of a chance, really, of driving back to the city tonight. Well, maybe he'd have time to do what he needed to do and still head back. If he managed to find Darden and warn him—and Frank, too—he might....

No. He was tired already and going to sleep while he was driving didn't seem like the brightest of ideas.

The road into Ponca took him by the Pioneer Woman statue—a marvelous piece of work, Walter thought. There were lights overhead in the little park it sat in and somebody had installed some kind of spotlight to illuminate it in the dark. He'd stopped at it before, just to look it over. It wasn't too hard to imagine his Grandma Cantrell as the woman in the statue. Well, except Grandma probably had never been that slim.

He passed the Marland mansion, too. A huge place. As far Walter knew, Marland still owned it, but he'd heard that the man cou afford to live there anymore. Instead he lived in a smaller house— an artists' studio or something—on the grounds. Marland was ru Congress now, and Walter supposed that he'd vote for him. really paid much attention to the man's platform—if he even Marland had put a lot of money in the hands of a lot of wo that had to count for something.

It was dark outside now. God, how had she so long? Callie looked at her wrist watch. Hell, it would be pacing up and down. Or he'd be remembered with more than a little embar Braman when he and Walter had looked al under the porch the whole time. Well, sh that was for sure. Dad would be furiou her before.

There were a bunch of guys standing around on the front porch of the big old house where the party was going on, and Callie had to walk past them to leave. They'd called out to her as she went by and one had tried to grab one of her breasts. She twisted away and went down the rickety steps toward the street. Somebody called after her, calling her a foul name and grabbing his crotch. She wanted to turn around and let the jackass know what she thought of him, but she knew that doing that would be a mistake. So she just kept walking.

She turned to her right when she reached the street, but there wasn't any good reason to choose one direction over another. Johnny's motorcycle was at the curb facing west. So it seemed to make sense to go east, back the way they'd come. If that was really the way they'd come; she'd been too busy just holding on to watch where they were going.

Where should she go, provided, of course, that she could find her way? She stopped walking for a moment and looked back at the house. No one was following her. Thank God. She stood there for a moment, letting her shoulders sag. She supposed that she'd have to call Dad.

But he didn't have a telephone anymore. She could call the camp and somebody would go tell him where she was. Hell. The camp offices wouldn't be open this time of night. Shit.

That left Frank. She had his address because she'd written him a couple of times, once to thank him for the blouse he'd sent her for her ___ She didn't really see how that could help her much, though. ___ name was one thing; knowing where the street *was* was

___ that dirty old camp. God, she'd seen
___ Ugh. And she damned well
___ he he was rich.

___ . Oh, yeah.
___ ections. That
___ she'd been to

___ head for the

___ what she thought

___ even be at home.
___ d him talking about
___ t that meant that he
___ it now, though, and it
___ be at work. His wife
___ o, but waitresses didn't
___ e.

___ as
___ dn't
___ uilt as
ning for
He hadn't
ad one—but
king men, and

managed to stay here
___ as after ten thirty! Dad
___ ut looking for her. She
___ assment the time back in
___ over for her and she'd been
___ e wasn't under any porch now;
___ with her. Well, he'd been mad at

She had to laugh at herself a little. She was worrying about whether anybody'd be at home and she didn't even know where that home was. She turned north at the first block.

There was a brick sidewalk here, so she didn't have to walk in the street. Some of the bricks, though, had sunk into the ground more than others, so walking on them in her high heels was awkward. Callie considered taking off her shoes, but doing that would almost certainly mean that she'd ruin her stockings. So she walked in the street anyway.

She'd had a little bit to drink, but not enough to make her wobbly. But it had probably been enough to make her sleepy. Of course it getting late, so being sleepy was sort of normal. But sleep was probably a long way off. Frank and Bobbie probably didn't even have a sofa for her to sleep on, so the next time she slept in a bed would probably be when she got back to Kaw City. And when that would be she had no idea. She probably should have just stayed at the party.

No. Johnny was too drunk to handle that motorcycle even if he woke up, and staying there all night would clearly have meant that she'd have had to fend off his drunken friends. Callie hadn't been a virgin for a while now, but that didn't mean that she was going to have sex with some stranger just because he wanted her to. So she kept walking.

Walter drew another blank.

Darden's old place of business was clearly shut down. There weren't any lights on, of course, but Walter could see by the headlights that the racks of pipe were gone; the lot was empty now, except for the shack that had been the office. The building's windows were boarded up, and the sign was gone. Of course. Darden had been bought out, but he'd thought there was a chance that the man was still trying to stay in business somehow. But, if he was, it wasn't here.

He didn't have a home address for Darden. He should have looked to see if there was a home address in their records before he left the city. No. There almost certainly wouldn't have been one. Hell, Darden probably wasn't even in Ponca any longer.

Well, he'd managed to waste a whole day and, with his luck running the way it was, there was probably some big crisis back at the office and things were going to hell while he was out here doing nothing. He shrugged.

So he found a telephone and called in.

No crisis. Gravel had called. Nothing new and he was staying in Konawa for at least another day. Dougherty and Garner weren't back from McAlester. Morgan had gone home, of course, so anything that he might've been told by anybody was unavailable. No, the night girl said, he hadn't left any message for Mr. Gage. And, no, there was no address for Darden in the files.

"Very well, then," Walter told her. "Leave a note on Agent Morgan's desk for me. Tell him I'll be back some time tomorrow and he's in charge until either I or Agent Dougherty show up. Got that?"

She did and she would.

Walter put back the receiver and sighed. He could just head home. Or he could get something to eat—when had he eaten last? And then try Frank's. And if he wasn't there, start checking all the taverns in town for Frank or all the eateries for Bobbie. Or both. Eating could wait, he decided; Frank might be in danger.

After ten o'clock. Whatever he was going to do later, he needed to call Crystal now.

Callie decided that she needed to find the café where Bobbie worked. If she wasn't there—and she probably wouldn't be, the way things were going—somebody there would know where she and Frank lived. She remembered the name of the place because she'd thought it was funny when she'd first heard it: Eagle Eats. She'd wondered then what eagles ate. Hamburgers? Prairie dogs? What *did* eagles eat, anyway?

There weren't any street lights on the block, so it was too dark to look at her watch. Probably eleven o'clock. Damn. Dad would have gone from being angry to being worried. Neither one of those things was good. Bad, but for different reasons. Callie considered that she might be justified in disobeying; after all, she wasn't a child any longer. But worrying Dad— maybe even scaring him—was clearly a bad thing.

The next block had some street lights along the curb. She checked her watch, but it told her only what she already knew.

The houses she was passing now were nicer than the oilfield houses she was used to, but they weren't fancy or big. Cars parked along the street or in the gravel driveways were mostly Fords and Chevrolets and none of them looked new. These were working people's houses. Probably the men who lived in these houses worked in stores or businesses of some kind. Not oilfield workers. If they had jobs.

She knew that jobs were sometimes hard to come by. Things were better now, Dad said, than they'd been a few years ago. But she'd been able to tell, sometimes, that he was worried about money. She wondered, briefly, how Johnny could afford his motorcycle. He did have a job, working at a place that sold tires. He just helped put the tires on the cars, though, so he couldn't be making much money. But he always seemed to have money for whiskey and for that funny stuff he smoked.

The light in the sky to the north was brighter now. Callie thought that that meant she was closer to downtown, but it might just be because the rest of the sky was so dark.

The street lights carried on into the next block and there was a sidewalk that looked safe to walk on, so she left the street. The houses she was passing now were older. Most of them had two stories, but they didn't look fancy. A couple of the houses had porch lights burning, so she could see that at least some of the houses had flowers or plants of some kind next to the door. She wondered for a moment whether she should just walk up to one of those houses and knock.

Maybe later. If she had to.

Then, after two more cross-streets, there were little businesses. A cobbler. Closed. A little grocery store. Closed. A little furniture store, the words on the window said, but there was a "for rent" sign on the door. A barber shop with a pole in front. Closed. Another empty storefront, this one with a cracked window.

And a gas station on the corner. All lit up, and they would have a telephone! She could call Dad. If she had to. If they'd let her use the telephone. It might be a pay 'phone. She stopped and looked in her purse. A dime, a nickel, and three pennies. Was that enough to pay for a call? She didn't know.

Oh, hell. How could she call somebody who didn't have a god-damned telephone? Jesus!

She shuddered at the thought, but she might have to go back to the house where Johnny was. He'd been passed out, but maybe there was somebody sober enough and nice enough to drive her home. Knowing Johnny's friends, though, and what had been going on back at the house, if she did find somebody to take her home, he'd probably expect her to have sex with him. She shook herself: only if she absolutely had to.

She could try to hitchhike, she supposed, but that was almost certainly a bad idea; it was a good way to get raped.

At the filling station corner she looked down the street both to her left and to her right. She couldn't see anything in either direction that looked like it might be Eagle Eats. But then she didn't know what kind of sign they had; if it was just a flat sign, maybe over the door, or just painted on the window, she couldn't see it from here. Hell, would they even be open this late?

She looked back at the service station. There weren't any cars at the pumps, but the place was lit up. It was probably safe. So she could ask for directions.

CHAPTER 54

Streams Converge
Ponca City, Oklahoma, 1932

Chief Galloway had almost certainly gone home for the day, but Walter decided to try the station anyway. If Crocker was really on some sort of revenge rampage, the police chief himself was a potential victim. Walter was quite sure the chief could take care of himself, but he should be warned, anyway. Besides that, Crocker was still a suspect in the murders of his wife and Lennon. Galloway needed to know, for more than one reason.

Galloway was in his office, as it turned out. He seemed glad to see Walter and stood up, walked around his desk, and shook Walter's hand.

"Good to see you," he said. "But what are you doing here this time of night?"

"Came to see you, actually," said Walter. "What are *you* doing here at this time of night?"

"Yeah, I know it's late," said the chief. "We had an oil tanker turn over out on 60, and we've got two men out sick. So—well, that's why *I'm* here." Galloway straightened up and pointed a finger at Walter. "Your turn!"

"Damn," he said when Walter had answered his question. "You think it was Crocker?"

Walter looked down at the chief's clean desk and considered how his own would look when he got back to the city. "There's no way to know for sure," he said, "but we have to consider it."

"Yeah," said Galloway, slumping into his chair. "Bastard."

Walter leaned forward. "Chief, if it is Crocker and he's trying to kill the people who put his brother and his uncle into prison, you're almost certainly on his list."

Galloway sat up straight. "I hope to hell that I am!" he said. "I'd like for him to come after me, so I could put a bullet between the bastard's eyes."

"Sam Persomoie didn't get a chance," said Walter. "He was shot in the back of the head. Rifle. Most of us can't see behind us. You have to be careful."

"I'm always careful," said Galloway, "but I appreciate the warning. You have any reason to believe he's around here?"

Walter shrugged. "No idea. We don't have any idea where he went when we put the others in the pen. We can't even prove he killed his wife and Lennon—or Inspector Taylor."

"Don't have any doubts, though, do you?"

Walter sighed. "Not really, but we couldn't even come close to proving it."

"Yeah," said Galloway. "And that's a good reason to just shoot the fucker."

Walter put his hands on the arms of the chair and pushed himself up. "I need to go, Chief. You be careful, hear?"

"All the time," said Galloway. "You, too."

Walter smiled at him. "Right. All the time."

At the door Walter remembered and turned back to the chief. "Say, Chief, you happen to know what happened to Darden? His old place is shut up and deserted. He still in Ponca?"

Galloway stood and took a couple of steps to a filing cabinet. "As far as I know, he is," he said, pulling open the top drawer. "One of our people stopped him two or three weeks ago. He'd had a little too much to drink and got pulled over. Ah, here it is!" He pulled out a file and opened it. "Got an address here. Don't know if it's still good, but it was—let's see— yeah, about two weeks ago." He brought the file to the desk. "I'll write it down for you."

Walter thanked him, took the paper the chief handed him, folded it once, and tucked it into his breast pocket. Then he turned, again, to go. "Be careful," he said.

"You said that," said Galloway, with a smile.

"Yeah, I guess I did."

Darden's house was out at the north edge of town, farther from the station than Frank's apartment, but Walter's car was pointed in that direction. So, for no other reason than that, he headed for Darden's.

He had no idea what kind of house Darden would be living in now that he'd recovered some of his money. He suspected, though, that he was renting.

The house, when he found it, wasn't surprising. It was a small white house with a small front porch and shutters over the windows.

It was dark.

Walter swore to himself. If Darden wasn't here, he had absolutely no idea where to look for him. The man definitely needed to be warned, but if Walter couldn't find him, well....

There was no answer to his knock. The man might be asleep, perhaps passed out from too much alcohol. So Walter knocked harder.

There was still no answer, so Walter tried the door. Unlocked. If Darden was asleep, he'd wake him up. He stepped quietly through the door.

The smell hit him immediately.

He was afraid of what he would find, but he searched the wall for a light switch. What he saw when the ceiling light went on was, if anything, even worse than he'd expected.

Darden's body lay face down in the middle of the small living room, surrounded by a lot of blood. Walter leaned over the body. The blood hadn't clotted completely, so whatever had happened had happened not too long before.

The wounds on Darden's back looked like exit wounds. He was tempted to turn the body over, but restrained himself. This was, at least initially, a Ponca City case; he shouldn't, then, do anything with the body.

Frank! Frank needed warning now more than ever!

First, though, he had to call the local police department.

Waiting for the police to arrive was one of the hardest things Walter had had to do. If Chief Galloway had still been in the office, Walter would have asked him to send a car to Frank's, but the officer who answered the telephone didn't really give him a chance to ask.

"Stay where you are," the man had said. "And don't touch anything!"

So he waited.

After the two officers in the patrol car arrived, Walter was told to stay outside on the porch and not to go anywhere. He didn't recognize either of the men, and of course they didn't recognize him, either.

His O.B.I. badge got no response at all. He went so far as to suggest they call the chief to verify who he was, but they simply ignored him, even when he tried to plead his case for warning others of the danger they might be in.

He understood their attitudes well enough; after all, he might even, from their point of view, be the shooter. That didn't mean that he had to like it. He was tempted to leave in spite of being ordered to stay, but decided that he really couldn't justify doing it.

So he paced. And looked at his watch. And paced.

People arrived with cameras. People came for the body. Time passed. Then Sergeant Cook arrived with another officer.

Cook was willing to listen to Walter's brief explanation why he couldn't stay. The other officer looked on in disbelief that his superior was letting someone—someone who might be a suspect—just leave.

"I'll be back," said Walter. "I promise. Just as soon as I can!"

He looked at his watch again as he opened the car door. Almost eleven. Damn. He shuddered at the thought that he might be too late.

Frank's place was south of the main drag and several blocks west. The streets Walter had to drive on, for most of the distance, were residential, so he had to control his speed. He turned off on Grand and had a few blocks of business district.

The man at the filling station—Callie thought that he might be twenty-five or so—tried to flirt with her a little, but she'd just kept smiling until he gave up and told her how to find Eagle Eats. The café, it turned out, was just a few blocks away. She thanked him and started down Grand Avenue.

She wished she were wearing different shoes. The high heels were fashionable and they looked good, but her feet were hurting. They'd been hurting for quite a while, actually. She considered once again the possibility of walking in her stocking feet, but decided against it. At least she'd get to sit down, for a while at least, when she reached the eating place.

Then what? If Frank's wife wasn't there? She let out a deep sigh. She'd have to try to call the camp, even if the office was closed. Maybe somebody would answer.

Then they'd either have to go get Dad to have him come to the 'phone or just tell him to come and get her. She could easily imagine his face if that happened. He'd not only be mad at her for taking off like she'd done but he'd be embarrassed, too.

What could she tell him? It'd have to be a lie. She shook her shoulders in exasperation: there couldn't be a story good enough.

Some teen-aged boys in an old Ford passed her and one of them leaned out of the window and waved and whistled. She ignored them, of course. She looked up ahead. Eagle Eats should be in the next block if the man at the station was right. Of course he might be laughing his rear end off right now while he imagined her heading off in the wrong direction.

But there it was. Finally. Despite her sore feet, Callie began to walk faster.

Walter had to deal with a truck blocking the way and then had to go around the block to avoid some sort of street work that was going on. This seemed to be his day for having to deal with obstructions—of all kinds.

He finally got back on track. Then he saw, just at the end of the block, headed in his direction, a familiar figure.

His sister Callie.

Couldn't be, he thought. Lots of girls nowadays bleached their hair and tried to look like movie stars. So he dismissed it.

The girl, whoever she was, started walking faster and then turned into a lighted storefront. As he drove by, he glanced at the building. Eagle

Eats. The name was familiar somehow. Oh, yeah. That was where Frank's wife, Bobbie, worked. Bobbie should be warned, too. And if Frank was out on the rig, she'd know where he was. He pulled to the curb.

The little café wasn't busy at this time of night. The movie show crowd would have come and gone. Anybody here now would probably be somebody who did some kind of shift work.

There was one waitress—not Bobbie—behind the counter, putting pieces of pie into a little glass cabinet. The pie looked good.

There were people in a couple of the booths, but the stools at the counter were all empty. So Walter took a seat at the counter and looked around. Just because Bobbie wasn't visible didn't mean that she wasn't here. She might be in the kitchen; she might be taking a break. He'd have to ask. He considered having a piece of that coconut pie, but reluctantly rejected the idea.

Before the waitress had finished what she was doing and turned to wait on Walter, he felt a tap on his shoulder.

"Walter?"

He turned. The girl with the bleached-blonde hair and the clothes that were too old and too flashy for her was looking at him expectantly.

"Callie! What the dickens are you doing here?"

Walter listened to Callie's story with a bit of astonishment. Imagining his baby sister involved with the people she described was difficult, even when he considered how she was dressed and her bleached hair.

"I'll take you home, Callie," he said, "but I have something I have to do first." There was no reason to tell her about the potential danger to Frank. Or about Darden. He was sure she knew about his work, but he wasn't sure how much Dad had told her. At any rate, she didn't need to know any more.

"Oh, thank you, Walter! Thank you! Thank you!" Then her face fell. "What'll you tell Dad, Walter?"

Walter met her eyes. "The truth, Honey. That's what I'd have to do."

She dropped her eyes. "I know," she said.

Walter pushed the pie plate away. When Callie had sat beside him he'd yielded to the coconut pie, in part because she was having some. "You stay here," he said. "I need to talk to the waitress. Okay?"

Callie nodded.

"Want anything else? Another piece of pie?"

"No," she answered. "I shouldn't be eating this one."

"Me, either," he said, patting her on the shoulder.

The waitress wasn't any help. "Bobbie Gage? I don't know who that is."

"Doesn't she work here?"

The waitress turned to the man at the grill. "Hey, Al," she said. "Somebody named Bobbie Gage work here?"

Al looked up. "Who wants to know?"

"I do," said Walter. "She's my brother's wife and I need to find her."

The man turned halfway back to the grill and began rubbing it with a rag. "That so?"

"Yes," said Walter, beginning to wonder if he'd need to show his badge.

"Brother's name's Frank, then?" asked the man.

"Yes," said Walter. "It is. So that means you know Bobbie, right?"

"Uh-huh. Don't work here no more, though. Quit a couple of weeks ago—maybe three."

"Well, you know where I could find her—them? It's important."

The man stopped wiping the grill and came over to Walter, wiping his hands on the cloth he'd been using on the grill.

"You're sure you're his brother? You don't look much like him."

"I'm sure," said Walter, "and the girl down at the end of the counter is his sister."

There was no reaction from the man.

"You want to see some identification?" asked Walter. He leaned over the counter. "Look. I need to find him. It's important! If you have the slightest idea in hell where I could find either one of them, tell me!"

The man backed away.

Walter backed away, too. He took a long, deep breath. "I'm sorry," he said. "I didn't need to yell at you." He dug into his jacket pocket and took a five dollar bill out of his wallet and put it on the counter. The man reached for it, but Walter picked it up again and waved it at the waitress, who was looking at him with something like alarm.

"This'll pay our check," he called to her, "and you can keep the change."

Walter looked at his sister and could see that she was trying not to laugh.

"Knock it off," he told her, "and let's get out of here."

CHAPTER 55

A Visit to Apartment 3
Ponca City, Oklahoma, 1932

Callie was giggling as Walter hustled her out of the café.

"All right, all right," said Walter, pushing her—gently—toward the car. Despite his concern for Frank, he had to smile a little. "You just saw your brother have a little temper tantrum. Remember, young lady, I've seen you throw a few of those!"

Callie just laughed.

In the car, though, when Walter told her as much as he thought she needed to know about the possible danger to Frank, she didn't laugh any longer.

Walter had never been to his brother's apartment, but he knew the street name and the house number—if it *was* a house rather than an apartment building. It wasn't all that far away, just part of a block off the main drag. He found the place easily. It was a house, the only one on its side of the street. The rest of the block was dominated by one-story brick buildings, stores of some kind, or perhaps offices.

"You stay in the car," he told Callie. "I'll just be a minute."

"Can't I go in with you, Walter? I'd like to see Frank!"

Walter almost agreed, but then considered how the conversation might go.

"No, Honey. Better stay here." He patted her shoulder. "I'll be right back, and then I'll take you home. Okay?"

Callie nodded, but Walter could tell that she didn't want to.

"I won't be gone long, so I'm going to leave the car running. But if you take off on me, I'll skin you alive, young lady!"

He left her and headed toward the house. There wasn't any yard as such; the house was right up against the brick sidewalk. There were seven or so steps up to the front door. The house itself was just about what he would have expected. It clearly needed a coat or two of paint; the steps were a bit shaky. A screen on one of the front windows was hanging by one hook. Yeah, it looked like a place Frank might live. A little fancier, actually.

He wondered about knocking. The place clearly contained a number of living areas, but it was possible that a family lived downstairs and rented apartments on the top floor. The height of the steps suggested, too, that there might be living quarters of some kind in the basement.

Perhaps, then, there was a second entrance, maybe at the side or rear of the house, for renters.

A glance through the full-length glass on the front door, though, showed a hallway with closed doors on each side—doors with numbers. 1 and 2. At the rear of the hall was a staircase. Frank's apartment number was 3, so it was probably upstairs. So Walter didn't knock. The door was unlocked. So far, so good. He went up the stairs.

How long had it been since he'd seen Frank? Too long; he should have taken more time for his family. Oh, well.

Apartment number 3 was on the right side of the hall at the top of the stairs. Walter started to knock, then noticed that the door was ajar. He knocked anyway and the pressure of his knuckles on the door caused the door to swing open.

The front room was empty. There was a beaten-up old couch and an easy chair with stuffing coming out of the frayed armrests. The place didn't look lived in. Bobbie might not have been the greatest housekeeper in the world, but there was absolutely no sign of a woman's touch.

Then the bedroom door swung open, and Walter heard a voice saying, "Gage! We've been waiting for you!"

Walter turned when he heard the voice. It wasn't Frank's voice. What he saw caused him to freeze.

CHAPTER 56

The Bottom of the Hole
Ponca City, Oklahoma, 1932

In the car, Callie was fretting. How mad her father was going to be didn't seem to matter. Something was going on—something bad. Walter had joked with her, but there'd been something about his face—something that told her that there was some kind of trouble.

Frank? He'd been in trouble before. Was he in trouble again? Yes, she'd been told to stay in the damned car. But she wasn't some damn' kid; she could damn well do what she wanted to do. She pulled down the handle on the car door and turned to get out.

And immediately stepped halfway on the curb and halfway off, turning her ankle. She sat down quickly and rubbed her ankle. She felt like crying. This was one terrible fucking night! Shit! What else could go wrong?

Walter stared. The man standing in the door was *Simon Crocker*. Beside him, just a step behind, were his brother Jack and a third man.

"Oh, it's you," said Jack Crocker. "We were waiting for your asshole brother!"

"This is even better," said Simon Crocker. "I think I've met this guy before!"

Crocker had changed. His sideburns were gone. The suit was gone; he was wearing rough work clothes that were clearly too large for him. He was thinner, paler.

"You're in the penitentiary," Walter managed to say, realizing almost at the same time that it was a ridiculous thing to say: the man was standing in front of him.

Crocker smiled. "You can see that I'm not."

Jack Crocker stepped forward and put an arm over his brother's shoulder. "As of about ten o'clock last night," he said, "my brother became a free man!" He smiled.

There were guns. Three of them, now all pointing at him.

Walter considered reaching for his own gun, but he knew that doing that would just get him killed more quickly.

"How'd you manage it?" he asked Simon Crocker, partly stalling and partly because he wanted to know. "You didn't get pardoned or paroled. If you had, I'd've known. What happened?"

Crocker smiled, an ugly smile. "I have friends," he said. He turned his head slightly toward the third man. "Hey, Ed," he said, "Say hello to the state police agent here, Ed. Remember, he's the one I told you about."

"We busted him out," said Jack Crocker, with a grin. "Fuckers let him go out on a work detail. Dumb sons-of-bitches!"

"Yeah," said Simon Crocker. "My good ol' brother here and old Ed just knocked a couple of those stupid guards in the head and here I am!"

Then he stepped forward and put the barrel of his pistol under Walter's chin, forcing it up.

"Good to see you again, asshole," he said, pushing Walter's head even farther back.

It was the chance Walter needed.

He jerked his head back away from the gun, slammed his right hand into Crocker's shoulder, and used his left wrist to push the gun away. The push turned Crocker halfway around and Walter immediately wrapped his left arm around the man's neck and squeezed, lifting Crocker a little and pulling him back, his right hand reaching for the gun.

He managed to turn Crocker so that he was between him and the others, shielding himself from their guns, at least for the moment. Then he had Crocker's gun.

But then it all went to hell.

Crocker had been trying to pry Walter's arm away from his neck without success, but now he grabbed Walter's left hand—his bad hand—and twisted.

The pain was excruciating. There was no choice: he had to let go. He raised a knee into Crocker's back and pushed hard, sending Crocker sprawling.

Walter raised Crocker's gun, hoping to hold off fire from the other two men. And, yes, they both stood there, wide-eyed.

But Simon Crocker had a second gun. He quickly recovered from his fall, and came out with the weapon.

But Walter fired first, and the bullet struck Crocker in the chest.

The others were firing now. The first bullet stuck Walter's right shoulder and the gun slipped from his hand. The second smashed into his chest. It felt like a sledge hammer. He staggered, fell against the door frame, then slid to the floor.

"We've got to get out of here," he heard someone say.

"I'm not goin' to leave my brother!" said another voice.

"He's dead, asshole! We got to go!"

Walter knew he should be getting up, but couldn't seem to move. Then he felt Jack Crocker's foot smashing into his side. The pain was like fire.

Then the door slammed. They were running. Somehow Walter forced himself to a sitting position and then managed to stand.

Reaching down for the gun he'd dropped wasn't, somehow, all that painful, but his coordination wasn't good. All he managed to do was to push the gun farther away.

He gritted his teeth. They were getting away.

His own gun! Damn. He managed to pull the pistol from his shoulder holster.

The pain was there, but it wasn't important.

He managed to take the few steps to the open door and looked out. The hall was empty, but he could hear the men on the stairs. Quick. Quick.

He stumbled once on the way down to the entrance hall, but managed not to fall.

To his surprise, when he burst through the door to the street, Jack Crocker and the other man were still standing on the sidewalk at the foot of the steps, yelling at each other.

"He's my fucking brother!" he heard one of them yell.

Walter raised the gun.

"Stop!" he shouted, but his voice was weak; they didn't even seem to hear him. Then they were turning away, leaving. They weren't going to stop; they were going to get away.

So he fired.

His hand was shaking, though, and the bullet went wide, slicing off the sidewalk.

Crocker ran, but the other man turned and fired.

Callie, sitting in the car with the door open, saw the two men come running out of the house. She watched them, but without any real interest. People ran all the time. She rubbed her sore ankle.

Then there was the sound of a gun firing and some kind of changing sound. She looked up to see one of the men turning back toward the house and raising his hand. With a gun in it!

He fired as Callie started to turn and to slump down in the seat, to hide. But as she started to slide, she saw Walter, standing at the top of the steps, with a lot of blood on the front of his shirt. Then he was falling, tumbling down the steps, and smashing into the bricks.

Callie screamed. Her first impulse was to run to Walter, but she saw that the men were running away. Bastards!

She slid to her left, slammed her left foot on the clutch and jerked the car into gear. For part of a weird second she was grateful that her skirt was so short; she could never had made the movement in the kind of dress Dad wanted her to wear.

Then the car was surging forward. Callie jerked the steering wheel and the car smashed against the curb and then leapt it. The impact threw her backward and she lost her grip on the wheel.

Then, directly in front of her—in front of Walter's car—a man turned, the man who'd shot her brother. Callie screamed vengeance at him; then the car was crushing him against the storefront.

"Got you, you bastard," Callie managed to say.

Then the storefront gave way. Bricks came crashing through the car's window at the same time Callie's head was jerking to her right. A brick smashed into her cheekbone and broken glass sliced into her face and neck.

CHAPTER 57

God-damned Guns
Northern Oklahoma, 1932

So it was that when Henry Gage came to Old John Blaine's house near the Arkansas River, he had, for his son Frank, both good and bad news.

He didn't bother with the good news—that Frank was not going to jail for the incident with the cop at Shidler; the bad news was too overwhelming.

He'd been awakened sometime around four a.m. by loud knocking at the front door. He'd felt Lizzie's movement as she got out of bed, and tried to go back to sleep. He had no idea what time it was, but he could tell from the way his body felt that he hadn't been in bed long enough.

Then Lizzie was shaking his shoulder. "Henry. Henry. You have to wake up. Honey, you have to wake up!"

Henry got up and staggered into the living room, with Lizzie holding his arm and propelling him forward. Carl Schlosser, the production superintendent—and Henry's boss—was at the door.

Had to be some kind of emergency. Well on fire? What?

"Henry," Schlosser had said, "your daughter...."

Then Henry had grabbed the man by both shoulders. Callie. He'd waited up and waited up until Lizzie had finally nagged him into bed. Fear roiled up inside him and, for a bit, he couldn't speak.

Schlosser reached up and took Henry's hands from his shoulders. "She's been in some kind of accident, Gage. She's in the hospital in Ponca City."

"What happened? What the hell happened?" Henry could tell that he was shouting, and he felt Lizzie's hand on his arm.

"I don't know. Just got a call," said Schlosser. "Some Ponca cop called and told me to find you and give you the message."

"Cop?"

"Uh huh." Schosser reached forward and put a hand lightly on Henry's shoulder. "He said it wasn't life-threatening or anything, but that you had to know."

"Yeah, yeah," said Henry. Then he turned and headed for the bedroom and his clothes. "I gotta go," he told Lizzie over his shoulder.

As he'd dressed it occurred to him that he ought to have thanked Schlosser, but it was too late for that.

He'd had to be really gruff with Lizzie. She'd wanted to come with him. "No, damn it!" he'd said. "You stay the hell here!"

Only when he was out of the drive and a quarter mile down the road did he wonder why he'd insisted she stay. She and Callie didn't get along, sure, but he knew Lizzie'd be worried, too.

Hell with it. He kept driving.

Callie was sleeping when he got to the hospital. He looked at her bandaged face and wanted to cry.

The young doctor—he couldn't be more than twenty-five or so, Henry thought—patted him lightly on the back. "She's going to be all right," he said. "Lot of stitches, but she'll be fine."

Henry looked at the bandaged face of his youngest daughter and knew that, no, she wouldn't be fine. There would be more scars. But at least she was alive. There was that.

"What happened?" he asked the doctor.

"I can't tell you that. But Chief Galloway's right down the hall. He's been waiting for you." The doctor put his hand on Henry's elbow. "Come with me. I'll show you where to go."

Henry resisted, but the doctor squeezed his elbow gently. "She'll be all right. I promise you."

And Henry'd let himself be led out.

The policeman in the waiting room shook hands with Henry. "My name is Galloway," he said. "I'm chief of police here in Ponca City." He gestured to one of the metal-legged sofas by the wall. "Have a seat, Mr. Gage, please. We have some things to talk about."

Henry's first thought was that Callie was in trouble. Perhaps she'd broken some kind of law. Car wreck. Wait. Who was driving the car? Whose car?

He sat, but before the policeman could say anything, he asked the question. "Who was driving? Is he all right?"

He watched Galloway take a deep breath, then sit on the adjacent sofa. "I'll get to that," he said. "There's a lot to tell you, Mr. Gage, and some of it—well, some of it isn't good."

It was far from good. Henry heard Galloway's first few sentences quite clearly, but after those words, they were mostly just a little noise, like a wind's shaking the window screen.

Callie. Walter. Walter!

Then he felt a hand on his shoulder and looked up. Galloway was standing, now, in front of him.

"You all right, Mr. Gage? Can I get you something?"

"No," said Henry. He stood up so fast that Galloway had to step away quickly to avoid a collision. "I've got to get out of here!" he said, and brushed by the chief, headed for the door.

"Wait!" said the chief. "You sure you're all right? Where are you going?"

Henry looked at Galloway and then looked at his own work shoes. He realized that he didn't have an answer to the chief's question. He didn't know where he was going.

"I think we need to call someone for you," said Galloway. "This has to be hard. Look, you probably shouldn't to be driving right now. It's not going to do anyone any good for you to hurt yourself."

"We don't have a telephone," said Henry.

Galloway just stood there and Henry realized that he wasn't making much sense. He shook his head and tried to find words. The best he could do, finally, was "I need to tell my people."

"Yeah," said Galloway. "Look, I know that people had to call around to find you, but somebody did get through to someone who could get a message to you. Can we call that person back? That do any good?"

Any good? Nothing was going to be *any good*. Hell, yeah, they could call Schlosser and he'd walk over to the house and tell Lizzie that Walter was dead and Callie was all cut up. What the hell good would that do? What could Lizzie do about it, then? She couldn't call Mattie and she couldn't call Claude and she couldn't call....

Frank! Frank was off somewhere hiding from the law. Henry mentally kicked himself. He'd have already told Frank he wasn't in any real trouble now over that mess in Shidler if he hadn't been sitting on his rear at home, waiting for Callie. Well, he had to be told. And he had to be told about his brother. All the telephones in the world wouldn't reach Frank right now. There was only one thing to do.

He had to find John Blaine's place and look for his son. Now.

The police chief had tried—nicely—to detain him, but it hadn't worked. Henry drove north out of Ponca City, heading in the direction of Newkirk and the Arkansas River.

It was almost nine o'clock when Henry turned onto the road leading to the old Indian's house. Where the hell had the time gone?

He didn't know. He hadn't thought about much on the trip north. He hadn't allowed himself to think. At first he'd kept getting images—memories of Walter as a boy, huddled over a book, his eyebrows knotted. Walter standing proud in his graduation robe. Walter with the biggest smile he'd probably ever had, looking down at Crystal on their wedding day. Henry fought the images away and tried to concentrate on the road ahead.

He'd expected to have to hunt for Frank out in the woods, maybe for hours. But he knocked at the old Indian's door, anyway, just in case. And Frank was there.

So Henry told him about Walter. "He's dead, Son, and Callie's hurt bad."

Frank had to force himself to concentrate to understand the rest. His own head was swimming, and Dad's voice was almost a whisper.

He understood enough, though. His brother was dead. Doing what he was supposed to do, damn it. His baby sister had killed a man and was badly injured. She'd killed the wrong man, though. That damned Jack Crocker was off somewhere. At least the other brother was dead. Small comfort. No comfort at all.

And Frank, the boisterous, loud, fearless, and sometimes angry son, shut down. For a minute or two, he just sat there. Henry wanted to reach out, to touch him, but something held him back, told him somehow just to wait.

Old John Blaine, though, didn't hold back. The old Osage stood and took a step forward. "These men—these men who killed your son—they are the murderers of my people. Is that not so?"

Henry looked up and met the old man's eyes. "I think so," he said. "That's what I understood."

Then Blaine was shaking Frank by the shoulders. "Gage! Gage!"

Frank turned his head to look up at the old man.

"Your brother—your sister, too—are heroes. They will be heroes to my people and they should be heroes to yours!" He stopped, then, and stepped back. "Be proud, Gage. Be proud."

Frank just shook his head. And Henry's emotions had, at that moment, nothing to do with pride.

Henry offered to take Frank back to Ponca City with him, but Frank wanted his car. He insisted, so Henry drove him as close to the car as he felt it was safe to do.

"Looks like you've had a lot of rain here," Henry said. "I don't want to take the chance of gettin' stuck out here. You all right to walk from here? You sure you're not goin' to be stuck yourself?"

"I'll get 'er out," said Frank, opening the door.

"I'll stick around and see," said Henry.

"I'll see you back in Ponca, Dad." And Frank moved through the weeds.

In just a few minutes, Henry heard the sound of a car motor starting up, and then the whine of tires, slipping in mud. But then there was Frank, moving past him and waving.

"Ponca," he heard his son shouting, and then he was gone.

So Henry followed, thinking now about Callie and wanting to be by her. She'd be scared, he knew. And she'd have to deal with more scars. Damn, damn, damn.

Frank was waiting for him where the drive from the Blaine place met the road. He rolled down his window as Henry pulled up beside him.

"Dad," he said. "You need to be with Callie, but I think you need Lizzie with you right now. So I'm goin' to go to Kaw and pick her up and bring her back to Ponca. I'll see you back there as soon as I can. Okay?"

Lizzie. Henry hadn't even thought about her. It made sense. At least he guessed it did. So he nodded and put the car in gear. Then he remembered.

"Frank," he called out. "I went to Shidler. There aren't going to be no charges filed."

Then he pulled past Frank and out on to the road.

Frank headed back toward Ponca City, wondering whether he should stop and see how Callie was before going after Lizzie. Or just go on to Kaw. He saw his father's headlights behind him, then they were beside him. He'd never known his old man to drive that fast before.

Frank didn't stop at the hospital. Instead he made the turn to head east toward Kaw City. He sometimes felt as if his head was coming off: so many thoughts—coming fast upon each other, overlapping, expanding, retreating. Walter falling beneath the wagon. Callie running and leaping into his arms. Walter trying to teach him the words to some song or other and how really badly Walter sang. Callie opening Christmas presents.

And Bobbie. Damn.

Frank drove right past Kaw City and into Osage County. He needed to see Callie, yes. He needed to pick up Lizzie, yes. But he had to see Bobbie. He needed to go to their place in Fairfax. Would she be there? Or would she be with that Perkins woman? Back in Shidler. Yeah, he'd check that first. Hell, he probably owed that Perkins bitch some kind of apology, too. Maybe.

But when Frank was pulling into the dying, almost dead town he'd always known as Whizbang, he thought of something, pulled into a beat-up, weedy driveway and turned around.

Gun. God-damned guns. Hated the sons-of-bitches.

It took almost half an hour, kicking weeds and stomping around through the ditch to find the gun—the policeman's gun, the gun he'd tossed out of the car. But there it was, hiding underneath a patch of sunflowers.

Frank picked it up and stuffed it under his belt.

PART NINE

SAND

CHAPTER 58

The Death Card, Upside Down
Wichita, Kansas, 1960

In front of a small wood-frame house on South Market Street in Wichita, Kansas, there is a wooden sign. *Fortunes Told*, it says, in bright red letters outlined in blue. A second sign, on the window of the front door, says simply *Madame Isabella*.

Inside, in what would have been, at one time, a small living room, two women sit at a folding card table. One of the women, wearing her coat in spite of the rather warm weather, is clearly nervous. Her hands keep moving, touching her coat, brushing back her bangs, running along the edge of the table. Her eyes dart around the room.

The room, small already, is made smaller by the number of *things* that fill the room. There is a large picture of the Virgin Mary on the wall to her left. On the fireplace mantel to her right is a stand holding a large crystal ball, a bowl of artificial flowers, and a small statue of the Buddha—no, the little lettered card in front of it says "Ho Tai." But it looks like a Buddha. On the wall behind the woman opposite her is a large crucifix.

"Please cut the cards," says the woman opposite—Madame Isabella, we presume. "No, with your left hand." When the cards are cut, she begins to deal them out, spreading them on the table, counting aloud as she places the cards in rows, five per row, with the fifth card turned face up, until there are seven rows.

"Now," she says, "we will see what the Tarot has for you in the future. Are you ready?"

The woman nods, but Madame Isabella can tell that she is nervous, so she reaches out and touches the back of the woman's hand. "We need to know," she says. "If there are bad things waiting for us—and there are always bad things—then we can be prepared. Please don't be afraid."

"I'm not afraid," says the woman, but it's clear that she is. She pulls back, a little, from the table. "How do I know this will work? Please. I need to know some things. I really need to know!"

Madame Isabella smiles at her. "We all do," she says. "I must be honest with you, though. The Tarot will tell us the truth, but it doesn't always tell *all* the truth. And I don't want you, at least for now, to ask questions. We don't know exactly what affects the cards, but it seems clear that anxiety on the part of the counselee can skew the interpretation."

"I can't ask you questions?"

Madame Isabella smiles. "It's better that you don't. If I'm thinking of your questions, I might be tempted to change my interpretation. It's better simply to let the Tarot work."

The woman slumps a little, apparently in resignation.

"All right," says Madame Isabella. "Now we'll begin." And she begins turning cards.

"The Six Cups," she says. "This usually has to do with memories."

"Memories? What kind of memories?"

"Ah, by itself, it means just that: memories. Let us see the next card, shall we?" She waits. Then the woman nods.

"The next card is Aaron." Madame Isabella looks at her customer with something like pity. "This card is both good and bad," she says. "You see that it is upside down. That means something is bothering you, worrying you. But it is next to the Six Cups, and that is good. Things may be bad now, but your memories will be good ones."

Madame Isabella looks up at her customer, who is now leaning forward, looking at the cards, her eyes bright.

Madame Isabella turns up the next card.

"The Egyptian Sudan," she announces. "A dark-haired man. May I ask if you're married?"

"No," says the woman. "That's one of the things I wanted to ask about." Her hands flutter.

"Wait," says Madame Isabella, and turns the next card. "The Order of Mopses," she says, and a big smile crosses her face.

Her customer leans forward. "What? What is it?"

"Someone loves you," says Madame Isabella. "But he hasn't told you. Perhaps he is afraid to, afraid of rejection. But he does love you."

The woman's mouth opens into a large O.

"But there is something else here," says Madame Isabella. "Gossip. You will be the object of stories about you. Perhaps the gossip will be about you and the man, perhaps the dark-haired man, but perhaps not. However, the gossip will pass and no great harm will be done."

The woman rocks a little in her chair and presses her hands together and holds them against her lips. "Oh, please, please go on," she says.

And Madame Isabella goes on, turning cards and explaining what they mean. Only rarely does she decide not to reveal some negative things.

So they sit there for a while, the young woman, nervous but eager, and Madame Isabella, wearing a robe covered with crescent moons, the right side of her face covered with scars.

CHAPTER 59

Sand
Lakin, Kansas, 1972

After Linda left to drive back to Kingman, where she was teaching English in the high school, Frank stretched his long legs out in front of him, and pulled his hat down over his eyes.

In a little while, it would be time to get up from his chair and walk down Main Street to the City Café for supper, but he wasn't really hungry. He thought about Linda's story. Dumb. He wondered why she'd ever believe anything like that. He brushed away a buzzing fly.

Bobbie, he thought. Pretty Bobbie with her little funny-painted lips and big ol' brown eyes. And her funny little giggly voice....

Vivian, from out in Wyoming. God, that woman could cuss and, God, how she made you feel like a man. That reddish-blonde hair and the smile that made fun of you and laughed with you at the same time....

And that pretty whore in New York that he'd caught trying to pick his pocket. Caught her red-handed, but she'd been pretty and kinda funny, so she'd wound up with most of his money, anyway; he'd boarded the plane to Libya with sixteen dollars....

And Ruby, who'd been a real bitch sober, but had been a hell of a good ol' gal after she'd had a drink or two....

And that little waitress in Russell....

And Margie, who wouldn't hardly let him have her any anymore, but who still fed him and gave him cigarettes and sometimes kissed his forehead when she thought he was asleep....

And Bobbie, who'd gone home and never come back. Her daddy had met with Frank at a café in Cedar Vale. "She's scared of you, son," he'd said. "She's afraid you'll hurt her sometime." His ears had roared like the river.

He looked up, then, for just a second, astonished. His big hands gripped the metal arms of the old lawn chair as he remembered.

Connie, from long ago, with the murdering son-of-a-bitch husband....

"Shit!" Frank tightened his grip on the arms of the chair, then lifted his right hand and looked at it. Worthless son-of-a-bitch husband. Yeah, right. "You should talk," he said aloud. "Bastards who hit women...."

Frank had to stand, then, and walk down the three steps onto the front walk and then to his left and onto the lawn—that needed mowing, he noticed. He kicked at the grass, remembering that time in Shidler. Remembering hitting that woman who'd come out of the bar with Bobbie. Jesus!

Then he just stood, staring into the past, seeing himself, back again at the raging Arkansas River, with the rushing water all white at the top and with the debris being hurled along. Standing on that bluff above the Arkansas River.

1940.
Frank looked out over the water.

The last time he'd stood here, on this bluff above the river, not far south of the Kansas border, he'd been running from the law.

He was older now. Wiser? He doubted that. He'd stared down at the water then, much like he was staring now.

Things were different now. Old John Blaine's house was empty; the old man was probably dead. The river was still here. The bed didn't look as full as Frank remembered, but the river, at least, was constant. Not much was.

Walter was still gone, of course. He'd stopped off in Oklahoma City on the way here—to visit Walter's grave. He'd been surprised to see that there was another headstone beside his brother's: Crystal Hemings Gage. Damn! Walter's woman and she was gone, too. What the hell?

Frank shuffled his foot against the bluff, sending a cascade of dirt down into the river.

Walter. He'd always called Walter "little brother," even though Walter had been older. He'd known that Walter hadn't liked it, and Frank regretted, standing there on the bluff, that he hadn't always been the kind of brother he should have been.

He couldn't do anything about that now, and he probably couldn't have done anything about it before, during the trouble. But there was one thing he could do, and he'd done it.

It had taken him a couple of years. A lot of traveling, a lot of time, a lot of patience, and a lot of jobs in a lot of oilfields, but he'd found Jack Crocker all right, down in Midland, Texas.

Frank reached into his jacket pocket and took out the gun that he was supposed to have returned years ago. He stood there, looking at it. "God-damned guns," he said, and then sent it flying in a high arc out over and then into the river.

Just two blocks south of where he sits now, in 1972, his feet up on the porch rail and his hat over his eyes, there is, on the highway to Ulysses,

279

a bridge over the Arkansas River. There is no water in the river; the bed is dry. There is nothing but sand. The sand is always there, even when the river is full and flowing. When the flow is gone, the sand remains.

AUTHOR'S NOTES

The Osage murders really happened, but the details of the investigation here are completely fiction, as is the rest of this book.

A number of real historical figures appear in the novel, though. The governors mentioned were real, as were several law-enforcement personnel and oil businessmen. Any appearances by them, however, is fictional.

Lucas Taylor, whose death occurred at the end of the previous novel was modeled, very loosely, after Luther Bishop, the agent who received the greatest amount of credit for the arrests and convictions. Bishop *was* murdered in life, and his wife was brought to trial and acquitted.

Some of the towns mentioned here no longer exist, except as, in some cases, scattered foundations on which buildings once stood. Others have, of course, in the ninety or so years that have passed, changed dramatically.

Some freedom has been taken with Oklahoma geography.

SOURCES

A number of works were essential in doing research for this book. Certainly among the most useful were *Early Oklahoma Oil* (Texas A&M University Press, 1981) by Kenny A. Ranks, Paul F. Lambert, and Carl N. Tyson, and *The Oklahoma Petroleum Industry* (University of Oklahoma Press, 1980) by Kenny A. Franks.

John Joseph Mathews provided two excellent sources: *The Osages: Children of the Middle Waters* (University of Oklahoma Press, 1981) and *Life and Death of an Oil Man* (University of Oklahoma Press, 1951.)

Also contributing two works to my research was Michael Wallis: *Oil Man* (Doubleday, 1988) and *Way Down Yonder in the Indian Nation* (St. Martin's Griffin, 1993).

John W. Morris's *Ghost Towns of Oklahoma* (University of Oklahoma Press, 1978) was absolutely essential, as was *A Primer of Oilwell Drilling, 6th Edition* (University of Texas Press, 2001) by Ron Baker.

Others were *Taming the Sooner State* (New Forum Press, 2007) by R. D. Morgan; *Big Bluestem* (Council Oaks Books, 1996) by Annick Smith; and *The WPA Guide to 1930s Oklahoma* (University of Kansas Press, 1986.)

I was fortunate to have in my possession (from who knows what source) *Oil Field and Pipeline Equipment*, a large, hard-bound catalog put out by the Oil Weekly in 1935.

Finally, to refresh my own memory of the area of Oklahoma where my family lived for many years, I looked at *North Central Oklahoma, Rooted in the Past* (two volumes, put out by the North Central Oklahoma Historical Association in 1995.)

GLOSSARY OF TERMS

Some of these terms are used in the story, and those would be, one hopes, explained in the process. Others were used, instead, as chapter titles and would be meaningless, perhaps, without explanation. Oil field language is often highly technical—and, just as often, a kind of jargon used only by and known by oilfield workers. Some of them don't occur within this work at all, but appear, instead, in the earlier part of this novel, which takes place in two separate parts.

Blowout—*an uncontrolled eruption of gas or oil that may occur when there is unequal pressure in the drilling hole. When such a blowout occurs in such a way that oil spews high into the air, it's commonly called a "gusher."*

Cable tools—*a heavy, chisel-like bit, attached to a cable, is simply repeatedly dropped from a height into the hole, pulled up, and dropped again, gradually deepening the hole.*

Christmas tree—after the well has been completed, the Christmas tree, consisting of valves and gauges, tops off the hole, maintaining control of the oil.

Derrick—*the metal (wooden, at one time) structure that is erected on the drilling site for the purpose of supporting pipe and machinery used during the drilling process.*

Doghouse—*essentially a little building on the rig floor, used largely as an office and store-room, but also often a place to eat meals, etc.*

Driller—*the worker in charge of the drilling crew.*

Drillstem test—*a lowering of certain equipment into the hole for the purpose of testing pressure and taking samples.*

Drip gas—*a condensation of natural gas that sometimes occurs in the pipes coming from the wells. Some people would open a valve, drain out the condensate, and use the product in the gasoline engines of their cars.*

Dry Hole—*simply a well that doesn't produce enough oil or natural gas to be worth finishing or maintaining.*

Fishing tool—*a tool designed to bring up equipment that has somehow become disconnected and lost in the drilling hole.*

Fracturing—*often called "fracking," fracturing uses a number of methods to create cracks in the rock layers in which drilling is taking place for the purpose of allowing oil to flow more freely.*

Hydrostatic pressure—*the pressure exerted by whatever drilling fluid is present in the drilling hole. This could be water, chemicals, or "mud."*

Idiot stick—*a shovel.*

Landman—*the person (and it may be a woman) who deals with the landowner to acquire the lease—the permission to drill on the land.*

Light, sweet crude—*oil that contains little or no sulfur. This is desirable.*

Location—*the drill site.*

Logging the well—*the record-keeping that occurs during the drilling process.*

Monkey board—*a small platform that is used to lift the derrickhand to the top of the derrick from where he can handle the top of the pipe going into the hole.*

Mud—*a fluid inserted into the hole while drilling. It may serve as lubricant, as a vehicle to lift cut particles from the bottom of the hole, and as a sealant to prevent water from entering the hole.*

Mud Pit—*at the time the story takes place, the mud pit was simply that: a pit dug into the ground near the well for the purpose of holding the drilling fluid that came out of the well during the drilling process—simply a place to store waste.*

Offset wells—*wells placed near already producing wells. The purpose may be to gather information about the extent of the oil reservoir. But they were, at the time of the story, also used to drain oil from the same source as the wells of competitors or simply to draw the oil from the ground more rapidly.*

Plug and abandon—*seal with concrete plugs the hole of the well that either did not produce or is no longer producing.*

Pumper—*the employee in charge of the actual maintenance of a producing well. He would, perhaps, do minor repairs to the pumping unit, check to see that it was working properly, clean the area, and perhaps gauge tanks (check the level of oil contained in them.) The pumper might be in charge of only a few wells or many.*

Rat Hole—*a hole in the rig floor through which the drilling assembly works.*

Rig—*the derrick and the surface equipment needed to drill an oil well.*

Rotary rig—*unlike the cabletool rig, which creates the hole primarily with weight and gravity, the rotary rig uses a rotating bit. This has several advantages. Speed is a factor, but probably more important is the fact that the bit is at the end of pipe through which the cuttings from the bit are forced upward and eventually out of the hole. One of the problems with cabletool drilling was that operations had to stop periodically to clean residue out of the hole.*

Roughneck—*just one of the "hands" on a rig.*

Roustabout—*an unskilled laborer, who may work at various jobs. He may unload trucks, dig pits, clean, or clear an area of shrubbery prior to drilling.*

Safety slide—*a wire device which the derrickhand, the man at the top of the derrick on the monkey board, can use to come down in an emergency.*

Sour crude—*crude oil that contains high concentrations of hydrogen sulfide. This oil is worth less than sweet crude because it takes more processing. If you ever pass a field producing sour crude, you will know it. The odor is fairly intense.*

Spudding in—*beginning the drilling process.*

Throwing the chain—*as the hole goes deeper, additional pipe (casing) has to be added. Since long lengths of pipe are involved (and considerable weight) the process involves "throwing a chain" around one length of pipe to control it.*

Toolpusher—*the person in charge of the drilling rig. (He's not the driller; the drillers work in shifts as the drilling process goes on twenty-four hours a day until completion.) The toolpusher may, in fact, be in charge of more than one operation at once.*

Tour—*pronounced "tower," simply a workshift.*

Tripping the pipe—*the process in which the drill stem (pipe and bit) out of the hole and putting it back in.*

V-door—*an opening at floor level in a rig that is used to bring pipe, drill casing, tools, etc., onto the rig floor.*

Wildcatting—*drilling where no earlier oil production has been found, an operation clearly with greater risk attached.*

Made in the USA
Coppell, TX
25 January 2023

11695661R00166